HOTTEST DEAL ON WHEELS

Paul's Gremlin was in silhouette, on a direct line between us and the sun. Several people had started tossing a Frisbee to the right of us, and the boom box had been cranked up another notch, playing a real nugget-'cause-you-dug-it: Norman Greenbaum's "Spirit in the Sky."

"Hey, Ellen!" Paul stood beside the Gremlin, leaning on the open door, face unreadable in the lee of the sun. "You ready for this?"

Ellen shielded her eyes. "Ready when you are."

"This thing had better fire up quick, or I'll sue you, Ben."

"Not to worry, kid."

He waved, then dropped into the driver's seat and bent over the wheel. The explosion blurred the car with a light brighter than bright. A white-hot pillar of flame shot hungrily toward the sky.

I found myself on my feet, running toward what was left of the car. Ellen was on her feet too, still as a pillar of salt. The Gremlin's hood fell from the sky onto the fender of a Dodge pickup a hundred feet away and crashed spinning to the pavement, sizzling like one of my well-done steaks.

Then Ellen screamed.

I0596934

Bantam Crime Line Books offers the finest in classic and modern American murder mysteries.

Ask your bookseller for the books you have missed.

Rex Stout

The Black Mountain
Broken Vase
Death of a Dude
Death Times Three
Fer-de-Lance
The Final Deduction
Gambit
Plot It Yourself
The Rubber Band
Some Buried Caesar
Three for the Chair
Too Many Cooks

Max Allan Collins

The Dark City
Bullet Proof
coming soon: Neon Mirage

Loren Estleman

Peeper
coming soon: Whiskey River

V.S. Anderson

Blood Lies
King of the Roses

William Murray

When the Fat Man Sings
The King of the Nightcap
coming soon: The Getaway Blues

Eugene Izzi

King of the Hustlers
The Prime Roll
coming soon: Invasions

Gloria Dank

Friends Till the End
Going Out in Style

Jeffery Deaver

Manhattan Is My Beat
coming soon: Death of a Blue
                Movie Star

Robert Goldsborough

Murder in E Minor
Death on Deadline
The Bloodied Ivy
The Last Coincidence

Sue Grafton

"A" Is for Alibi
"B" Is for Burglar
"C" Is for Corpse
"D" Is for Deadbeat
"E" Is for Evidence
"F" Is for Fugitive

David Lindsey

In the Lake of the Moon

Carolyn G. Hart

Design for Murder
Death on Demand
Something Wicked
Honeymoon with Murder
A Little Class on Murder

Annette Meyers

The Big Killing
coming soon: Tender Death

Rob Kantner

Dirty Work
The Back-Door Man
Hell's Only Half Full
Made in Detroit

Robert Crais

The Monkey's Raincoat
Stalking the Angel

Keith Peterson

The Trapdoor
There Fell a Shadow
The Rain
Rough Justice

David Handler

The Man Who Died Laughing
The Man Who Lived by Night
coming soon: The Man Who
                Would Be F. Scott
                Fitzgerald

Jerry Oster

Club Dead
Internal Affairs

Benjamin Schutz

Embrace the Wolf
The Things We Do for Love
A Tax in Blood

MADE
IN
DETROIT

Rob Kantner

BANTAM BOOKS
NEW YORK · TORONTO · LONDON · SYDNEY · AUCKLAND

MADE IN DETROIT
A Bantam Book / June 1990

ISBN 0-553-28458-4

Published simultaneously in the United States and Canada

Bantam Books are published by Bantam Books, a division of
Bantam Doubleday Dell Publishing Group, Inc. Its trademark,
consisting of the words "Bantam Books" and the portrayal of a
rooster, is Registered in U.S. Patent and Trademark Office and
in other countries. Marca Registrada. Bantam Books, 666 Fifth
Avenue, New York, New York 10103

PRINTED IN THE UNITED STATES OF AMERICA

RAD   0 9 8 7 6 5 4 3 2 1

for Nancy and Malcolm Kantner,
Mother and Dad:
the first book read.
And for Valerie, my sweet accomplice.
I love you.

Publisher's Note

Chapter 1

One steak left; one customer left.

Perfect planning, for once.

I speared the T-bone, dropped it on Randy's plate, and closed up the grill. Time to transform from Ben Perkins, chief cook and bottle washer, to Ben Perkins, party person. The weather was perfect, the occasion was perfect, and I was in an absolutely perfect mood. Nothing could spoil it. Nothing.

"I toldja *rare*, Ben," Randy said, squinting at his steak. "What are ya, deaf?"

"Jesus Christ, Randy, any rarer than that and I'd have had to serve it to you right out of that ice chest."

"Can't stand overdone meat," he grumbled, serving himself some potato salad from the large bowl on the picnic table.

On the other side of the pool, someone put a new tape on the boom box, sending the good solid guitar sounds of Mr. Joe Walsh's "Rocky Mountain Way" around the Norwegian Wood recreation area. Randy was still studying his steak suspiciously. I leaned toward his plate, stared, and said, "See there? It wiggled."

"Oh, bullshit." But for a second there, he looked spooked. Randy's a member of my Norwegian Wood maintenance crew. A hard worker, a street-smart thirty-year-old and a connoisseur of all species of female—but no intellectual giant.

"It wiggled, I swear," I insisted. "And I'm sure I heard it moo as I turned it over on the grill a minute ago."

"Oh yeah, right," Randy said, then burped. "Sorry, pal,

1

this ain't what I call rare. For what I call rare, you lean close, say 'heat,' and then serve."

I looked around dramatically. "Where's my ball bat? May have to stun it to even up the odds between you."

He grinned. "Screw it, I didn't come here to eat, anyway." But he kept his plate as he sauntered away, looking for a place to sit at one of the picnic tables, eyes a-prowl.

I threw my utensils into a plastic washbasin, rescued myself a Stroh's beer from the ice tub, fired up a short cork-tipped cigar, and stood there on the lawn, arms folded, looking at the festivities. A pretty sight. I'd say we had about three dozen Norwegian Wood tenants there, the people who knew Paul and Ellen best. Some swam in the Olympic-size pool; others were involved in a fierce game of volleyball on the lawn; the rest sat at picnic and deck tables, eating, drinking, and talking.

Could anything be better than this? It was Sunday, the tail end of the Fourth-of-July weekend. Perfect weather, a perfect occasion, and the perfect crowd to celebrate it with.

"Hey, Ben!"

I turned to see Brian, my other full-time maintenance kid, amble toward me across the pool deck. Beside him was Debra Clark, his roomie. For an uptight EPA clerk, she looked splashy in a snug Tahiti-print swimsuit. Brian wore khaki shorts, sunglasses, earring, and little blond pigtail. They looked relaxed and happy and Brian even looked like he was starting to get some color, finally.

"Hi, guys," I said. "Buy you a beer?"

"Got it covered," Brian said, digging a pair of them out of the tub of ice. He cracked them, handed Debra hers, and said, "Where's the newlyweds?"

"Paul's working the crowd. Ellen was with him, but I don't see her now...oh yeah, she's over there with Clare and Beth."

"Here's our contribution to the savings bond," Debra said, handing me a sawbuck. "Thanks for handling all the arrangements. You did well; this is a lovely occasion." Her smile was small and looked like it hurt; I remain not exactly one of Debra's favorite people.

Brian, tapping a bare foot in time to the music, nodded agreement and asked, "You going stag today, Ben?"

"Yeah, Carole's doing the duty thing up at her mother's at Elizabeth Lake. I'll be catching up with her later."

Somebody cannonballed into the water, sending a hail of warm chlorinated water our way. We stepped back to the lawn. I looked Brian up and down and said, "You're looking pretty healthy there, kid. You're back on the clock when? Tomorrow?"

"Week from tomorrow," he corrected.

"Got another whole week off to skate, huh?"

Debra said, in a voice that brooked no dissent, "The doctor told him to convalesce till the fourteenth."

I looked him over. Long tall Brian with the honest, earnest face. Looked pretty good, considering that just five weeks earlier he'd been flat on his back at Detroit Receiving Hospital, at death's door from a bullet that, in a kinder, gentler world, would have hit me instead of him.

I remembered how guilty I'd felt, watching him lie there in intensive care as Debra sobbed in misery and anger beside me. I remembered the relief I felt when the doctors ruled that he'd recover fully, and how elated I was when Brian got home from the hospital, limping and weak but all in one piece.

And I said to him, "Your coming back don't exactly send me into ecstasy, pal. For one thing, now Randy's bitching 'cause he won't be getting all that nice juicy overtime anymore. If you'd have croaked, I wouldn't be having that personnel problem."

"That's why they pay you them big, big bucks, Mr. Hotshot Maintenance Manager." Brian's grin was bright in his long tan face. "To solve those kind of knotty personnel problems."

I pointed my cigar at him. "Go ahead. Laugh while you can. But next week your soft flabby ass is getting put to work, youngster. I have been saving up the scungiest, most disgusting fix-up and cleanup jobs just for you."

Brian laughed. Debra glared at me and took Brian's elbow. "Marcie's over there, let's go say hi. Excuse us, Ben."

Brian waved at me and they strolled away. I heard him say, "He was just kidding around, Deb." I didn't hear her reply, which was probably just as well.

I hooked my cigar in my teeth and strolled along the grassy verge by the pool deck, watching the festivities. Paula Heintz was the life of the party today; Joe Depp and his brother Mick took her by the wrists and ankles and tossed her, fully clothed and shrieking with laughter, into the deep end. Randy was getting close up and personal with a girl who couldn't have been more than sixteen. Paul Reardon, the birthday boy and newlywed, was talking excitedly to Ahmed Senatkor and his wife, eliciting a beaming smile out of Mrs. Senatkor, a woman normally about as expressive as a brick wall. The Colonel held forth at the far picnic table, no doubt telling his three cronies once again how he'd won the war in Europe. Several young moms sat on blankets back by the play equipment, keeping an eye on their toddlers.

As I ambled along, I got a friendly greeting from just about everyone I met. That wasn't because I'm by nature popular or gregarious; it was because I'm Norwegian Wood's manager of maintenance and security. Have been for a lot of years now; been here longer than most of the tenants, all but Mrs. Janusevicius, the Colonel, and a couple of others.

To them, I'm like the furniture. They know I'm here, they use me without thinking about it, occasionally they realize that I'm useful but mostly they don't notice me. When they're friendly, it's mostly business; storing up points against the day when they'll need me to come trotting over about 3:00 A.M. to fix a runaway faucet or something.

I know that and it doesn't bother me. In fact, I make it a point to avoid getting close to tenants. Being friends with them can get real sticky. For one thing, Norwegian Wood's definitely for people at the upper edge of the social and financial scale. I wouldn't live there in a million years if my apartment didn't come free as part of the job. For another, today's pal could be tomorrow's evictee. Who needs that?

So I rigorously enforce this "no friends with tenants" rule—with some exceptions, such as Paul Reardon. But then Paul was special. A guy you instantly relaxed with. A man literally without an enemy or a detractor in the world. A person who could be nice without making a big deal out of it.

We'd become real pals, all right. Now that he was officially married, that would, no doubt, change. Nothing can screw up a good friendship like marriage. . . .

Ellen Reardon, the bride in question, sat at one of the permanent cement picnic tables with a big yellow umbrella angled a bit to shade her from the bright afternoon sun. She smiled at me coolly as I cruised up. "Care for company?" I asked.

"Have a seat," she said. Typical Ellen. Not friendly, but not gushing either. There was a distance in her, a wariness that always had the faint odor of fear.

I grabbed a folding chair and sat down in the shade next to her. The boom box had flipped over to Mr. Jeff Beck's cover of "People Get Ready," with Rod Stewart on the vocal. Paula Heintz had finally succumbed to the exhortations of the Depp brothers and stripped off her wet clothes. Their anticipation turned to disappointment when it developed that she was wearing a green one-piece swimsuit underneath.

Randy and his new lady friend had disappeared, leaving their full plates to take care of more urgent appetites. Brian and Debra were sitting in side-by-side folding chairs at the pool's edge, holding hands and dipping toes. Paul Reardon had made his way to a chaise lounge occupied by Mrs. Janusevicius, who'd not only come to the party but had also set her needlepoint down to talk with him.

I looked at Paul's new wife. Ellen was a picture of youthful vitality, five feet six of well-built young woman fairly glowing from the effects of eating right and jogging five miles a day. Her short blond hair, streaked white in places, was pulled back into a casual ponytail that reached to the collar of her white "Hard Rock Café/Detroit" T-shirt. Below that she wore light blue pocketless shorts and sandals.

"I'm disappointed," I told her. "I expected you to show up in your wedding gown, with veil and bridal train and children scattering flower petals and the works."

"We didn't go that route," she answered. "Kept it real simple."

"Oh, really. What do you think this is, the sixties? The full-blown formal wedding is all the rage now."

"Not for me, thanks," she said. "And even if I'd gone formal, I'd certainly change out of my gown before coming out here."

"Too bad. We'd have taken commemorative pictures, gotten our wedding kisses, then pitched you ass-over-appetite into the deep end. That's the way we do things in Detroit, not like out here in these weenie suburbs."

She did not smile. "Since you were organizing the party, I had a pretty good feel for what the dress code would be. Somehow I knew you'd wear sneakers, raggedy cutoff jeans, and a T-shirt with something really vulgar printed on it, like—what does it say? It's all scrunched up, I can't make it out."

" 'Eat Right, Stay Fit, Die Anyway.' "

She stared at my chest. "That's not what it says."

"Sorry, bad guess." I tugged it flat so she could read all the words: "I Don't Give a Shit. I Don't Take Any Shit. I'm Not in the Shit Business."

"Something sweet, like that," she said.

"My motto for the summer," I answered.

After a moment's thought she said, "I think I'll adopt it, too. Now that all that wedding bullshit is over and done with."

I grinned. In so many ways Paul and Ellen were yin and yang. He was dark, she was fair. He came from money, she came from nothing. He was confident and secure, she was twitchy, watchful, like a rabbit in the dark. He was the amiable, sensitive sort who could never utter a negative word to anyone, where she was almost compulsively direct. "Know what I think your problem is, Ellen, is you bottle up your feelings inside way too much."

I looked at her and caught a fleeting grin, but she said nothing. My cigar had gone cold; I fetched a fresh one out of the rear pocket of my cutoffs and fired it up. "How'd the wedding go?"

"Let's just say it went, and it's done, and I'm glad."

I said nothing, hoping she'd spill, for three reasons. First of all, I'm nosy. Second, I wanted her to unwind, let off a little steam for once. Third, I really wanted to be friends with her. Not that I was hot for her body—though I admit I'd always felt a long-distance, low-grade longing, the kind you think about and nurse along, knowing full well that you'll never act on it. I wanted to be friends with her because you always want to get along with your pals' spouses, tough as that can be sometimes.

She examined her short fingernails for a moment, then, eyes far away, began to talk softly. "The problem is Paul's father. If I ever seriously considered *not* marrying Paul, Lance was the reason. He's one of the creepiest, Ben, I'm not kidding."

I whacked a hunk of cigar ash toward the grass behind us. "Not that I'd know personally, but in-laws are never a treat."

"I've heard that, too," she said. "But this is a special case, I think. The problem isn't me, really. The problem is that Lance really hates Paul. Hates his own son."

This was news to me. Paul had never talked about his dad. Ellen must have read skepticism in my expression. "I know it's hard to believe," she said, "but it's true. He ridicules Paul's ambitions as an artist. Belittles Paul's advertising work. Makes nasty comments about the fact that Paul lives here in Wayne County when 'people of quality,' as Lance puts it, live in Oakland or Washtenaw. And, of course, he has nothing but contempt for me." Her face went hard. "A rootless foundling from Chicago, probably the bastard offspring of a hooker and a dope pusher—"

"He said that about you?"

"Not exactly. He did ask me, at dinner a couple of weeks ago, what ethnic extraction I was. Of course, being adopted, I have no idea. So he sat there at the table—this is at the Lark now; he's ridiculed me at all the best places—running his beady little eyes all over me, loudly evaluating my features one by one. He concluded that I'm probably a Belgian Jew with a little Scandinavian thrown in, 'most likely from a horny Norse raider,' according to Lance the real-estate geneticist, the instant expert on everything."

"Sweet guy." I drank off the last of my beer, musing over the contrast between Paul as I knew him and his father as Ellen described him. Talk about yin and yang. It explained a lot about Paul. "Hate to tell you this, but you're stuck now. For better or for worse, as I believe the saying goes."

"This comes under the heading of worse," she answered. "If I had any illusions that our marriage would improve Lance's treatment of me, he dispelled them nicely at the end of the wedding luncheon today. He gave me a fatherly embrace, put his big hand on my tit, and said he was sure I'd get knocked up soon because I have the right hips for it."

I had no reply to that. I mean, what could you say?

Paul Reardon had finished up with Mrs. Janusevicius and had moved on to chat with Brian and Debra. The party had grown, if anything, louder, as more people joined the turbulent volleyball game that dominated the grassy verge between the pool area and the parking lot.

Ellen pulled a foot up onto the chair and rested her chin on a shapely tanned knee. "It all comes down to money," she said after a bit. "As long as we owe Lance money, we'll never be rid of him. But, as of today, the trust fund from Paul's grandfather kicks in. That'll take some of the financial pressure off us."

"Unless Paul's daddy tries to block it," I said.

She looked at me darkly. "I know you're a private detective, trained to look for trouble, but I'm not worried."

I didn't bother to tell her that I hardly ever have to go looking for trouble. It sort of finds me on its own. "Good."

"The bequest is very straightforward, as far as I understand it," she said. "Paul has to be twenty-five and married. As of today, both conditions are met."

I grinned. "Ms. Moneybags! Don't forget us small fry you met on the way up."

She shook her head patiently. "It's only ten thousand a year. All it means is I may be able to quit the nurse-aide gig and go back to school. And we can start paying Lance back—"

I waved her silent as I spotted Paul Reardon making for our table, a Stroh's can in each hand, floating on bonhomie and beer. Like Ellen, Paul was the very picture of wedding-day formality. He wore a purple tank top, white shorts with blue trim, and thongs. He was about five-ten and, like his new wife rawboned and exercise-honed. Normally he was a religiously clean liver, but this afternoon you could hear the beer sloshing inside him.

"Hey, Ben," he said, nearly breathless as he dropped into a chair between me and Ellen. "Fresh one for ya, big guy," he added, setting an unopened Stroh's on the table.

"Thanks," I said, cracking it. "Doing all right, kid?"

"Oh yeah. Doing fine." He slugged down the last of his beer, then lunged at Ellen and kissed her hard. As they broke apart, laughing, I thought, as I had in the past, about how right they looked together. Young, vigorous, bright-eyed, and good-looking—Barbie and Ken with an edge. Paul clanked his empty on the table and lurched to his feet. "Time for the big speech."

"Speech?" Ellen echoed, puzzled.

Paul rapped his beer can on the table several times till some semblance of quiet dropped over the crowd and faces turned expectantly toward us.

"Sorry to butt in," he said in public-address mode, "but I got something to say and I'd better get it out now, while I've still got the nerve." Someone turned the boom box down and Paul lowered his voice. "First of all, I want to thank you all for coming to this party to help celebrate my birthday and Ellen's and my wedding today. We'll never forget your kindness."

A ragged spray of applause sprang up. Paul nodded, smiled, held up his hands. "Also want to thank you for the savings bond you all chipped in for. That'll come in mighty handy a few years down the road."

A little more applause this time. Then Paul said, "There's one person I want to thank publicly. That's the man responsible for setting up this party—my good friend, and the one who keeps us all maintained and secure here at Norwegian Wood: Mr. Ben Perkins!"

This time the applause was mixed with what I hoped was good-natured booing and hissing. I half rose, made a foolish, embarrassed grin, and sat back down, hoping to hell the kid was done.

He wasn't. "Here's an example of the kind of pal Ben's been to us. Just yesterday, he finished dropping a new engine into our Gremlin, and he would only charge us for materials, not for his labor. How about that?"

Applause again, mostly dutiful. I sat there on my chair, profoundly embarrassed, wishing I could vanish off the face of the earth. Paul, half-drunk, went on to extol Norwegian Wood, the city of Belleville, the weather, you name it. Finally he ran out of gas and sat back down between me and Ellen as the party got back under way.

Ellen had been watching me. She touched Paul's arm and said, "I have a feeling you embarrassed Ben to death."

He squinted at me, head cocked. "Oh, I'm sorry, Ben. That's the last thing I wanted to do."

"Forget it."

"No, seriously," he said. He skootched his chair back and propped one ankle on the opposite knee, squarish tanned face intent. "It's just that I want all of these people to realize just how important you are around here, how much you do for everyone. I think they pretty much take you for granted."

"They're allowed to. I'm a hired hand. I thrive in the background, so leave me there, okay?"

He smiled crookedly. "As your friend, and as an advertising professional, I feel it's my duty to elevate your image—"

"Image? What's wrong with my image? I've spent years building this image, buddy. It's simple and straightforward: Under this rough exterior beats a heart of stone."

"That's your image, huh?"

"It is, indeed. Keep your mitts off it."

"Okay. I will."

Ignoring the furtive grins the newlyweds exchanged, I busied myself fending off the volleyball that came screaming at our table, thanks to one of Connie Faber's errant serves. When I looked back at the two, they were holding hands and smiling at me innocently. I reached into my back pocket, pulled out a business-sized envelope, unfolded it, and tossed it in front of him.

"What's this?" he asked, picking it up. I shrugged. Ellen

leaned close to Paul, watching as he tore the envelope open. Out fluttered about a zillion tiny blue scraps of paper.

He look dumfounded for a second, then murmured, "That isn't the check I gave you for the engine job on the Gremlin."

"Uh-huh. I got a little clumsy with it, evidently. So I figured, what the hell. Happy birthday."

He stared at me, stricken. "Ben, I can't accept this. You've got to take the money. You already gave us the labor free, and that's more than enough."

I shook my head. "Free labor was your wedding present. Free parts is your birthday present. Today's your birthday, I seem to recall. Plus"—I shrugged—"I'm a little flush right now, and I know you guys are always scraping."

Ellen, arms folded, was watching me coolly. But Paul really looked upset. "Eight hundred bucks! I can't take this. Number one, the labor was generous enough already. Number two, we're not all that broke right now, things are pretty good in the money department. I'm gonna write you another check."

"You keep writing 'em, I'll keep shredding 'em."

As Ellen watched him, bemused, Paul sat there looking lost for a minute. Then he brightened. "Well, as a matter of fact, I probably shouldn't be paying you for the work just yet, anyway."

"Why's that?" Ellen asked.

"We haven't even driven the car yet," he told her. "How do we know Ben's work is any good?"

"'Cause my work is always good," I growled. "I'll have you know, I did a great job on that car, even if it is an AMC and not a Ford car like it should be."

"Yeah, but till I test-drive it I won't know for sure," Paul said, smiling innocently. "Where is it? We'll settle this right now."

"In the lot over yonder," I answered, jerking a thumb.

Ellen said, "Come on, Paul, you can do that later. This is our party."

He was on his feet, smiling in anticipation. "Take just a

minute to wheel her around the lot once or twice, make sure old Ben did the job right. Got the key?"

I fished it out and handed it to him. "Baby it, huh? It needs five hundred miles or so to break in good."

"Right." He gave me an intrepid, very British salute, then looked at Ellen. "Want to come along?"

"No, thanks, I'll let you handle it," she said.

"Okay, See ya!" He turned and jogged up the grassy verge to the waist-high chain-link fence, which he vaulted effortlessly. As he walked across the parking lot toward the bottle green Gremlin, I felt Ellen's hand touch mine.

Her blue eyes were serious. "Thank you for the "birthday" present," she said.

"De nada."

"What Paul said about us not needing the money . . . I don't know why in the *hell* he said that, 'cause it's not true. We're as strapped as ever. It's so generous of you to—"

"Skip it, okay? It's done and I'm glad to do it for you guys."

The sun was dropping in the afternoon sky, still brilliant but not penetrating. Paul's Gremlin was in silhouette, on a direct line between us and the sun. The volleyball game was still going great guns on the other side of the pool, several people had started tossing Frisbee to the right of us, and the boom box had been cranked up another notch, playing a real nugget-'cause-you-dug-it: Norman Greenbaum's "Spirit in the Sky."

"Once that trust fund comes through," Ellen murmured, "we'll be doing okay. But that could take six months—"

"Hey, Ellen!" Paul stood beside the Gremlin, leaning on the open door, face unreadable in the lee of the sun. "You ready for this?"

Ellen turning to look, shielded her eyes against the bright glare, and called, "Ready when you are."

"This thing had better fire up quick, or I'll sue you, Ben!"

"Not to worry, kid."

He waved, then dropped into the driver's seat, pulled the door shut, and bent over the wheel. The explosion blurred the car with a light brighter than bright, followed a split second later by a blast that lanced my ears and rattled windows all over Norwegian Wood as a white-hot pillar of flame shot hungrily toward the sky.

I found myself on my feet, taking jerky steps toward the Gremlin and forced myself to stop.

Steve Anders splashed to the surface of the deep end to find the world stunned silent. "Hey! What the hell!"

Ellen was on her feet, too, still as a pillar of salt.

A baby began to cry.

The Frisbee thwacked unnoticed to the concrete deck.

The Gremlin's hood fell from the sky onto the fender of a Dodge pickup truck a hundred feet away and crashed spinning to the pavement, smoking and sizzling like one of my well-done steaks.

Then Ellen screamed.

Chapter 2

I'd begun that glorious, flawless Sunday with a morning visit to Bloomfield Hills. Not pleasure, but business, wrapping up a small assignment for a longtime client.

Like everyplace else, Detroit has its new money, its old money, and its very old money. Joann Sturtevant is a living example of all three. Despite her Dutch name, which I think she inherited from one of her three husbands, she's of French extraction. Her family dates back to the "ribbon farms" that comprised the original settlement called Fort Pontchartrain du Détroit, circa 1703. So, right off the boat she ain't.

From what I gather, in the succeeding years her family managed to make a buck or two off every Detroit industry of consequence: mining, timber, leather, shipbuilding, you name it. In the early part of this century they invested tidy sums with guys like Ransom Olds, David Buick, and the greatest of them all, Mr. Henry Ford. If they ever guessed wrong, there's no record of it. So old Mrs. Sturtevant's never had to worry about clean sheets to sleep on, and the *Free Press* never, ever spells "Joann" with an "e" at the end.

Mrs. Sturtevant's been no slouch in the fortune-building department herself. She was one of the first woman graduates of the Wharton School and has invested wisely, wheeling and dealing in commodities of all kinds. She likes land. She likes shiny little high-tech firms. She's also liked—and perhaps even loved, but most assuredly found good use for—three men whom she went so far as to marry, and then, in the natural course of things, bury.

The last of these was a leading Big Three executive big shot who also logged some time as secretary of defense a few Republicans ago, enabling Mrs. Sturtevant to add D.C. connections to her already extensive Detroit network.

A network that includes politicians, business people, entertainment figures, and, off to the side, little old me.

Unrealistic as our relationship may seem—she's blue blood and I'm blue collar and usually the twain don't meet— we have more in common than you might think.

Like Mrs. Sturtevant, my family has a long history in America. According to my late mother, who spent years looking for something about our family to brag about, the Perkins family hit America in about 1733, when one James Oglethorpe populated the settlement of Savannah with the dregs of Britain's debtor prisons. Allegedly, one of them was a Perkins. The only reason I buy any of this is that bill trouble is not entirely unknown in our family.

As the story goes, when the colonists headed south to fight the Spanish in the swamps, my forebear, showing uncommonly good sense, headed north to the hills around Brasstown Bald. There, Perkins people scuffled and scratched out various forms of a living till 1915, when the man who was to be my daddy migrated north to Detroit to get a job at Mr. Ford's car factory.

The Ford Motor Company got into the family's blood

and stayed there. Daddy did ten years till Ford's laid him off and never called him back; he finished up as a trim carpenter for the old Kerns Casket Company. But my uncle Dan put in forty years there, and my older brother Bill is still going strong after thirty years. As for me, I did a few years on the Ford line myself, till the day I was hired away to be a "personal assistant" (sanitized term for "enforcer") for Emilio Mascara, of the Beck/Hoffa/Fitzsimmons persuasion of union leaders.

Mascara ended up in the pen and I ended up on the street. I took a "strictly temporary" job as maintenance and security man for Norwegian Wood out in Belleville, a far western suburb. Shortly after that I wandered into private detective work. That was better than a dozen years ago, and was also when I met, and started handling discreet assignments for, Joann Sturtevant.

These assignments have been many, varied, and lucrative. I've often acted as her bodyguard at major public events. I've done courier work for her and background checks on various potential business associates. I've been her all-around driver and personal escort. The most exciting assignment was the time she hired me to track down $100,000 cash that had been embezzled from her; by the time I caught up with it, it had grown to nearly half a mil. My share was four grand and two dead friends.

Down through the years, I suppose you could say we've developed an unspoken amount of arm's length affection for each other. Further than that it could never go. To me, she was always Mrs. Sturtevant; to her, I was always Perkins; but we had the best of business relationships, one based on the exchange of fair value.

Till the previous week, I hadn't heard from Mrs. Sturtevant in over a year. This didn't worry me. She was a busy woman, always traveling; I thought maybe she'd locked herself away for yet another face-lift and general physical overhaul. It wasn't just me she was shunning; I noticed that her name appeared in the papers less frequently than in the past, misspelled or otherwise.

When she finally called with an assignment, delivered in

her typical terse tones, it was a locate job. The subject was her godson, a man named Marty Stempel. She had lost track of him and wanted him found.

Aside from the fact that Mrs. Sturtevant had never given me a locate job before, I thought the whole thing was routine. And it was—till I found him.

My first sight of Mrs. Sturtevant that Sunday morning, out on the deck behind her lavish Bloomfield Hills home, confirmed one suspicion. She had, in fact, had another face-lift since the last time I saw her. Aside from that she didn't look much different. She was an average-height lady composed mainly of skin and bones and very long blondish-gray hair that was always intricately bundled and tied up to the back of her head. Her face was narrow and wise, highlighted by sharp gray eyes that always understood even if they seldom believed.

This morning she wore a short-sleeve white silk crepe de chine blouse over battleship gray slacks. Being as it was Sunday, she was low-key on the jewelry, just a fine gold chain around her neck. This was about as informal as Mrs. Sturtevant ever dressed, at least when I was around.

She looked up from her *New York Times* as the maid escorted me toward her across the pool patio and intoned, "Mr. Perkins, ma'am."

The old woman gave me a wintry smile and said to the maid, "See if Mr. Perkins would care for some coffee or perhaps something stronger, Claire."

"Mr. Perkins would indeed care," I answered. "Mud straight up."

"Coffee, black," Mrs. Sturtevant translated. The maid nodded and left. "Have a seat," she said, folding up her newspaper.

I took a lavishly stuffed deck chair across the table from her. I felt nervous; I didn't want to tell her what I had come here to tell her. I got the feeling she was nervous, too. I knew why. She hadn't leveled with me, not at all, and she was wondering if, and what, I'd found out.

"How's my favorite tycooness?" I asked, just to break the ice.

"Very well, thank you," she said with rote formality. Always a get-down-to-it lady, she added, "So! You found him, I gather."

"I did." I pulled a short cork-tipped cigar, snapped a match alive on my thumbnail, and fired up the smoke. "I'm pleased to report that Mr. Marty Stempel, your godson, is alive and, so far as I could determine, well."

"Where is he?"

"Not that far away, oddly enough." Claire brought my coffee then, in a plain sturdy ceramic mug, and topped off Mrs. Sturtevant's from a sterling silver decanter. "Much obliged," I said. "Anyway, he's down in Bolles Harbor, right below Monroe. Living on a yacht called the *Blue Water Rambler*."

A long silence, broken only by the long hoot of a mourning dove from somewhere in the long grass beyond the fence. Mrs. Sturtevant asked softly, "A yacht?"

I got out my little spiral pad and flipped through some pages. "Yeah, pretty nice one, too. Great bit mothah, goes sixty feet if an inch. Registry says Port St. Lucie, Florida, but I checked the paper, it's in his name, all right." I looked at her. "Your godson's doing pretty well for himself. I mean, a boat, jeez. What is it they say, a boat's a hole in the water into which you throw money."

"I'm aware of that," she intoned. "I own several myself."

No doubt she was wondering, as was I, where Stempel got the scratch. If she'd asked, I'd have told her about the other signs of deep pockets, such as his candy-apple red Mercedes with the vanity plate that said VIP ON BOARD. But she didn't ask, so I didn't say.

Her gaze came back from far away. "Very well," she said crisply. "Thank you." Her checkbook was to hand, and she opened it and began to write with a heavy gold pen in her finishing-school calligraphy. "How did you find him?" she asked as she wrote.

I took a deep pull of the rich coffee. Whoo-whee, was it strong. Good, too. "Well, interestingly, he didn't make all that earnest an effort to disappear. Kept using his credit cards, for one thing."

"I see." She opened her check registry and began to write in that. "So, all one would need to do is call directory assistance and—"

"I've got his phone number right here," I said. "I'll give it to you if you want. But I wouldn't bother to call him, if I were you."

"Why not?" She started to tear out the check.

"I just wouldn't, ma'am." I took a deep, bracing hit of cigar. "Trust me on this one."

She looked up at me and her face was now real woman, not Bloomfield Hills. "You talked to him?" she asked, voice low and slow.

"Yes, ma'am," I replied, bracing myself.

"I said for you not to. I specifically instructed you to *find* him, Perkins. And then come back here and tell me where he was. I specifically told you not to talk to him."

"Yes, ma'am."

"You son of a bitch," she said, almost inaudibly.

"Yes, ma'am."

She got up and walked toward the edge of the ice blue pool, clutching herself as if someone had just thrown her down a flight of stairs.

I inhaled some cigar smoke and blew out a long thin stream. "If it matters, I'll tell you why I did it." No response. "Something smelled about the whole thing. Number one, you and the 'godson' story. Number two, the smell he gave off. I didn't like it. I wanted to find out what was going on. It's not that I wanted to butt into your private business. I only wanted to help."

"I pay you to do what I tell you to do," she answered, back to me at the edge of the pool. "Nothing more."

I shrugged lazily. "I don't do halvsies. You take me on, you get the whole shot. Your trouble is my trouble, and all that. I smelled trouble, so I talked to him."

She dropped her hands, turned, and walked stiffly back to the table. Her face was a white rigid mask, and she did not look at me. I couldn't tell if she'd been fighting tears, and I didn't want to know.

As she resumed her seat, she asked, "No point in my contacting him at all, then? Is that what he said?"

"That's essentially it," I answered, uttering my first total lie of the conversation.

For what he'd actually said was, "Godson! Is that what that dippy old cunt told you? Shit. Well, ain't that something. Listen, Perkins, you tell her something for me. You tell her I don't need to screw rich grandmas for my supper anymore. I mean, let's be honest, the money was nice. And the living was even nicer. Almost nice enough to make up for having to ball her every day. Almost. But I got sick of that shiny gold leash, so I got myself a whole new deal. And I'm doing pretty good, as you can see. I'm doing high-class work with high-class people, so she's gonna have to get her dick someplace else. You tell her I said that, Perkins."

Right.

I looked as blandly as I could at Mrs. Sturtevant. She searched my face, then cleared her throat as a steely expression took over and she got her ducks back in a row. She folded the check in half, crisply, and handed it to me. "Thank you, Perkins," she said.

"You're more 'n welcome." I got to my feet, put away the check, dropped my dying cigar in the ashtray. I wanted to add something else, like an apology, or something sympathetic or whatever, but I've learned that the only thing you can do about another person's pain is to keep it from happening. Once it hits, there's no helping them. "I'll show myself out the back way. See you around."

I'd reached the brick arch at the southeast corner of the lawn when I heard her call me. I strolled back. She was on her feet again, arms folded, walking slowly along the edge of the pool, glowing in the morning sun.

She stopped and looked at me. "Have you ever killed anyone?"

Hell of a question on a Sunday morning. "Yes, ma'am."

"How did it feel?"

I looked down, searching for an answer, and while doing so rescued the cold cigar from the ashtray and relit it. "Necessary," I said finally.

"What do you mean?"

I scratched my head. "They were heat-of-the-moment situations. Kill or be killed, that kind of thing. I guess the main emotion was relief that they'd bought the big one instead of me."

"Crimes of passion," she murmured. "What a convenient rationalization."

"Look," I said, not bothering to conceal the bite in my voice, "I know you're hurting right now and all that, and I'm sorry. But you got no call to say that to me. Just because I've killed people doesn't make me a killer."

Her smile was cold and knowing. "What about Wakefield?"

The name startled me. I hadn't heard it, or thought about it, in years. "What about him? That's got nothing to do with this."

"Oh, yes, it does. I remember what you said you were going to do to him. It was right here on this very deck when you said it. Remember?"

"I sighed. "Oh, jeez, that was what? Five years ago?"

She began to stroll, emoting to the pool at large. "Vince Wakefield. The man who killed your lover, as well as one of your friends. He'd escaped the country, as I recall. And you sat here and told me, 'I haven't won till Wakefield is dead. If you ever read in the papers how they find his stiff in a car trunk somewhere, tell them to look up one B. Perkins, Belleville, Michigan.' Remember?"

"Sounds like me all right. So what?"

"Did you ever go through with it?"

"Oh, hell no. I was upset, I'd just come off some pretty tough times, I said a lot of goofy things."

"You sounded sincere."

"Number one, I don't know whatever happened to the guy. He might have died over there in England, for all I know. Or he might be back home across the river in Windsor. And number two, even if he had come back, I wouldn't just up and kill him. No way. I don't just knock off people."

An odd look was growing on her face. "You don't?"

I guess I was a little slow that morning. It was only now

that I realized what this conversation was really about; what she was really asking me to do.

"No," I said. "I don't."

One jeweled hand went to her neck. "Not for revenge? Or love?"

I shook my head.

Her voice went almost inaudible. "But what if I asked you to?" I stared at her as her face brightened. "Of course you will. You'll do anything for me. Anything I ask. You always have, and you won't let me down now. I know you."

"Mrs. Sturtevant," I said, fighting to keep my voice steady, "I'll be seeing you around."

She was nodding, smiling, waving as she said gaily, "Thank you, Ben, thank you so much!. You've taken such a load off my mind."

I got the hell out of there.

Chapter 3

Under New Management, my favorite dark 'n' dingy drinking hole on Ecorse Road near I-275, wasn't doing too badly for 12:10 on Sunday afternoon. The usual contingent of Sunday-noon gotta-have-it boozers was there, as well as an assortment of carousers who'd begun celebrating the Fourth of July on Friday morning and were determined to make it last through tonight.

I stopped off there on my way home from Mrs. Sturtevant's because I had some time to kill; I didn't need to start setting up for Paul and Ellen's party till around two. I knew that my good buddy Bill Scozzafava would be manning the stick, and a couple of brewskis were just the thing I needed to settle the road dust. Last, but not least, I was hungry, and Under New

Management had, in an unprecedented move, expanded its offerings beyond booze and chips and was now serving lunch.

You heard right, friends and neighbors. Mr. Eddie Cabla, the owner, was up to his old tricks again, screwing up his perfectly good saloon with a stupid gimmick. Just like the time he decided that the secret of success was to establish the place as a hot spot for young dating couples, so he inaugurated "Ladies Night," which was a total bust. We got women, like always, but no ladies. And no couples, either. Well, that's not strictly true. People seldom arrived in pairs, but they often left that way.

Eddie insisted this lunch thing would make him rich. The consensus around the saloon was that he was dreaming. We thought he should stick with saloon food: chips, peanuts, Slim Jims, and microwaved ground rounds, nutritious stuff like that. When you're talking an honest-to-God meal, Under New Management is way down the list, well behind the Burger Barn and the Captain Chickie's Bird Curb that are within a mile of the place.

But Eddie considers himself the Lee Iacocca of saloon owners. He even looks a little like old Lido. He's taken to smoking big cigars, has been seen pricing toupees, wears glasses for no good reason, and has ordered a new sign that allegedly reads IF YOU CAN FIND A BETTER BAR, TRY IT. Anyway, according to Eddie the marketing whiz, lunch would draw people like flies. More important, it would get the drinkers started earlier.

So back in June he bought some equipment, laid in supplies, hired a cook, and sprang his innovation on an unsuspecting public, announcing it via a piece of plywood nailed to the side of the saloon with the word LUNCH spraypainted in red.

We're not talking haute cuisine here. Mainly sandwiches and soup and stuff, served on paper at the bar; you had to wait on yourself. The menus were cardboard mimeos scattered on the various tables. The Anonymous Gourmet hadn't written up the place yet. But it seemed to be working, at least today. Three people in the saloon proper were chomping on

sandwiches, and several empty stools to my left sat a grease
monkey in a jump suit, studying the cardboard mimeo menu.

Bill Scozzafava greeted me, drew a Stroh's dark, and set
it in front of me. He's one of those lucky bartenders who can
double as his own bouncer, without resorting to the sawn-off
ball bat hung below the bar. Bill is six-five, two-twenty, solid
muscle courtesy of the National Football League and Nauti-
lus. His head is a symmetrical, on-end rectangle, with short-
cropped brown hair graying at the temples, small sleepy
eyes, a heavy brown mustache, and a very direct jaw. Though
he won't talk about it unless you press him, he was once one
of the Chicago Bears' most feared linebackers. Now he runs
his own bump-and-paint shop in Romulus, tends bar at
Under New Management, and knits for relaxation. He's the
only serene person I've ever known. I've never seen him
angry. I've never heard him raise his voice or use bad words.
I've never known anyone to cross him. Must be nice.

"So what's up, Benjy?" he asked, gnawing on a toothpick. "you gonna eat or what?"

"Yeah, gimme a minute." I fired up a cigar. "We got the
pool and barbecue party for Paul and Ellen later, remember?
You coming over?"

Bill's sleepy eyes lit up a little. "Maybe I'll stop by.
Sounds nice."

"I'm cooking the steaks."

"This *today* you're talking about? Sorry. Can't make it,"
he said, smiling.

"Wiseass." I drank some more beer and studied the
small menu. "Guess I better eat something, it's what I came
for."

The grease monkey to my left said in a high, whiny
voice, "Hey, barkeep, is this all the damn food you people
serve here?"

"That's it, pal," Bill answered.

"Ugh. The chili any damn good?"

I glanced at him. "Well, I had some the other day, didn't
kill me." Good old Helpful Perkins.

"Chili in July?" the grease monkey argued. "Never
heard of such a damn thing." He turned his back to us.

"Ah," I said to Bill, "get me some chili, I guess."

He nodded and stepped to the archway behind the bar. "Chili, Vinnie," he said, then came back. "Really wish I could make it tonight. Paul and Ellen are nice kids. Give 'em a big hug for me. Especially Ellen. Nice long hard one for her."

"Watch it, now. You're a married man."

"No law against looking."

"With you there oughta be. You got a rep. All you have to do is look hard at 'em and they get pregnant."

Bill extracted the toothpick. "Now now. Not true."

"Ya got nine kids, for Chrissake! And those are the ones you own up to."

Bill inspected the end of the toothpick and said in a low voice, "True enough, but there won't be no more. I'm getting it taken care of this week."

"Which one, you or her?"

"Me."

I grinned. "The big snip, huh?"

I wasn't sure, but I thought that big bad Bill, once the meanest, nastiest member of the Bears' infamous Gorilla Gang, paled just a bit. "What happened was, Sue had another close call last month. If she can't come around finally, I swear the poor gal'd have taken a coil of rope into the woods. Shoot, my oldest is pushing thirty and my youngest isn't even in school yet. So we talked real serious, and the choice was her getting the tubes tied or me getting a vas—a vas—"

"Ka-*chunk*," I said helpfully. "Soprano city."

Bill didn't think it was funny. "A vasectomy," he said with dark precision. "Anyhow, when we come right down to it, there wasn't much choice. Sue feels like she's paid her dues, bearing the nine of 'em and everything."

"Uppity slut! I wouldn't take that shit."

"Yeah," Bill said without changing expression, "it seems fair to me, too. Besides, what the heck. A couple of shots, a few hours of soreness, and it's all over, big deal."

I stopped in mid-drag on my cigar and looked at him. "Plus the throbbing. And the itching. And feeling so weak you can't hardly raise a beer to your mouth. And let's not forget the real fun part: ice packs in the crotch, yes indeedy, a sensation not to be missed."

"Since when are you such an authority?"

"Since I had mine done, a few years back."

He blinked, which, for him, is equivalent to a fainting spell. "Are you serious? You never told me."

"Well, I mean, you don't go around wearing a sandwich sign or—"

"But why? You're not even married or anything."

"Let's just say I'm an advocate of zero population growth. Let's also say that I feel that it's only fair that I share the burden of contraception with the women with whom I associate. Let's say further that I felt it important to protect my assets and my estate from the threat of malicious paternity suits."

Bill waited me out patiently. "And the real reason?"

"I was offered one for free."

A couple of guys were waiting at the bar. Bill took their food orders and pulled their drinks with more than his usual briskness, and came back to me. "Free? How'd you—"

"Hey," the grease monkey whined, "how long does it take to get food in this damn place, anyway?"

Bill turned very slowly and said, "Our fine cuisine takes time to prepare." His voice dropped to a low hiss. "First, however, you have to order something." He turned back to me. "Spill it."

I shrugged. "Nothing really mysterious. I got it in trade, that's all. This urologist, Slater, hired me to collect his winnings from a sports bookie who'd disappeared. I found the book, collected the dough, gave it to the doc. Then he came up with a bad case of the shorts inasmuch as he owed this Shylock the bread. So he offered me a vasectomy, with all the trimmings."

Bill looked sour. "I don't know if I'd have touched that one, man."

"Why not? I'm not married, never going to be, and there ain't no kids in my future, that's for sure. Besides, I take stuff in trade all the time. Cash ain't everything. That's how I got my season Tigers tickets last year. I mean, you'd be amazed the stuff people offer. Once I had a shot at a live-in masseuse."

"You accept?"

"Naw. You got to draw the line somewhere. She was fifteen."

"Nice wholesome work you're in, Ben."

"It's a livin'. Anyway, so when's the big day, Pegleg?"

He winced. "Wednesday afternoon."

"So you're taking the rest of the week off?"

"You kidding?" He picked up my empty mug. "I'm backed up with work at the shop, I'm working a shift here, and I got a softball game that evening. I was lucky the doc was able to fit me in." He went to the tap and started pulling my refill. "What's so funny?"

"You play catcher, right?" I asked in a strangled voice.

"Yeah, so?"

I regained control. "I'm sorry, bro. This really isn't very funny."

"What isn't? What the heck you talking about?" He brought my beer and set it on the bar, overly hard.

I squashed out my cigar. "Do yourself a favor, Bill. Forget about working here that day. Forget about the softball game. Matter of fact, forget about doing much of anything for a couple of days afterward. You won't be in any shape for it."

He smiled. "Maybe I'm tougher than you."

"Funny thing about tough, it has a way of disappearing when they start whittling on your weanie. Fact is, you start wanting your mommy real quick."

"My doctor says there's nothing to it."

"Your doctor ain't the one getting shaved. But do what you want."

"Yeah." Bill nodded. "I think I will." Good luck, I thought. "'Nother beer?" he asked.

"Ain't but half-done with this one. How's that chili coming?"

"Our fine cuisine—" Bill began.

"Takes time to prepare," I finished for him.

A couple of food orders came out of the kitchen, neither one of them mine. Bill served them to people named, evidently, "Roast Beef Sandwich" and "Two Coneys, Hold the Onions," and came back to me. "What're you grinning like that for?" he asked suspiciously. "I'll make it through this vasectomy, no sweat, and—"

"I know, bro," I said. "Ever occur to you, maybe I'm grinning because I'm feeling pretty good today?"

"No. Maybe because that's so rare. Usually, you come in here moaning and groaning about one thing or another. The Norwegian Wood work, or woman trouble, or a tough case, or woman trouble, or car problems, or woman trouble—"

"Well, life ain't always peaceful, that's for sure. But here's the thing, bro." I raised my hand and showed him the thumb and forefinger, about an inch apart. "Right now I'm in this teeny little calm window of my life, and it feels good. No problems, no worries, just a nice long quiet summer ahead."

He unsnapped his rag and wiped at the damp rings around my beer mug. "No cases, huh?"

"Most especially, absolutely positively, no cases. Oh, maybe a background check for Psytech along the way, but other than that, nothing. Face it, Bill, it's already been one hell of a year. I had that Skinhead thing last month, which was a whole lot of ugly, Brian getting shot and all."

"Not to mention your little fling with Barb," Bill said.

"Yeah, right. And last winter there was that whole business with the radio announcer—another big dose of ugly—"

"Not to mention your little fling with the TV lady," Bill said. He gave me that serene, Buddha smile. "Does a pattern emerge, or what?"

I deliberately missed his point. "Yeah. I've been hitting it too hard this year already. So after that Skinhead thing was done, I figured, take it easy the rest of the year. No more heavy mysteries. I'm doing a lot of Detroit Tigers, a lot of flying in the ultralight, maybe some camping up north come August."

"Not to mention your little fling with Carole," Bill said.

"Does everything come back to sex with you?

"No, but it seems to with you. Actually, I think the Carole revival's nice. Fate, or something," the big man mused.

"You were together, then you split up, now you're together again. Who'd have figured it?"

"I sure wouldn't have."

"Chili's up," came a harsh voice from the kitchen.

Bill fetched the bowl and set it down in front of me along with plastic utensils wrapped in a tissue napkin. The aroma wafted up and over me, and my stomach did one of those odd little adjustments, like it was bracing itself. "Actually," I said, "I'm not sure I'm all that hungry anymore."

"Do what you want," Bill said. "It's three ninety-five regardless."

"Yeah, fine." I pushed the bowl away. "Guess maybe chili in July wasn't such a hot idea, after all."

"Hey," the grease monkey said, "I'll take that damn chili if you don't want it."

I shrugged. Bill took the chili and utensils to the other man and strolled back, looking thoughtful. "Who knows?" Bill said placidly. "Maybe you and Carole ought to face up to it, admit you're perfect for each other, and tie the big knot."

"No way, man. Not going to mess up a nice thing with a lot of mush. We used up all that serious shit the first time around. Now it's cookouts, and movies, and hanging around on the deck, and waking up with a friend, which has its points, you know?"

"I know," Bill said.

"Headed for a perfect summer, like I said."

"Well," Bill said, "all kidding aside, I'm glad for you."

"Thanks. Guess I had to luck out sometime." I swirled the last of my beer in the mug, then dumped it down my throat. "Better get going. Got a lot of setting-up to do for Paul's party." I stood, wrestled my wallet out of my back pocket, and tossed a couple of twenties on the bar. "Throw that at my tab, willya?"

Bill stared at the money like it was an alien life-form. "What is this? Legal tender from Ben Perkins?"

"Yeah, wonders will never cease, I guess. See you around, pal." I started for the door and looked back. "Stop by the party later, if you get a chance. It'll be a real blast."

Chapter 4

And now, this.

I sat in the small Norwegian Wood sales office, outside the closed door of the conference room. Carole Somers sat beside me. We didn't talk; we brooded.

Though two hours had passed, my ears still rang from the explosion. The stench of fuel and high explosive filled my nose. My arms stung with scratches I'd incurred while wrestling Ellen Reardon to the ground, to keep her from flinging herself into the roaring blaze that had instantly erased her new husband.

I think the only other time I felt that numb was back in '67, when they told me that my mother had been killed in the Detroit riot. I was no stranger to sudden death. I'd seen it happen and even caused it once or twice. But getting accustomed to it was an art I hadn't yet mastered. One instant Paul was there, the next he was gone. And "gone" (*dead*, the kid is *dead*, better get used to that), though bad enough, wasn't the worst part of it. He'd been murdered. Someone had wired a bomb to the engine of his car and blown him away.

The conference-room door opened and Paul Heintz came out, white-faced, shaking, sobbing. Carl Portman, a young, swarthy city of Belleville detective, looked at me with annoyance. "When's your lawyer getting here, Perkins? Chief's getting pissed."

"Mr. Perkins's lawyer is here," Carole said.

Portman's expression was just this side of a leer. "Oh. My humblest of apologies, Counselor." He opened the door wide. "Please step this way. Chief Hatfield would like to confer with you."

We walked into the conference room. Jack Hatfield, Belleville police chief of detectives, stood squat and immobile at the head of the conference table, hands jammed into the pockets of his gray suit coat, which hung open around a plentiful belly. A gray fedora was shoved back on his close-shaved blocklike head and an unlit cigar jutted from his meaty lips as he studied notes on a small pad with his tiny, weathered eyes.

Another man, middle-aged, balding, and dressed in shirt sleeves, sat at the table. Otherwise, the room was empty.

Hatfield looked up at us, let his notepad drop to the table, and removed the cigar from his mouth. He didn't greet me; he didn't need to. We'd met before. "Have a seat," he grunted.

Carole restrained me with a hand on the arm. "If I may, Chief, a couple of orders of business first?"

Hatfield smiled, a gallant old sea dog. "Certainly, Counselor. I don't believe we've met."

"Carole Somers," she said. "First order of business is, have you advised my client of his rights?"

Carl Portman, leaning against the closed door, answered. "Yeah, we Mirandized him, twice already. Fair enough?"

"Thank you," Carole said. "Next, Chief, I'd appreciate it if you'd advise your detective over there that I'm not the only woman lawyer in the United States, in Michigan, or in Wayne County. In fact, and this is just a wild guess, I'm most likely not the first woman lawyer he's ever seen. I'd also like you to advise your detective—"

"Now, hold it," Portman said.

"Advise him, please," Carole bore down, eyes on Hatfield—"that I am not the first lawyer in history to have been called away from a day at the lake to a crime scene, without time to change into more formal attire. I'd like you to encourage him, if you'd be so kind, to keep his mind on the business at hand and to wipe the asshole smirk off his face."

In a way, you couldn't blame Portman for giving Carole the once-over. She's a big vivid woman, with blond Princess Diana hair, creamy skin, dark Mediterranean eyes; today she wore a white cotton jump suit with sleeves and cuffs rolled

up, over a hot-pink top. But Hatfield, who'd remained expressionless, didn't mention any of that. "Carl," he said, "you
heard her."

The detective shrugged and rolled his eyes and returned
to his place at the door. Hatfield beamed at Carole. "Any
other business before we take up my agenda, Counselor?"

"Yes, Chief. I'd like to know who this is," she said,
indicating the balding man seated at the table, who was
watching us with reddened eyes.

"This is Mr. Lance Reardon," Hatfield rumbled, "the
father of the victim."

Reardon, a big soft man in his fifties, wore a white-on-
white shirt, a tie loosened beneath an open collar, big fat
suspenders, and dark formal trousers. His face looked swollen
and puffy around reddened, mean-looking eyes.

Carole took a deep breath. "Well, while it goes without
saying that this gentleman has my most heartfelt sympathies,
I most strenuously object to his presence here. I mean, what
the *hell*, Chief?"

Reardon was staring at me. "You're dead, you son of a
bitch."

Portman took a cautionary step toward him. I said
unsteadily, "Your son was one of my best friends. I'm as upset
about this as you are, and—"

Reardon rose and kicked his chair back onto the floor.
"You *killed* him, you son of a bitch! You were the only one
who ever went near that car!"

Portman sauntered toward him. "Please sit down, sir."

Reardon shot a finger at me. "I want him locked up right
now."

"Mr. Reardon," Hatfield rumbled, "please sit down and
compose yourself. I know this is difficult, but—"

"Chief," Carole said hotly, "this is not going to work, and
I think it's outrageous and inexcusable to have Mr. Reardon
here."

Reardon said, "I want Perkins's ass in the jail at once."

"Well," Hatfield drawled, holding up both hands, "as it
happens, this is my little sody-pop stand, and I'll run it as I
see fit, if it's all the same to all of you." No one answered. "All

right," he grunted. "Now that we're all acquainted, let's sit down and get on with it."

Portman uprighted Reardon's chair and he sat back down. Carole and I took seats across the table from him. Jack Hatfield remained standing, studying his raggedy little pad. Carole flipped open her leather portfolio, extracted a gold pen, and wrote on the yellow legal pad: *Why Reardon?*

I knew the answer to that, or thought I did. Reardon was a rich man, rich to the point where he had never had to work, and occupied himself with spreading beneficence, like fertilizer, upon the bowed heads of politicians across the state. No doubt, he'd taken pains to apprise Jack Hatfield of the power and prestige of the friends that he had on high. Hatfield's no whore, but he's also careful not to annoy the rich and famous needlessly.

My mouth was dry and my heart was pounding. I wanted a cigar, I wanted a beer—make that several beers—and most of all, I wanted to start the day over, with Paul Reardon back.

Hatfield looked up at us from his pad. "Well," he said in his smoke-thickened voice, "ain't we got a mess?"

No one argued.

"Question is," Hatfield said rhetorically, "what do we got here? What we got here is one hell of an explosion in a 1974 AMC Gremlin, instantly killing Mr. Paul Reardon, aged twenty-five, of Apartment 308, Norwegian Wood, Belleville.

"My officers and I have been interviewing witnesses. Our forensics people have been collecting physical evidence. Not that there's much to examine, given the power of the explosion. But we have determined that the explosion was caused by a bomb consisting of as many as a half-dozen sticks of dynamite, wired to the ignition of the Gremlin."

Reardon stirred. "Get to it, Hatfield."

"Easy, Mr. Reardon." Hatfield examined his cigar critically. "We have developed information as to two facts." He looked at me. "One: It would appear that the dynamite may have come from the Norwegian Wood maintenance shed. We found two sticks in there. Any comment, Perkins?"

Carole said, "I don't think we—"

"Wait a minute," I cut in. She gave me a long look: *It's your funeral.* I said, "Two sticks? There's supposed to be fifteen. That's what I had left over."

"Fifteen, huh?" Hatfield said happily. He took a pencil stub from behind his ear, licked its point, and wrote something on his pad.

"We had some dead trees along the lakeshore," I said. "I topped 'em and dropped 'em, and used the dynamite to blow the stumps. Somebody must have stolen those missing ones."

"Fine, thank you," Hatfield said. "Thirteen sticks missing," he murmured as he wrote.

Carole did not like where this was headed. "Chief," she said, "there's no reason to presume that Mr. Perkins had anything to do with Mr. Reardon's murder."

"There's the missing dynamite," Hatfield said, "which Perkins admits he was using. Then there's the fact that Perkins was putting a new engine in that Gremlin for the Reardons, and that he was, so far as we can determine, the last person to touch that vehicle. Any argument with that?"

Ignoring Carole's threatening expression, I said, "I finished the job yesterday afternoon, pretty late. Took the thing out, put a half-dozen miles on it, made some adjustments. Then I parked it in the lot by the pool area. I had this notion of tying a big bow to it . . . never got around to that. . . . "

"Ben," Carole said, "did anyone use that car or touch it, after you finished with it?"

"No, not that I know of," I answered softly. "But somebody went near it. Somebody sure as shit did, and wired it up, and—"

Reardon evidently could restrain himself no longer. He stood, visibly shaking. "Why are you being so deferential to this thug? Lock him up!"

My heart was hammering and I felt like killing something, or someone. But I clamped down on myself, maintained icy calm, and chose my words carefully so as not to make a bad situation worse. "I realize you're distraught and out of control, Reardon, so I'll just overlook that, you stinking greaseball."

Carole grabbed my wrist and squeezed it to the point of pain. "Enough!" she hissed.

"Just keep him out of my face."

Carl Portman appeared behind Reardon and put his hands lightly on the older man's shoulders. "Keep your ass to the chair, would you please, sir?"

Reardon sat. Carole, face dark with impatience, let me go and said, "Chief Hatfield, I repeat my objection to Mr. Reardon's presence here."

"Noted," Hatfield rumbled. His tiny eyes were on me, pinprick bright with interest. "So tell me, Perkins, if you didn't blow up the victim, who did? Got any thoughts on that?"

"Yeah, come to think of it. How about Reardon? Give that a listen."

Reardon sagged in his seat as if slugged and gaped at me. "You're out of your mind."

"Oh, I don't think so," I said maliciously. "There's the matter of that trust fund your son was to come into as of today. That was from your side of the family, from your father, if I remember correctly. Since Paul won't be getting it now, wonder where it's going to go?"

Reardon's face was getting ruddy. His fingers writhed like snakes on the table in front of him. Portman was poised to intervene, but Reardon gave no sign he was going to move. "This is outrageous. To even *suggest* that I'd murder my own son—"

I turned to Hatfield. "Follow the money," I said, "Rule number one in the book of 'whodunit.' In this case, the money leads straight to good old Daddy over there. A daddy who likes to live big and splashy. What's his personal finances like right now? Inquiring minds want to know. Is it true, as informed sources have told me, that he detested his son? Sure be interesting to find out. Has he ever had any experience with explosives? The world wonders."

"I've never been around such things in my life," Reardon said pointedly. "As opposed to you, Perkins."

"Have to admit," Hatfield said, "on the question of experience and ability, you got him beat all hollow, Perkins."

"This is the absolute *depth* of irrelevance," Carole said.

Hatfield ignored her. "When was that now? Five years ago?" He picked up his cigar and studied it intently. "Young woman was found strangled to death in the closet of Perkins's apartment here. Named Cinnamon somebody. Cute little redhead."

"Cinnamon Grajewski," I answered, voice dry. "Turned out an ex-boyfriend had snuck in and killed her and tried to pin the rap on me. He was—"

Hatfield beamed. "I remember now! You run him over with your John Deere riding mower after he tried to strangle you in the maintenance shed. Chopped him to hamburger. Remember that, Carl? 'Nothing runs like a Deere,' was what we all said."

"I remember, Chief," Portman answered.

Carole looked about as pained as I felt, but did not interrupt. Reardon was staring hotly at me with his red-rimmed eyes. Hatfield, grinning, mused, "Yeah, you sure have had your moments, haven't you, Perkins? There was that old security guard of yours, several years back. Gunned down out in the security shed by a couple of guys'd come looking for *you*."

"Yeah, well, I took care of that one, too," I said. "I ran the perp clean out of the country, for your information, and he ain't been heard from since."

"What's the point?" Carole asked Hatfield wearily.

"Point is," the chief said, sobering, "we been bagging a lot of bodies in these parts, thanks to your client here."

"That hardly qualifies as evidence against him," Carole retorted.

"Just observing, counselor."

"Lock him up," Reardon said.

"You've got nothing," Carole said. "It's all circumstantial, and you know it."

"Lock him up," Reardon repeated in a harder voice.

Hatfield's lined face scrunched up intently, then smoothed. "Well, as it happens, Mr. Reardon, the lawyer here is right. We don't have anything solid on Perkins. Not at the moment."

"I'm telling you to lock him up."

"We just can't do that today," the chief answered gently.

"Right now," Reardon said.

Hatfield slowly stuck his cigar back in his teeth and then went motionless. "Or, what, sir?"

Reardon's smile was icy. "You ever heard of Frank J. Kelley? Attorney general of the state of Michigan? It so happens that I'm close pals with several of his deputies. You wouldn't want to have this *incompetence* of yours reported to the state people, would you?"

With lightning speed, Hatfield went into his jacket pocket, took out something, and tossed it to Carl Portman, who caught it one-handed. "Open it, Carl," he said.

Portman opened the wallet.

"Read it out loud," Hatfield said, turning his back.

"'City of Belleville Police. Chief of Detectives,'" Portman read from the badge.

Hatfield spun back to face Reardon, put both hands on the table, and leaned forward, his voice gaining like rapidly advancing thunder. "Thought I remembered it right. You hear that, Mr. Reardon? Chief of detectives. That's me. City of Belleville. That's here. Now: I sympathize with you, losing your boy. I'm sworn to find the perpetrator, and since nineteen and forty-seven I've always been true to my oath." He leaned even further forward, face just two feet from Reardon's now, and his voice went raspy. "But you coming onto my turf and threatening me with some horse's ass state action—no, sir, that will not do."

Lance Reardon visibly wilted. He tried to speak, but was unable to force words past his dry mouth.

"You're excused!" Hatfield boomed.

Reardon rose. His face was glacial. "We'll just see, Chief," he said, and left the room.

Carole flipped her portfolio shut and said brightly, "Well! That concludes the festivities, I believe?"

Hatfield looked at us distantly. "You know you're number one on the list, Perkins."

I stood. "I didn't do it, Chief. I mean, get serious now, just between us: do you really think I did?"

The old cop squinted. "Bottom line? Doubt it. And not

because you're pure as driven snow. I been around, I know better."

"My client has never been convicted of a crime," Carole said.

Hatfield rolled his eyes. "So he's been lucky. Amazing how much you can get away with when you have a good lawyer and a good line of bullshit."

Carole smiled. "I prefer to think of it as blind justice working its will. But I'll accept the compliment, Chief."

"You're more 'n welcome," Hatfield growled. "By none of this do I mean to suggest that I think Perkins is some kinda angel. I just figure, if he was of a mind to whack somebody, he'd do it smarter than this."

"Well, I've heard more glowing endorsements in my time," I said, "but I'll take it. Can we go now?"

"I guess. Let's wrap it up, Carl."

Carole and I headed for the door. Hatfield said, "Stay real handy, Perkins. As in don't leave town."

"Got no plans to, Chief. Thanks for the advice, anyhow. Can I offer you some?"

"Shoot."

"Check old man Reardon out. Follow the money."

"We'll do that. And now, Hatfield added, "just another teensy-weensy bit of advice for you. Butt out of the investigation."

"Don't tell me what to do," I said pleasantly.

His face reddened. "Now, looky here—"

"'Looky' nothing, old man." I felt my face grinning. "Just stay plenty clear of me, would be my advice."

"Ben," Carole said.

"I'm cutting you a shit load of slack as it is," Hatfield rumbled.

"He was my friend. I'm going to piss on the flowers of whoever did this." I pointed a defiant finger into his face. "Any of your boys interfere, they're gonna get hammered."

Carole stepped between us and physically nudged me toward the door. "Have to go now," she said brightly. "Thanks so much, Chief." As we walked through the door she seized my arm and hissed into my ear: "Keep moving, butthead."

We burst out onto the sidewalk. The daylight was fading rapidly, but not rapidly enough to suit me. I wanted this evil day over. As we walked briskly toward my building, the surge of violence that had nearly swallowed me receded, leaving only regret and a sour sense of guilt. I took Carole's hand. "Thanks, babe. I appreciate your—"

She snatched her hand away. "We have to talk," she said, eyes averted.

"Yeah, I know, we got a mess on our hands, but—"

"A mess?" She snorted. "You think that's a mess? Oh, no, buddy boy. That's nothing. Wait till you hear. Just *wait* till you hear."

Chapter 5

My apartment was a disaster area, but what else do you expect? I'm a maintenance guy, expert at cleaning other people's messes, never my own.

I closed the door behind us. Will Somers, Carole's seven-year-old, sat in front of the TV, surrounded by cast-off sections of the *Detroit Free Press,* old pizza boxes, overloaded ashtrays, and various brands of empties. He paused in his game of Dig-Dug and looked at us. "Hi. Is Ben's trouble all fixed?"

"No," Carole said. "It's just beginning."

I still had no idea what she was talking about. She'd refused to elaborate on the walk over here. But it didn't sound good.

"Don't worry," Will said cheerfully. "Ben'll take care of it. He's a real good fixer."

"From your lips to God's ear," I said.

"I think you need a drink," Carole said. "No, don't

bother to offer," she added, before I had a chance to. "I'll bring them out."

She went into the kitchen. I walked past Will, who'd returned to his game, and went out on the deck, leaving the window-wall door wide open to let some breeze inside.

It was the day's last stanza. The sun, by now a fireball, was headed for its daily showdown with Ford Lake. A light warmish breeze breathed on me. Going to be a warm night, a humid night, a sleepless night.

I stood at the deck railing, looking absently down the long grassy avenue that ran toward the big grove of trees lining the lakeshore. A sour smoldering ache was building in the center of my chest. A slight tremor owned my hands. I was physically tired and emotionally done for. Worst of all, I did not know what to do.

Everyone's life is built on a structure of certainties. Funny thing is, you don't know what those certainties are till one of them has been proven false. Which was what had happened to me today. I learned I'd always been certain that twenty-five-year-old men don't get blown up on their wedding day.

I fired up a cigar and put my hands on the deck rail. I wanted to do one of two things. Go out to the bars, sing obscene songs, tell tall tales, and get window-smashing, pissy drunk. Or, even more appealing, I wanted to stay here, hide from the world, sit and stare, maybe cry a little, and get pissy drunk.

Well, there'd be time for that, once Carole went home. In the meantime I had to get this latest "bad news," whatever it was. Couldn't be worse than what had happened already, right? The world never gives you more shit than you can handle. Right?

Carole came out onto the deck and handed me an ice-cold Stroh's tall boy. I noticed she'd gotten a 7-Up for herself, which surprised me. She's not one to get pissy drunk, but on an evening like this I expected her to hoist one or two.

I thanked her for the beer, popped it, drank. No taste,

but I didn't want taste, just effect. I sucked down half of it as Carole sat in one of the lawn chairs and kept my back to her till I felt I had some semblance of control. Then I faced her. She was watching me curiously, the setting sun creating a halo in her blond hair. "Are you all right?" she asked.

"Yeah. Sure. Look, thanks for coming down and keeping me out jail and stuff."

"Glad to do it. For one thing, it got me away from my mother's just when things were starting to get deadly up there. Will was getting cranky, and—"

"Hey, Ben!" Will said, galloping out onto the deck. He wore red shorts, a red top, and his blond hair in a buzz cut. A big brawny boy, he got his mother's eyes and maybe his height came from her, but the rest of him was handed down from his dad, whose name was, so far as I've been told, Asshole. "You wanna play Dig-Dug?"

"No thanks, kid, not tonight."

"Bet I can whip your ass."

"Will," his mother said wearily.

"Yeah, kid, keep it clean. This is a class joint, act respectable. And while you're up, fetch me a fresh cold one and a cigar, if you would."

"Okay, Ben." He scooted back inside.

"Good kid," I said to Carole.

Her face was unreadable. "I'm pregnant," she said.

I froze, then raised the tall boy and drank it down. My first thought was unworthy, a stab to the heart: Oh God, she's been with another guy after all. Another one of those unacknowledged certainties shot to hell.

I looked at her again. No change, except now she looked watchful and appraising, her rich brown eyes aimed at me beneath the sweep of blond hair that crossed her forehead. I cleared my throat and said, "Aw Jesus, Carole." I sighed. "I'm sorry for ya. Gonna be a tough one. Told the guy yet?"

"Here you go, Ben!" Will said as he came out onto the deck. He gave me a fresh beer and a cigar, looked at the two of us uncertainly, and, with the keen instincts developed as a refugee from a broken marriage, retreated indoors. After a moment Dig-Dug started up again inside.

Carole answered, "Yes. I told him today."

That lance of pain again. Well, what do you expect, I asked myself roughly. You got no hold on her, or she on you. It was just for laughs, this time. That's what you said and that's what you meant. I opened the beer. "Is he gonna fall into line, or do I have to go beat him up?"

A strange smile crossed her face. "I don't know yet."

"Well, what'd he say when you told him?"

Her eyebrows arched. "He said, 'Aw Jesus, Carole. I'm sorry for ya. Gonna be a tough one.'"

My grin hurt. I really was trying to be an adult about the whole thing. "Or words to that effect, eh?"

"No. Those were his words exactly."

Finally it registered. I really wasn't tracking all that well. I laughed sharply. "Aw no. No way, Carole, uh-uh."

"Yes."

"It's friggin' impossible and you know it."

She spread her hands, inviting an inspection. "And yet here I am, knocked up bigger than hell. You figure it out."

I waved the wrong hand, sending a slop of beer splashing to the deck. "I had a *vasectomy*, remember?"

"Or so you thought."

"Whaddya think, I dreamed it or made it up or—"

"All I know," she said softly, "is that I am pregnant, and I haven't been with anyone but you since winter."

"Wow!" Will shouted from inside. "I'm doing great, Ben! Fifty thousand points!"

"Come on," I said, stepping into deep shit, "You had to've been with somebody."

"Oh," she said dangerously, "you think I had a one-leg quickie, six to eight weeks ago, and it just slipped my mind."

"That's not what I said."

"You really can be an asshole."

"What I can't be is a father, Carole."

She took a sip of pop and looked away from me. "Well, you're not going to be, anyway. I'm getting an abortion, of course." Her eyes found me again. "If it's all right with you."

"What've I got to say about it? I'm not the dad."

She rolled her eyes. "Look, I'm thirty-six years old. No

way do I need another kid. I'm just finally getting my law practice off the ground, getting it to the point where I can make a decent living with it, maybe even take on a partner or an associate."

Carole's specialty is women's legal issues: spouse abuse, sexual harassment, unfair labor practices, you name it. Her zeal for those issues sprang from her own experience as a battered wife and a down-and-out divorcée raising a baby boy by herself, working crap jobs while attending University of Detroit Law School. As an honors graduate, she'd been offered numerous cushy jobs with large corporations eager to beef up their inventory of female executives; instead, she'd continued with what she called her "tradition of poverty," hung out her own shingle, and virtually invented her specialty. For years, few people took her work seriously. Now that was changing. She was starting to make it.

I said, "Hey, kid, I'm not arguing with you."

"Besides, I've got Will," she said. "I'm not like these precious yups who hit their midthirties childless and then panic, believing that the world as we know it will cease to exist without the benefit of the issue of their loins."

I'd forgotten all about my cigar. I stuck it in my teeth, flared a kitchen match, and lighted up. "Whatever you want to do, Carole, is fine with me."

She'd lost all track of me. "And Jesus God, at least Will's in school full-time! The thought of having an infant to take care of . . . oh Lord . . . I've done my share of that and it's all over."

I leaned back on the deck rail. "Okay."

She looked at me, her face drawn, her eyes remote. "So I'm going to abort. Okay?"

"Whatever you want to do. It's your life, your body, your kid."

"Yours too," she said softly.

"Can't be," I answered as gently as I could. "You're my friend and I'll do anything I can to help. But there's no way the kid is mine."

She slowly stood up from the deck chair, rising to her

glorious altitude of five feet nine. Her face was flushed, body poised, eyes flashing. "So I'm lying, is that it?"

I stood, too, thinking, Jesus Christ, another one of those patented no-win situations. "I didn't say that."

"Might as well." She glared at me. "Listen, mister. You and I have tested that 'vasectomy' of yours under real-world conditions, and it flunked."

As civilly as I could, I answered, "For the record, this here vasectomy has been tested with at least a half-dozen other women, and I ain't had no complaints yet."

She tossed her head, folded her arms, looked past me. "Yes, indeed, there's never been any doubt of your promiscuity. Which is why you've got a hell of a nerve accusing me of sleeping around."

"I did not accuse you of that," I shot back. "Although you've got a track record to be sure, like that time with my friend Eddie way back when."

"Oh yeah?" she shouted. "How about you and that lady cop that you were doing the back-door dance with? You bastard, you dirty son of a bitch."

She marched to the sliding door, grabbed the handle, and ripped it open. Tossing my cigar away, I went to her quickly, took her hand and shoulder, and turned her to face me. Red highlights showed starkly in her pale face and her brown eyes were moist and seemed extra large as she glared at me defiantly. "Look," I said quickly, "I'm sorry, all right? I'm sorry."

She leaned her forehead against the doorframe. "This is just such a mess," she whispered, "and I don't know what to do."

"So take your time and sort it out. Meanwhile I'll get myself checked out and then we'll see. I'm with you, kid."

She straightened, nodded, cleared her throat. "Okay."

Will, just inside, was still playing Dig-Dug, elaborately ignoring us. I said, "Want to get something to eat?"

"We have to be going," she said dully. "Will starts his summer day camp tomorrow, he's got to get to bed." She looked in at her son. "Will, close it up now, we're going home."

"In a minute," he answered, "I'm doing real good here."

We stepped inside. Will was still hard at it on Dig-Dug and doing pretty well. Carole stood beside me and watched him, and I reflected on how, just that morning, I'd been looking forward to nothing more than a pleasant summer party and eight weeks of baseball games, sailing, flying, and relaxation. Now, I was the principal suspect in the murder of my best friend, and my lady friend was accusing me of being the father of her unborn child. I mean, things have turned to shit before; but it usually doesn't happen all at once.

Carole said to me, "By the way, if this Reardon thing gets any uglier, I'm going to bring in another lawyer to work with us. We may need a real gunslinger this time."

"Hope not," I said. "They got nothing on me, right?"

"At the moment," she answered. "Will, come on, dear. We've got to go."

He cranked his head around looked at us as the game chirped merrily. "Oh, Mom, can't we stay awhile? I just got a new life."

I said, "We should all be so lucky."

I eased the Mustang into its semi-enclosure, shut off the engine, and sat back in the bucket seat. "Well, I guess that's it."

"I guess it is," Ellen said softly.

"You okay?"

"As okay as I'll ever be."

"Takes time," I said. "So take your time."

"Time heals, is that it?" she asked, her laughter the sound of breaking glass. "Can you come in for a while?"

"Sure, if you want."

We got out of the Mustang and walked across Norwegian Wood's central parking lot toward Building 3. The day was pitilessly hot and humid and I was beginning to swim under my navy blue pin-striped suit. Ellen didn't seem to feel the heat. She didn't seem to feel anything at all. She looked like she was being operated by remote control, an automatic woman in her simple deep purple dress and plain black pumps.

This was Wednesday, the third day of Paul's death and the day we buried him. Hump day of a week that had started off rotten and was only getting worse.

Monday the story of the bombing hit the papers. A terse story that gave only the name of the victim; the police withheld all further comment. I worked maintenance jobs all day with Randy, who was noticeably remote with me, as was everyone else I encountered around Norwegian Wood.

Tuesday the complex's general manager, Simpson, dragged me into his office and told me that he'd fire me if I was convicted and sent to prison for murdering Paul. Company policy; he even showed me where it was written in the manual. Reassuring. That afternoon Ellen called to ask if I'd escort her to Paul's funeral. What could I say?

And today we buried him, in what was about as uncomforting an exercise as I'd ever witnessed. The service was held in an ice-cold Episcopal church in Farmington Hills and was conducted in hard-edged, robotic tones out of some sort of prayer book that sounded papist to my Southern Baptist ears. Evidently the whole thing had been arranged by Lance Reardon, and he threw in a sadistic reminder to Ellen as to where she stood in the scheme of things: instead of having her seated with the family, he had her (and everyone else associated with her) seated across the aisle from the family, as if we were unclean.

Well, damned if I know how I got through it without breaking someone's head. The numbness of Sunday was wearing off. I felt twitchy and anxious to break loose.

Ellen and I went upstairs and into Apartment 308. It looked about the same. Maybe cleaner than usual. It was one of Norwegian Wood's smallest units, a one-bedroom with small rooms and no deck. The small living room had Paul written all over it. His aquarium; his framed charcoal sketches on the wall; a framed, autographed poster of ex–Detroit Tigers catcher Lance Parrish standing next to a crouching, grinning bengal; a large wood bookcase standing between two windows, loaded with stereo equipment and Paul's collection of oldie LPs; the big, well-worn easy chair on the far wall facing a stand holding the twenty-inch Sony Trinitron.

And his guitar. It leaned against the wall next to the easy chair. I remembered a night just a couple of weeks ago when Paul and Ellen had been over to my place for pizza, and Paul had brought his guitar and entertained us with an excellent version of Jonathan Edwards's "Hang Around the Shanty."

That guitar got to me.

Ellen seated herself in the corner of the sofa. The air-conditioning felt invigorating to me, but she seemed only more tired. Her streaked blond hair was braided and bound tight to the back of her well-formed head. She wore no jewelry except for her wedding ring and a fine gold chain around her neck. She looked older, thoroughly beaten, out of it.

"Get you anything?" I asked.

She stirred. "A diet, if there's any in there. Help yourself, too, Ben."

I went into the tiny kitchen, opened the fridge, and rescued drinks. On the trip back to the living room, I noticed that the entire place was immaculate. Ellen had probably spent several hours scrubbing the place sparkling, in anticipation of the visitors whom she had fully and reasonably expected to stop by after the funeral. A miscalculation, as it turned out.

It took Ellen a moment to realize I was holding a pop out to her. "Thanks," she said. "Go ahead, have a seat."

I loosened my tie, sat down uncomfortably in the big easy chair, and twisted the top off the Labatt's Blue I'd found in the fridge. I wanted a cigar. I wanted out of my suit.

And, to be totally honest, I wanted to go home. But I was raised in a culture that was very strict about how to behave during a friend's bereavement. You don't just cut and run and hide somewhere till it blows over. You go to the person and you stay with her, and you help her and watch out for her till she gets back on her feet again.

You hang around and help, no matter how bad it gets.

Ellen said abruptly, "Now I know why I've never been to church since I was sixteen."

"Why's that?"

Her light eyes were wide and unseeing. "Did you hear that funeral service? The tone of it? The church always assumes that people are naturally evil and bad. That's what I really resent. Paul wasn't evil."

"No, he wasn't."

"I had trouble sitting there and listening to that prayer-book drivel that was trying to convince me that God had actually done Paul and me a big fat favor by taking him away from me."

"They said that?"

"One of those prayers, toward the end. I remember the line clearly. 'Most merciful Father, who hast been pleased to take unto thyself the soul of this thy servant.' They said God was *pleased*."

"I don't think they meant it quite like—"

"And that other line," she drove on, "where they describe death as falling asleep in Jesus. You were there, Ben, would you describe the way Paul died as falling asleep in Jesus?"

"I guess they mean figuratively or something," I said uncomfortably.

"And God?" she said, voice rising, looking past me. "I don't know about you, but I don't think *God* took him. I don't think God put that bomb in the car, do you?"

"No."

"I also don't think the police will find out, because they don't care."

"That's not true at all, Ellen. I know Hatfield. He ain't downtown, but he gets the job done."

"So," she said, looking directly at me for the first time, "I want you to find out who murdered Paul."

Looking into her eyes was almost more than I could do. Saying what I had to say was even harder. I didn't want to make her any promises. I didn't want her counting on me. "Listen, Ellen. I'm a suspect myself, and—"

She waved a hand. "Suspect! That's a joke, and you know it. What you are, Ben, is a private detective. A professional. And Paul's best friend—"

"That's just the point, I'm not objective enough." The rationalization sounded weak, even to me. "And frankly, there's not much in the way of clues to work on—"

She smiled then, and it was not pretty. "Clues? Oh yes, there are clues. I can't figure them out, but maybe you can."

Chapter 6

"What kind of clues?" I asked.

"He started acting strange, the past few weeks, for one thing," she said. "Weird. Different. Remote—"

I hooked one leg over the other and rubbed my jaw. "Look, kid. I hate to sound negative, but Paul was about to get married. Not that I'd know personally, but that's enough to make anyone weird and different and remote."

She was nodding. "Oh, I thought of that. I thought maybe he was getting cold feet. I even thought—I mean, I know how silly this sounds—I even thought maybe he was seeing someone else."

"What made you think that?" I asked carefully.

"Nothing special. Silly idea, really." She licked her lips. "But there's evidence, all right. I don't know what it means. Want to see it?"

I nodded. She left the room. I stood, lighted a cigar, paced a path around the coffee table, walking through my own clouds of smoke. Ellen came back in and sat down. She had a catalog-size clasp envelope in her hand. She undid the clasp, upended the envelope, and two items slid out. "Take a look."

The first was a thin blue-backed legal document. I folded it and read the heading: "Last Will and Testament." It was less than a legal size page long and very standard as far as I could tell. Paul Stanley Reardon, born July 6, 1951, in Sydney, Nova Scotia, and now a resident of Belleville, Michigan, thereby left everything he had to Ellen. All duly signed, witnessed, and as official as could be.

I let it drop. "So, he wrote a will. Makes sense to me."

"I didn't know about it," she said. "Look at the other."

This was a thin gray savings account passbook, still shiny and new, issued by Detroit Bank and Trust. I flipped it open. One entry. An initial deposit. Five thousand dollars.

"Hoo boy," I said.

"I didn't know about that either," Ellen said.

I remembered what Paul had said at the party, just minutes before he was killed: "Things are pretty good in the money department right now."

I'd say.

"No idea where this came from, huh?" I asked Ellen. She shook her head. I sat down on the sofa next to her and arrayed the two items on the coffee table so I could examine them. "You found them where, exactly?"

"In one of Paul's art portfolios. You know, those great big leather things he carried pasteups and mechanicals around in."

My eyes ran absently over the documents. "Do you think he was really trying to hide them from you?"

"Well, he knew I never had reason to look in his art portfolios."

"Why did you this time?"

"I don't know," she said wearily. "I had this goofy idea of getting a bunch of his free-lance things together for a scrapbook or something. I thought there might be some things in there. Anyway, I know he didn't want me to know about these things, because he never told me—"

"The dates," I broke in.

"What?"

I gestured at the documents with my smoldering cigar. "Look at the dates. He opened the savings account just last Wednesday, and executed the will last Thursday."

"I see," she said, voice small.

I poked a finger at the witness signatures on the will. "Who're these people?"

"Curt Goldflower is the man at the agency that Paul

free-lanced for. Never heard of that other person. Probably works at the agency, too."

I felt I'd been sitting around for a month. I got to my feet and paced again, burning down the cigar. "So he got the money somewhere. Then he decided to draw up a will. I guess to make sure you got the money if something happened to him. Which suggests that he had reason to believe something might happen to him."

"You think so?"

I waved a hand. "Just thinking out loud." I about-faced and paced back toward her. "And that Curt Goldflower fella who witnessed the will, he might have interesting things to say. But forget that, too, I'm not going to go poking around."

"Ben," Ellen said directly, "I want you to."

"Well, I think we should wait and see what the cops turn up. What did they say about this will and everything?"

"Nothing. I haven't told them about it."

I looked right at her and put all the steel into my voice that I could. "Tell them, Ellen. They've got to have all the facts."

She swallowed. "So you won't help me?"

The words came hard. "I can't make you any promises. I've learned that lesson the hard way—"

A pounding sounded from the apartment door. When Ellen made no move, I said, "I'll get it. Probably somebody wanting to sit with you for a while."

She straightened herself and patted absently at her hair as I hoofed heavily to the door and opened it. Two men stood there. Strangers. The older one was stout and gray, the younger was tall, angular, and dark. Both wore bored expressions and an air of implacable purpose. Cops, or a reasonable facsimile thereof.

"Paul Reardon, please," the older one said.

I blinked. "No," I answered stupidly. "He's—"

"Who're you?" the younger one asked.

"Perkins. Friend of the family. What the hell is this?"

"Reardon here?" the older one asked.

I gaped at them and then said softly, "He's dead, for God's sake."

"Ben?" came Ellen's voice from behind me. "Who are they?"

"Good question," I said.

The wallet materialized in the older man's hand. Michigan State Police. "Kilkenny," he said. "This is Daws. Can we come in?"

"Listen," I said rapidly, "I don't know what this is about"— but rest assured I was dying to know—"but Paul Reardon was killed last Saturday and we buried him today. It's just me and the widow here, and she's in no shape to—"

They wore identically skeptical squints. "So he's dead," the older one, Kilkenny, said. "How very convenient."

"Whaddya think, Kil?" the other one asked.

"I think we'd like to come in and chat," Kilkenny said. "Would that be all right with you, Mr. Perkins?"

I was badly torn. On the one hand, I wanted no new problems for Ellen, especially today. On the other hand, I was consumed with curiosity and a fresh dose of dread. These guys weren't involved in investigating Paul's death. Unbelievable as it might seem, they hadn't even known about it. They wanted him for some other reason.

I stood back. "Okay, for a minute." I focused on the older cop. "And be goddamned careful what you say and do. The widow's in a bad way."

"Certainly," Kilkenny said.

"And afterward I want you to tell me what this is about."

"Absolutely," Daws said.

I stood back. Kilkenny and Daws walked past me and I shut the door. They stood in the center of the living room, glancing around, missing nothing. Ellen was on her feet by the sofa, hands knotted together in front of her, pale face set and fearful.

"Mrs. Reardon," Kilkenny said, holding up his shield, "I'm Sergeant Kilkenny, Michigan State Police. "We're here to see Paul Reardon."

"For God's sake!" I thundered. "I told you, Paul is dead. He died in a car bombing last Sunday. It was in the *Free Press*. You guys been hibernating somewhere?"

"We don't read the *Free Press*," Kilkenny said. "We're not from the immediate area. Where was the funeral held?"

It was all I could do to say the words civilly. "St. Michael and All Angels in Farmington Hills. I could probably get a note from the priest if you want."

"Nah," Daws said, "we'll take your word for it."

Kilkenny looked at Ellen, whose face was so drawn you could see the bone structure under her pale skin. "Our condolences, ma'am."

She nodded just once. The policemen exchanged looks, turned as one, and started for the door. I trailed them. "So what's the bit, boys?"

"Routine inquiries," Kilkenny said, opening the door.

"Sorry to've intruded, ma'am," Daws called back to Ellen.

"Hey, we had a deal," I insisted. "What's this about?"

"Police business," Daws said curtly, following his partner out the door. Helpless, I watched them walk away up the hall. Then I shut the door, overly hard.

"What was that about?" Ellen's voice was quavery.

I turned to face her. Her face was flat white, her eyes glittering pools ringed in black. "Damned if I know," I said.

"I'm scared," she said. "It's like—it's like the whole world has gone out of control."

"Take it easy."

She crumpled back down onto the couch and hugged herself as she pulled her legs up under her. "Tell me what to do. Please."

"Just hang in there," I said. "It's all you can do."

She took a deep breath and let it out in stages. She looked around the room, as if seeing it for the first time. "Everything's coming unglued," she said softly. "I can't afford this place. I have no money and my nurse-aid job won't pay the rent. No family either."

"You got Paul's family. And you got that five grand in the savings account."

"Paul's father hates me," she said. "Just like he hated Paul. And that money—I can't touch that—I don't know where it came from." Her eyes were shining brighter and her voice was hoarsening, and I thought: Here we go, over the top to the long slope down, all the way to the bottom, the trip she had to take, sooner or later. "We didn't even have any life insurance. Paul was only twenty-five, we didn't even think about things like that." She examined her hands a moment, then rubbed an eye and laughed roughly. "I don't even have a car. I mean, what are you in Michigan without a car? A nonperson."

"That I can fix up for you," I said, relighting my cigar. "I've got a handful of old crocks stashed at a car wash in Detroit. I'll ferry one of 'em out here for you. Nothing pretty, but it's wheels and it'll run and it's yours."

Her eyes found mine. "You'd do that for me?" she asked in a small voice.

"Sure."

She blinked rapidly, rubbed an eye again, and said shakily, "What about a husband? Got a spare one of those?"

"Come on, Ellen," I said gently.

She masked her face with her hands and sobbed, her shoulders shaking, her elbows clamped to her flanks, feet twisting together. I never know what to do in those situations. I mean, do you go hug the person, or do you leave them be? I can never tell.

So I made myself useful by getting tissues and a glass of water from the bathroom. She took the tissues, daubed her eyes, drank a little water, set the glass down. The storm had passed, for the moment, and she looked wasted and whipped and about a hundred thousand years old. Her fingers kept playing with the wedding band on her left hand.

"So the deal is this," I said finally, looking down at her.

Her eyes were red and just barely interested, if not exactly curious.

"You turn over the will and the savings account books to the cops," I said. "Give 'em a shot at it. Meanwhile, I'll do some low-key checking around. Okay?"

She blinked, "Okay," she said carefully.

I started whomping out my cigar in an ashtray on the coffee table. "I'm making you no promises, except that I'll try."

"Okay." Voice and face brighter now.

I got a fresh cigar out of my jacket, along with my little spiral pad and a pen. "Maybe I can at least find out what the deal is with those state cops just now. Meantime, you better tell me everything you know about the past few weeks."

Ellen straightened on the sofa and cleared her throat. "You mean, about Paul?"

"Yep. Everything that's happened. Plus how you've felt, what you've sensed, all that kind of off-the-wall stuff."

"Okay," she said uncertainly. "You'd better take off that jacket and loosen your tie. We're going to be here for a while."

It was a typical Perkins summer evening tableau. Slouched in a deck chair, cigar in hand, half-empty six-pack at my feet, the good gritty blues of Duane Allman and the Band drifting out the screen door.

I'd changed into T-shirt and cutoffs and lounged there alone, smoking and drinking, studying my notes of the conversation with Ellen. Precious little. Precious goddamned little.

Well, if I couldn't sort it out, maybe the cops would.

God, what a terrible thought, counting on the cops to do anything. I mean, they were in business for themselves, no question. Like those state guys, Kilkenny and Daws, who'd dropped in at Ellen's. I didn't like the smell of that. I'd called my friend Dick Dennehy, a state police inspector. Dennehy had never heard of them but he promised to check and let me know what they were working on.

The wireless phone whistled at my feet. I picked it up and switched it on. "Yo, Perkins's 'Unsolved Mysteries' here, Ben speaking."

"Jack Hatfield," rasped the senior Belleville detective.

"Yessir, Chief, how can I help you?"

"How about telling me what became of the rest of the dynamite?"

"The hell you talking about, Chief?"

"You said there was fifteen sticks in the shed. There's

two left. Lab people say seven or eight sticks done the dirty deed on Reardon. That leaves five or six unaccounted for."

I tried to puzzle it and got nowhere. "Beats me," I admitted.

"Us too. I'm also afraid," he went on heavily, "that your little theory about Mr. Lance Reardon has died without regaining consciousness. I'm sorry, son."

I straightened in my chair. "Oh, come on, Chief! Reardon's dirty, I can just feel it."

"I have to admit, Reardon looked good for it at first," Hatfield said. "We had our fine-print boys go over all those wills and trust documents and whatever. Deal is that Paul's grandfather—Lance Reardon's father—left the proceeds of a trust fund to Paul. Income of ten grand a year, thereabouts. Two conditions. Paul had to be married and he had to've turned twenty-five."

"Yeah, I knew all that, the widow told me."

"As it turns out, the trust instrument is worded very specifically, see. Our fine-print boys feel that Paul Reardon did not live to meet both conditions. The income from the trust will revert to Lance Reardon."

"What do you mean?"

"According to his birth certificate," Hatfield said patiently, "Paul Reardon was born at five-thirty P.M. on July 6, 1951. He died at exactly five P.M. on July 6. That means he was half an hour shy of turning twenty-five."

"Oh, brother. Who'd split a hair like that?"

"Reardon's father, if he wanted to."

"And if he does," I said, "Ellen won't get the money."

"She can't have what Paul Reardon couldn't leave to her," Hatfield agreed.

"Hey, all this just bears out what I've suspected all along. Lance wanted the money, so he whacked the kid."

"Oh, come on!" Hatfield exploded. "What do you think this is, 'Murder, She Wrote'? The idea's too cute, too convenient. Besides, Reardon may have hated his kid all right, but I doubt he's going to have him whacked for a measly ten grand a year. That's pocket change to a guy like our friend Lance."

"I don't care," I said stubbornly. "I like him for it."

"Our investigation further shows," Hatfield said, "that Lance Reardon was on the West Coast all last week, didn't get back here till about two hours before Paul's wedding on Sunday. Doesn't give him no opportunity, far as I can tell."

"Big deal. Reardon would've hired someone for it."

"No evidence of that at all. We can't even figure where Reardon would know anyone who could do this thing for him. He's a lavish spender all right, but it ain't on interesting things like ponies and broads and baccarat. He buys art and shit. And looky here, Perkins. Lance may be an insufferable shit, but that don't make him guilty of killing his kid."

"You're just not digging deep enough," I insisted.

"What I am," Hatfield rumbled, "is pretty goddamned tired of feeling like I have to justify anything to you, young fella. You being the prime suspect and everything."

"Oh," I said hotly, "so I'm still that, huh?"

"You're still that."

"You've got squat, Jack."

"We'll see, sonny." He hung up.

I switched off the phone, set it down, drained the last of the current Stroh's, staring blindly along the darkening grassy avenue toward the lake.

Scratch the cops, I thought. It's up to me now. As usual.

Chapter 7

I cruised up to the reception desk and signed in on the clipboard. The sharp-featured nurse-receptionist with the Rosie the Riverter hairdo studied my scrawl and then peered at me over her half-moon glasses.

"Perkins," I said, by way of interpretation.

"Very good, Mr. Perkins," she said briskly. "Have a seat, the doctor will see you shortly."

Sure. And the check's always in the mail.

It was 7:55 the next morning and here I was, in the waiting room of one Amin Abbas, M.D., who billed himself as a physician and surgeon specializing in urology. If I was in a sour mood, it was because I hadn't managed to drop off to sleep till three in the morning. Then only my body slept, leaving my mind free to romp through one dandy of a nightmare.

I was running down a wide, brightly lighted hospital corridor. Gurneys loaded with patients lined the walls. I wore a green surgical smock that flapped around me as I ran. At the end of the corridor I turned left and dived through a pair of swinging aluminum doors.

The large room was also brightly lighted. In the center stood a bed, surrounded by lights and equipment and a doctor and a nurse. On the bed lay a woman with her feet up in stirrups, her face averted from me, her belly bare and distended. The doctor, who wore a face mask, looked up from his examination of the woman. "About time you got here, Perkins," he growled. "Get into position, we're about ready."

I darted around to the left side of the bed. The woman, who wore a surgical top and nothing beneath, was Terry Lowe. This can't be, I thought. Carole's the one who's pregnant. But there was Terry, very much alive, making that unforgettable smile, which abruptly turned to agony as a contraction hit.

She began to gasp and scream and buck and thrash on the bed. The nurse wasn't there anymore, it was just me and the doctor. He was doing something between her legs. Suddenly Terry went absolutely still and I heard the doctor say, "I'm sorry. She was born dead."

I looked at the doctor. He held something unspeakable in his hands. When I looked back at Terry, her surgical top was gone. Instead, she wore a snug white short-sleeve shirt and soft blue prewashed jeans. The clothes were all bloody. She'd been shot in several places and she was breathing very slowly and hoarsely and with tremendous effort. Panicked, I looked back at the doctor, whose face mask was off now. It was Vince Wakefield, smiling wolfishly and pointing a pistol at me. . . .

I picked up a copy of *Popular Mechanix* from the rack next to the doctor's couch and flipped it open. That dream had had a nice mix of influences. Mrs. Sturtevant had mentioned Wakefield. That in turn had brought to mind Terry Lowe, an old and painful memory, the kind you don't ever recover from but merely shut out.

As for the delivery-room scenario, that was easy to figure out. Carole, and her pregnancy, and my alleged role in it.

Which was why I was here in Dr. Abbas's office, bright and early on a Thursday morning.

At least the good doctor was prompt. Three minutes after the nurse escorted me into the examining room, he came in and shook hands with me. "Amin Abbas," he said. "A pleasure, Mr. Perkins."

I liked his looks right off the bat. He was in his fifties somewhere, with dark leathery good looks and the distinguished profile of a sheikh. His lined, dark-eyed face was intelligent and calm, exuding the air of a man who'd seen plenty and was still in there swinging. I got the impression that here, at last, was a doctor who gave a shit. Incredible, if true. They should have a section devoted to such in the Yellow Pages. It would be a short one.

Abbas seated himself on a stool and folded his arms across his thin, white-jacketed chest. "How may I help you?" he asked.

Here goes. I explained the situation briefly: my vasectomy, Carole's pregnancy, and the suggestion that my vasectomy hadn't, uh, taken. Abbas watched me closely as I talked, then made a couple of notes in an open folder on the supply table next to him. Finally he said. "And your vasectomy was not performed by me, unless I'm greatly mistaken. I never forget a face."

"Never thought faces figured much in your work, Doc," I said, grinning. His thin smile was dutiful and brief. Hastily I added, "It was performed by Dr. Slater, in Taylor."

His eyes flickered. "Ah."

"I'd have gone back to him, but he doesn't seem to be there anymore. His number's disconnected. Must have moved away or retired or something."

Something tugged at a corner of his thin mouth. "Mm," he said.

"So I looked in the Yellow Pages and there you were, number one under urologists. Advantage of having a name starting with a *A* and two *B*s. Great marketing ploy, I must say."

He was scribbling again. "Oh?" he asked absently.

"Ever heard of Slater, Doc?" I asked.

He closed the folder and looked at me seriously. "But that is not important, is it? Our task is to determine whether or not you are fertile, and if so, to what degree. Simple enough. We'll collect a semen sample from you this morning and have it analyzed. The results of that will tell us what to do."

"When will you know?"

He rose briskly. "This is Thursday? Come back Monday morning. We'll have the results by then." We shook hands. "The nurse will be right with you," he said, and bustled out.

She was, too. Either I was incredibly lucky, or they were incredibly efficient around there. Rosie the Riveter handed me a very small plastic container that could have been Tupperware. "Collect the sample in this," she said briskly, "and drop it off at the desk on your way out." She peered into my face over her half-moon glasses. "This isn't funny."

"I know," I said hastily. "It's just that I ain't never heard the word 'collect' used quite that way before."

Expressionless, she silently handed me a large open-flapped manila envelope. I peered inside. Magazines. *Playboy* and *Penthouse*. Well thumbed.

"Odd," I said. "I didn't see these on the table while I was waiting out there."

"Drop them off at the desk as you leave," she ordered, and blew out of the room.

Like I said: efficient.

* * *

Ellen and I had managed to put together a rough outline of the last two weeks of Paul's life. Everything Ellen knew about where he'd been and what he'd done during that time was sketched out in my little notebook.

Not much to go on.

I skimmed the material as I motored east on Michigan Avenue toward Ypsilanti. The sun was halfway to zenith in a cloudless sky; the morning rush hour had ended, and the road was now host to truckers and grannies, kids playing hooky and guys out of work, moms in big station wagons and cops. I played it docile, kept the Mustang down to sixty—which for my baby gal is fast idle—and glanced at my notes at each stoplight.

Professionally, it had been a very busy period for Paul. He'd had practically full-time graphic-arts assignments for TGB Advertising, a little outfit over in east Ann Arbor. He'd also, according to Ellen, taken on a couple of freebie jobs for the Torch Drive campaign and was just finishing them up at the time he was killed.

Not much to go on. I've heard that advertising is a cutthroat business, but Paul worked strictly on the creative end, and I had trouble picturing bespectacled writers and geeky artists wiring a bomb to his car in the dead of night just because he'd missed a deadline or drawn an ugly picture or something.

On summer weekends, Paul had set up his easel at Hart Plaza in downtown Detroit and peddled charcoal portraits to patrons at the weekend ethnic festivals. He charged ten bucks a pop for these and never came home with less than a couple hundred. Lucrative, perhaps tax exempt, and Paul genuinely loved the work.

There seemed little to go on here either, except that two weekends before Paul was killed—I had no trouble nailing down the date, because Ellen said it was the Lithuanian Ethnic Festival—he'd come back to his parked Gremlin to find that someone had vandalized it pretty badly, flattening a tire and slashing the backseat to ribbons. On my advice, he'd bought a brand-new secondhand previously owned backseat at WorldWide Auto Parts, a glorified junkyard on the west side of Detroit, and installed it himself.

Big deal, right? I didn't see anything all that earthshaking. But Ellen felt differently. She said it was that very weekend that Paul began "acting weird." She felt strongly that the whole incident—the seat slashing and the replacement—had something to do with how and why Paul died.

Well, maybe. Personally, I was a lot more interested in the five grand he'd obtained somehow, somewhere. I mean, five grand equals five hundred charcoal portraits, and though the ethnic festivals are popular enough—hell, even I'd go if they had a Welsh one—something told me he hadn't earned the dough that way.

Then there was the will he'd written. Evidently it had been executed at TGB Advertising, which was also Paul's principal free-lance client. For both of those reasons, TGB sounded like a good place to start.

The ad agency occupied the top level of a fairly new four-story building on Plymouth Road just west of U.S. 23. The building, otherwise occupied by lawyers and dentists, was a squeaky-clean, cold-sober, dead-silent place. As I rode up the elevator to the fourth level, I expected to find some action. Maybe some signs of life. I was wrong.

TGB Advertising's office smelled of new carpet and was ringed with furniture: chrome-and-glass tables, couple of stuffed chairs, and a sofa. None of the seats was occupied except for one at the back, filled in plenitude by a young, well-dressed woman wearing the kind of anxious expression you see at Sears package pickup, on the faces of people wondering if it'll *ever* come and will the goddamned thing fit.

I sauntered on the springy carpet up to the reception desk. Its owner was an emaciated young woman dressed in brilliant red, which coordinated well with the barrette in her spiky blackish-brown hair, the lipstick, and especially the fingernails, which were as long as the tines of a meat fork, and just as sharp. She was too busy to tend to me just then, though. A man was bent over the desk, backside to me, whispering something in her ear; something that evidently was not making her happy.

When I'd gotten tired of examining the man's ass, I cleared my throat. He stood and turned. He was a youngish fella in denims. Not new, not old; ex-student vintage, I guessed. He looked to be in decent shape—youth forgives all, I thought—but there were telltale signs of beer bloat in his skin. His brown hair was unfashionably long and had been eggbeatered into submission. He wore a scrub of beard and even from six feet away I caught a whiff of that popular ablution that we call Miller's after-shave. He kind of edged away from me, scowling at the intrusion.

"Sorry to butt in, pal," I said. He didn't answer. I looked at the receptionist. Her complexion was deathly white and her red-tipped fingers were trembling as she fidgeted with a Bic Ink Stic. Pressure job, answering the phone and shit. I said, "Ben Perkins, I'd like to see Curt Goldflower, please."

"He's interviewing," she said. Her eyes flicked to the man in denim, who hovered within springing distance to my right. "Typesetter or keyliner?"

"Huh? Oh. Well, neither," I fumbled. "Private detective. Need to talk to him about Paul Reardon."

Might as well have said Jack Sprat. "I'll tell him," she said tonelessly. "Have a seat."

The man's eyes were on us like spotlights. I could hear her breathing, that's how dry her mouth was. I leaned a little closer and murmured, "Are you all right?"

She nodded abruptly and turned from me. I drifted to the back of the room and took a seat next to the very large young lady with the anxious face, pageboy haircut, deep blue business suit, and snappy leather yup portfolio. I hung one ankle over the opposite knee and tossed out that time-honored icebreaker: "Typesetter or keyliner?"

"Typesetter," she answered, smile as gentle as her Kentucky accent. "You?"

"Oh, I mainly fix things for a living." The man in denim had gone back to the receptionist and was giving us the blue moon again, face close enough to the woman to kiss her. Judging from her expression, I didn't think he was about to do that, though. I didn't think what he was whispering were sweet nothings. "Tell me," I said to my couch mate, "what in the world does a typesetter do, anyhow?"

She started to tell me, but I didn't hear a word. I watched the receptionist as the man, still whispering intently, poked her hard at the top of her sternum with his index finger. Then he straightened and glared down at her. She stared up into his face, seemed to gather her strength, and shook her head, defiant and tight-lipped.

He clenched a fist, whispered something else, then whirled and slammed out of the foyer through the emergency exit.

My couch mate was still talking nervously. I smiled and nodded, watching the receptionist as she seemed to sag in her seat, all the tension running out her. She found a tissue and daubed at an eye; she picked up the phone receiver once and put it down. My couch mate had run out of talk by then. I excused myself and, pretending to stretch my legs, ambled over to the wall and took up position just inside the emergency exit.

It didn't take long. The fire door flung back and the man charged back in toward me. He had one hand under his denim jacket, but I didn't notice much else because I was on the move. I walked straight into him like a bulldozer and plowed him back through the door onto the dim landing of the fire stairs. He snarled and came out with his concealed hand. I took and twisted it over and back the wrong way, sort of using it like a crank, and he bent and cried out and released the pistol into my other hand. I shoved him away. He lunged at me and rammed his nose squarely into my right fist. His proboscis popped like a ripe tomato and he said "Ahh" and bent, cupping it with both hands as it squirted red like a defective faucet.

The weapon was a cheap-ass no-name snubnose, a .32 or a .38. "Hey, dipshit," I said. "It's against the law to shoot this thing inside a building within the city limits. Shame, shame, shame."

He was too busy crouching and spouting blood to reply. There'd have been no point anyway, because just then the fire

door opened behind me, a woman shouted something, and
suddenly I was being swarmed by the receptionist, kicking
me, beating me with her fists, slashing at me with those
fingernails, hissing curses. I pointed the pistol at Dipshit,
caught hold of one of her wrists with the other, doubled her
arm up behind her back, and jammed her against the wall.
That shut her up. "What the hell's wrong with you?" I
barked.

"Leave him be! He's my *husband*!" she yelled, squirming.

Dipshit took that opportunity to take off running, down
the stairway, around the corner, out of sight. I considered
shooting him, but decided not to. I'm not that good shooting
southpaw—not all that great right-handed, if the truth were
known—and I'm leery of strange pistols. With my luck the
thing would have blown up and taken my hand with it.

I let the receptionist go and held up the pistol. "Great.
This is what he was bringing you just now, little symbol of his
love." I opened the cylinder and spun it, raining bullets out
onto the floor. "Loaded, too. Thoughtful sort, ain't he?"

"It was none of your business," she retorted. She couldn't
take her eyes off the pistol. "He was just trying to scare me,
that's all."

As I bent to retrieve the bullets, the fire door opened. A
youngish man, casually dressed, goggled at the two of us.
"Della? What's going on?" He looked at me blankly and then
back at her. "Was David here again?"

Della's face was stark white, solid, and expressionless as
putty. "He didn't mean anything, Mr. Goldflower, we're just
not getting along so well right now—"

"Yeah," I cut in, holding up the pistol, "and he brought
this along as a negotiating tool."

Goldflower recoiled slightly. "Who're you?"

"Ben Perkins. Here to see you about Paul Reardon. You
want this thing?"

"God, no." He looked at the receptionist. "Della, you
remember what I said before. One more problem and it's the
police. You call them now."

She nodded dumbly.

Goldflower held the door back. "Come on, Perkins, we can talk till the cops get here."

I allowed Della to precede me into the reception area. My heavy young friend with the Kentucky accent was just getting on the elevator. For some reason she'd decided against applying for a job there.

Goldflower noticed that, too. "Good thing it wasn't a client," he muttered.

Curt Goldflower was a medium-size, fine-boned man in his midthirties with bushy dark hair and rimless glasses. He also wore a beard; either that, or he hadn't bothered to shave the past few days. He wore dark corduroys, loafers, short-sleeve open-collar dress shirt, and a wisp-thin, loosely knotted tie. My initial take was midlevel grunt, the busy energetic non-aggressive sort who'd do well around Ann Arbor but had never had a shot at the big time over in Detroit.

But I had to revise my impression when he escorted me to a large corner office. Midlevel grunts don't work alone in large corner offices. A honcho, seemed like; maybe even one of the top people. Maybe he was the *G* in the agency's name.

Goldflower's cluttered desk looked more like a plank on two pedestals. A small personal computer hummed on a table to one side. At the other leaned a huge oak drafting table, a real monstrosity that must have required eight men to lug in here. My arms ached just at the sight of the thing.

Goldflower still seemed unnerved at the sight of the pistol in my hand. "Set that thing down over here, would you?" I put it on his desk and he threw a file folder over it. "Tell me, Mr. Perkins, do you make a career out of protecting women from their violent husbands, or was this a onetime shot?"

I shrugged. "Had nothing better to do at the time."

Goldflower studied me silently. "Have a seat."

I took a guest chair. "'Preciate your seeing me. I hear you're pretty busy."

Goldflower dropped into a chair behind his desk, fired up a cigarette, leaned back, and hung his loafers on the edge of the desk. "Hiring, man. Business is going nuts. But frankly

I'm sick of interviewing. After a while all these people start to look alike. You're a refreshing change. I mean, the ad game's dangerous, but—"

"Always glad to bring variety into people's lives."

Goldflower sifted a big pad from the mess on his desk, propped it in his lap, and started to doodle on it with a big fat pencil. He did it casually, hardly looking at it, maintaining some sort of eye contact with me the rest of the time. "So, I gather you knew Paul?"

"Yes. He was a close friend of mine. Police don't seem to be getting anywhere finding his killer, and—"

"And you," Goldflower said, smiling, "the intrepid private detective, are going to find the perpetrator and avenge your dead friend."

"That," I agreed mildly. "Plus, the cops seem to think I might have had something to do with it, so I got a little extra motivation to find the perp. Plus which, there's an oddball item the cops don't know about that I want to check out with you."

Goldflower did not change expression. "That being?"

"The will he made out, which you witnessed."

"What about it?"

"Whatever you can tell me."

"Nothing to tell," Goldflower said, scribbling and scratching on the pad. "He told me he was making out a will, asked me to witness it, I did. End of story."

"Did he say why he needed a will?"

"No. Didn't ask him, either. Seemed obvious. I mean, everybody's going to die, Perkins. So everybody needs a will. Nothing weird about that."

"Did you read it?"

"Nope. I'm an art guy." He grinned. "Words don't matter to me."

I leaned back in the chair and studied the brilliantly sunny view through the large window. Dead end on the will. Jeez. Well, long as I was here, I decided to go on a little fishing trip. I mean, you never know. I fired up a cigar and said, "I hear he worked for you a long time."

Goldflower operated his pencil with one hand, his cigarette with the other. Coordination. "Yeah, hell of an AD. We used him as much as—"

"Hold it. Only AD I know of is Adrian Dantley with the Detroit Pistons."

"Sorry. Stands for art director. Graphic artist, does layout, keylining, illustrating. Like me, I'm an AD."

"Gotcha."

"Anyhow, yeah, he did a lot of work for us the past couple of years. He was good, really good, and I did everything I could to persuade him to come to work here full-time, but he wouldn't. I mean, in his quiet way Paul could be stubborn as hell. He wanted free-lance, period. So I threw him all the assignments he could handle."

"Nice of you."

He grimaced. "Nice got nothing to do with it, actually. Free-lancers, even the good ones, work cheap. You don't have to buy 'em a desk. You don't have to pay 'em insurance or vacation or sick time. They're hungry and they'll come through for you. I got a soft spot for free-lancers anyway; that's how this business started, me and my partner were both free-lancers when we threw in together. TGB Advertising, stands for 'Two Guys in a Bar,' because that's where we had most of our meetings before we got our own office."

"You did advertising in the bars?' I asked, grinning. "And they came out coherent and everything?"

He glanced at me and scribbled some more. "You ever been to Tattoos, Boots & Motorcycle Parts in Willow Run?"

"Sure." Makes Under New Management look like the lounge in the Westin.

"We've won two Addys and a Clio," Goldflower said, "and all three campaigns were created in that saloon."

"Gawd. Never woulda guessed."

The art director stopped scribbling and looked at me. "For God's sake, don't tell anybody what TGB stands for. We're doing a lot of project work for Domino's Pizza, and Monaghan over there is pretty conservative."

"Hey, your secret's safe with me." I looked at my pad. Blank. "Did you get to know Paul pretty well?"

Goldflower flipped a page of his pad and began doodling again. "Professionally, anyway. Just a flat-out nice guy. Polite, you know? Dependable."

He took a last hit off his weed and pressed it out in a jammed ashtray. His glasses had slid down his nose a bit, and he looked at me over them. "Personally, we weren't all that close. I knew he came from money, but he and his dad didn't get along. I knew about his portrait work at Hart Plaza. I met his live-in girlfriend, Ellen somebody, right?"

"Right."

"And I knew about the other woman he was seeing."

I froze, halfway through a doodle of my own.

"Oh," Goldflower said, leaning back, "I guess that's news to you, huh?"

Chapter 8

"You bet your ass," I answered when I'd found my tongue. "I don't know anything about that. Nobody else knows anything about that. I guess what I'd like to know is, how you know about that."

Goldflower's eyes narrowed. "Hey, Perkins, I'm no gossip. I take no pleasure in this. I just figure, if you're investigating, it's the kind of thing you need to know about. Correct me if I'm wrong."

I mentally kicked myself. This shows why you should never do a case that you're involved in personally. Your perspective gets warped, you make rookie mistakes. I held up a hand. "You're right. Didn't mean to come on all hardcase. So, this woman: who is she?"

"I don't know." Scribble, doodle.

I sighed. "Tell me what you saw, where, and when."

Goldflower dropped his pencil and busied himself lighting another cigarette as he talked. "It was over at Tattoos, Boots & Motorcycle Parts, a couple of weeks ago. We were trying to come up with some fresh creative on a toilet-bowl-cleaner account. Tough creative challenge. I mean, somebody's already doing singing toilets that look like Buddy Holly; what's left?"

"Got me hangin'."

"Well, anyway, my partner and I were hoisting a few, and who should I see in a corner booth but Paul Reardon."

"With the woman," I prompted.

He slid the pad back onto his lap and commenced to scribbling, the cigarette smoking in his thin lips. "Well, I didn't get a look at her then, just saw this blond hair. Her back was to me. I knew right away it wasn't Ellen; this woman was taller, wearing a business suit. A few minutes later I managed a better look when I went to the can, and it definitely was not Ellen."

"Okay." I drew a series of question marks on my pad. "What makes you think that he was boinking her?"

"Well"—Goldflower grinned—"he didn't mount her right there in the bar, if that's what you're asking."

"Seen worse, in that place."

"That's for sure. But no, I didn't catch 'em in a flagrante. It's just that, you know, you get a feeling. They were leaning close together, shutting out the world, just the two of them. Believe, me Perkins, I've been around and I can tell. He was screwing her, I'd bet my biggest account on it."

As a private detective, I should have felt elated. I'd hit the street looking for the private underside of Paul Reardon, and here it was on a platter. Who knows, this was an angle that might lead me to whoever killed him.

But I felt no elation at all. Just a kind of grumpy resignation. Everybody screws around. Everybody cuts corners, dicks with the system, and is in business for number one. Everybody is corrupt, the only question being one of degrees. Everybody including yours truly. I should not, therefore, have been surprised to learn this about Paul.

But I was. Another one of those unacknowledged certainties blown out of the water.

My cigar had grown a knuckle length of ash. I tapped it off and took a hot, hostile hit. "You seen the woman before? Or since? She work in the building here? Or in the neighborhood anyplace?"

"No, on all counts."

I wrote *Check Tattoos* on my pad, knowing in my heart that asking questions over there was pointless. I'd try anyhow. Detective work is like everything else; ninety-nine percent of what you try doesn't work. "You can describe her?"

"I can do better than that." Goldflower turned his pad around so I could see it. I nearly dropped my cigar.

Goldflower had drawn a series of sketches. In the center of his pad was a full-length sketch of a woman somewhere in her thirties. Her hair was straight and smooth, pinned here and there and layered to her shoulders. She wore a simple, clean-tailored business suit and some kind of thin chain around her neck and around one ankle. Her figure was very good. So were her legs.

In this sketch, Goldflower had caught her walking, in the act of glancing back over her shoulder. Arrayed around this sketch were three drawings of the woman's face: head-on and both profiles.

I saw what Goldflower meant about the slight resemblance to Ellen, but there were definite differences. This woman, whoever she was, was older and more voluptuous— no whipcord-thin jogging look for her. And there was another difference, something Goldflower had captured in the cast of the woman's face. There was resoluteness there. Confidence. You never saw those qualities in Ellen. She always seemed ready to bolt. Though she covered it well, in her eyes you sensed fear, the glow of the headlights of an oncoming, runaway truck.

I decided that the woman in the sketches was more alluring than anyone in Dr. Abbas's magazines. You got the feeling, even in black and white, that this was an icy lioness, coldly intelligent and passionate as hell, too. She reminded me of the actress Theresa Russell. Some guys have all the luck—for a while.

"Hell of a job, Curt," I said quietly.

He bobbed his head modestly. "Some things you can't get across in a sketch. She's blond, the real kind straight through. Five-seven and about one-thirty, lot of woman and it all hums."

"You got that across all right."

"Moves like she's in pretty decent shape. And green eyes—you wouldn't believe those green eyes." Goldflower lighted a fresh cigarette from his old one with almost unconscious movements.

I was making notes. "What did she drink, did you see?"

He rolled his eyes back, thinking hard. "Hard to say. Something clear. Could have been 7-Up. Could have been gin."

"How about Paul?"

"Beer. Oh yeah, and he was really diving into it, too, he must have ordered three or four just in the half hour they were there."

Weird. Paul was no drinker. After two or three he'd get silly and stupid; any more than that and he'd fall asleep where he sat. Well, I figured, if he's out on the street sneaking around with a gorgeous broad behind Ellen's back, maybe he needed extra sauce to help settle his nerves. This whole thing was reminding me of the innumerable infidelity cases I'd investigated over the years, and the questions came to mind as readily as if they'd been written on a sheet. "How did he pay for the drinks?"

"Well, he didn't," Goldflower said. "She did."

"She did?" I asked, puzzled.

He was scribbling on his pad again. "Yeah, I saw it plainly, she put a twenty on the table and they walked out together."

Very strange, but what the hell, it's an enlightened age. "Did they drive away together or separately?"

"I don't know. I lost track of them when they walked out."

"Had they come together, do you know?"

"No idea. They were there when my partner and I arrived."

I pressed out my cigar in the ashtray and leaned back in my chair, skimming notes and scratching my head. "Oh yeah, one other thing. Exactly what day was this? Do you remember?"

"Christ, I don't know," he retorted. "I barely know where I was yesterday, let alone a couple of weeks ago."

"Try to remember. Timing could be important, and—"

He held up a hand, smiling at me. "Not to worry, I know how to find out." He pressed a button on his intercom and said, "Della, what day was it the D drive went out on the typesetter?"

"I don't know, Mr. Goldflower," came her voice through the squawk box. Her voice sounded shaky. "Mr. Goldflower, the Ann Arbor police just got here."

"Fine, we're just about through," Goldflower said patiently. "We'll be out in a minute. Listen, find out when that drive went. Go through the files or the payables or whatever and get me the date right away, got it?"

"Okay, Mr. Goldflower."

He stood up and stretched. "Well, Perkins, guess we'd better go talk to the fuzz. You ready?"

I folded the sketch carefully, tucked it into my pad, and put both away. "Ready when you are," I answered as I stood and rescued the pistol from Goldflower's desk. "'Preciate your help with this."

Goldflower tore the top sheet off his big pad and folded it into quarters as he talked. "Glad I could do it. About time somebody was around asking about Paul. I thought maybe the cops had caught somebody already, and—"

"You mean, the police haven't questioned you about this?" I broke in.

"No."

Oh boy. That could mean only one thing.

Goldflower handed me the sheet he'd been doodling on. "Little present for ya."

I unfolded it. There in the center, as big as my palm, was a pencil sketch of my face. Being black and white, it didn't get across the dark blue of my eyes, but Goldflower had caught everything else. The heavy black medium-length hair. The strong bones. The weather, squint, and grin lines. The nose that had been forcibly adjusted several times over the years. And he'd caught something else, a facial expression that I suspected was pretty typical these days.

Bafflement.

On TV, investigations proceed in orderly little twelve-minute chunks, each concluding with a little cliffhanger to keep you glued to the set during the commercials instead of going for a squirt or a fresh beer or whatever.

In real life, investigations lurch along. You spurt ahead here, fall back there. Insight and intuition are often meaningless. People lie routinely, even when they don't have to. Memories and impressions are flawed from the instant they're born and get more so with the passage of time. Just when things seem to be falling into line, they fall apart on you instead.

Such was the case now. For, after my relatively successful visit to Curt Goldflower at TGB Advertising, I came up goose egg at Tattoos, Boots & Motorcycle Parts. I showed my snap of Paul and my fresh-minted sketch of his lady friend to the sleepy bartender and the handful of late-morning drinkers, and got nothing but shrugs in return. If anyone knew, they weren't telling.

Which didn't really surprise me. It's that kind of place.

I picked up I-94 at Rawsonville Road and motored east at an easy seventy mph, hugging the center lane with my wrists dangling over the Mustang's deep-dish wheel. I had the Scorpions' new one on the tape deck, but I paid no attention to it. I was thinking through what I'd learned—or trying to.

So Paul had a lady friend on the side. That much seemed certain. But there it ended, at least for now. I had Goldflower's testimony about what he'd seen. I had his sketches of what the woman looked like. I had the date of their meeting: Monday, June 23, about two weeks before Paul died, a week and a half before he took out the will and opened the bank account.

That was it. So what now?

I could hang around Tattoos and keep showing the snapshot of Paul and the sketch of his lady friend. Who knows, maybe I'd stumble onto someone drunk enough or stupid enough to talk.

I could sit down with Ellen, level with her, tell her about the lady friend and see if she had any fresh insights.

I could go downtown to Hart Plaza this weekend and hang around the ethnic festival, flash Paul's picture, see if anyone wanted to talk about him.

Lousy percentage plays. I had a better idea. Not much better, but it beat going back to Norwegian Wood and sitting around stewing about Carole and her pregnancy, Ellen and her widowhood, me and my sperm count, and those state cops who came calling for Paul the day we put him in the ground.

All big fat questions with no answers on the horizon.

Don't let the grand name fool you: WorldWide Auto Parts is a junkyard. A mighty big junkyard, but still a junkyard. It's on the northwest side of Detroit, within sight of the Jeffries/Southfield Freeway interchange, the Massey-Ferguson complex, the C&O yards, and the eastern segment of Dynamite Park. It needs no advertising; its mountains of twisted old auto iron rise into the sky, visible for blocks around.

Sure, it's ugly, but I love the place. It sort of square-ends the Detroit dynamic. All those thousands of cars: made in Detroit, scrapped in Detroit. Fitting. Furthermore, the place is a gold mine to a perpetually broke, compulsive auto tinkerer like yours truly. Hell, I practically rebuilt the rear end of my Mustang from parts scavenged there.

Today I was hoping that the place would be as good a resource for information. For, according to Ellen, it was after Paul bought his replacement backseat at WorldWide that he began, as she put it, to "act weird."

I wheeled up Westwood and slowed to a crawl as I snaked through a procession of idled tow trucks, each with fresh booty on the hook. As I passed, I thought about how each of these wrecks was once someone's bright shiny dream.

Each was saved for, chosen with care, haggled over, driven home, parked in the driveway, and admired by family and friends. Each had been "the car" to someone. Now each was a wasted, depleted shell: bashed up, rusted out, dragged in ultimate indignity by its front axle at a forty-five-degree angle that was almost sexual in its submissiveness, numerals scribbled in soap across its cracked or starred windshield.

Whereas I and my Mustang, two hard-edged, made-in-Detroit retreads, were still alive and kicking. That thought gave me a good feeling as I found a parking space by WorldWide's flat-topped cinder-block office building, got out, and hoofed inside.

The room was small, square, and dim. There'd once been windows but they'd been bricked over long hence; the only light came from asthmatic-sounding fluorescent fixtures in the dingy drop ceiling. A big table dark with bits and pieces of obscure machinery ran to my left; at the opposite end was a slapped-together counter a-tumble with big reference books. Behind it ran a wall broken by the mouth of a hallway which led eventually to daylight, as well as a nudie calendar showing a woman playing with some parts and, evidently, enjoying herself.

The room hung heavy with the compressed stench of sweat, tobacco, and grease. Within the thick walls the only sound to be heard was the intermittent coughing of the light fixtures, an occasional diesel scream from outside, and the murmuring of WorldWide's owner, Gary Muhleman, who was leaning behind the counter with the phone in his face.

He spotted me, gave me a just-one-minute finger, and went back to his conversation. I went to the counter, leaned, and lighted a cigar. Gary and I go way back, all the way back to Redford High School, where he was the jittery first baseman and I was the ice-cold hot corner commando who loved to torment him by waiting till the very last second before gunning the putout over there. We were good. Real good. Too bad his daddy died and he had to take over running the junkyard. Too bad I went to work for Ford's at night. We'd both been scouted by the bigs and, who knows? We might have made it all the way to double-A.

Gary hung up the phone and, as usual, the sight of him made me want to run to a mirror and check myself out. He looked a good ten years older than he was; his face was shrunken and wasted, all except for the nose, which was, shall we say, prominent. His hair, an indeterminate brown, was less of a problem as the days went by, since the bald spot in front was about to form a union with the bald spot in back, and what was left was flattened down and pushed back behind his jutting ears. He wore a baggy blue twill jump suit with "WorldWide" embroidered in white on one breast and "Big Boss" on the other. He also wore an expression that made you wonder who'd insulted his mother.

No one had. That's just the expression he wears when he's emotionally neutral. It doesn't mean anything, but it unnerves the uninitiated, giving him a negotiating edge that the rest of us only dream about. "Hi, Benjy," he said, my childhood nickname sounding perfectly natural coming from him.

"Hey, Gare, what's shakin'?"

He honked and spat into something on the floor behind the counter. "The automotive recycling business is god-awful terrible these days."

I gestured toward the front. "How so? You got fresh inventory lined up all the way to Campus Martius out there."

"City sweep." He nodded, expression even more venomous. "Thank God for Mayor Young, he keeps scooping up the wrecks and shipping 'em to urban conservationists like me. Wasn't for that, I'd be dead flat out of business."

I grinned. "You always been a fretter. Always said you'd die young."

"Too late," he observed mournfully.

"That's God's own truth. So what's the problem? Foreign competition?"

"Sure, there's that," he acknowledged. "They make cheap-ass shit-quality parts and dump 'em here below cost, and that puts a shit load of pressure on the price of reconditioned." Gary's word for "used junk," evidently. "But there's a worse problem than that, Benjy. The kids."

I exhaled smoke. "You lost me. What kids?"

"The kids today," he said, voice rising. "They got too much money, see. And nobody's brought 'em up right. To them, if something breaks, no problem! You just throw away and buy new. That's what you do, you throw away and buy new. In fact, it's not just the kids, it's everybody. Nobody fixes things anymore. Nobody cares about making things last. If it's old, or a little worn, or you're tired and bored with it, no problem! You just throw away and buy new."

Even in the lousy light I could see flecks of red on his cheeks. I said, "Not meaning to argue, but I don't think—"

"And that's hurting my business," Gary said, the words marching like little well-trained soldiers. I got the impression this wasn't a new notion with him. "I mean, remember back when we were kids? Our first cars? We *lived* in places like this. Scavenging parts and fixing up our cars. But the kids today, oh, no goddamned way, they wouldn't be caught *dead* around here, let along with a wrench in their hand. Shit, they wouldn't even know how to fix anything. 'Cause no one's teaching them. You know what passes for fixing things, today? Keep replacing parts till the problem goes away. Not the way we were taught, Benjy."

"Well, I've have to admit I've used that strategy more 'n once."

He wagged a finger. "But you don't have to, 'cause you got the skills. You know how to fix, Benjy. It's a dying art. When you go, it'll be all gone."

"I promise to use the power only for good," I said dryly. "Now listen up, I got a situation here." I got the snap of Paul out and laid it on the counter. "Ring any bells?"

I got the feeling he didn't want the subject changed, but he looked at the snapshot, if grudgingly. "Yeah, like, 'bing.' Customer, I think. Last month sometime. He looked at me. "Friend of yours?"

"Well, he was," I answered mildly, "till he got killed."

Gary's venomous expression softened and he shook his head. "Sorry to hear that. You on the job, Benjy?"

"Real unofficial and real quiet, dig?" Gary nodded. "Okay, you remember anything about when he came here? Anything unusual happen?"

Gary rubbed the back of his neck. "Tellya the truth, I remember him being here but I'm drawing a blank on—"

"Give you a hint," I said. "Backseat of a Gremlin."

His look of dark puzzlement was shattered and he positively beamed in a way that knocked twenty years off him. "Oh, yeah! Sure! Seventy-five Gremlin, right."

"Seventy-four, but close enough."

Gary stabbed a greasy finger at Paul's smiling face. "Sure, him. Nice kid, hell of a nice kid. Gremlins aren't all that common around here, I was glad we had a seat to sell him. We ripped it out, sold it to him for twenty, and he went away happy." Gary's expression went crafty. "I sure hope he turned a good buck on it."

For a second what he said didn't register. "Turn a buck? Whaddya mean, turn a buck? Who in the world would buy it?"

Gary looked at me, startled at the tone in my voice. "Well, there was this woman, see."

Chapter 9

Not this again. Not twice in one day.

"What woman?" I asked faintly.

Gary was still grinning, his venomous visage gone for the moment. "Well, she come in here a day or two after this feller Paul did, looking to buy the backseat of a Gremlin, too. Same model. Same year. Same everything."

I worried the end of my cigar with my mouth, toking and blowing and thinking hard. "How come you remember it so well, Gary?"

"Well, shit!" he exploded, gesturing grandly at the room.

"Look at this dump! You think we get so many broads come in this place that I have trouble recollecting any?"

"S'pose not."

"'Specially like this one." Gary charged on, eyes alight with the memory. "I mean this one was a straight-up beaut, Benjy, I kid you not. Tall and blond, with a porch you could stand on and legs running all the way from her ass all the way to the ground. Wore this business-type suit which is my favorite kind, makes me think about stripping it off her, piece by piece."

A hard ringing was going in my head. I almost went for the sketch, held off, then thought what the hell. The day isn't complete till you've made an ass of yourself just once.

Silently, I got the sketch out and unfolded it on the counter. Gary looked at it. His eyebrows arched and he gave one abrupt and lascivious whistle. "Yessir."

"'Yessir' what, Gary?" I prodded, barely allowing myself to breathe.

"That's the chick. That's her to a T, and I mean T as in 'bazooms.' Jesus Christ, Benjy," he said, looking at me with fresh respect, "this is nice work, I didn't know you was such a good drawer."

I didn't bother to correct him. I was too busy marveling over my sudden good fortune. Besides, everybody needs a little mystery in their lives. "So," I said, trying hard to sound casual, "she asked about the same kind of car seat. What then?"

"Not just the 'same kind,'" he corrected. "That exact one. Said she'd been told we had one here."

"Now, how would she know that?"

"Beats shit out of me. Anyway, I told her I was sorry as hell but that I'd just sold it. Pissed me off, Benjy; I wanted her to hang around. But she wasn't in no hurry to leave. Asked me to tell her who bought it, she'd contact the person and offer to buy it off him."

I stayed as neutral as I could, leaning and smoking, every nerve on full alert. "So, did you give her Paul's name?"

"Not right then. I couldn't find the sales slip," Gary explained. "She left her number, and I had to call her back."

My cigar was singeing my fingers. I dropped it, squashed it, and kicked the remains into oblivion. "You called her, then?"

"Sure did. Called her, gave her the guy's address and phone number off his check. Well," he amended, "I didn't actually talk to her, I left word on her answering box."

Big deal. "You wouldn't by chance still have that number, wouldja?" I asked.

"I don't know. If I did, it'd still be with the sales slip from when your friend bought the backseat. Want me to look?"

"If you'd be so kind."

"What the hell, Benjy," he said, sounding hurt, "we're old pals, I'm glad to do it. Hang on."

He disappeared into the hallway. I guessed he'd gone into an office back there. I lighted up a cigar and paced, thinking: there's nothing like a case when it's starting to cook. It's just like the feeling you get before you go to bed with a woman for the first time, that moment when you first know it's going to happen, it's just a matter of when instead of whether. I allowed myself to savor the anticipation. I didn't trouble myself with the very real possibility that even if I tracked this mysterious blond down, it would turn out that she had less than nothing to do with Paul's death.

Gary shuffled back into the room, pink paper trailing from his hand. "Here it is. Want me to read it?"

I had my pad and pen ready. "Shoot."

Gary read me the phone number—a Detroit exchange. "Her name's Angie, it says here," he added. "So there you go."

"Thanks, Gary," I said, snapping my pad shut.

"More 'n welcome. Won't do you a lick of good, though."

"Whaddya mean?"

Gary looked past me, took a deep breath, exhaled. "I done tried to call her several times after that. Wanted to ask her out, you know? Couple of beers or whatever."

"So what happened?" I asked, feeling grim already.

"First two times her box was on, I left word but she

didn't call back. After that I got one of those weird phony computer voices, said the number was disconnected."

"Oh. Well, too bad, I guess." I put away my pad, the pen, the sketch, and the snapshot of Paul. Idly I asked, "So she knew you had that Gremlin here, huh? Did she say what she wanted the seat for?"

"No. Just said she wanted it. Real bad, too."

"Huh. The well-known Gremlin seat fetish."

"Well"—Gary shrugged—"maybe she lost her cherry on a Gremlin seat, wanted one for a memento."

Or, I thought, maybe there was some other, far less sentimental reason. Keeping my tone casual, I asked, "Anything special about the car that seat came out of?"

He glanced at the pink sheet. "Nope. According to the inventory prefix, it's just another Detroit police impound."

"Which means what?"

"Could mean anything. Or nothing. Some people abandon perfectly good cars for reasons nobody can figure out. On the other hand, a month or so ago one of my boys found what he thought were a couple of life-size baby dolls in the trunk of this Dodge. Turned out they were real babies. Dead ones. They'd baked to death in that trunk, sun had rendered 'em into mummies."

My stomach did a slow painful turn. That surprised me. Normally, it's as fidgety as the Joe Louis fist. But the afternoon was pressing on and I'd had nothing to eat all day. I gave Gary my thanks and got out of there.

Ninety minutes later my day ground to a total halt as I cooled my heels on a fifth-floor hallway bench at Detroit police headquarters downtown.

The place was jumping, but when isn't it? Uniformed and plainclothes officers marched along with hard-edged purpose. Civilians—perpetrators and perpetratees—wandered to and fro, colored various shades of dread. Sleek, well-fed, smug suits of both sexes conveyed their briefcases from one place to the next, faces aglow with the art of the deal. It was one big marketplace in which the currency was power and the commodity was people's lives.

I shared my bench with a skinny, older black man wearing a sawn-off T-shirt, black pants, and a safari cap. He busied himself disassembling a Tareyton cigarette filter while humming "The City of New Orleans" in a loud, nasal voice. I felt better now, having gotten outside a Burger Barn double cheeseburger and a Coke on the way down there. I'd also put in a call to Pat O'Shay, my mole at Michigan Bell, to get a location on the phone number of the elusive and intrusive "Angie" who'd expressed such an interest in a certain Gremlin backseat and then, evidently, sucked some face with Paul before he bought the big one. Now I had one more avenue to pursue, and then—

"Perkins!" boomed a deep male voice. I looked up to see Elvin Dance, the squat, hard-nosed, hard-packed Detroit police homocide chief, pounding up the hall toward me. He already looked furious, and I hadn't even asked him anything yet. "Whatchoo bothering me for, boy?"

He was jacketless today, wearing a black dress shirt and a black and white paisley tie over ebony and white linen trousers and black alligator shoes. Gold winked from his teeth. Gold shone brightly against the cocoa color of his fingers. Gold flashed from his cuffs and his tie tack. Stainless steel glinted from the ivory handled Smith & Wesson Military & Police .38 revolver that hung high on his right flank. That was it. Otherwise, Elvin Dance was a study in monochrome: as dark as his mood.

"For the pure pleasure of seeing your smiling face," I answered. "Why else?"

"Drag it along, Jack," he growled to my bench mate. The black man lurched to his feet and wobbled away, humming "Alice's Restaurant." Elvin brushed the bench with his hand, sat down, and leaned his forearms on his knees, glaring at me. "What do you want, Perkins?"

"Well, let's see. Hit the Lotto for a couple mil. A dusk-to-dawn with Stephanie Zimbalist. High-test at thirty a gallon. And," I said, getting out my pad, "some info on a car the police impounded a while back."

"Sheeit," Elvin said. "I don't know nothing about impounded cars. I run homicide, remember?"

"Yeah, but you're the only ranking contact I've got here at the department.

"Lucky me." He got to his feet, put hands on hips, and paced a semicircle around me. "What makes you think I should drop everything and do your homework for you?"

I leaned back on the hard bench. "Oh, let's see. Could be because we go back what, fifteen years now? Call it old times' sake. Or, could be because you're a public servant and I'm a taxpayer."

"Not in this city you ain't."

I ignored him. "And last but not least, could be because you owe me."

He stopped walking. "Owe you what, asshole?"

I locked eyes with his. "You know."

"I do not know."

I made my hand into a handgun, pointed it down, squeezed off an imaginary shot, and looked back at him. I did not smile.

Nor did he. "You'd use that?" he whispered. "I thought we was friends, back of it all."

That surprised me. "Ain't business a bitch?"

His expression went remote. He held out a hand. "Gimme."

I handed him the slip of paper with the numbers. He stormed up the hall and disappeared. I sat and waited and thought, Fancy that, Elvin Dance asking for a break on the basis of friendship. We got along all right, but it was purely business. If I'd ever asked him for help in the name of our "friendship," he'd have laughed himself to death.

Ten minutes later he was back, and he wasn't laughing. "In my office, boy."

The "office" was really a sort of half-assed conference area, a big wood table with mismatched chairs in a room bounded by wood and glass partitions. The decor was traditional underfunded public service: battered filing cabinets, an ancient coffee machine, a cigarette machine, and a coatrack with but a single occupant, a leather number that looked like it'd been hung the same time as John Brown. Elvin took a chair at the head of the table and I sat kitty-corner from him wondering why I'd suddenly been promoted from hallway heel-cooler.

Elvin consulted a long jagged sheet of pulpy yellow teletype paper. "I'll just give this to you," he said, "and then, like a nice boy, you're gonna tell me what you're doing with it. Okay with you, Perkins?"

We'll see, I thought. "Fine with me," I said.

Elvin squinted at the faint printing. "Car's registered to one Davey Jackson. Deceased. He was peaceably stopped at a traffic light on Adelaide when person or persons unknown shot him to death with a nine-millimeter handgun, make unknown. For once, somebody called in the squeal real quick and, lo and behold, there was an RMP in the area and, believe it or not, they weren't smokin' or jokin' or coopin' somewhere, they was actually on the goddamned *job*, praise the Lord, and they got to the scene just five minutes later only to find Mr. Davey Jackson done bled to death from a single close-range head shot, the perpetrators of such head shot being long gone."

I waited for more. Elvin set the paper down and looked at me neutrally. I cleared my throat. "Sorry, Elvin, but that ain't all that interesting. I mean, people get killed in Detroit all the time, remember? Leastways this one must've been over sixteen; that's progress."

"Well, yeah, I did leave out one little detail. Mr. Davey Jackson was, according to my friends in vice, a major distributor for good old organized crime, Detroit chapter."

I resisted the temptation to say "Oh-ho." "By George," I said, "now we're onto something. Distributor, huh? Dude with some rank on him. Crack, I presume?"

Elvin drummed his fingers. "No. Regular old cocaine. And he wasn't no street operative. According to our people, he was a little more upscale than that. He had a downtown circuit: the utilities, the banks, the law firms, the City-County Building, you get the idea."

"Well hey, those people need their drugs, too. So, he got whacked. Was he holding?"

"Clean as can be, it says here. Nothing on his person, nothing found in the car. They did think it was mildly hilarious, though," Elvin added with a quiet smile, "a man of his professional stature driving a ratty-ass old Gremlin."

"Don't laugh, it's paid for," I said.

"But this whole thing's got us wondering if maybe there ain't a drug war starting to brew. The investigation is, as we say, continuing, which means we ain't got shit to go on. Till just now"—he grinned—"when you come in here. What's your interest in this car, Perkins?"

Detective rule number eighteen: when you're about to lie your ass off, take your time. Inexperienced liars give themselves away by rushing. I fired up a cigar, got it going well, and then talked. "Well, it's like this. Evidently that car was schlepped over to a west-side junkyard after y'all were done with it? One of the fellas over there found some personal effects inside. Hired me to track down the owner to return them." I was proud of this story, even prouder that I'd taken the time to dream it up before coming down here. Preparation is all.

"Oh horseshit," Elvin said.

I spread my hands. "Straight scoop, I swear to God, I mean, my client didn't know there was drugs and murder and shit involved in all of this."

Elvin closed his eyes, rubbed his forehead with all ten fingers, and mumbled, "I can't stand it." He looked at me. "Who's your client?" he asked neutrally.

"Now, you know I'm not going to tell you that. Get real."

"What'd he find?"

"Some rings. A watch. A locket with some engraving on the back, said 'To my loving son' or something like that."

"And a partridge in a friggin' pear tree," Elvin growled. "So all this 'client' wants is to return the stuff to the rightful owner, huh? Right thoughtful of him. Downright exceptional in this day and age and city."

I shrugged. "The whole world ain't like you and me, Elvin."

Either Dance really half believed me, or he wanted to buy into the story in order to avoid having to deal with me further. I was capable of blowing smoke and laying trails of prisms and mirrors for him all afternoon, and he knew it.

"Just one hell of a coincidence," he grumbled, "that this car happened to belong to the big-time drug distributor." He eyeballed the yellow sheet with annoyance, then said abruptly, "Anything else you want? We're just slightly on the busy side today, Perkins."

"Matter of fact, yes," I drawled. "This Jackson person leave any next of kin? I got to return this junk to somebody, or I don't get paid."

"Had a live-in, it says here," Elvin said, standing. "Talk to her and see if she knows about any kin." He read off the address, in the 3700 block of Brainard. When I was done writing it down, I saw that he was really grinning at me now. "Cass Corridor," he noted.

"I know," I said as I put the pad away and stood. "Thanks for the cooperation, Captain."

"The Detroit police," he intoned, "welcome every opportunity to serve."

He'd murdered a man, was what it was.

Let's put it this way. In the legal sense it was murder, inasmuch as Elvin intentionally deprived a person of his life without due process of law. Put more plainly, he'd put his foot on the man's chest and splattered his head with a single close-range shot.

I'd helped cover it up. In fact. Elvin was all ready to turn himself in, but I persuaded him not to. I suggested the cover-up, I orchestrated it, and it had stuck as tight as a lid on a used paint can.

If it hadn't, Elvin would have gone to prison and so would I. I'd have felt badly about that, but I didn't feel in the least badly about the cover-up. The "victim" was about as deserving of death as anyone I've ever encountered. My only problem with his execution was that it was too quick and clean.

Kind of like Davey Jackson's, I thought as I motored out the wide expanse of Grand River. A shot to the head. Pro work, all the way. I regretted his passing, not because I carry any grief for drug dealers—quite the contrary—but for selfish reasons. I'd have liked to have questioned him to see if he knew anything at all about Paul, anything at all about the voluptuous and very busy Angie.

My only hope was that Jackson's live-in would shed some light. I wasn't filled with eagerness, though. In fact, what I felt at that moment was foreboding. I'd ask the questions, because you go where the thing takes you. But I knew I would not like the answers.

Tomorrow would be soon enough. The afternoon was wearing away, I had no desire to spend an evening in the Cass Corridor, and I needed to get back to Norwegian Wood to check on the day's work.

First, though, one more errand to square-end this long, long day.

Chapter 10

The door to Apartment 308 eased back moments after my tap. Ellen Reardon stood there, face blank, and from her expression you'd think she hadn't recognized me. "Ben," she said, barely louder than the sound of "Goodbye Yellow Brick Road" crooning from the stereo. "What is it?"

I dangled a pair of keys in the air. "Your vehicle, ma'am."

She blinked. "What are you talking about?"

"Remember I said I'd get you a car? It's outside."

Her oval face loosened just a little, almost looked benign. "Well, that's—oh, I'm—listen," she rushed, "come on in for a minute."

I trailed her inside. She turned down the stereo and began fussing some newspapers into a pile on the coffee table. She wore a bright blue knit crop top with a wide elastic waistband, over matching boxer shorts. The top hugged her breasts, was scooped in back, and ended two bare brown inches above the shorts. Overall she showed about as much healthy, youthful skin as she would have in a bathing suit. Her blond hair was unkempt. She wore no makeup. From the looks of the living room—glasses, plates, empty pop cans, newspapers, and a couple of spine-up romance novels—she's spent the day vegetating.

"Hey," I said easily, "you don't have to straighten up for me. You've seen my place."

She smiled dutifully and sat herself down onto the arm of the couch, clearly not inviting me to stay long. She crossed her firm legs and exercised her toes, examining them intently. "You brought me a car?" she prompted.

I handed her the keys. "Yeah. It ain't much, now. A bright yaller three-on-the-tree Pinto with a bad squeak in the front end, a bald sneaker in the trunk, and two hundred K on the clock. The frame's a tad bent and the back window caught a rock somewhere along the line, but there's gas in the tank and paperwork in the glove box and it'll get you from here to there and back, as long as you baby her."

She'd brightened a little at the forced gaiety of my discourse, but there was something heavy weighing on her, and I wondered if I was going to hear about it. "Thank you," she said. "How in the world did you manage it?"

"Well, I keep three or four junker types at a car wash in northwest Detroit, cars I pick up at police auctions. Come in handy for surveillances and stuff. A couple of the guys at the car wash helped me ferry it out here." I didn't tell her that ferrying the car out had set me back twenty bucks—about what the Pinto was worth. I also didn't tell her about the "Explodes on Impact" sticker I'd scraped off the back bumper. I figured she didn't need that kind of reminder.

She jingled the worn Ford keys and said, distractedly, "At least something has gone right today." Her colorless eyes found me. "The Reardon family lawyer called this morning. I won't be getting the trust-fund income. Paul died a half hour before 'the instant' he turned twenty-five, so the conditions of his grandfather's will weren't met. According to them, anyway."

I'd already heard that from Jack Hatfield. It had bothered me then and it bothered me now. Not just because it was a tightfisted, mean-spirited decision—these were accountants and lawyers here; what do you expect?—but because a little tiny bell had gone off in my head while talking to Hatfield. A bell that signaled that something wasn't right. Damned if I could put a finger on it.

Ellen was still watching me. I thought she'd raise her voice, swear, cry, maybe even throw things around. She didn't. She made Tom Landry look like Jimmy Swaggart. "So, it's a clean sweep, isn't it, Ben?"

I wanted to hug her or something, but felt I might get a knee in the balls for my trouble. "I don't know what you mean."

She took a deep breath. "My husband's gone. Any possibility of making a decent income is gone. Pretty soon I'll lose this place. What'll I have then? A 'yaller three-on-the-tree Pinto with—'"

"The car's yours as long as you need it. And as for the apartment, we ain't gonna evict you right away, I can stave that off for—"

There it was, that glint in her eyes, the glow of the headlights of an oncoming, runaway truck. "Sure, you're my 'friend' now, but you're just like everyone else. Sooner or later you won't be my friend anymore."

"I'm here, aren't I?" I asked quietly.

She blinked. "What about your investigation? What have you found out?"

There it was, the question I dreaded. The only progress I had to report was that Paul was seen getting drunk in an out-of-the-way saloon with a stunningly attractive blond, identity unknown, just a couple of weeks before he was killed. I didn't think such a disclosure would brighten the mood around here any. "Odds and ends," I said lamely. "Nothing worth discussing yet."

"Oh, brother." Ellen stood. "Do me a favor, huh? Let's get it over with now. Good-bye, Ben."

After a moment I said, "I'll go. But you know where I am. Thirty seconds away. Don't forget it."

The words just bounced off her. I finally took the hint, turned on my heel, and left.

                          *   *   *

Here's Perkins's handy tourist guide to today's Detroit.
You've got downtown, where big money is cashing in with the
Renaissance Center, the Millender Center, Harbortown, Stroh
Place, Joe Louis Arena, Cobo Center, and the People Mover.
Then you've got the suburbs, which are going chrome, glass,
and treeless as fast as the developers can whistle up the
'dozers.

In between the two is a vast belt known collectively as
"the neighborhoods." Most of the people left living in this
belt are people who can't leave. They exist in a war zone,
watching the infrastructure crumble around them as their
institutions are ripped up by the roots and hauled away.

Say good-bye to dozens of Catholic churches. Say good-
bye to Olympia Stadium, Uniroyal, the Stroh Brewery, Vernor's,
Clark Street Cadillac, Fisher Guide, Dodge Main. Say good-
bye to the Detroit (Pontiac) Lions and the Detroit (Auburn
Hills) Pistons and, inevitably, to the Detroit (Ann Arbor)
Tigers.

The way things are going, pretty soon all the neighborhoods will look like the Cass Corridor, our research-and-
development center for urban blight.

The Corridor begins near downtown and runs, in a swath
several blocks wide, almost due north a mile and a half or so,
where it runs smack into Wayne State University, which was
put there to keep the Corridor from engulfing GM headquarters.

You can see there was money in the Corridor once. The
streets are wide, the houses two-story brick or stone, some
quite ornate, set back behind big lawns. But every second or
third house is obviously abandoned, invariably vandalized,
and sometimes burned out completely. The lawns are litter-
strewn, scraggly, and brown. Junker cars line the curbs, the
last refuge of the soon-to-be-homeless.

But you can't say that there isn't commerce. Even early
Friday morning, when I went down there to question the
live-in of the late Mr. Davey Jackson, there were people,
mostly black, hanging around on porches, standing in silent
trios on the sidewalks. Waiting for buses, waiting for jobs,
waiting for action, waiting.

Brainard Street begins at Vest Pocket Park and runs west under the Lodge Freeway to the Jeffries Projects, that symbol of "urban renewal" whose high rises improved poor people's view if not necessarily their living conditions. Davey Jackson's address was roughly at the halfway point, a few doors up from Second Boulevard. So far, so good.

I parked my Mustang behind a rusted white step-van sitting on four flats and walked across the front yard toward the porch. I felt the dogged resignation you get when a lead is sputtering and dying out on you. Davey Jackson, cocaine distributor, had owned the Gremlin whose car seat was coveted by the elusive Angie. She, in turn, obtained Paul Reardon's address from Gary Muhleman and, in fact, was seen schmoozing with Paul in Ypsilanti. Nice and neat, but there it fell apart, because Davey Jackson was dead and, therefore, unavailable as a source. Somehow I doubted that his live-in would be willing—if able—to give me any information, either. But I had to try.

The house was a two-story dark brick with a wide porch that wrapped around the north and west sides. Two chimneys flanked the high peaked roof. The windows were not only intact, but also closed and halfway clean. You didn't have to be a detective to know that it was occupied. All you had to do was look around. Its neighbor to the east was boarded up and decorated with spray-painted swastikas, triple-sixes, and the exhortation BON JOVI. The next one over was fire-gutted and sagging. The next one was gone completely.

Now, the neighbor to the west, that was a different story. I was astounded to see that it was in the process of restoration. All the window frames had been knocked out; the roof had been reshingled; a new aluminum siding had risen about halfway up the walls, and a bulbous silver Toyota van sat in the driveway. I could hear the twin whines of a power saw and power sander floating over to me—almost alien sounds in this sort of neighborhood.

I mounted the steps and walked to the door. It was an old-fashioned oversize double door, heavy when new and heavier today with the big bars bolted to it. The mailbox on the wall looked like the face of someone who had died puking; its lid was jammed open and mail had been brutally jammed in till it spilled out on the cement floor of the porch.

I felt a little tingling in my spine. I looked around and saw no one suspicious; listened and heard nothing but the whining of the skill saw next door. I gave the door one solid knock and felt it give under my fist, easing back an inch.

Now this wasn't right. I looked around again, then leaned toward the door and called, "Hello?" No answer, except for the faintest of scents wafting out.

I reached under my denim jacket for the .45 automatic that I'd stuck in the waistband against my spine. Cocked the piece and held it against my chest. Pushed the door open with my foot, trained the weapon at the darkness inside. No reaction. I stepped into the foyer and the smell fell on me, strong enough to burn my eyes; a smell with history to it, going back to the time my mother's freezer shorted out, causing two hundred pounds of beef to go bad.

The search didn't take long. Five minutes later I was back on the porch, standing at the rail, hyperventilating fresh air. Then I bent and retched over the rail, and kept retching till there was nothing left.

Finally the system calmed down. I felt shaken and drained, and my only thought was to get the hell out of there. I'd call it in to 911. No way was I going to hang around and—

"Yoo-hoo!"

I looked out toward the street. The woman stood on the yard between me and the bulbous Toyota van. She was one of the urban pioneers from next door, and she looked the part: a short, chubby lady in her forties with a milky always-indoors complexion, wearing a white shirt with big floppy sleeves, baggy mustard shorts, and white Reeboks. The morning sun glinted off her oversize aviator glasses and a tired breeze played with strands of her long grayish-blond hair, which was only technically restrained by a knotted blue bandanna.

I felt better by then. A little. I gave her a casual wave and trotted down the porch steps, bound for the Mustang and a long way out of here. No time for chitchat.

The lady was gutsy, I'll give her that. She marched over and headed me off, forcing me to choose between stopping or running her over. I stopped. "What are you doing at the Jackson's house?" she asked. "Are you with the city?"

Well, I was born in Detroit. "That's right."

"Oh," she said, relieved. "Checking on Charnelle, huh? We haven't seen her for a while. Is she all right?"

"I think her troubles are over."

The woman was really pretty attractive, for the chubby bookish sort. Nice smile, real presence, soft melodious voice. "That's such a relief! I was so worried after that other social worker was here. Sounded like Charnelle and David were having real troubles."

The numbness of the sight in that upstairs bathroom was fading away, replaced by that tingling of curiosity I knew so well. Here she was, the private detective's best friend: a nosy motormouth. I squinted at her. "What social worker?"

"The one who came here. You ought to know." She turned toward her house, cupped her mouth with a palm, and screeched, "Hey, idiot! You coming or what? We're going to be late!" Her eyes narrowed as she looked back at me. "Come to think of it, you don't look much like a social worker."

"Well, you don't look much like a resident of this neighborhood, so we're even."

She ignored me. "Who are you?"

Behind the slightly dense half grin on my face, the old brain was cooking afterburner. "I'm with the Outer Drive Council on Neighborhoods. We coordinate with the social-work people, but I didn't see anything in the file on a previous visit."

My use of words like "council," "coordinate," and "file" was, evidently, reassuring. This woman looked like she'd done plenty of time inside ivy-covered buildings and developed a respectful, even protective attitude toward bureaucracy. She said, "Well, a social worker was here, all right. I talked to her myself."

I rolled my eyes. "Do you believe it! Another darned paperwork screwup." I gave the lady a long-suffering look and, with hands that wanted badly to tremble, got out the sketch and unfolded it. "Is this the social worker you talked to?"

The lady looked at the sketch, then back at me, eyes wary again. "That's her. Do you typically carry around pencil sketches of social workers?"

I prefer being the asker instead of the askee. Besides, I had no decent answer to her question, offhand. "Exactly when was she here?"

"June the thirteenth," she said immediately. "I remember because it was Friday the thirteenth and Josh and I joked about whether it was bad luck to come and work on our house that day." She watched me put the sketch away. "Is there some kind of trouble?"

Josh. Figured. Bet her name was Annie. "I'm sorry," I said, "I didn't catch the name."

"Maggie," she said. Close. "Maggie Corbett-Hollingsworth."

"That's odd. You don't look much like a law firm."

"And you don't look much like a comedian, so we're even. I asked for your name, sir."

"Elvin Dance," I answered. Hers was a vigorous hand-shake. "There's no trouble, Maggie. Not for you or me, anyway. That worker you talked to, I'm going to have her written up. She didn't file any reports on the previous visit, and without that kind of inter-agency coordination, we just can't get our jobs done."

A skinny, bald man in a black curly Noah beard and Oshkosh B'Gosh bibs came trotting out of the house toward the van, keys jingling in his hand. Maggie caught sight of him and screeched, "'Bout time, you moron! Fire it up and wait a minute, I'll be right there."

When she returned her attention to me, her voice was soft again and her blond head was bobbing vigorously. "Oh, I know exactly what you mean. And I'm so delighted to hear about your association. With groups like you, and people like us moving down here, we'll turn Detroit around."

The man had clambered into the Toyota and started the engine, which flatulated pleasantly in the warming morning. I wanted to rush her along, but I had to stay in character. "Oh, so you're going to live here?"

"Of course. Josh and I believe in the Detroit renaissance. We've supported it at a distance for years. Finally we decided to put our money where our mouth is, and here we are. It's so convenient, too; I'm finishing my doctorate in modern culture at Wayne State, and this is *so* much closer than Novi."

"Indeed," I said judiciously. "And, if you're looking for modern culture, you've come to the right place."

The Toyota horn hooted. Maggie turned and screeched, "Cut it out, Josh, you'll bother the neighbors!" She turned back at me, face alight, and cooed, "The turnaround has to start somewhere, Elvin. Somebody's got to be first. If not us, who? If not now, when?"

She gave me that bonecrusher handshake again, smiled gaily, and marched to the Toyota. I waited till it had farted itself out of sight up Brainard, then went to the Mustang to call 911.

Elvin Dance—the real one, this time—strutted down the rickety back steps of the Jackson house and ambled across the yard to where I was leaning, waiting and watching. He wore a black-on-black pinstripe suit over gleaming wingtips, set off by gold winking from his fingers, his tie stickpin, and the watch chain that stretched across his vest. He was dressed grim enough to officiate at a funeral, which was fitting, considering the line of work he was in.

"You're right, Perkins," he said. "She's dead."

"Well, I'm no expert, but I thought it was a good guess."

He scooped his black felt hat back from his high forehead and turned his face so the sun would catch it. "You guess torture, too?"

"Wrists wired up to the shower spout," I said. "Exploratory surgery. Various parts, standard equipment, missing. Ankle-deep in a lake of dried blood. Yeah, I figured somebody had some sport with her."

Elvin lighted a Kool cigarette with a shiny gold Zippo. Not for him your thirty-nine-cent Bic throwaways. "You know," he said wearily, "you shouldn'ta gone poking around in there.

You shoulda called it in the minute you caught that smell. You been around, you knew what that was."

I didn't argue. Elvin will lecture and you have to let him. Especially if you want information. "How long ago you think it happen?" I asked, voice in maximum idle.

"We'll never narrow it down close. Heat in the house and shit, screws up all the tests. The maggots and the flies've taken up residence in her, though. My guess'd be two to four weeks she's been like that. Listen, Perkins."

"Yeah?"

His brown eyes weren't too tired to bore into me. "You gonna keep those belongings you was hired to return? Or you gonna level with me and tell me what's really going on?"

I looked at the police detective and said, with absolute honesty, "I don't have the slightest goddamned idea what's going on, Elvin."

He rolled his eyes. "Funny how every time I bump into you, you ass-deep in some heavy shit but you gimme that palms-up angel talk, as in, 'Who, me?'"

I ignored him. "Anything else I can do for you today?"

"Yeah," he said. "Disappear."

"'Bye." I hoofed down the driveway, squeezing between the meat wagon and the house, headed for Brainard, the Mustang, and home. It was pushing noon now. Lunchtime, allegedly, but I had no appetite. I wanted out of there, to get away where I could think and figure out what to do next.

I was unlocking the Mustang when an officious voice called from behind me: "Hey you, hold it!"

I turned. It was a young uniform, hatless, clambering out of one of the RMP cars parked in front of the Jackson house. "What's up, Officer?"

He slammed the car door, grandly checked his billy stick and sidearm, and strutted on leather heels across the street toward me. "What're you doing with that car?"

"This car?" I looked at it and back at him. "What I thought I'd do is drive it home. Why?"

"This car your car?"

"Of course it's my car. You think I'm going to steal a car with you sitting right over there watching?"

He'd reached me by now and he stood unnaturally close, an intimidating pose, to compensate, I suppose, for his shortness, his pudginess, and the soft mama's-boy lines of his face. "Prove to me you own this car."

I sighed. "Listen, sir, Captain Dance knows me, and—"

He had his palm out. "Paperwork, buster. Now."

I reached slowly for my wallet and handed over registration, proof of insurance, driver's license. He studied each in turn, taking his time. He compared my face with the license. Then he compared the plate number and VIN with the registration. A good cop, a thorough cop, a credit to his profession, a total goddamned pain in the ass.

"This a routine shakedown," I asked, "or is there something special you're after?"

He handed the paperwork back to me. "When I rolled in, there was a man on his hands and knees, peering under your front fender over there. Bent over and poking around."

I took a slow, deep breath. "You see what he was doing?"

"No. I just figured it was his car. Natural assumption. One thing I do know, though. Aside from the fact he was white, he didn't look a thing like you, Mr. Perkins."

Chapter 11

I gave the Mustang the once-over lightly, and found no equipment or options that hadn't been installed by either the Ford Motor Company or myself. Nor did I find wear, tear, or damage beyond the normal. My officer friend helped out by leaning against the side of his RMP car and watching me. At the end, as I prepared to start the engine, he shut his eyes, plugged his ears with his index fingers, and smiled.

Hilarious.

I rolled up Brainard to Third and swung north. From the sound of the engine, all systems were go. Whoever it was the cop had seen, he hadn't hurt the car any. Hell, maybe he was just a car buff. My car is, after all, a '71. Last winter a woman described it as a "classic." I'd never thought of it that way, but there sure aren't that many left on the road anymore.

At the Forest Street red light I scribbled some dates and notes on my pad, tore a bunch of the small pages out, and sorted them into a different kind of order. What I had was this.

Davey Jackson, cocaine distributor, was killed June 8, just over a month ago. Angie, the enigmatic blond with the porch you could stand on, was seen at Jackson's house on June 13. Paul Reardon bought his Gremlin car seat at World-Wide the next day. Angie was there "a couple of days later"—say, the following Monday—asking about the seat. Gary Muhleman gave her Paul's name and phone number a short time after that. Finally, Curt Goldflower, the Ann Arbor ad man, saw Paul and Angie schmoozing in a bar on June 23.

It all fit. Sort of. I had some pieces on the table, and they had some semblance of a sequence. Lots of pieces missing, but—

The light changed and I swung left. One other piece seemed to fit, too. Elvin Dance's guess was that Charnelle, Jackson's live-in, had been killed four to six weeks ago. June 13, the day Angie was seen at the Jackson house, was exactly four weeks ago.

Chilling thought. Could Angie have killed Charnelle? Why the torture? What did Jackson's career as a drug dealer have to do with this?

I beat the red light and swung right on the Lodge service drive. Why was Angie after that Gremlin car seat? Was there something important or valuable in it, like a load of cocaine?

I floored the Mustang and speed-shifted into fourth gear as I roared down the entrance ramp to the northbound Lodge Freeway. Did Paul find the cocaine? Did she track him down to get it back? Did all of this lead to his death?

I was edging over into the center lane, doing about sixty,

when suddenly the wheel felt weird. The car kept veering left and was starting to shake. I dickered with the wheel, got only a feeble response. I'd just started to react to that when suddenly the whole front end started to shimmy, then buck, as if a motor mount had let go. I came off the gas and locked my hands on the wheel as a great pounding sound commenced from the front end and the whole assembly up there dived left and stayed down, with an ungodly shriek of metal.

Thank God I didn't hit the brakes. If I had, I'd have lost it for sure, spun her and flipped her. As it was, I had a hell of a time fighting the wheel, trying to keep some kind of control as the car bounded over the curb onto the center median, skirting the cement barricade, grinding and screaming, the back end wanting to tear loose as the car slowed. I got a glimpse of one of the wheels gone off on its own, leading the Mustang, rolling like a fat chocolate doughnut ahead of me up the median. It collided with the center barricade and fell over and began to spin in place as the Mustang finally slid to a halt and choked itself dead in the center median, just shy of the Edsel Ford Freeway cutoff.

I'd lost the left front wheel, for some reason.

Shakily, I got out of the car. Traffic was flying past on the Lodge, a lot of it coming very close to the Mustang in order to get on the westbound Edsel Ford. I trotted up the center median, rescued the loose wheel, and rolled it back to the car. Inspected the wheel assembly and it looked okay to me. Scraped all to hell, but okay. The lugs themselves were completely undamaged. Only the lug nuts were missing.

Gee, I wonder what happened to them?

I had spares in the trunk, along with tools, and as I quickly remounted the wheel I thought about the man the cop had seen "peering" around under my car just a little earlier. I'd figured him for some kind of weirdo car buff. Now it seemed likely that he'd loosened my lug nuts, just for sport. Hell, I use better than a hundred pounds of torque to crank the things down. Lug nuts are like pregnant women: sure can't unscrew themselves.

Question was, who was he? Why'd he do it? How slowly was I going to kill him, if and when I ever found him?

I piled into the Mustang, fired it up, and eased back onto the expressway. The front end had definitely taken a licking. There was a constant, low-grade shimmy and leftward pull in the wheel, and a noticeable thumping that began at thirty mph and eased off at forty. My old gal wasn't up for any precision driving or high-speed chases, but at least she was still drivable.

I decided to head for home. Grab a late lunch, catch up on the maintenance work, see to the Mustang, think about what I'd learned. Just as I settled into the center lane of the westbound Edsel Ford, my cellular phone rang. Pat O'Shay, my mole at Michigan Bell, with the location of the telephone number Angie had left with Gary Muhleman.

She confirmed that the number had been disconnected, so odds were Angie wasn't around there anymore. But it was definitely worth a look. And there was no time to waste; the trail was already almost three weeks old. I exited at Livernois and headed north.

The address was an older two-story office building on Pulaski, just east of Livernois about a mile north of the Tenth Precinct station house. The building had no name, just a number, and no parking of its own. I scrounged a curb space about half a block east and sauntered back, looking the place over as I approached. For this area—a commercial/residential swath, gradually sliding downhill—the building didn't look bad. Gray brick with sorry-looking shrubbery, burglar bars on the ground-floor windows, opaque glass on the top-story windows. As I neared the entrance I realized there was no outside directory, and I wondered why. The entrance also had two doors: an outer one for looks, a much heavier one for security, and I wondered about that, too.

The foyer was small, dark, cool, quiet, and empty except for a desk that was attended by a uniformed security guard. Video cameras peered at me from upper corners at the left and the right. The guard wore a revolver, a walkie-talkie, handcuffs, and billy club. He wore no insignia, which made him purely private, like me.

"Help you, sir?" he asked, voice polite and gentle.

In one of those instant decisions you make, I decided to play it straight. Well, mostly straight. "Yeah, my name's Perkins, private detective working out of Belleville. I understand you either have, or had, a tenant here named Angela Barnes, and I need whatever information you've got on her."

The guard's complexion was leathery and very black, making him almost impossible to age. Even sitting, he looked to be in good shape, big shoulders, big arms, big hands. His face was placid and his eyes slow, a man who would never be surprised by anything ever again. I noticed that his desk was bare, except for a telephone console. No magazine, no smokes, no radio, no TV. All he did all day was, evidently, sit there and wait.

He looked me over incuriously. "May I see some identification, please?" The words sounded rehearsed.

I showed him my private detective license. He looked at it for a long time. Then he handed it back. I put it away. The guard did nothing but stare past me, toward the door. The silence stretched on. Finally I asked, "Well, can you help me, or what?"

"I don't know," he answered.

I looked over my shoulder. Nothing there to see. Back at the guard, who caught my expression and gave me a wink. The phone console purred and he picked up the receiver and listened for a moment, said "Very well," and hung up.

"Ms. Barretta will see you," he said, standing. "This way, please."

He led me up a narrow hall which dead-ended at a steel fire door. He unlocked its two locks with separate keys, swung the door open, and led me up two narrow flights of cement stairs. At the top he unlocked another fire door with another pair of keys, and now we entered a carpeted hallway with a bright window at one end and an ornate mahogany door dead ahead. He didn't unlock this one. It purred when he reached it—I spotted another video camera, watching us with a glass eye—and we stepped inside.

This was a sort of anteroom, occupied by a plush conversation set consisting of a sofa, love seat, two chairs, and a coffee table. Modernistic prints lined the walls and the royal blue carpet sank beneath my feet, like a soaking wet lawn. The room smelled lemony and the air had the bite of air-conditioning in it. The guard closed the door behind us and folded his arms, looking expectant.

A canned female voice spoke out of nowhere. "He's armed, Bruce."

I flinched, involuntarily. Jesus Christ, they must have had a metal detector in one of the doorframes. I held up both hands in a surrender gesture as the guard looked at me. "Sorry, I didn't know it was a problem."

"May I have it, please? I'll return it as you leave."

I didn't like it, but I got out the .45 and handed it to him butt first. He opened the inner door—just one key, this time—and I went inside.

The room looked like the lounge of an exclusive men's club. Two complete conversation groups of furniture—low-backed leather sofas, love seats, club chairs, coffee tables—held down area rugs to the left and to the right. The corner to my right was occupied by a small bar, the one to the left by a white baby grand. The far wall featured a large bay window, dominated by a brass telescope on a tripod. Black-and-white TV monitors hung from the ceiling there. A desk held a tiny personal computer with a screen like E.T.'s head, a police scanner radio, an intercom console, plus a telephone. A wood entertainment center contained a big boxy Magnavox and two VCRs. All of this was arrayed around a huge leather recliner, in which was seated an even huger woman.

"Come in, Mr. Perkins," she said briskly. I strolled toward her, trying not to gawk. She was probably the largest woman I had ever met: five-ten if an inch, a good three hundred pounds floating serenely under an expansive sleeveless smock in a blue floral print that ran all the way down to her ankles. Her red hair was tied in a bun high on the back of her head. You got lost in her face, there was so much of it, and the features were drowned, rendered indistinguishable, by all of that fat. You did pick up on the eyes, though: sharp and intelligent way back deep in there.

I gestured around at all the gear. "Looks like a security outpost here, Ms. Barretta."

She reached out and shook my hand with her cool heavy one. "Call me Gail, please," she said, voice melodious. "An unfortunate necessity if one is to survive in Detroit today." Like most old-time natives, she pronounced the word De-TROY-yit.

"Got a lot of crime problems here, huh?" I asked sympathetically.

Her eyes were cold. "No, I don't. That's the whole point." She had a little remote in her hand, and she pointed it at one of the VCRs. Abruptly, the Magnavox began rolling tape, showing good old yours truly at the guard desk downstairs, then switched to me handing over my .45 to the guard. "I don't get that many visitors," she said. "I like to avoid surprises." She shifted in the recliner, which gasped and creaked under her bulk. "No two-bit crack freaks are going to rip me off."

"Hell, it'd take a squad of commandos, and even then it would be iffy," I said.

She smiled, pleased. "I keep track of the street, too." She pointed out the bay window across the street. "See that brick Cape Cod? Someone started dealing crack out of there. I helped shut it down. The officers at the Tenth Precinct know me very well."

"That's what you do all day? Stand guard and stuff?"

Her shrug could move mountains. "I have nothing else to do. And I have plenty of money. My grandmother was a niece of the Dodge brothers, and enough filtered down to me. Plus I rent out the four offices downstairs." She arranged the folds of the smock over her lap and gave me an annoyed look. "Sit down, for heaven's sake. Smoke if you want to, and tell me what you want."

I sat in a straight wood chair, facing her. I did not smoke. For some reason, I felt like I'd been called to the principal's office. Given Gail's obvious interest in crime, I decided to give her the full treatment. "This is a murder investigation. A woman by the name of Angela Barnes is, according to my sources, a good suspect. A phone in her name is listed at this address."

Gail didn't change expression. "If it's a murder investigation, why are you working it instead of the police?"

That caught me off guard. "They don't buy my theory—"

She wagged a finger. "The only place I know of where private detectives are permitted to work murder cases is in cheap, trashy novels, Ben. You should turn it all over to the police."

Just my luck: a Jack Webb knockoff. I tried to keep the irritation out of my voice. "Nothing would please me more. And I will," I lied, "as soon as I've got something solid to give them."

"If there was anything solid to your theory," she said stiffly, "the police would be investigating it. You're obviously on a wild-goose chase." She stared out the bay window for a minute. I thought I was sunk. You couldn't make this broad spill with anything less than a stick of dynamite.

"Angela Barnes," she said absently. A whiny little motor sounded from somewhere and her recliner swiveled till she was facing her PC. She reached to the keyboard and tapped some keys rapidly. It clicked and stuttered and the screen went from blue to green, with tiny little letters in white. She squinted at them. "Gave her address as 881 Twelve Mile Road in Royal Oak," she said. "Don't bother writing it down. It's fake. I checked."

Very carefully I asked, "How long has she rented here?"

"Took Suite 3 on February 1 on a six-month lease," Gail said, consulting the screen. "Has not responded to our written requests to renew, so I assume she's letting it run out this month. Which wouldn't surprise me. She rented the place but she never used it."

"What?" I asked, startled.

She looked at me, face knowing. "Angela Barnes—if that's her real name—only came here once. I keep track. She came to sign her lease, pay the six months in advance, and put some things in her office. That was it."

I got to my feet and walked to the telescope, staring blindly out the bay window toward Livernois. "Did she tell you what she wanted the office for?"

"Number one, I didn't see her, at least personally. Bruce

dealt with her. Number two, she told us she was a free-lance researcher and needed a private office. Maybe it was true, it probably wasn't, but who cares? I got my money."

I had the sketch out. "All right if I show Bruce this?"

She smiled. "We can do better than that." She consulted the computer screen again, then slid open a door below the computer and extracted a videotape from a huge rank of them in there. She handed it to me. "Stick that in the left-hand VCR, will you?"

I did so. She fiddled with her remote. After a few minutes the screen showed the foyer downstairs, the back of Bruce's head, and a head-on shot of a woman speaking silently. It was Angela, all right. Tall and blond with a body by Fisher. The essence of female came through loud and clear, despite the severe business suit she was wearing.

I watched Angie talk, and said absently, "So she's only been here the once, huh? Any ideas on how I can track her from here?"

"I have her license plate number." I turned and gawked at the fat woman. "That's what the telescope is for," she explained. "People coming to this building have to park in the street outside. I record all the license plate numbers. Never known when they might come in handy." She consulted her computer screen and gave me the number. I wrote it down. "Hopefully it won't just lead you back to that phony address in Royal Oak," she said.

"Hopefully not," I agreed. I did some scribbling on a blank page of my pad, tore it out, and handed it to her. "Those are my numbers. If you see Angela, or hear from her, or anything, give me a call, will you?"

Gail took the paper and set it next to her computer keyboard. "Certainly. And, in return," she said, with a piercing look, "you will give all this information to the appropriate law enforcement agency as soon as it's developed well enough. And get back to peeping at adulterers, or whatever. Got that?"

"Yes, ma'am. Oh, one more thing?"

"Yes?"

"I'd like a look at Angie's office downstairs."

"I can't allow that. Landlord's allowed access only with twenty-four hours' written notice, Mr. Perkins."

"Come on, cut me some slack here."

"I don't approve of snooping!" she thundered. "Besides, even if I let you in there, all you'd find is an empty desk, a dead telephone, and a cheap answering machine. No papers, files, letters, or clues. So don't ask me again."

"All right," I said, "I won't."

I was pretty excited now. Angie's "office" in Barretta's building was clearly a blind drop, a place to get phone calls, and perhaps mail, anonymously. This is not the kind of setup employed by one with nothing to hide. Now all I had to do was find her. Simple.

The afternoon was hurrying ahead. My hunger was near terminal, but fortunately there was a Burger Barn at Livernois and Fenkell. Before starting to eat, I put in a call to Dick Dennehy in Lansing. As I was wadding up the litter, he called me back.

"You didn't tell me you blew up a tenant, last time we talked," he said. "This a new form of eviction you're trying out?"

"Very goddamned funny." I fired up a cigar and leaned back in the Mustang seat. "How'd you hear about it? Don't tell me it made the papers up there, too."

"Nope. Found out from Fat Bob."

"Who the hell's that?"

"New computer system. Among other things, it compiles a digest of local crime reports statewide. Tracks pattern crimes and pattern perps. You'll be pleased to know that you have your very own file in there. Whenever the spirit moves me, I key up one Perkins, B., file D-380890, and get the latest skinny on ya."

I rolled my eyes. "Man, that's about the best news I've had all week."

"Fat Bob hasn't decided whether you blew Reardon up or not," Dick went on. "You're his principal suspect, though. How 'bout it, Ben? You do the dirty deed?"

I felt unreasonably angry. "Shit no, Dick, get real, willya?"

The state police inspector sounded doubtful. "Doesn't matter what I think. What matters is what Fat Bob thinks. I'll tell him your side, but I can't promise—"

"Enough of Fat Bob. I'm sick of the son of a bitch already. You find out anything on those state cops I called you about? The ones who visited Reardon?"

"That was just two days ago. Haven't gotten to it yet."

"Christ," I muttered. "Well, d'ya think you can trouble Fat Bob for a name and address belonging to a license plate number?"

"Hell, why not?" Dick said expansively. "After all, it was your tax dollars paid for him, haw. Give it to me."

I read him the license number Gail Barretta had given me. In a moment Dick said, "Well, looky here! Jalopies to Go, Metropolitan Airport."

Car rental. Another sign that Angie was one very smooth, very careful professional. "Thanks," I said.

"Glad I could help. So, you gonna give Uncle Dick the lowdown on the bombing and your investigation and so forth?"

"I gotta run, Dick. Thanks for the help."

"Sure, I know you're busy. Don't worry about it. We'll have plenty of time to talk about it on visiting days."

Chapter 12

Jalopies to Go operated out of an old Quonset hut on Wickham Road, right across I-94 from Metro Airport. In my own mind I'd more or less pictured a seedy little joint renting wheezing oil burners, like that Pinto I'd lent Ellen, to folks of a less than affluent persuasion. Imagine my surprise to find the Jalopies to Go office bustling with blue suits of both sexes, as well as tourists, fresh off shuttle buses from Metro. They were doing a regular land-office business out there.

It had been a busy day and I guess I was getting tired, for I could think of no reasonable con that would get me information on Angela Barnes's rental last March. I could just walk in and ask, but then they'd probably say no and that would be that. I had no moles, no leverage, nothing. Depressing.

I decided to wait and watch awhile. I sat in the Mustang at the edge of the driveway. With my beat-up 7×50 binoculars I watched the action inside the office through the big plate-glass window, as L-1011s and 747s screamed by overhead.

The office was staffed by two people. One, a man, was clearly in charge. He was in his fifties, balding, very officious, lots of teeth in the grin and a slight tear in the seam of his gray sport coat. The other counter person was female with very long, dark, wavy hair and a full friendly face. She wasn't a day over twenty and she wore, pinned to her black uniform vest, a big button that said "Please Be Patient—I Am New."

Now there was help, just waiting to be had, if I played my cards right.

I waited awhile longer. Another shuttle bus arrived and disgorged customers—just four this time; things were easing up. More planes screamed by. An ambulance wailed out on I-94. My eyes and my ass—the private detective's two most important tools—started a friendly competition to see which was going to get sore first.

Presently, the customers were taken care of. The man inside suddenly filled my binoculars and I saw his name tag: "Hi! I'm Fred!" I dropped the glasses as Fred came out the front door. He bustled toward me and got into a white Ford Thunderbird three cars over. The T-Bird backed out and gunned past me toward the exit, and I caught a glimpse of the business ends of golf clubs peering over the top of the backseat.

I checked the time: 5:30. He might be gone three

minutes or three hours. Either way, I had to try. I got out of the Mustang and walked inside.

The Jalopies to Go office was furnished economically, not to say cheaply. The walls were fake walnut paneling, the floor was cement covered by a day's growth of carpet, the ceiling was a Styrofoam drop job pocked with fluorescent lights. The counter ran the width, broken at three places by built-in computer terminals, and the puzzling Jalopies to Go logo glowed red on the back wall. The clerk was poised like a bird dog at the far terminal. "Yes, sir?" she called with a sunny smile as I came in.

I sauntered down there. "Where's Fred?"

"He had to step out. May I help you?" she asked brightly. She had a good voice, good teeth, and a face that hadn't been hurt too much yet. According to her name tag—which was pinned next to the one advertising her rookie status—her name was Connie. Appropriate, since that was roughly what I was about to do to her.

"Yeah," I said heavily, "I got another hummer, you wanna run it for me?"

"Another what, sir?" she asked, smile dimming a little.

"Hummer." I blinked at her. "Oh, I guess we haven't met yet. I'm O'Gannon, from the home office, how's it going?"

She shook my hand tentatively. "If it's something special you need, maybe you should come back when Fred's here. I'm—"

"Yeah, I know," I said gently, "you're new, but that's okay, all right? Fred's told me how great you're coming along."

She brightened. "Fred talked about me?"

"You bet," I said heartily. "Just the other day. He told me you were working well, even if his putter wasn't."

She laughed along with me, even though I don't think she thought it was any funnier than I did. "What do you need, Mr. O'Gannon?"

"A 'hummer' is a slang term for a phantom complaint. That's when people claim that one of our rented cars did damage to property of theirs. Fred clue you in on that?" Of course Fred couldn't have, since I had made the whole thing up. But Connie, anxious to be a good trouper, watched me intently and nodded eagerly. "Okay," I went on, "I got the license number here and I need to find out who the renter was back on February 1."

Her face was alight. "I know how to do that!" she said. "Give it to me, I'll have it for you in a jiffy."

I handed her the slip from my pad with the license number. She bent over her computer terminal and tapped some keys very slowly, very carefully, the pink tip of her tongue peeking between her lips. After a moment's silence the computer printer began its Gatling gunning, making me jump. When it stopped, Connie tore off a piece of soft printer paper and handed it to me. "There you go!" she said proudly. "Is that what you need?"

I studied the heavy, all-caps printing and found what I wanted, under "driver's license information":

ANGELA ELEANOR BARNES
77 CURTIN TERRACE
DETROIT, MICHIGAN 48207

"Oh yeah," I said softly. "I think this is pret' near perfect."

I drove like a madman through rush-hour traffic and ended up waiting the evening away.

Curtin Terrace is smack in the middle of Harbortown Place, the swanky new development just a stone's throw up the Detroit River from downtown. Ironic. I'd begun my day in the Cass Corridor, Detroit at its most real; I was ending it in Harbortown, Detroit as the land of Oz.

The street was lined with two-story brick townhouses, each with a bay window, driveway, porch, and set of solar panels. Number 77 sat about four doors up from me. Gradually, people returned home to the other places. Gradually, the sunlight started to fade in the west. Gradually, I began to accept that I'd tapped out.

Then she arrived.

The car was a deep red four-door sedan, chunky and anonymous looking. It could have been any of about eight American cars, but it happened to be a Dodge Dynasty. It wheeled up the street toward me, swerved smartly into the driveway of Number 77, and parked at the garage.

I squashed out my cigar and picked up my Canon AE-1 off the passenger seat. A blond head appeared above the roofline of the Dodge, and even before I peered through the Canon telephoto, I knew it was her, Angie, in the flesh at last.

She wore a dove gray blazer over a shirt and skirt in blue-black. Her blond hair was pinned and bunned as it had been in Curt Goldflower's sketch. Her oval face was unsmiling and intent. She really did look a little like Theresa Russell, with a taller and stronger build. I snapped shots as fast as the Canon would film, catching her for a dubious posterity as she went onto the stoop, took mail out of the box, opened the front door, and gave the street one final suspicious glance before disappearing inside.

I set down the camera and gave one long, hissing sigh. If Paul was banging her, I didn't hardly blame him. Sometimes the ice princess bit is a turnoff. Other times it isn't. You wanted to take that hair down, take those clothes off, and then take her to, and on, the nearest available horizontal surface.

Down, boy.

I flamed a cigar, fired up the Mustang, and started the long drive home to Belleville. I felt good. It looked to be a clear, relatively cool evening; the weekend was upon us (though I had maintenance catch-up work to do); WABX was playing Rare Earth's cover of "I Just Want to Celebrate"; and I'd run the bitch to ground.

Now that I had her, what was I going to do with her?

I needed a plan. And, by the time I got home, I had one.

"Want my opinion of this, uh, plan?" Carole asked after a moment's thought.

"From that tone of voice, I think I know already," I answered.

It was Sunday evening and we sat on the deck, having wiped out a couple of Little Caesar's largest and finest pizza pies. Carole reclined on the lounge, sipping a diet 7-Up; I sat facing her near the rail, working on Stroh's tall boys; Will was inside playing video games, as usual. About as close to a family setting as I ever get.

Carole looked stunning in a denim sundress that hugged her long body from bust to thighs. It made me wonder if she was planning to spend the night or not. I was looking for a way to ask, but she was all business at the moment. "You have absolutely no evidence that Angie killed Paul," she pointed out.

"Granted."

"All you know is, Angie and Paul were seen together once and may have been having an affair. You know that Angie was seen at the Jackson home, about the time his live-in was murdered—"

"Tortured and murdered," I said.

"Right. And, finally, you know that Angie has gone to great pains to keep her activities from being traced back to her. All very suspect, I agree, but these things do not make her a killer."

"Well, we'll see," I said. "We're just gonna turn her upside down and shake her by the ankles, and see what comes out."

"I'm surprised Captain Dance is going along with this harebrained idea of yours."

Boy, was she in a negative mood. "Maybe my old buddy Elvin knows a great piece of detection when he sees one. Maybe my old buddy Elvin has a lot more faith in my ability than some people I could mention."

"Maybe—in fact, most likely," Carole said with a piercing look, "you've got some kind of leverage over your old buddy Elvin. I'd love to know what it is."

I lighted a cigar, drank some beer, and did not answer.

She sighed. "I've lined up a co-counsel to help represent you. Classmate of mine. Shaughnessy Levin."

I grinned. "Whoa. Now there's a culture blend for you. Daughter of Jacob Levin and Annie O'Leary, I presume."

Carole did not smile. "She's good. Hell of a lot more criminal litigation experience than I have. Tough as bark. Number two in our class at U of D."

I didn't have to ask who'd taken down number one. "Well, good," I said lazily, "but I have a feeling we won't need her."

She waved a hand. "I wouldn't count on your plan to succeed, if I were you."

"Even if it doesn't, it's been a week now, and the cops haven't pestered me at all. They got no case on me and they know it. They're just letting the whole thing slide. Which is why I'm working on it, because it's not right, the person who killed Paul walking around loose, I won't sit still for it."

She waited me out and said calmly, "Don't count your chickens just yet. They could still indict you. That's why I've got Shaun on board, just in case."

I was tired of talking business. I'd been catching up on maintenance work all weekend and I wanted some relaxation, maybe even some fun, before the shitstorm began anew tomorrow morning. I went straight to the issue of the hour. "Love the sundress, Carole."

She grimaced. "Thanks. It's really not for evenings, but I'm wearing all of my snug things now, before I get too fat to fit in them."

"Oh." Pause. "So," I said carefully, "you're going through with it." She nodded. The words "But you said" were on my tongue. I held them back. That was then. "I see."

She took a good shot at smiling. "I figure I've gotten through so much already, I can get through this. When I left Asshole, I had no job and no education and an infant to take care of. I got through law school and started building my practice while raising Will. I haven't done badly, right?"

"You've done great, kid."

"So there's no reason why I can't handle this, too."

"Well," I said, trying not to sound uneasy, "this time you're not alone." She looked away. "I took the test," I added. "I'll have the result tomorrow morning."

She did not answer.

"Not that it makes any difference, Carole. I said I'd be around and I meant it."

She set her glass down and stood. I did likewise. She faced me, expression a mask of remoteness. "No, you stay here. I need to cry and I don't need an audience."

I stood there, helpless, as she left the deck, sliding the screen door shut behind her. I walked to the rail and leaned down on it, staring out at the meadow that ran between the buildings down toward the lake. I thought over what she had said, what I had said, and couldn't see where I'd done or said anything wrong.

If that was true, why was I out here alone, and she was inside crying? Will I *ever* get this right?

The game ended at eleven, another humiliating loss for the Detroit Tigers, an 11–3 thumping by that American League powerhouse, the Seattle Mariners. This season many chickens had come home to roost. It was clear that the glory of '84 was, as Ernie Harwell would say, "long gone!" It was also clear that I could just abandon any hope of seeing a fourth World Series championship this year. Maybe this century.

I snapped off the radio and cruised the dark deck, picking up empties, and carried them inside. Will Somers, who'd listened with me till the cause was hopeless—the second inning—lay slaunchways on the big couch, watched over by the poster of the scantily clad lady with the champagne and the Rolls-Royce and the caption that said "Poverty Sucks." The big little boy wore blue shorts, blue sneakers, and a red University of Detroit T-shirt, and he was snoring with the sound of an energetic crosscut saw. I slipped off his sneakers, covered him with a sheet, secured the doors, and headed back to the bedroom.

Carole lay facedown on the big bed, eyes closed, breathing evenly. The hem of her denim sundress was hiked up a little, and those glorious miles of legs glowed in the low light of the bedside lamp. I went into the walk-in closet and collected the sleeping bag, air mattress, and pillow. I was opening the bedroom door as quietly as I could when her voice broke the silence.

"Where do you think you're going, buster?"

She hadn't moved, but her eyes were open and fixed on me. "I'm sorry, I didn't mean to wake you."

She hiked herself upon one elbow. "I've been awake for an hour." Her smile was one of female certainty. "Lose that stuff. The bed's over here."

I dropped the items where I stood and went over to the bed. She turned on her side, facing me expectantly with a hand out. I took it and reclined on the bed beside her. Instantly she hugged me with arms and legs and we kissed, one of those endless events, four hands exploring as our breathing went hot.

In my wanderings I discovered that she wore nothing under the sundress. I broke the kiss and said, "You temptress. You came here ready."

"Just a common slut, what can I say," she breathed.

"That's what got you into this fix you're in, you know."

"So the damage is done already." She smiled. "I've never screwed a murder suspect before."

"I've never screwed a pregnant lady before. Just a couple of virgins, that's us."

She arched her back. "Get this thing off me. Quick. You know what I'm like when I wake up horny."

We were working on each other's zippers when the phone rang.

"Let the box get it," Carole said.

The phone kept ringing. "*Shit!*" I snapped. "I forgot to turn it on." I disengaged from Carole, lassoed the receiver, and dragged it to my ear. "What!" I barked into it.

"Ben?" came an uncertain voice. "It's Ellen, Ellen Reardon."

"Uh-huh." My eyes were on Carole, who'd dropped the straps of her sundress and was on her back, dragging the snug garment down over her hips.

"I know it's late," Ellen said, "but I need to talk to you."

"Right now? What about?" Carole shunted the sundress down past her knees and, with a scissor kick, sent it away over the foot of the bed.

Ellen's voice rose. "I can't talk about it on the phone. Can you come over?"

Carole sat up on her haunches and knee-walked to me. Her breasts were on full alert, her eyes alight, lips parted and moist. I took a deep breath and said to Ellen, "Can't, not right now, I'm sorry."

"Please!" she said, a helpless edge to her voice. "Things are happening and I don't know what to do."

Carole tugged my shorts down to my thighs. Then, with almost surgical precision, she pulled my underwear down as if lifting a lid. She mimed a look of exaggerated surprise and delight at what she saw there. "It'll have to wait," I said into the phone, faintly.

Ellen sounded like she was about to lose it. "See?" she sobbed. "I knew it. I knew you wouldn't be here for me."

Carole mounted me, aimed me, and took me home with a long, smooth stroke, her eyes intent on mine all the while. After a silent moment in full genital lock, she snatched the receiver from me and growled, "He's can't talk now" into it, then hurled it away from the bed, dragging the rest of the phone to the floor in a ringing, clattering crash.

She put her palms down on either side of my head, kissed me almost primly, shook her head to loosen her hair, smiled, and said, "Wanna fuck?"

"Thirty million," Dr. Abbas said.

I blinked. "Thirty million what, Doc?"

He closed the file folder. "Your sperm count, sir."

"Is that enough?" I asked, feeling stupid.

"It's very, very low. Perhaps twenty-five percent of normal. But, to answer your question, one is enough, sir."

I closed my eyes for a long moment. "But I had a vasectomy. What happened? Did it go bad?"

Dr. Abbas set the folder down on the examining table. His lined, kindly face was dead serious. "Vasectomies do not, as you say, 'go bad,' Mr. Perkins. When properly performed, that is. They can be surgically reversed through microsurgery—I myself have an eighty-percent success rate in that area—but—"

I felt my face hardening. "Properly performed. So, what you're saying is, Dr. Slater is a quack."

The doctor flinched. "It's hard to say what went wrong. Most likely, one of the vas was not completely severed, and—"

"He's a quack, right?"

"It is not within my purview to assess the qualifications of a fellow practitioner, sir."

"Just answer the damn question." At his expression, I sighed and shook my head. "I'm sorry, Doctor. It's just, my lady friend is pregnant. She said it was me, and the only damn reason I doubted her was this vasectomy. Jesus Christ. Problem isn't that I'm twenty-five-percent fertile. Problem is that Carole's a hundred-percent pregnant."

"I sympathize," Dr. Abbas said, and from his look I could tell he really did. "I'll be happy, of course, to complete the procedure—"

"Little late in the day, wouldn't you say?" I looked at the doctor and kept my voice as light as I could, even though my hands were locked into fists. "Now tell me what you know about Slater."

Dr. Abbas's slight shoulders lifted beneath his white jacket. "It's a matter of record that Dr. Slater's medical license was revoked some time ago. There'd been complaints—"

"I'll just bet!"

"He left the state," the doctor said softly. "The last I heard, he'd set up practice in Ohio."

"Figures. Where in Ohio?"

"Columbus, I think." He looked distressed. "You're not considering going back to him to complete the work, are you?"

"Nah. I got other plans for him."

"I don't think you'd prevail in litigation, Mr. Perkins."

"He's gonna *wish* I'd sued him. Real bad."

"Now, Mr. Perkins—"

"I think I'll take a crack at urological surgery myself. With a busted beer bottle. Learn by doing, my daddy always said."

Chapter 13

Fifteen minutes later I'd joined the I-94 bumper-to-bumper club, bound for downtown Detroit. The Monday-morning rush hour was in full cry: four solid lanes of iron flooding east at better than sixty miles per hour, each vehicle a bare half-length from the next.

I drove on full automatic pilot. The radio blasted something juicy and throbbing by the Fine Young Cannibals. I was on my way to help Elvin Dance put my "Angie" plan into action; with any luck, by day's end I'd have the answer to what had happened to Paul Reardon, and why. But I wasn't listening to the music, and I wasn't thinking about the work.

I was thinking about Carole and her pregnancy, and a little chorus kept playing in my mind: Daddy, daddy, Ben's gonna be a daddy.

It wasn't that I'd doubted Carole's claim of fidelity. It's just that I'd counted on that vasectomy, and while that was there, any possibility of my being the father seemed remote and arm's length. Now it was reality.

A *baby*, for Chrissake. Mine. I knocked her up. Thirty million, the doc said. And one of them little rascals had made it.

I didn't know how to feel or what to think. There'd been a lot of years and a lot of women, a lot of effort devoted to avoiding such a thing. Starting with high school. Condoms in the billfold and the glove compartment. Like taking a shower with your socks on. I remembered the time with Gretchen when the skin gave at the ultimate moment: SNAP! We sweated it out for a couple of weeks, then never saw each other again.

Coitus interruptus: a bad way to have sex, a good way to

get pregnant. Nudges, leers, and braggadocio in the locker room. Girls who went away to "live with her aunt Elaine in Port Huron" for a year. Police spotlights shining through the back window of my '51 Ford Deluxe Tudor. Sneaking in the back door of Beth Heinzeroth's Roxford Street house in the dead of night. A chance encounter with the allegedly virtuous and unavailable Debbie Somebody, cheerleader captain, at a rowdy Metro Beach picnic, ending up in the back of my Ford—no protection, no nothing, but go for it: Pump and Pray was the name of that game.

Then later, my first lengthy relationship, with Charlotte, the lady I lived with in Jefferson-Chalmers. She was a devout Catholic who played the rhythm game expertly, counting days, taking her temperature, and exercising such strict willpower during the infamous and all-too-frequent "bad periods" that I remember nights when we did everything but bang our heads against the wall to keep our hands off each other.

In the years since there'd been the pill, diaphragms, IUDs, and foam. Then I had my vasectomy, eliminating all worry and all responsibility. Or so I thought.

Through the interchange area, traffic slowed to about ten. My clutch foot was starting to ache. I checked the time: 8:40. Could be Carole was in her office by now. I punched out her number on the cellular phone and she answered on the second ring. "Somers Law Office."

"Hey, kid, so you made it in."

"Well, I'm here. You got me up so early this morning, it was almost yesterday."

"You said you had a lot to do. Everything took care of?"

"Oh yes," she said evenly, "it's gone as expected. Will and I came home, I got him dressed for his first day of summer camp and gave him breakfast. Then I showered, dressed, threw up, and came to work. How's your day so far?"

I winced. "Gettin' there, babe. Listen, whaddya say we kick out the jams tonight?"

"After last night," she said coolly, "I think my inventory of 'jams' is going to be a little low for a while. And all I want to do is get this day past me. If I didn't have a bail review hearing at the Thirty-sixth this afternoon, I'd pack it in right now."

"What I'm suggesting here," I said, improvising rapidly, "is dinner. I'll drop by after work and fix it. The whole nine yards."

"As delicious as it is, I don't think I could keep down even one bite of Perkin's World-Famous Tonna Spaghetti. Sorry."

"We're not talking spaghetti. We're talking every food-type item you love the best. And you don't have to lift a finger. Aside from feeding yourself, that is."

"Well," she said listlessly, "just so you don't expect me to entertain. I'm just not in the mood."

"Just dinner and conversation." Especially conversation.

"Well." She suddenly seemed conscious of her cold tone. "It's sweet of you. Fine. See you then. Is today the day you carry out your big plan with Elvin Dance?"

"Today's the day. This morning, in fact."

"I hope it goes well."

"I think it's gonna go fabulous."

"It's goin' down the toilet," Elvin Dance growled.

We were in that same half-assed conference room as the last time. Elvin sat on the edge of the battered wood table, face stormy as he lighted a Kool cigarette. Today he wore a white shirt with faint vertical purple pinstripes, a purple paisley tie, and dark beltless slacks over calfskin boots. As usual, gold winked from everywhere. I wondered idly, and not for the first time, if Elvin took. I doubted it, but you never know.

"Calm down, Captain," I answered. "What's the problem?"

"That witness you was telling me about? The neighbor lady with the last name like a law firm?"

"Yeah. Maggie Corbett-Hollingsworth." I had a sinking feeling. "What about her?"

"Dead." Elvin exhaled smoke.

"What? Oh, shit," I murmured. I went to a wood chair

and sat down heavily. "I knew she was nuts for living in that neighborhood. What happened?"

Gold winked in one of Elvin's teeth. "Neighborhood didn't kill her, Perkins. Fact is, that house of hers on Brainard went up in flames night 'fore last. Hell of a fire. Husband got out all right, firemen found him standing across the street watching it, calm as could be. Place was totaled, not much left except solid stuff like bathtubs and plumbing and stuff. That's where they found what was left of Maggie. In the bathtub."

"Got trapped, huh?" I said, thinking about how those old houses had a lot of wood in them, dry tinderbox wood.

"Sort of. She was handcuffed to one of the fixtures."

I squinted at him, momentarily at a loss for words. "You are shittin' me, Elvin."

He showed me both palms. "Not me, no sir. Husband admitted the whole thing. He handcuffed her to one of the fixtures in the tub, filled the tub with water. Said it was so she'd 'cook for a good long time.' Then he scattered ten gallons of Amoco Ultra unleaded on all three floors, tossed a burning rag through one of the windows, and strolled across the street to watch."

I remembered Maggie screeching at Josh, the odd looks Josh gave her when she wasn't looking. I suddenly felt a little more used up. Impatiently I said, "That's a real shame, but we're still on for this morning, aren't we?"

Elvin looked glum. "Officers are on their way here with Angie Barnes right now. If I'd've known earlier that your star witness got smoked, I'd have canceled this whole thing. Even with the witness we didn't have much on Angie. Now we got squat."

I was upset for more than one reason. I paced, thinking furiously, and said, "You can still roust her. You know. Say you got a witness, et cetera, who saw her near that house the day Jackson's live-in died. Tell her you like her for Jackson's death, too. Throw the fear of God in her, maybe she'll spill something we can use."

Elvin was shaking his head slowly. "Rousting isn't as easy as it used to be. People are awful sensitive these days, they feel like their rights are being violated when the police question them without probable cause, they get lawyers and stuff."

"Cheer up, Elvin, could be the prints'll match."

"We'll do some quick criminalistics. But I wouldn't bet the farm on anything working out there. This whole thing is a sorry-ass mess, Perkins, and I wish to God I never got involved."

I stopped pacing. "But you're going to do this anyway. Because you owe me."

"Yeah," he said unhappily. "I'm gonna do it against my better judgment. I'm gonna do it despite the fact that you failed to tell me about Maggie's statement to you. That's withholding evidence, and—"

"Slipped my mind. What can I say?"

Dance rolled his eyes. "I'll do my best here. But once it's over, we're square." He stood very close to me and poked my chest with the heel of his fist. "That incident we been alludin' to, the one that never happened, is history. No more comebacks. You read me?"

"Sure, Elvin. Christ. Don't get so worked up."

"Being into you ain't the most pleasant situation in the world," he grumbled. "Something else I'm curious about, white boy. This Angela thing have anything to do with that car bombing out in Belleville, the one the police out there like you for?"

Great. Elvin had spent the weekend asking around. "Angie and the victim had sub rosa contact," I said. "She's the best suspect around."

"Aside from you." Elvin grinned.

The observation room was dark, dusty and airless, and stank of cigarettes and sweat. It was equipped with a couple of chairs, a video camera on a tripod, and some recording equipment, all of it dark and silent. The only light came from the big one-way window that gave a full view of the interrogation room on the other side. At the moment it was empty. I sat on a chair, got out my pad and pen, lighted a cigar, and waited.

Presently the interrogation-room door opened and Elvin Dance came in, followed by Angela Barnes, another plainclothes detective whom I did not recognize, and a faceless uniform. "Have a seat," came Elvin's voice through a tinny speaker on the ceiling of the observation room.

Angela Barnes sat down silently at the left-hand side of the long gray steel table. She wore a sky blue suit, the jacket a one-button job, the skirt vented in the back and descending snugly to midcalf. The blouse, also snug, was a soft warm peach. The whole getup was totally business, yet totally female. This held true as well for the blond hair, pulled back so tight it looked painted on, and just the subtlest shadings of makeup on her round face, her pouting lips, and her colorless, watchful eyes.

She was something, all right. I'd seen her in sketch, on TV, though a viewfinder, and now, through a one-way window. This was the closest I'd gotten to her, and she got nothing but more gorgeous.

Elvin and his anonymous partner sat across the table from her. The uniform posed next to the door. Elvin, half-smiling, gave Angela the obvious and almost sarcastically appreciative once-over. She endured it with an expression that was unafraid without being defiant, absolutely neutral. Finally Elvin said, "Ms. Barnes, my name is Elvin Dance. I run the homicide section here at the Detroit police. My associate is Sergeant Zindlar, and—"

The door opened and a tall, middle-aged white man came bustling in, briefcase in hand. "Here you are, Dance!" he barked. "Goddamn it, I've been chasing all over the building looking for you."

Elvin stood. Though he hid it well, I could tell he was just a tad shook. "Mr. Hite. Um—are you representing Ms.—"

Hite nodded abruptly at Angie, who hadn't changed expression, and took the chair next to her across from the detectives. "My client. What's the scoop here, Captain?"

The lawyer was white-haired, florid, athletically built, and a vivid presence in the small interrogation room, tricked out in a charcoal gray, immaculately tailored double-breasted suit. His arrival did not please me. What pleased me even less was the way he and Angie reacted to each other. Fact is, they didn't react at all. Didn't even nod at each other. It was as if they were about to play a scene they'd already done a thousand times.

Elvin said, "We're developing some information on a couple of murders, and since Ms. Barnes's name has been mentioned once or twice, we thought maybe she could help us."

Hite's smile was a full grille of capped teeth. He glanced at Angela Barnes, who didn't move, change expression, or even blink. "We're ready," he said. "Let's get on with it, shall we?"

Elvin addressed Barnes. "Your address is 77 Curtin Terrace, Detroit, Michigan, is that correct?"

"That's correct," Hite answered.

Elvin squinted at him, consulted his notes. "Ms. Barnes, where are you employed?"

"Ms. Barnes is a technical researcher for Barkley Enterprises, 26880 Northwestern Highway, Southfield, Michigan."

Elvin sighed audibly. "Ms. Barnes, are you some kinda mute?"

"I'm her legal counsel," Hite said, as if addressing a child. "Ms. Barnes is not accustomed to this kind of proceeding. She's too upset at this unwarranted intrusion in her private life, her lawful affairs, to answer directly. I most strenuously object to your brutal attempts to abrogate her legal—"

"Save it, shyster," Dance said wearily.

Hite, unmoved, said. "I'd like for us to get down to business now, Captain. Who's the stiff?"

"Two stiffs. Number one," Elvin said, consulting his pad, "was Davey Jackson. Shot to death in his car on the morning of June the eighth."

Hite and Barnes leaned together, she whispered a moment, then they straightened. "My client has no information about that alleged matter," Hite said. "For the record, she was at the Pontchartrain Hotel, a guest at a brunch given by

Wayne County Commissioner Seymour Shreyer, on that morning."

Dance let the silence string out, an indication of his skepticism. "Then there's Jackson's companion, Ms. Charnelle Blais," he said. "Found tortured to death in their house on Brainard Street. A witness has positively identified you, Ms. Barnes, as a visitor to that house on Friday, June the thirteenth. That perfectly fits the medical examiner's estimate as to the time of death."

Hite and Barnes leaned, whispered, straightened. "My client knows nothing about that alleged incident. For the record, she was attending a meeting of the Windsor Italian Friendship Club at that time."

I sat, smoked and watched, growing more glum by the minute. Those two were as rehearsed as Burns and Allen, but not quite as funny.

Elvin seemed to concur. He folded his dark knuckly hands together and glared at the woman. "Let's cut the crap, Ms. Barnes. We know that Davey Jackson was a major cocaine distributor. We're sure that his murder was related to that activity. Bein' as you were positively identified at the scene of his live-in's death, we—"

"Who's your witness, Captain?" Hite asked briskly.

"That's confidential for now, Counselor."

"What physical evidence do you have?"

"We're still developing that."

Hite sat back, folded his arms across his chest, and said, "So what you got is zero. And what you're on is a fishing expedition."

Dance indicated Barnes with a nod. "If she's clean, she's got nothing to worry about, cooperating with us."

Hite's face exhibited amazement. "But she is cooperating, Captain! She's come down here at your request, voluntarily, and answered all of your questions, been totally cooperative. She's done this because she's a public-spirited citizen, and, I might add, one hell of a nice young girl." Then he smiled, his expression almost eager. "Whereas I, as you know, Captain Dance, am one nasty son-of-a-bitch bastard who likes nothing better than rubbing cops' faces in their own shit. Now, I realize that my role here is to advise Ms. Barnes, not you, but nevertheless my advice to you, sir, is to book her or kick her."

Elvin scribbled for a moment on his pad, then said without looking up, "We'll be in touch. Thanks for stopping by."

He stood and walked out, followed by Zindlar, the uniform, the lawyer, and Angie Barnes. As she went through the door, she looked over her shoulder and, it almost seemed, directly into my eyes. She winked, smiled, made a kiss with her lips, and was gone.

"Happy now?" Elvin asked, voice a low slow rattle.

"What do you think?" I retorted.

"All I know is, I pissed away half a morning here on doodly, but what else is new in this fucking work?" Elvin was in shirt sleeves, smoking a cigarette as he wandered the confines of the tiny observation room. "We got zip on the fingerprints, as I suppose you gathered."

As I watched Elvin I felt badly for having arm-twisted him. He'd embarrassed himself to help me, and I couldn't blame him for being upset. "Look, Elvin, I really thought I was onto something. I thought maybe we could pop Angie loose, and—"

Elvin stopped still. "Oh, you onto something all right. No doubt about it." He gestured angrily with his cigarette hand. "That honkie lawyer? Hite? Don't that tell you something?"

"Tells me she came down here prepared, more's the pity."

"Never heard of him, huh?" Elvin's expression was a mask of angry disgust. "He's an organization man. Through and through. Bought and paid for." I guess Elvin thought I didn't understand, because he leaned down to me and said very distinctly, "Organization, Perkins! As in mob, La Cosa Nostra, Mafia."

Chapter 14

I stood up and went to the one-way window, staring at the chair in which Angie had sat. I replayed a mental videotape of the proceedings and it all made sense. Every move Angela Barnes had made had been utterly professional. I felt a chill. What the hell did you get yourself mangled up in, Paul?

I turned and looked at the burly black detective. "She said she works for something called Barkley Enterprises. That a mob front, far as you know?"

Elvin's face was showing a sheen of sweat in the small hot room. "Beats me."

Something clicked in my memory. "Well, what about that address she gave? Northwestern Highway in Southfield, twenty-six-thousand block. That sounds awfully close to the Titanium Tower, doesn't it?"

"Could be."

I thought about Davey Jackson, the dead drug distributor; Charnelle Blais, his live-in, tortured to death; Paul Reardon, blown to oblivion out in Belleville. In all three cases, Angela Barnes had been involved either before or after. Coincidence?

Elvin was on a track of his own. "You realize, Perkins, that it ain't nice to play guilt by association. We can't be positive that your friend Angie works for the mob. Don't know if she's into drug traffic or killing or whatever."

"Yeah. Sure. She could be pure as driven snow."

"One thing I do know, though. If Hite's her lawyer, she's sure as shit guilty of *something.*"

* * *

The crack had begun down low on the north wall of Building 5. I'd first noticed it in '84, and since then had watched it creep along the mortar joints, zigzagging aimlessly up and right, up and right. Now it had reached the height of a full-grown man and I figured it was time to do something about it.

Brian was with me that Monday afternoon, my sole student in the fine art of repairing a damaged mortar joint. This was his first day back on the job after his long convalescence, and he'd handled it well. In fact, he really seemed to enjoy it.

I, on the other hand, felt frustrated and foul. For one thing, it was hotter than hell's hinges that day, ninety-plus heat and humidity; as I informed Brian, if I wanted to live in fucking New Orleans, I'd move there. For another, I'd been unable to reach Ellen Reardon. It made me uneasy, wondering what she'd meant the night before when she said, "Things are happening and I don't know what to do." Not only that, but tonight was dinner at Carole's, in which I'd tell her the results of the sperm test. This would be the ultimate in anticlimaxes—a line I would probably *not* use on Carole, most likely.

Finally, I was at a total dead end on Paul's murder. Angie, my latest brainstorm, had come up empty, just like the notion that Paul's father might have been the perp. I had a bunch of facts, but they all just lay scattered around like a mess of pickup sticks. I only knew three things for sure. One, Paul was dead. Two, Angie had something to do with it. Three, I was still the best suspect going—hell, *I* would've suspected me if I hadn't known better.

What I didn't know was what the hell to do next.

So I took refuge, if not pleasure, in physical work, and in teaching the kid how to do it right.

I gave the cold chisel a couple of final licks with the ball-peen hammer, then brushed my goggles up onto my forehead and said, "You see what I mean, kid? Gotta whack all that old mortar out of there, widen the crack so it's big enough to fill."

Brian nodded, long handsome face intent. "The entire length of the crack, huh?"

"Yep." I handed him the hammer and chisel. "You try it now. I'll mix up some mortar and patch in behind you."

"I notice I get the tough half," Brian said, grinning, "while you get the easy. That's okay, old men deserve a break."

"We'll trade off," I said darkly. "Get going. Put those goggles on first."

"Yes, Mother," Brian said. He began to chisel with short strong strokes, the hammer meeting the chisel with a piercing *ping, ping, ping* that echoed off the other buildings. I measured some portland cement into the wheelbarrow and was just adding lime when a voice called behind me. "Hey, Ben, you got a visitor!"

I turned. Randy, my other crewman, stood on the long grass, alongside an older man in navy pants, white shirt, red tie, carrying his jacket slung casually over his shoulder. He smiled and waved. I stared and waved back, thinking, Oh-ho.

"Got a minute, Ben?" Carlo Infante called. "Somebody wants to see you."

Somebody, huh? Wonder who? But I wasn't worried. Carlo wouldn't double-cross me. Or would he?

"I wouldn't double-cross you," Carlo said as he motored the Honda Civic along Huron River Drive. We were approaching Belleville proper now; to our left was the blue expanse of Belleville Lake, to the right were fields and an occasional house. "That's why Rick had me come along, so you'd feel safe. So don't be nervous."

"I'm not nervous," I lied. "I'm just not exactly dressed for the occasion, you know?" I felt dirty and grubby and sweaty in my twill shirt and pants. Hell of a thing, looking like this on the way to an appointment with the operations chief of the Detroit organization. "What's it about, Carlo?"

His glance flicked at me. "I don't know, Ben. I can tell you he isn't happy. You been up to no good lately?"

I shrugged. "You know I stay clear of you guys. I want nothing to do with your action."

We entered Belleville, heading for the rats' nest of

intersections at the center of town. "Just talk to him and stay cool," he counseled.

Good advice, and I could take Carlo's word to the bank. He was a midlevel finance and computer grunt, in the brains—not muscle—end of the organization. I helped him out once a long time ago with a personal problem, and since then he'd been my low-key contact within the organization; he had, in fact, helped grease a couple of bad scrapes with them in the past. That was, of course, no assurance that he would help me out of a jam now. But I wasn't worried yet. I'd stirred something up, and I was anxious to find out what.

"Here we go," Carlo said, wheeling onto the grassy shoulder at the east side of the triangular Victory Park. He indicated a picnic table by a clump of trees near the large white gazebo. I got out and sauntered into the park, pleased that the place was so public, practically in the center of Belleville.

Rick Savastano saw me coming and stood as I approached. He was six-four and had that lean, honed greyhound look. His brown hair was thick and conservatively cut. His face was still fighter-pilot handsome, though I thought he looked tired around the gray eyes. He wore an oyster suit with a pink hankie in the pocket, over a cream shirt split by a medallion paisley tie. His suit was worth more than all of mine combined.

He nodded in greeting. I said, "Hey, Rick, what's cooking?" We did not shake hands, just sat down on opposite sides of the picnic table. I did not smoke, knowing that Savastano had a violent hatred of it and wishing not to hack him off just yet. There we sat with nothing to do but talk—an odd-looking pair there in the center of Belleville, engaged in an odd business.

Savastano folded his tanned hands. "What's your interest in Davey Jackson?" he asked.

I tipped my head back and squinted. "Davey Jackson," I murmured.

Something hot flared way back in Savastano's eyes, just for an instant. "You know what I'm talking about. Let's not play games. I have sources of information within the Detroit Police Department."

I grinned. "Tell you what. You tell, then I'll tell."

The slightest throbbing began in Savastano's temple. "I

don't have to dick around with dirtbag detectives like you, Perkins. I can have you squashed."

I stared at him, dumbstruck, then allowed myself the smallest of smiles. "Rick, old son," I said, "I'm real ashamed of you, coming on all grade-B movie like that. You're supposed to personify the new Mafia, all business, Harvard MBA. In fact, if memory serves, you are a Harvard MBA and a JD out of U of M besides. You're supposed to be a slicked-down smoothie, not an old-time goombah."

The mob operations chief looked away from me, pressing his lips, and said finally, "I'm easy to piss off lately."

"I don't want any trouble with you," I said evenly. "I've never wanted any trouble with you."

Savastano was unimpressed. "Indeed? Then what about State Senator Borrello—"

"Now Congressman Borrello."

"And Commissioner Carlson—"

"*Former* Commissioner Carlson. But I don't think of those as conflicts. We reached an accommodation, you and I."

He looked at me again, neutral as a newscaster. "You've been dancing along the razor's edge with me a long time. Now I want an answer. What's your interest in Davey Jackson? Make it quick, I've got to get back to Southfield."

"I toldja already," I said. "You tell, then I'll tell."

As he looked at me, I saw how much he'd aged. Weary with the sins of the world, eh Ricky boy? The fencing made me tense and dry-mouthed. It would have been easier just to play the game his way. But I'd learned one thing a long time ago about these guys. You don't back down and you don't give in. Ever.

After a moment, Savastano's eyebrows arched. His shoulders shrugged. His whole being broadcast, *Okay, all right, whatever it takes to make the temperamental little child happy.* "He was one of mine, okay?"

"So what else is new?" I drawled. "Story I hear is he was moving 'caine in the high-pockets turf, the banks and the utilities and the newspapers and the City-County Building."

"That's not important. What's important is that a lot of pressure has been building in that channel, and—"

"Pressure!" I snorted. "I'll say! Pressure as in Davey gets blasted by a nine-millimeter while sitting in his car on Adelaide. Pressure as in his live-in gets gutted like a twelve-point buck while handcuffed to her shower nozzle. Pressure like that."

"We're in a competitive business," Savastano observed. "Now it's your turn. Spill."

I trotted out the pretty little story about the belongings found in the Gremlin that I was being paid to return. "But with Davey and Charnelle both dead"—I shrugged—"the case is closed, as we say in the trade."

Savastano's fighter-pilot face was sad. "That's about the sorriest story I've ever heard out of you, Perkins, and I've heard a lot of them."

"You don't like the answers, don't ask the questions."

He checked his gold Necco Wafer watch. "I've got to move along," he said grimly. "But hear me well, Perkins. You know that pressure I was talking about? Well, I'm not going to sit still for it much longer. We will respond. And we're not going to be particularly careful about avoiding damage to half-wit hillbilly detectives who stroll in the way by accident. You hear me?"

"Yeah yeah yeah," I said, standing. "Is that it? Can I go now?"

"Carlo will take you back. Remember what I said."

"Sure. Consider me filed under 'Terrified.'"

"He on the rag," I asked, "or what?"

Carlo drove the Honda with one hand, the other cradling a pack of True cigarettes and a Bic lighter. You'll die frustrated waiting for him to smoke one. I've known him ten years; he likes to handle the smokes but I've never seen him light up. "Things happen," he said. "We're in a competitive business."

"So I hear." I leaned back in the uncomfortable seat, notched the window, and lighted a cigar, projecting an air of nonchalance that was entirely false. "Off the record, Carlo."

His eyes flicked at me once. "All right."

"What's with him?"

Carlo slowed and stopped at a red light. "I'm not with him very much, and even if I was, I—"

I waved a hand. "Understood."

Carlo sniffed. "Steve's bird-dogging the P and L pretty close, giving Rick face on a pretty regular basis, or so I hear. Plus there's a fresh one on Steve's lap, guy named Tagucci, been popping up in Rick's rearview, got him nervous, it looks like."

So Steve Ritchie (né Ricci), the de facto boss of the Detroit organization, was unhappy with Savastano's business results and appeared to be grooming a successor. "Rick's performance as bad as Steve's acting like it is?"

The light changed and the Honda motor whined us forward. "It's not the greatest," he conceded.

I smoked a moment, gnawed the cigar tip, and asked. "You guys still working out of Titanium Tower?"

"That's not for me to say," Carlo answered. Which was his way of confirming.

"Where does Angie Barnes fit into all of this?" I asked, sending off the ultimate in shots in the dark.

"You lost me."

Which could have meant anything.

After showering, I called Ellen Reardon's number. No answer. On the way out, I checked the parking lot. The Pinto was there. I was running late, but I went to the door of Apartment 308 and knocked loudly enough to wake the dead. No answer.

Dinner was an exercise in the power of the MasterCard. Rolf's-on-the-Dock in St. Clair Shores catered a full-course surf-and-turf dinner for three to Carole's house in Berkley, and we ate the rare steak, shrimp, asparagus tips, and tossed salad with fine appetite.

That is, I had a fine appetite. Will wrinkled his seven-year-old nose at the asparagus and shrimp, and Carole skipped the wine and the coffee. But she did clean her own plate and polish off Will's leftovers besides.

When we were done, I tipped the caterers and left them

to clean up the mess, then followed Carole out onto the patio with a Stroh's tall boy in hand.

She was dressed on the casual, nonprovocative side tonight: a white polo shirt with wide pink horizontal stripes over new acid-washed jeans. As she sat on a chair in the shade of the giant sycamore tree that huddled over the patio, I saw signs of fatigue everywhere. Her eyes were dull, her smile occasional and forced, her posture uncaring and almost beaten. I'd never been around a pregnant woman before—except my mother, with Libby, and I was only three then—and it suddenly hit me what a bitch pregnancy must be.

I walked to the edge of the patio and looked around the small backyard, trying to figure out how to say it. Will came flying out of the house and darted into the backyard, tossing a baseball into the air and catching the pop flies over and over. I thought, Oh, just do it, ya jerk. I turned to Carole. "Well, you're right, kid, it's me."

Her dark eyes found me. Her look was steady and neutral and she did not change expression.

"Test came back," I plunged on. "Thirty million. Doc thinks the joker who did the vasectomy screwed it up—heh—or whatever, who knows."

She propped an elbow on the arm of her chair and leaned her chin on her fist.

I drank some beer. The yard was quiet except for the leathery slap of the baseball landing in Will's mitt and the darting of his big bare feet in the grass. "You know what I think," I said, "is that it must have happened downtown. You're what, about ten weeks along now?"

She nodded, examining the fingernails of her left hand.

"Must have been at the Pontch, after the Red Wings game."

"Evil omen," she murmured. "I hate hockey."

"Well,"—I grinned,—"as I recall, it was you who suggested we stay over Saturday night, too. You even arranged for Mrs. Miracle to stay here and take care of Will—"

Carole broke in. "If what you're hinting is that it takes two to tango, I'm fully aware of that, thank you."

"Come on," I said gently. "I'm just reminiscing here,

sort of. I mean, this whole thing has really made me think. And I've been thinking, well, if this had to happen, it could have gotten started anywhere. Here in Berkley, or at my place in Belleville. But instead it got started downtown, which is sort of fitting. The kid's gonna be like you and me. Made in Detroit."

Her face had gone absolutely unreadable. Seemed as though my effort to lighten things up wasn't working. She said, "How interesting."

"Well, yeah." I drank some more. "I been thinking also about the money part, and I want you to know I'll be good for my end. How's a hundred a week sound? Is that fair?"

"I don't know."

I took a deep breath and said, "What I'm trying to do here, in my own clumsy way, is let you know that I'm in this with you, that I'm gonna be around, that I'm not going anywhere."

She nodded. "Now that there's no doubt as to paternity."

"Now wait a minute, I said I'd help you before, too. This was just something I had to find out."

"And now you've come around to warm, sentimental feeling about the whole thing," she said, almost dreamily. "After a lifetime of catting around, you find the idea of being a daddy warm and appealing."

"I'm only trying to—"

"You're even willing to part with a hundred dollars a week! My, oh my! How will the beer industry survive?"

I closed my eyes for one long moment, then opened them. "You trying to make some kind of point here, Carole?"

"Is it my turn to talk now? Thank you." She got to her feet, locked her hands in front of her, and walked toward the house. "I guess now I'm supposed to feel warm and wanted and protected and reassured. I'm supposed to fall into your arms and be grateful that you've stopped being such a suspicious shit."

I felt my face heating up. "Hey, I never claimed to be any good at this. It's never happened to me before. I'm making it up as I go along."

She faced me and hissed, "Let me clue you in on

something, mister. *Nothing* is happening to you. It's happening to me. And I know how it goes because I've been through it before." She jabbed a hand in the direction of her son, who was still running around the yard playing baseball with himself, elaborately ignoring us. "It was different with him. I was young and stupid and gullible. I also had a husband. Not much of a husband, I admit. He'd already slapped me around some, given me a shiner, broken one of my fingers, *snap* like a bread stick. But I figured having a child would change him. I found out differently."

"I'm not Asshole," I said, "and you know it."

She spread her arms, inviting a full-length inspection. "Now here I am, thirty-six and pregnant again. What do I do? What in the *hell* do I do? There's my practice to consider. How am I going to run it and raise a baby, too? There's my seminar work. And I've been approached to write articles and maybe even a book. How am I going to handle all of that—plus a damned kid? And there's Will to think about."

I didn't answer.

"Well," she said in a low voice, "it's obvious what I have to do. The only problem is, when I look at Will, it breaks my heart to think that I could easily have done it to him, too."

"Done what?" I fumbled. "You talking about—"

"I'm having an abortion, Ben. It's on for Friday."

The words "But you said" were on my tongue. I held them back. That was then. "I see."

"It's the only sensible thing," she said, face resolute. "Especially when I remember what I've learned about men over the years: they come and then they go. In the end, I'm always alone. I've learned not to need anyone, and I don't need you." She turned and went into the house, ripping the sliding door shut behind her.

I stood there dead still for a minute. Then I lighted a cigar. I felt drained. I realized that I'd rather take on a half-dozen liquored-up chain swingers than go through that again.

Will came walking toward me, tossing the baseball in the air. His round, open, innocent face understood everything. I puffed smoke and said, "Guess I blew it, huh, kid?"

"It's been easy to do lately," he answered.

Chapter 15

"So what happened then?" Bill Scozzafava asked.

I took a belt of beer and wiped my mouth. "Just what you'd expect. I went into the house, followed her to the bedroom, soothed her and sweet-talked her and got her between the sheets and gave her the ride of her life. That's what I did."

"Good for you. You acted like a man." He gave the immaculate bar a wipe. "Now tell me what really happened."

"I went home."

It was noontime Tuesday, the day after my disastrous "date" with Carole. I was grumpy; felt like hitting something. Not much had gone right since last night. I'd hit the sack early and slept fitfully, dreaming over and over of men in smocks kicking me in the head. I overslept, rushed to work, tackled the inventory of maintenance jobs with less than my usual zest. This was not going to be the best Monday of my life.

Of course the Reardon investigation was bugging me. Two promising theories had bellied up and no new ones were in sight. Dick Dennehy was dragging his feet on finding out exactly why the state police were, evidently, investigating Paul. And that mystery blond out there, Angela Barnes, danced just out of reach: puzzling, tantalizing, infuriating.

Add to that the Carole dilemma. Plus a brand spanking new problem: Ellen Reardon.

Upon reaching home last night, I'd called her once again. No answer. I stomped over to her building. The Pinto was still in the parking lot, right where I'd left it. I pounded on the door; no answer. Used my passkey to get in. Illegal, of course, but I was really worried by now. I had visions of Ellen Reardon wired to the shower nozzle like Charnelle Blais, her breasts whittled with such exquisite care. . . .

Apartment 308 contained no such horrors. As far as I could tell, nothing was disturbed, out of place, or missing. Nothing but Ellen. The dry sinks and the unexamined mail said she'd been gone at least twenty-four hours. She hadn't been thoughtful enough to leave a note as to where she'd gone and how she'd gotten there without a car. Just one more thing to fret about . . .

Under New Management was downright deserted today. Some trucker was taking a snooze in the corner booth; Kate Leffingwell was waiting for her boyfriend over by the juke, and at the first table behind me Harry Moscone and Norris Johnston were loudly debating a critical issue of our time: what's the greatest love song ever recorded? They didn't think much of my opinion that there are two: "Unchain My Heart" by Ray Charles and "Jealous Guy" by John Lennon. The rest are just pale imitations.

Bill took the toothpick out of his mouth, examined it, then went to worrying it again. "Thank God Sue and me never had no debates about abortion. That'd be the worst."

"There's no debate about it. If that's what she wants, that's what she gets. Period." I squinted at him. "And you 'n Sue are out of the baby biz now, if everything went on schedule, am I right?"

Bill nodded. "Yep. Had it done last Wednesday, as advertised. And you oughta be ashamed of yourself, trying to scare me the way you did."

"Get me another beer and tell me about it."

Bill grabbed my mug and started pulling a fresh Stroh's into it. "I went in and he did the deal. No sweat. From there I went out to CLEATS in plenty of time for batting practice. We were home team and I was catching, like usual. First batter came to the plate and I took the first pitch, low and inside. Next thing I knew, I was back home."

He'd said it dryly, with a completely straight face. I laughed. "Fainted, huh?"

Bill nodded. "Boys hauled me home on the back of Stevie's stake-body." He set the mug down in front of me. "So you was right. Congratulations."

I shrugged. "I been through it. I know what it's like."

Bill winced and shook his head. "I'm mobile now but I still ain't a hundred-percent *me* yet. Ask you something?"

"Shoot."

He glanced around. No one was within earshot. "While they were doing yours, did the, uh ... did the nurse keep putting cold cloths on your forehead?"

"Yeah, she did."

His voice was almost inaudible. "And ... did she hold your hand, and tell you everything would be all right?"

"Yep, uh-huh."

He gave me one close look, then nodded abruptly, snapped his towel, and began to shine the immaculate bar. I kept as straight a face as I could while firing up a cigar. "Well," I said, "now that I'm on my second beer, guess I'd better have some lunch. What's good today?"

Bill stopped wiping. "Oh, you hadn't heard. Health department closed the kitchen."

"Why? Food's no nastier here than anyplace else."

Bill's face was troubled. He stepped over to me and said softly, "A guy died, and they say it was from something he ate here. Ground glass in the food. He got sepsis and—"

"Jesus H. Christ."

"You ain't kidding. Health people come swooping in here, confiscated all the equipment, interviewed me and especially Eddie, they grilled his bony little butt. Couldn't talk to the cook, though, he'd quit on us, took off for parts unknown." The big bartender shook his head. "It's really bad. They could close us down behind this."

"Never happen. This bar belongs in the National Register of Historical Places."

Bill's face flickered in annoyance. "A guy died, Ben. That's nothing to laugh about."

"Times like these, buddy boy, it's either laugh or suck on your muffler."

Bill nodded. "Does seem like the world's gotten a whole lot uglier since you were in here the last time."

The bar door opened and Jimmy Joe Putnam called, "Hey, Benjy, better get your ass out here, son."

"What's up?"

"Just get out here. Quick. It's your car."

Words that strike fear in a Detroiter's heart. I hit the door on the fly and skidded onto the gravel parking lot. The scrawny little Jimmy Joe was over on the berm by Hannan Road, looking north. The Mustang sat right where I'd left it, next to Bill's eminently practical Ford Escort station wagon. It looked undisturbed, except for one thing. The hood was notched up a couple of inches.

Jimmy Joe trotted toward me, long greasy hair swinging. "Damn. Couldn't get the plate, he was moving too fast and my eyes ain't so good since Nam. Agent Orange, you know."

I was in no mood for another of Jimmy Joe's self-pitying lectures. "Who was he? What was he doing?"

Jimmy cowered. "I don't know, Ben, I come pulling in here and saw your car with the hood up and here's this guy at the front and it sure wasn't you. I asked him what gives and he took off running."

"Oh boy," I muttered. I went to the Mustang and hoisted the hood. Bill and Jimmy Joe trailed along behind me. I looked over the engine. Nothing missing, added, or tampered with. Checked the chassis the full length, the drivetrain back to the axle. Gave special attention to the lug nuts. No damage, as far as I could tell.

I got back to my feet. The men were looking at me, Bill puzzled, Jimmy Joe nervous. I was wired up heart-pounding tight. "What'd he look like, Jim?"

"Just a guy. I only got a quick look."

I started toward him. "You better do better than that."

Bill got between us and put his massive hands on my shoulders. "Come on, Ben. Cool it. You know Jimmy Joe, he'd help you if he could."

I closed my eyes and nodded. "Yeah, okay."

He released me. Jimmy Joe beelined for the safety of the

bar. I hoofed over to the door of the Mustang and opened it. "Catch you on the next one, Bill."

He said seriously, "Too bad you don't have one of those remote starters, just to be on the safe side."

"Wouldn't use it if I did," I said as I climbed in. I slammed the door. "If the Mustang's going, I'm going with her."

The Mustang and I didn't go anywhere except west on Ecorse Road, bound for Norwegian Wood. Jimmy Joe must have interfered before the stranger got a chance to tamper. *If* that's what he was planning.

No way of knowing if it was the same man who'd loosened the lug nuts. But it could have been. No way of knowing if all of this was related to the Paul Reardon case. But it could have been. I'd thought I was at an impasse in the case. But Rick Savastano had made a point of touching base with me to issue the usual threats. And now somebody was messing around in my backfield. The lug-nuts episode had occurred last Friday and this was Tuesday. Was there really a pattern, or was I imposing one on an array of coincidences?

I wished I knew what it all meant. But one thing seemed pretty certain. I was doing better on the case than I thought. I'd touched a nerve and upset somebody, which was almost as good as getting a confession—

I blinked out of my reverie and straightened in the seat, lightening up on the gas pedal. Up ahead on the left sat a white, unmarked Chevy panel truck. On the right shoulder lay a blue, girl's ten-speed bike. Just beyond that, two heavyset men, one long-haired and the other totally bald, were wrestling with a young, blue-jeaned teenage girl.

This stretch of Ecorse Road was undeveloped countryside. The two-lane road was deserted, aside from me. There was never any question in my mind. I stood on the brakes, shrieking and skidding the Mustang to a smoky tail-weaving stop twenty feet beyond, and landed slantways to the shoulder. I popped the door, jumped out, and stomped toward the group. The long-hair had the girl in a from-behind bear hug and was trying to drag her across the road toward the truck.

The baldy was trying to grab her legs, dodging her kicks as she screamed at him.

"Hey!" I yelled. "What the hell's going on?"

The girl struggled and kicked, her long brown hair flying wildly. "Help me! Please!"

The bald man dodged one of her kicks, stepped in, and slapped the girl across the face. The long-hair, whose arms were locked across her chest, snarled, "This is private business. Beat it."

"If you love something," I said, "let it go. If it comes back, it's yours. If it doesn't—"

"Hold her, Del," the baldy said, and turned to me. He was strong and squat, and wore jeans, a tailless athletic shirt, and a scraggly Fu Manchu mustache. Gold twinkled in his teeth as he grinned. "This is my little sister Gracie," he said, walking toward me with a gait that was almost jaunty. "She's been selling go-fast and blow jobs to the truckers out at the Detroiter. I'm taking her home to give her a little lesson in how to live right. So bug off, mister."

I stopped and braced myself. "He your brother, Gracie?"

She twisted and kicked in the strong grip of the long-hair, who was obviously enjoying groping her prominent breasts. "Hell *no*," she muttered. "Let me *go!*"

I sighed and shrugged. "You heard the lady."

The baldy grinned. "Here we go." I squared myself, in good balance, arms loose, fists ready. He came straight at me, low and hard, intent on mowing me down. I dodged as he came and raked a kick at him, but my safety shoe only glanced off his shoulder. I danced around to face him as he tumbled in the high grass and expertly flipped back to his feet in a grappler's pose, the grin fixed on his face. He wasn't even breathing hard.

I decided to wait and take him on his next try. This was going to be a breeze. Hell, he had no gun, no chain, no knucks, no knife, not even a pool cue. Child's play. As I braced, I realized the sound of struggle had stopped behind me. The baldy feinted and froze, eyes flickering from my face to something in my backcourt. I started to turn, heard Gracie say, "Take him, Del," and dodged sideways, way too late. An incredible blow caught me at the base of my skull, exploding a bomb in my head like a grenade in a punch bowl. Bluish-red light, a sheet of pain, I bellyflopped and ate weeds.

I kept winking in and out. I saw the men coming toward me. Then they were dragging me up and along, across the road toward the panel truck. I saw Gracie sitting on the berm, cross-legged, bright-eyed, looking for all the world like a spectator who was enjoying herself hugely. She really did look like a truck-stop mama in her tank top and tight cutoffs. Her body was lush and ripe, but her freckled face, beneath the makeup and the wisecracks, was fifteen, sixteen tops. Somebody's little girl, once.

When I blinked on again, we were at the rear of the truck. One of the men yelled, "Come on, Gracie, let's move it." I felt blurry, pain-soaked, numb—where's the rest of me?—and, chiefly, ridiculous. Big tough Ben Perkins, zapped limp and about to be trucked to God knows where. Hopefully not a landfill. Hopefully, if they wanted me dead, I'd be explaining myself to St. Pete already. Hopefully.

The truck door clattered up. The two men were manhandling me up onto the bed. I felt a remote impact. Del, the long-hair, said "Oh." A fountain of blood exploded through his T-shirt and he went down as if his legs had been removed. In the distance, as an afterthought, sounded a gunshot. The baldy let me go and vanished. I lost my balance and fell out of the truck in a twisting, anyways *splat* onto the hard macadam, which was suddenly spreading red from the corpse of the long-hair lying next to me.

All was silent for a moment except for crickets in the woods behind us.

"Where'd that come from?" I heard Gracie ask from somewhere.

"Dunno," the baldy said. He was crouched behind the rear wheels. "Long ways. Rifle. Got Del dead-bang center."

"We got to get out of here, JoJo!" she said urgently. I saw where she was now, up by the front of the truck.

"No shit," he answered. Silence. "Wait a minute. Look at that. Little van just pulled out of that lane, four hundred yards up thataways. Headed away from us now."

"Think that was him?"

"I dunno," he said grimly, "but there's one way to find out. Get down here, Gracie, help me with this."

In the meantime, I'd been implementing my great escape and had managed to slither maybe about thirty inches along the macadam away from the truck. JoJo took me under the armpits and hauled me up. "Get his legs," he said tightly. "We'll just chunk him on in there and get the hell out of here."

I tried to struggle but it was no use. Gracie took my other half and they dumped me into the truck like a roll of carpet. Gracie hopped inside and slid me back into the darkness toward the back of the truck. Strong girl, stronger than she looked. In the dim light I caught her grinning at me oddly. I decided to wait and rest.

I heard a couple of grunts and a heavy wet thump. Sounded as though Del, the late long-hair, had joined us. "See you back there, Gracie," JoJo called. "Remember to do your thing."

"Oh yeah." She laughed. The back door clattered down, leaving us in darkness: me, the woman-child, and the corpse. It was the black on black of a velvet blindfold, a basement closet, or a coffin.

Presently the truck shook, the motor cranked and fired, and we began to move. I concentrated on lying still, battling the pain, gathering whatever strength I could for whatever was ahead.

Something rustled near me. I tensed, bracing my hands on the rough wood floor. More sounds, a soft ruffling. Then a gentle weight settled on my midsection. I reached up quickly and encountered warm moist skin, sleek flanks, heavy bare breasts. I dropped my hands as if I'd touched a live wire.

"Hi, baby," came her voice in the darkness. "It's Gracie." Open lips found my jaw, and she expertly tongued her way to my mouth and seized upon it, pressing down on me as she kissed me, humming way back in her throat. She tasted like Trident and tobacco. I reached back along her and it was as bad as I thought: she was bare-ass naked the length of her. Talk about instant physical rehabilitation. I took her shoulders and turned her off me gently onto the vibrating truck floor. I said, voice dry, "You outta your mind? Cut it out."

"But it's yours, baby," she said, taking my hand. "Call it a token of respect. They're not going to hurt you. They just want to talk."

"Who's they?"

She guided my hand to her warm pubic thatch. I snatched it back. "You'll find out who 'they' are," she said, voice pouting. "But we got lots of time to play first."

It was like a freakish dream, lying there in the darkness of death with the headache of a lifetime as the truck vibrated and swayed and the nubile young girl offered me the ultimate in casual sex. "If they just wanted to talk," I said, "why didn't they pick up the phone and call, like everyone else?"

With a sudden movement she unbuckled my belt. I caught her wrist as her hand dived under my pants, but I was too late. Her fingertips found my penis, which wasn't difficult, but hard.

"They didn't think you'd come on your own," Gracie's voice said softly. "But you know something? I think you will."

Chapter 16

At long last the stop-and-go ended. The motor shut down and faint male voices sounded from outside. I heard Gracie stir across from me. "Remember, you promised," she said sullenly.

"I'm a man of my word, darlin'," I answered.

"You let on we didn't do nothing, I'll get thumped."

"Don't worry," I said, getting to my feet. "The terrible secret is safe with me."

I was still in pain. I still felt highly disoriented, trapped in this truck by persons unknown with a hot young chick who'd done her best—which was very good indeed—to seduce me. I was also more than a little scared. I reassured myself, once again, with the thought that if they'd wanted me dead, I'd be gone already.

The back door clattered up, drenching the interior with light so bright it almost hurt. A tall young black man stood there with JoJo the hairless, who was saying, ". . . *who* it was or *where* he was shooting from, but looky there, got Del dead-bang center, blew his heart up. Poor motherfucker never even heard the shot."

The black man eyed Del's corpse incuriously, then looked at me. "This way, Perkins. Watch your step at the edge here. You too, Gracie."

I edged around the corpse and dropped heavily to the cement floor, grabbing the bumper to steady myself. We were in a vast warehouse. Absolutely the largest, and emptiest room I'd ever seen. Pale light shone in through a bank of windows that ran high up the walls, thousands upon thousands of dirty panes girdling the building all the way around. Steel girders rose from the cement floor thirty feet up to the ceiling, which was crisscrossed with struts, pipes, and ducts. The place smelled of dust, mold, and old fuel, and was dead silent except for distant, echoing footsteps and the perversely cheerful chirping of faraway birds nesting in the ceiling struts.

The size of the place was eerie. The dissociative effect was total. I resisted the temptation to blurt all kinds of anxious questions at the black man. I just waited there, under his watchful eye, while Gracie sat on the bumper examining her fingernails, till JoJo returned. "This way, Perkins. Hang tight, Eli," he said to the black man, "we're gonna have chores."

"'Bye, darling," Gracie said, smiling knowingly, waving with her fingertips.

I followed JoJo around the truck and across the bare cement floor. Way off in the distance, located precisely in the center of the huge room, was a plain card table. It was attended by two old-fashioned wood swivel chairs. In one of them sat a short, burly man in his late fifties. The light wasn't good in there, and I'd only seen him once before, several years ago, at a distance, in a rocking, stomping Ann Arbor saloon called Hill Street Booze—but I made him right away. Ezra Goforth, boss of the Pontiac branch of the organization.

His operation is a direct and very unfriendly competitor to Savastano's Detroit group. Their coexistence is, to put the best face on it, uneasy, principally because Goforth is known to be just as vicious and ruthless as Savastano—the only difference being, Savastano pretends to be a businessman, and Goforth doesn't bother. Oddly enough, recognizing him lowered my anxiety level somewhat. At least now I was getting a handle on what was happening.

Goforth did not rise as we approached him. "Seddown, Perkins," he said, voice a raspy air hammer. "You know who I am?" I nodded, and remained standing. Goforth looked at JoJo. "You and the coon go plant Del in the landfill."

"'Kay."

"And listen," Goforth added, aiming a weathered finger at JoJo. "Pass the word. Everybody carries till further notice. Especially if they're holding assets. I'm not looking for initiative, y'understand? No Lone Ranger shit out there, but nobody gets the drop on us no more. Sumpin' smells, ya hurt the person, end of sentence period. Now go."

JoJo walked away. Goforth looked at me with eyes that were the merciless blue of oceans. "'Preciate your dropping by, Perkins," he said with no evidence of humor.

"I don't suppose it's worthwhile complaining about your scheduling methods," I said.

"Hey," he said, half-grinning, "ya make appointments with guys, half the time they don't show up. This way, the snatcheroo, assures that guys are punctual." He looked me up and down, smiling with beneficence. "Whaddya think, we was gonna hurt ya?"

"The thought occurred to me."

He shook his head vigorously. "Just a straight snatch. Ha! Speaking of snatch, how was Gracie? Something else, huh. G'wan, sit down, let's discuss things."

I did so. Goforth leaned back in his chair and we sized each other up. I don't know what he saw. What I saw was a short, muscled cylinder of a man whose bullet head was balding at the top, fringed with bristly reddish-gray hair. He had a lot of face, but its features were compressed toward the center of it, giving him a bookish look that was belied by the large, closely grouped and very cold blue eyes. He wore a short-sleeve blue pullover shirt and only a wedding band on his rough workman's hands. His voice was a hard metallic hammering and very hoarse, as if he'd spent years making himself heard over the roar of heavy diesels.

I glanced around the warehouse. We were surrounded by ten million cubic feet of dead-silent empty. I said, "Saw a picture of Hitler's office once. Wasn't much bigger 'n this."

"This ain't my office," Goforth said. "Conference room."

"Where at?"

He smiled coldly. "Somewhere. Anywhere. Could be Bay City, could be Toledo, could be right around the corner from where we metcha."

That was true. We'd been in the truck a good hour and I'd completely lost my sense of direction. "So what's this about?" I asked, doing my best to sound casual.

He gestured grandly. "Go ahead. You wanna light up a cigar, light up a cigar." He grinned at my expression. "Yeah, we know a lot aboutcha. We know you was a union goon once upon a time. We know you call yourself a private detective whenever you ain't busy unplugging toilets. We heard about how you hammered that video snuff operation a few years back, for which we thank you profusely, being as you erased a potential competitor for us. We know you're a sucker for the kinda street theater we put on for you out on the road there. We know you're screwing a blond lady lawyer. For which I congratulate you, incidentally. Usually with lawyers it's the other way around."

I had a cigar going by now. Ah, blessed relief.

"The only thing we haven't figured out," Goforth continued, "is what work you're doing for that fucking little three-suit weenie, Richard el Sleazo Savastano."

It made me want to chuckle, Goforth calling Savastano a

sleaze. But I didn't, which no doubt was prudent. "I don't work for him," I said.

"Now don't be bullshittin' me. I hate it when people bullshit me," he warned. "We know you was with him just yesterday."

I maintained a steady, bored expression. "A bit I been working tracked across some action of his, and he asked for clarification. That's all. We walked away clean." My voice hardened. "I don't work for guys like him. Never have, never will."

He nodded finally. "Yeah, that's the word, too, you're definitely the antisocial type." He leaned forward on the card table. "But being as you got a 'in' with that cocksuckin' little assfucker, you're in a position to do me a service. That's why this little conversation today."

My first impulse was to rear up on my hind legs and tell him to shove it. My second impulse was to sit tight and hear him out. I was, in effect, a captive. Job one was to get away clean. I exhaled smoke and asked, "What kind of service?"

He leaned back in the chair, folded his arms across his chest, and stared off into space. "You saw how Del got hurt out there on the road? That's Savastano's work. I know that. And I know why he done it, too."

"Why?"

His eyes found me. "He's been losing cocaine distributors lately. 'Bout a half dozen by now. He thinks we done it, and he's hitting back. Could turn into an all-out war unless we put a stop to it right now."

Nothing would have made me happier than for Savastano's group and Goforth's group to knock each other off. "What's this got to do with me?" I asked, smoking.

"Even before today," Goforth said, "I knew Savastano suspected us of hurting his people. I been reaching out, trying to get word to him, through my people upstairs in Milwaukee and his people upstairs in New York. Plus, even though I work up here these days, I was made in Detroit, I know lots of people down there, I been leaving word for him around town, but the dick-faced little pig poker has stayed outta reach. So, when I heard about your meeting him, I thought: Here's the guy to go-between for me."

After a long silence I said, "So you want me to convince Savastano that—"

The mob boss's voice rose to a shout. "That we're not hurting his people!" He pounded the table. "We don't want no war! We got other problems! We got the niggers and the spics and the fuckin' Ay-rabs and even the high-school seniors going all entrepreneur on us. We got enough headaches without our own kind hurting each other. I mean, what separates my guys and Savastano's guys is Eight Mile Road. Beyond that we got certain interests in common. Such as not hurting each other."

I sat there as still as I could, looking as bored as I could, but the little relays were clicking away like mad. So, Davey Jackson wasn't the only distributor that Savastano had lost. Somebody was picking them off, one by one. No wonder Ricky boy was nervous and upset and in trouble with his boss. A drug war seemed to be brewing, and it looked as though Paul Reardon had wandered into it somehow. The link, of course, was Angie Barnes. I still didn't have a solid handle on her. I'd begun to wonder if I ever would. Here, on a platter, was a chance to learn more—if I played my cards right.

I edged my chair closer to the card table and leaned an elbow on it. "The deal with Savastano, it had to do with a woman," I said.

Goforth's eyes were unimpressed. "Get out of town. He don't do girls."

"I don't think sex entered into it," I said patiently. "Woman by the name of Angela Barnes. Hint I got was that she works for him. Name sound familiar?"

"Nope. But I can sure's hell find out. You help me, I'll help you," he added, making a smile that cracked his face.

"How about this?" I fished out my wallet, extracted the sketch, and unfolded it. It had been riding around with me for quite a while by now and the pencil markings were blurring up. Goforth took the sketch and held it gingerly, at arm's length, and squinted at it, moving his lips even though there were no words to read. "Seen her before?" I asked.

The change in expression was so quick, I'd have missed it if I hadn't been watching the mob boss closely. For an instant he looked surprised. Almost scared. "Yeah," he said, clearing his throat. "Wasn't using 'Barnes,' though. And she don't belong to Savastano. She's free-lance. And I didn't think she was working the Midwest no more, she'd pretty much shown her face to death here." He gestured at the sketch. "You seen her around here lately, Perkins?"

"Uh-huh." There was nothing I could put a finger on, but the sketch had really thrown the guy. "What kind of work does she do?"

Goforth drummed fingers, then said, "She hurts people."

I leaned back in my chair. I wasn't all that surprised. I never thought her visit to Charnelle Blais, about the time the hapless woman was tortured to death, was any coincidence. I said, "Free-lance, huh?"

"Absolutely," Goforth said. "One of the best, too. I'll tellya, Perkins, if you been doggin' that lately, you oughta thank your lucky stars she didn't turn and gun. She can put one up your nostril at a hundred feet."

"What does she like?" I asked.

"Purely traditional. Twenty-two with a suppressor," Goforth said, making a pistol with his hand, "*phip-phip* and outta there."

"Nothing fancy, huh? No wet work with knives? How about pyrotechnics?"

"Purely traditional, far as I know." Goforth stared at me intently. "So your word is she's hooked up with Savastano now?"

"I heard it mentioned. That would be at Titanium Tower, right?"

"Yeah, it would," Goforth said dubiously, "but forget it, Perkins. She ain't working for Savastano. If she was, I'd know. I got moles in there like you wouldn't believe."

I dropped my cigar to the cement and squashed it. New answers give birth to new questions, but I couldn't ask them here. What I had to do now was disengage, as gently as possible, and there was only one way to do that. "Listen," I said, staring into the mob boss's eyes," I want you to know I'm not for hire. Not by you, not by Savastano, not by anybody in your type of enterprise. You got that?"

"Yeah, yeah," he rasped expectantly.

"But you want me to pass word to Savastano that you're clean on these killings, I'll do my best. Assuming the payback is decent, that is."

Goforth snorted. "You wanna know the payback? The payback is, you do this thing for me, and I give you an indulgence, like one of the old-time popes."

"Huh?"

"You can cash that indulgence in for a service sometime," he said patiently. "Think of it like the 'get out of jail free' card in Monopoly, or the 'free spin' gizmo in 'Wheel of Fortune.' You hit bankrupt, you cause me a problem sometime, that free spin gizmo gets you out from under the hammer."

"Sounds okay to me."

"There is, of course, a downside." Goforth's face went empty. "Remember, I got a mole in Titanium Tower, I'll be checking on what you do. If you don't do this thing, or if you're not enthusiastic enough, then I'll send some people around, some real experts, and they're going to hurt you." He sat back and folded his arms, face cold. "So what'll it be?"

The next morning's chore list was pretty light, which was a good thing, because I was in no mood to work. I divvied the jobs between Randy and Brian, spent a couple of hours on paperwork, then retreated to the old cinder-block shack in the Norwegian Wood back forty. Put on WABX, which was doing an all-morning Eric Clapton retrospective, and busied myself doing maintenance work on my toys.

My old Harley Sportster needed a new valve-cover gasket. The Mustang needed plugs, wires, rotor, and distributor cap—like most high-performance engines, mine gleefully burns up those things every couple thousand miles. The carburetor on my ultralight aircraft needed cleaning and adjusting. I hadn't taken the aircraft up in a couple of weeks.

I didn't think I'd have the chance to do so till the weekend.

I was, of course, wrong.

Chapter 17

The maintenance work busied my hands and occupied part of my mind. With the rest I sorted through the debris of my life as it stood at this moment. Not a pretty picture.

To start with, there was Carole and her pregnancy. Looking back at what had happened the past couple of weeks, I could see in grim detail that every move I had made had been wrong. At the same time, upon reflection, I couldn't see what I could have done that would have worked out better.

Then there was the disappearance of Ellen Reardon. Yeah, she was still gone, I'd checked the evening before, after returning from my unscheduled visit with Ezra Goforth. I was really worried. She might have split under her own power but, distraught though she was, I didn't think she'd do so without leaving word. I didn't know what to do about it except file a missing persons report with the cops if she didn't show up soon.

Another problem was the pair of strange little incidents involving the Mustang. The loosening of the lug nuts in Detroit; the seemingly harmless intrusion at Under New Management. I didn't know for sure if the incidents were connected. I assumed that they were, and the whole thing had me jumpy: it was evident that the perpetrator didn't exactly wish me all the best.

As to the case—my "investigation" of the murder of Paul Reardon—I had candidates for who, the principal one being Angela Barnes, the alleged free-lance killer. It was the why part that still had me thrown. I seemed to be making progress in fits and starts, but I hadn't found the smoking gun, the key you sometimes stumble across that makes everything fall magically into place.

As I slaved away there in the hot shed, taking refuge in routine and heeding the ancient training of the demanding old daddy for whom maintenance had been a religious rite, I got the feeling that I'd fallen out of sync with the world. It seemed that everything I did made things worse. Carole was upset with me and Ellen was obviously pissed off. Jack Hatfield wanted my scalp, Dick Dennehy was gleefully watching me through the electronic surveillance of one Fat Bob, and I'd probably been X'd off Elvin Dance's Christmas-card list. Rick Savastano was unhappy with me and Ezra Goforth expected me to help him, *or else*.

So, at this point, I was on the shit list of the two women I cared about most, plus the Belleville police, Detroit police, and Michigan State Police; as well as two rival factions of the Mafia. Not bad for a few days' work. Now, I'm not so foolish or naive as to expect sweetness and light in all things. But right about then I could have used a friendly face to talk to—

"Hey, asshole!"

I looked up from the Mustang engine to see Dick Dennehy marching toward me across the long grass of the back forty. I finished tightening the new oil filter and wiped my hands with a rag as Dick reached me, puffing from exertion. "Well, well," I said sourly, "what rat hole you been hiding out in? I been trying to track you down for days."

Dick's naturally hard face hardened further. "Don't fuck with me. It's been a difficult week and it's only Wednesday."

"What you don't know about trouble would fill a book." I sneered. "Anyways, like they say, any day above ground is a good one."

"Times like these I'm not so sure." He loosened his nondescript tie. "Got anything to drink? Hotter 'n a virgin's crotch out here."

I'd brought an iced-down six-pack of Stroh's with me. I stripped the first out of the plastic bra, gave it to Dick, and requisitioned one for myself. We tore tabs, saluted silently, and swigged. The ice-cold elixir worked its magic almost at once. Suddenly I wasn't in quite as much trouble. Suddenly I felt a little more confident. Suddenly the stifling heat and humidity didn't matter quite as much. To everything, as my mother would have said, there is a purpose.

"Aahhhh," Dick said as he came up for air. He's a big guy, a tad over six, a smidge over two hundred, but a little out of shape. That's because he's more of an executive than a street cop these days, flies a lot of steering wheels and large mahogany desks. He wears gray suits from Calvin's of Taiwan. His hair is short and grayish blond. His face, adorned by aviator glasses, is hard and lined. A seen-it-all face. A cop face.

He stripped off his jacket and slung it over the Mustang's rag top. His white shirt was limp and crisscrossed with the straps of the holster that held his Colt Python loosely under the damp left armpit. He gurgled down some more beer, sighed again, and said, "I got the poopy for ya on the state police detectives that were after your dead pal. But it wasn't easy, and I been busy besides, which is why it took this long."

"No need to apologize."

"I'm not apologizing. The Michigan State Police don't owe you doodly squat, pal. I've done this for the usual reason: I'm still naive enough to believe that you occasionally mean well."

"Come on, Dick," I said wearily. "It's been as rough for me as it's been for you, and I don't need any, whatchacallit, invective. Okay?"

"Just so we understand each other." Dick fired up a Lucky straight end. "*Jesus*, it's hot! Anyplace cooler we can talk?"

"Shady spot outside, but—"

"Sold. You bring the brewskis."

I shrugged, picked up the six-pack—make that four-pack now—and followed him outside. Around the corner on the east side was a big patch of shade cast by the roof of the shed. Dick hunkered down with visible relief, leaned against the cinder-block wall, and took a long swig of beer. I remained standing, watching him, wondering what was up.

"Your friend Paul was dirty." He announced it as if it were the day's Dow closing number.

"Oh yeah?"

Dick pulled some folded papers out of his back pants pocket. "Cocaine dealer," he said, unfolding the papers as the cigarette bobbed in his lips. "Kilkenny and Daws had him nailed, dead-bang certain."

My legs felt weak. I walked over to the shed wall and slid down it to a sitting position on the grass, about a yard away from the state cop. "Oh boy. So what were they doing that day, coming to arrest him?"

"Not quite that simple. Let's back up." Dick consulted the paper. "Daws is an undercover. Evidently, he was working a place called Jugg Poltiss's Texas Time Saloon—"

"I know the place. Down in New Boston."

Dick drove on: "Behind tips about some low-level cocaine traffic going on there. Anyway, on 18 June he's approached by an individual, later identified as Paul Reardon, soliciting to sell a sizable quantity of cocaine. Key and a half, it says here."

Whoo-ee, I thought. Lotta lady.

"They cut a deal and agreed to meet, taste, and close on Saturday, June 28, at Dynamite Park," Dick went on. "Joint task force of state guys and Detroit PD was set up to tape the meet and then nail the perp. But he never showed."

I said nothing. I was staring across the grassy field toward the fringe of trees that runs along the lake. I was thinking about Paul Reardon. You dumb-ass son of a bitch, I thought wearily.

"Never showed up at Poltiss's again either," Dick noted. "Kilkenny and Daws decided to brace him at his house, question him, see if they could buffalo him into—"

"But they were too late," I observed. "Paul was dead."

"Yep. Case closed."

I drained my beer and opened another. I knew how Paul must have looked at it. It was sheer coincidence that he'd found that cocaine in the Gremlin seat. He needed money to stay out from under his daddy's thumb. To him it must have seemed risk-free. A little work for a lot of bread. He just couldn't pass it up.

And he'd gotten the money. Some money, anyway; five

grand. Peanuts for that much snow. Who'd he sell it to? Then somebody had wasted him. Who? Angie, If so, why?

I looked at Dick, who was watching me closely. "Thanks," I said. "Satisfies my curiosity."

The cop's gray eyes narrowed. He shook his head very slowly. "Oh, no, you don't," he said. "You aren't getting off that easy."

"Whatever do you mean?"

"'Whatever do you mean!'" he mimicked angrily. "You're going to tell me, forthwith, what this is about, what you're up to, and what you know. Chapter and verse."

I shrugged. "Frankly, I don't know what makes you think that I've got anything worth telling."

"Because I know you!" he exploded. "You're poking around into this thing and you've been poking around into it for a couple of weeks now. I have a feeling you've found out plenty, and now you're going to, as the shrinks say, 'share' it with your old buddy here."

I was hot and tired and upset, and I needed no static from Dick or from anyone else just then. "Even if I knew something, theoretically, why should I spill to you?"

"Why? Theoretically?" Dick clambered to his feet and paced his way into the sunshine, squinting as he looked back at me. "Because this is bigger 'n you, pal. Bigger 'n anything you've ever dreamed of. Because just this once you're gonna let the police do the job, and you're going to be smart and stick to your own line of work."

Having him shout down at me was unpleasant. I stood and faced him. "Okay. You tell me what you got, and I'll tell you what I got."

Dick grinned, relieved. "Good. Glad you're being sensible about things for once." He sat back down, ground out his cigarette in the grass, and flattened out his notes against his knee. "We think we got Paul's affiliation figured out. He worked for an ad agency, right? Saw lots of big-time clients all the time?"

"Well, he was a free-lance guy, and—"

Dick was nodding. "Fits the pattern to a T."

"What pattern?"

"There's this cocaine network," Dick said. "A big-time class all the way. Our boys've been calling it the 'silk stocking network' because, unlike the cracksters, this one's aimed at the upscale people. Doctors, lawyers, politicians, white- and gold-collar types. Product they're moving's a little different, too. A lot purer, more powerful. For those discriminating yups who demand the best. Who," he went on, almost snarling, "expect maximum performance out of their cars, their women, their deodorant, and their cocaine. You follow?"

I nodded. My face revealed nothing, but I was remembering that Elvin Dance had described the late Davey Jackson as a distributor who handled the downtown Detroit banks, utilities, and government offices. Silk stocking, for sure.

"Your friend Paul was one of the distributors," Dick went on. "It's the only thing that makes sense. And it's why he got whacked. Been a big epidemic of that lately."

I turned away from him and hung my hands in the back pockets of my jeans. Now Dick was echoing Ezra Goforth, who'd talked about how Savastano's group was losing cocaine distributors.

"I heard something about that. How many've got it so far?"

"Five, including your friend Paul." Dick squinted at his notes. "First one was May eleventh in St. Joe. Victim was a registered nurse, d'ya believe it? He took a .22 long rifle in the ear. Next one was the twenty-fifth, a business consultant in Grand Rapids. No more till June the eighth, when—"

"Davey Jackson," I said. I had my pad out and was scribbling like mad. "Detroit. Right?"

"Right." Dick grinned at me. "You been doing your homework. I'm proud of ya. Then we had a U of M assistant prof bite the big one in Ann Arbor on the twenty-second, followed by your buddy Paul on July sixth."

I squinted at my notes. Something didn't add up. "You said the first one, the nurse, got shot. Aside from Paul, were the others shot, too?"

"Yeah. So what?"

"Different MO," I pointed out. "Paul was blown up. The others were shot."

"So"—Dick shrugged—"maybe a different hit man took over starting with Paul. Maybe the next few'll ride the big ker-boom into the sky. Who knows?" He pressed out his cigarette, opened a fresh beer, and said, "Okay. Your turn. Spill."

"Well," I said slowly, "aside from what I said about Davey Jackson, I don't know anything at all, Dick."

He lowered the can, swallowed, and said hoarsely, "Don't jerk me around, buddy."

"I'm not." I put my pad away. "Honest to God."

Dick stood clumsily. Grass clippings clung to his gray pants and his face looked puffy from the heat and the drink. His eyes were smoldering and a vein throbbed in his left temple. But when he spoke, his voice was soft. "Let me tell you the facts of life, Ben. You're out of your league."

I just looked at him.

"You think you've took on tough guys," Dick went on. "Guys like Ernest Ecke, the video king. Then there was Vince Wakefield, who killed your lady friend. Not to mention Rick Pacquin the serial killer and those white supremacy nuts. Tough guys, sure. And you beat 'em. But they're fuckin' pansies compared to the guys you're dealing with now in this drug thing."

"I never said I was dealing with anything," I said.

Dick ignored me. "What I always secretly liked about you is, you give a shit and you put your ass on the line. Rare these days. Rare any day. But this thing you're into, this is just plain foolish. Come on in, Ben, give me what you got and get out clean. While you can."

"Very moving," I said. "Wish I could oblige."

The throbbing in his temple quit. His whole body seemed to slacken. He reached a fresh Lucky to his lips and lighted it up.

We stood there in the silence of the hot summer day. Then Dick said, "You know, lately I been thinking a lot about Nam. Couldn't figure out why for a while. Finally I figured it out. This whole drug thing, it's exactly like Nam. Different turf. Different day. But same shit."

I flamed a cigar to life. Dick hung his fists on his hips and stared raptly at the woods in the distance. "We're pouring in endless tons of money and effort. But it's lost already, and everyone knows it. There's no way we can win this thing. Ever. You know why? There's just too many people getting too fucking rich. The business is awash with so much untraceable, untaxable cash money, everybody's corruptible. The drug trade has become a permanent part of our society because people don't really want it to go away."

"I think you're right," I said.

"This isn't for publication," he said. "Us officers are supposed to be upbeat and positive at all times. But it's over already, Ben. The bad guys won. Worse than that. They're taking over. Turning our world into one big battleground. Rival dealers shooting at each other, vigilantes shooting at the dealers, cops shooting at everything that moves."

I couldn't argue. Some places I've seen are like that already.

"Everybody'll have to choose sides," Dick said. His eyes cleared, went piercing sharp again as he looked at me. "What I'm saying to you is, if you send me away now empty, you've chosen your side. Which means you're one of them. You get no sympathy and no help from me. You get jammed up behind this thing, don't call. You get whacked, I won't come to your funeral, and I won't visit your grave."

At first I wasn't going to answer. But I couldn't help myself. "Let's say you're right, and I'm on the job," I said softly. "It was my best friend that got blown up. It's my ass that's on the line for it. Put yourself in my place. I don't think you'd set back and trust the cops to take care of you, Dick. In fact, I know you wouldn't."

Dick Dennehy did not change expression. He flicked his cigarette into the field, turned on his heel, and walked around the corner into the shed to retrieve his jacket. Then I heard his footsteps as he stomped across the field away from me, toward Norwegian Wood.

*   *   *

The boys were gone by the time I got back to the maintenance office. I checked through the job slips, dispensed with the day's time sheets, then sat down behind my desk and propped my feet up and smoked a cigar, thinking.

Dick Dennehy, for all of his skill as a cop, was wrong. Paul was not a cocaine distributor. He was a young kid with money trouble who'd seized an opportunity that had fallen into his lap out of nowhere. And he'd paid for it. Dearly.

I wondered why he hadn't come to me when he found the cocaine in the Gremlin car seat.

I wondered why he didn't confide in me when Angie made her approach.

I wondered who he'd finally peddled the coke to. I wondered what he'd done to deserve getting killed.

I wondered if the cops would ever make a case on me, or if I'd ever definitely clear myself—or would things just stay stuck in neutral like they were now. . . .

I flinched and my vision cleared. Jack Hatfield stood at the office door, facing me with a neutral expression on his craggy face. Behind him stood Carl Portman. He was smiling, from ear to ear.

Chapter 18

"Are we all here now?" Jack Hatfield wheezed.

Evidently so. Once again the old Belleville police chief had set up shop in the Norwegian Wood conference room. Once again his personal goon and my personal nemesis, Detective Carl Portman, was stationed at the door. Once again Carole Somers sat beside me at the table, wearing a houndstooth check suit, black belt, and worried look. We hadn't had a chance to talk privately, but I knew what she was thinking. Hatfield had reached some sort of decision about Paul Reardon's murder, a decision that did not bode well for good old yours truly.

And once again there was a stranger in the room. And not Lance Reardon this time.

"I'm sorry, madam," Hatfield said to the woman seated across from us, "but I haven't had the pleasure."

She rose and extended a pink hand. "Shaughnessy Levin," she chirped, nodding and smiling gaily as she shook hands with the cop. "Mr. Perkins's co-counsel, assisting Ms. Somers, Chief."

She was a pale-complected butterball of about Carole's age, wearing a generously cut suit of bright jade over a fuchsia blouse. Her carroty hair was curly and unfettered around a face that was so gleeful you almost wanted to smile along with her, till you reached those icy blue eyes that watched, waited, and missed nothing. I remembered how Carole had described her: "Tough as bark." If so, and I had no reason to doubt it, she wore one hell of a disguise.

Jack Hatfield nodded at Levin as she sat back down. "Goddamn," he mused to no one in particular, "the lady lawyers is everywhere these days."

Shaun Levin gave me a grin and a wink as she folded her chubby fingers together. Reassuring, I guess. Carole said in a bored voice, "Chief, if we could get on with this, please?"

"Oh, sure," Hatfield said, stuffing both hands into the shapeless pockets of his jacket. "Fact is, ladies and gentlemen, some new evidence has come to light in the death of Paul Reardon. On the basis of that new evidence, I am forthwith placing Mr. Perkins under arrest, and will charge him with the murder of Paul Reardon."

"Aw, jeez. Come on, Chief!" I blurted.

Carole touched my arm. Neither she nor Levin looked surprised. Levin, who hadn't bothered with a pad—apparently she was leaving note taking to Carole—said, "I'm advising my client not to say a word. Not one."

"Okay," I said thickly.

Her reddish eyebrows shot together. "Not *one!*" she snapped.

I nodded, heart pounding.

"Now," Hatfield drawled as if he hadn't been interrupted, "you all are prob'ly asking yourselves, why did old Chief Hatfield brang us here to Norwegian Wood 'stead of the station house? I'll tell you why. Because I wanted to have a little informal discussion first, go over this evidence with Mr. Perkins in a relatively low-pressure situation, see what light he can shed on it."

"Decent of you," Levin said, her smile utterly without feeling, "but you've got nothing as it is, Chief, and you know it."

Hatfield squinted. "Well, in a kind of backward way we do have something, Counselor, when you think about it. What we have is all kinds of physical evidence linking Perkins with that Gremlin."

"Of course you do," Levin parried. "We're willing to stipulate that Mr. Perkins did mechanical work on that car. It's quite natural that you'd find—"

"But what we don't got, Ms. Levin," Hatfield went on, raising a hand, "is evidence that anyone else touched that car. See what I mean? Plus there's the missing dynamite from the supply that Perkins was responsible for. The same dynamite that was used to blow up the Gremlin."

Shaughnessy Levin grinned at us and tossed her head. "Go ahead, Chief. Take us to court with that. It'll be good clean fun, eh, Carole?"

Hatfield's gaze roamed the room. "Perkins had the means. Perkins had the opportunity. What I haven't been able to figure is, what was the motive? Why would Perkins want this young man dead? I couldn't figure it. Till now, that is." He withdrew a small cassette recorder out of his pocket and set it end up on the table.

No one said anything. Hatfield glanced around at us again. "There's a sworn and witnessed transcript of this testimony on file in the prosecutor's office, Counselors. I'll skip over all the identification routine and get right to it." He pressed the PLAY button.

—long have you know Ben Perkins?

Two years.

Describe the circumstances under which you met him, please.

When we rented our apartment at Norwegian Wood. He's the manager of maintenance and security there.

How shortly after moving in did you meet him?

About a week or ten days later. Our dishwasher was leaking around the door. I called the maintenance office, and Ben came and fixed it.

Your friendship with him began on that day?

No. I barely spoke to him. But Paul happened to be home—

Your husband?

Well, we were only living together at that time. We weren't married yet.

Thank you. Go ahead, please.

Paul happened to be home, and he and Ben chatted for quite a while. Paul made friends easily, people liked him. He and Ben began to associate. Ben took him to a bar he hangs out in. Paul invited him to dinner a few times. We all went bowling together—

The three of you?

Well, not always. Mr. Perkins sometimes brought a date. There was a woman named Jeannie, I remember. Another one named Laurie, I think it was. And of course lately he's been going out with Carole Somers. She's a lawyer.

Mr. Perkins never lacked for female companionship, is that a fair assessment?

He's always seemed to have a steady person. And he's never seemed to be a one-woman man. Not by a long shot. There's a woman at that bar, Barb Paley. Someone named Annie, I don't know her last name, she's a nurse at Annapolis. And over at Norwegian Wood there's a rumor he's tight with Marge, the rental agent. That's only talk as far as I know. I've never seen them together.

Very good, Mrs. Reardon. Now. When was the first time Mr. Perkins showed any, shall we say, interest in you?

Well, that first day it showed. I mean, he didn't say anything. It was just his look. The way he talked to me and smiled at me. He was very friendly, more friendly than maintenance people usually are. Believe me, I know. Maintenance people usually treat you like shit.

You felt Mr. Perkins was attracted to you?

Yes.

And were you attracted to him?

(inaudible)

Please speak up, Mrs. Reardon.

Yes. I was attracted to him.

Very well. Tell us, if you would, how your relationship developed from that point.

Well, he stopped by the apartment a few times. Always when Paul was away at work. Ben said he wanted to make sure we were settling in all right. But we'd talk—talk about all kinds of things. He'd bring drinks, beer for him and wine for me. He brought a surprise lunch once and we ate at the grove by the lake. Once I had the flu and he brought some soup—

Was your husband aware of any of these visits?

We weren't married at that time.

Was your fiancé aware of these visits?

Paul wasn't my fiancé then either. We didn't get engaged till last New Year's Eve.

I'll rephrase once more. Was Paul Reardon aware, Mrs. Reardon?

. . . No.

You concealed what was going on?

For God's sake! Why are you badgering me? I'm only trying to help you!

Mrs. Reardon—

You're not making this any easier for me!

Turn it off! Turn that damn thing off for a—All right. Are we on again? Fine. Mrs. Reardon, when we took our break, we were talking about your developing relationship with Ben Perkins. Is it true that you concealed what was going on from Paul Reardon?

Yes . . . I enjoyed being with Ben. It was—it felt dangerous and exciting. I didn't want it spoiled.

Let's move on. Describe the events that led up to the change in your relationship with Ben Perkins.

Uh . . . well, he took me for a flight in his ultralight.

That's some sort of airplane?

A real little bitty small one. Like a kite with a motor. He keeps it in an old shed at the back of Norwegian Wood. I remember it was August the year we moved in. He asked if I wanted a ride in it.

You agreed?

Yes. We went up. It was—oh, I can't describe it. It was like riding a motorcycle in the sky. Two little seats, one in front, one in back, and no floor, no walls, no cockpit at all. You're just out there, practically naked in the air. He took us up a couple thousand feet. We cruised from one end of Ford Lake to the other. We saw the Hydramatic plant, Willow Run Airport, the freeways, and—oh, it seemed like forever up there. And it went so quickly. And it was the most terrifying and exciting thing I've ever done in my life.

What happened when you landed?

I felt shaky and weak. I could hardly walk. He helped me to my apartment. We got inside. He put his arms around me. He felt so good, so strong—

And you became intimate with him.

Yes.

And the affair continued, is that a fact?

It wasn't an everyday thing.

How many times did you have sex with him?

Please. That's not—I have no idea.

Surely you must have some idea. Was it fifty times? A hundred times?

All right, probably, yes.

How long did the affair continue?

Till late May.

Roughly a month, perhaps six weeks, before your husband was killed, is that correct?

He wasn't my husband till the day he died! Don't you understand that?

I understand, Mrs. Reardon. What you're saying is, during the course of your affair with Mr. Perkins, you weren't married. Therefore, your relationship with Mr. Perkins did not constitute infidelity.

Yes. No. I don't know. It was just—something special and fun and just for me. I wasn't looking for a lover. It just happened.

All right. Please describe the circumstances under which this clandestine affair with Mr. Perkins ended.

Well, I told him we had to stop. I'd decided once and for all to marry Paul.

There'd been some question of that?

No, not really, not from my standpoint. But Ben had been hinting at, well, maybe if I got myself free, we could move in together. "Make things semi-official," is the way he put it. It was really out of the question. I loved Paul, not Ben.

I see—

And even if I'd considered it seriously, well, I wasn't sure I could ever get serious about him. How can you get serious about a man you can't trust? After all, he was close to Carole Somers at that time, yet he was sneaking around seeing me. And maybe others, who knows. I wasn't sure he'd change his ways for anyone, even me.

How did Mr. Perkins react when you broke it off?

He was angry. Very, very angry.

What did he say?

Well, he didn't yell and scream and throw things. That's not his way. But there's a dark side to him, a real dark, violent side. I've known violent men and I can tell. He used to be some kind of union goon, you know. And he's a private detective. There's a part of him that—well, you know, a deceitful side. He can be so smooth. Often he'd sit there on our deck and be friends with Paul, so nice to him, yet look at me knowing he and I had been in bed together just hours before.

What specifically did he say when you told him it was over, Mrs. Reardon?

He looked at me. And his eyes were sort of empty and gone-away someplace. And he said, "Darlin', all things can be fixed."

Did you take that as a threat?

Not then.

Do you think Mr. Perkins killed your husband in order to secure your affections for himself?

I'd like to say no. But—

But what, Mrs. Reardon?

The day of the funeral, he—he came to my apartment . . . and he took me to bed.

Did you submit willingly?

You bastard! You son of a bitch! Of course not! But what choice did I have? I was a woman, alone in the world, with no friends, no family, no protection at all. In my heart I sensed that Ben had killed Paul. I was afraid he'd hurt me, too, if I didn't go along. I was so terribly afraid.

That was a couple of weeks ago. How do you feel now, Mrs. Reardon?

The son of a bitch killed my husband, and to all intents and purposes, he raped me. He should pay for it.

Hatfield snapped the recorder off. Silence owned the room. The chief looked solemn. His sidekick was beaming. My lawyers were the very picture of indignation: Carole was staring glumly at the table and Levin was examining her fingernails.

As for me, I felt as though the contents of my stomach had turned into cement. It seemed hard to breathe and there was a faraway ringing in my ears. I wanted to kick the table over. At the very least, I wanted to say something. But I was under orders.

"There's your motive," Hatfield said. "Older 'n running water. Goes back to David and Bathsheba, I believe."

Shaughnessy Levin's glance swept by me like I wasn't there. "Fine witness you've got there, Chief. She questions the moral character of my client while blithely engaging in an illicit love affair behind her fiancé's back."

"You dance with who you brung," Hatfield shrugged.

"Now," I said, "just hold it one goddamned minute—"

"Hush," Levin said, face icy.

I waved a hand. "No, no. Uh-uh. I don't buy this shit, everybody gets to talk but me, it's like I'm not even here or whatever."

I expected Carole to jump in, but she was doodling aimlessly with her Cross pen as if waiting for the class bell to ring. Shaun Levin, on the other hand, was totally focused. "We will have our turn!" she lashed out. "Now is not the time for—"

"Forget it, Counselor." I sneered, getting to my feet. "I'm gonna say my piece, so just set still." She thumped back in her chair, rolling her blue eyes in disbelief. I looked at Hatfield, who seemed eminently pleased. "Okay, chief, I'll grant you. Ellen tells a crackerjack story. Nice and juicy, ya hang on every word. There's just one slight problem. It's a lie."

I was looking at Carole as I said that. Her eyes found me for one brief moment and her expression said, *Maybe. But you always did have trouble keeping your pants on, buddy boy.*

Hatfield was silent and expectant. I said, "Oh, she's clever as hell, how she puts it together. How we met, all that's true, far as I remember. The bowling, the going out to the bars and stuff, that's all true. I did bring her soup once when she had the flu and Paul was out of town. I did tell her, after Paul died, that I was only thirty seconds away. And sure, I've had my share of girlfriends. Why not? I'm a grown man."

Portman snickered.

"But lunch by the lake?" I charged on. "Nope. Ride in the ultralight?" I laughed. "No, but here's how cute she is: that was *Paul* I took up that time and it was *Paul* who described it as being like riding a motorcycle in the sky." I looked at Carole. She steadfastly refused to look at me. I said, "And I never went to bed with her. Not a hundred times, not fifty, not even once. Not by force, by mutual consent, or by accident. Not after the funeral or before it. Not ever."

Carole skidded her chair back, stood, and left the room without a sound except the clicking of the door behind her.

Hatfield squinted at the closed door, then at me. "You tell a pretty impassioned story yourself there, Perkins. But I gotta go with what I got. We'll have a chance to sort all this out at trial. Meantime, you got a date at the jailhouse. Carl?"

Portman swaggered over. "On your feet. Palms on the table, legs spread."

No choice at all. Slowly I got to my feet, bent and braced myself. Portman's hands poked, prodded, and raked over me. He relieved me of my wallet and keys, then jerked me upright and cuffed my hands behind me. Levin cruised around the table, car keys jingling in her chubby little hand. "I'll be at the arraignment," she said briskly. "Be silent till then." She left.

I looked at Hatfield, whose face gave away nothing. "What about that instinct, of yours, Chief?" I asked. "The one that said I didn't do it?"

The chief put a burned out, chewed-up stub of cigar in his teeth and worked it slowly. "Well, I have to believe if you were going to kill, you'd do it smarter than this." He withdrew the stub and spat a scrap. "But there's a school of thought that says maybe you were figuring we'd figure that. You can chase your tail like that for days, but in the end it comes down to politics."

"I don't believe this," I lied.

Hatfield looked bleak. "Old Lance Reardon's been bitching to anybody who'll listen, in Lansing and Detroit and everywhere else. For a while I kept the lid on, but this testimony of the wife clinches it. I need somebody for this, Perkins, and you're it."

Portman took my arm in a steel grip and jerked me. "Come on, let's go."

"Hold on, Carl," the chief said. We faced him again.

"You been looking into this yourself," Hatfield said. "You found out anything? Anything at all?"

Something about his tone, his expression, the fact that he'd asked the question at all, encouraged an idea I'd been toying with. "Not a thing," I said, grimacing. "But listen, Chief, can I have just one favor?"

"You got nothing coming, wiseass," Portman said.

"All I'm asking," I said, "is to stop by my place on the way out, change clothes, and wash up. I don't want to go to jail looking like this. How about it, Chief?"

"Jesus Christ," Portman spat.

Jack Hatfield said, after a moment's thought, "Just be real quick about it. And Detective Portman's gonna escort you. Can you handle it, Carl, or d'ya want a hand?"

"I can handle this scumbag just fine," Portman said.

Which was music to my ears.

Chapter 19

"Was she good, Perkins?" Carl Portman asked.

We were walking up the sidewalk toward the door of my building. I didn't see fit to answer. My wrists were starting to ache from the hard bite of the cuffs, and my fingertips were starting to tingle. Two unmarked city of Belleville police cars sat at the curb in front of Building 1. Two black-and-whites were in position in the no parking zone near the exit. They were taking no chances with me, your friendly local Public Enemy Number One.

Portman opened the door for me and pushed me inside ahead of him. "I hope she was good," he said. Dark glee colored his voice. "I hope she was the best piece of ass you ever had."

We passed the stairs and turned left down the first-floor hallway, bound for the elevator, which I never use.

Portman's voice continued its quiet taunting behind me. "Because it's the last legit nooky you'll ever have. Where you're going, the fuckin' ain't nearly as nice, and you'll probably be on the receiving end of most of it."

The elevator doors stood open. We stepped aboard. Portman punched the second-floor button and then leaned in the corner of the car, watching me as the doors hissed shut. His dark face was bemused as the car lurched us upward. "I been waiting for this, Perkins. I been waiting to nail your ass for a long time."

I looked at the switch panel. "Aw, looky there, Carl! You hit the wrong floor!"

"What?"

I reached out both cuffed arms, index finger extended, and hit a button.

Not a floor button. The emergency stop button.

The elevator bucked and lurched and quit. Portman said, "Hey, what the—" and then my two locked fists swung up and smashed him in the neck between the shoulder and the jawbone. He was tough, tougher than he looked, and the blow, which had every ounce of my strength behind it, didn't take him out. He dropped to his knees and made a half-strangled "Aaaaccch" sound as his hands scrabbled at the chrome passenger handle. I kneed him in the jaw, cracking his head soundly against the elevator wall, then swung my knotted fists again and bashed him to the floor.

The next move was obvious. Stomp his head. I dearly wanted to do it. The fury was awesome, but with great effort I managed to restrain it. Who says I'm not civilized?

The elevator hung there frozen and silent between the first and second floors. I got my breathing under control and bent to the coldcocked cop. Blood was running from his mouth and his breathing was wet. Evidently he'd bitten his tongue in the struggle. I rescued my keys and wallet, used his keys to uncuff myself, then cuffed one of his wrists to the brace of the passenger handle.

Then I inserted a utility key into the control panel and

twisted. The elevator hummed to life and continued its rise. At the second floor it stopped and the doors hissed open. I checked the hallway both ways. No one in sight.

Portman was still out cold, sprawled anyhow on the elevator floor, seemingly hanging by his cuffed wrist. I mashed the first-floor button and strolled rapidly down the hall as the elevator doors hissed shut. I trotted around the corner and to the end of the hall, where the building's main breaker cabinet was built into the wall. I unlocked and opened the cabinet door and flipped the third breaker to OFF. The hum of the elevator stopped abruptly. It was somewhere in no-man's-land between the second and first floors, and there it would stay till somebody figured out what had happened.

Not perfect. Perfect would have been Portman suffering a convenient heart attack in retribution for his nasty attitude. But it would do.

I figured I had maybe half an hour, tops. I went to my apartment. The floor just inside was scattered with mail and the answering machine message light was blinking like mad, but I didn't care. I went back to the bedroom and changed into road clothes: clean jeans, high-topped work shoes with steel inserts in the toes, pullover shirt. I put together all the cash I could find: close to sixty bucks. Not good. I had an ATM card, but using it would be like buying a billboard on the Lodge Freeway: HERE I AM, COME AND GET ME. Well, I could always get cash advances on my credit cards. If I was careful. If my credit lines weren't maxxed out. If, if, if.

Finally, I stuffed a small vinyl airlines bag full of fresh underwear, along with my .45 automatic, extra ammo, extra cigars, and all the change I could find. That took care of the essentials. I also packed my binoculars, camera, and the scraps of notes I had collected on the case along with the sketches and pictures of Angie. I surveyed the apartment one last time, wondering when I'd be back. No way to tell. I wasn't even positive about "if" at that point.

I went out the fire exit in the back of the building. No one was around except for a foursome over on the seventh fairway, and they were too interested in searching for their balls to care about me. I set out across the bristly grass toward the back forty, feeling very much like a target, expecting any minute to hear a loud voice behind me: FREEZE!

Nothing. My luck—what was left of it, tiny little scraps waving feebly in the wind—was holding. I reached the shed, slid open the door, and rolled my ultralight airplane out. I unfolded the wings, snapped them into place, and did only an abbreviated preflight inspection; then fired up the 350cc Zenoah engine with a tug of the pull rope.

Five minutes later I was in the air, climbing through the three-hundred-foot level, the warm breeze tearing at my hair. As I made the big sweeping banking turn, I could see Grove Road, Huron River Drive, the edge of Ford Lake, and the buildings of Norwegian Wood down below. I could even see the rooftops of the four Belleville police cars, still vigilant, still guarding the exit to the complex as I flew by overhead.

I resisted the temptation to waggle the wings. Instead I took a northeast bearing and continued to climb, bound for the city of Detroit.

Consciousness grew like the coming of daylight and the tortured dream I'd been having faded away into nothingness. I opened my eyes and saw, printed in faded black felt-tip on the dirty plaster wall:

COCKROACHES
Killed: 8
Wounded: 13
Missing in Action: 5
Prisoners of War: 3

I closed my eyes again and it all came back to me: the tough landing on the northbound lanes of Telegraph Road near Seven Mile; the short taxi into the driveway of the Shine Inn car wash; and the debate with Phil over which of my remaining police auction relics was likely to live the longest.

I'd finally settled on the 1964 Buick LeSabre. I picked it mainly because it was a yacht on wheels, from those halcyon days when we built them big, brawny, and here. Consequently it was plenty roomy in front and in back, which was good; I had a feeling I'd be living in the thing for a while. It had four decent tires, brakes I could get by with, good glass all the way around, and an exhaust system that was only just starting to go. I could have lived without the automatic Power Slide transmission, and the 300 V-8 was an oil hog—I had to add two quarts before starting out—but the car was powerful, anonymous, legal, and, best of all, paid for.

I locked the ultralight to a rusted standpipe behind the Shine Inn and Phil and I tarped it over. He agreed to keep an eye on it. He agreed that I'd never been there. He agreed that I could owe him the hundred bucks. With my backfield about as secure as it ever is, I threw my stuff into the Buick and headed downtown, ending up here at the Czar Nicholas Hotel.

I opened my eyes again. The cockroach scoreboard had not changed. I hoisted myself upright, blinking my grainy eyes in the dimness of the sunless light that diffused through dirty windows. The room was maybe twelve feet square and as high as it was wide. The air smelled as if dead things were stored in there from time to time. The mortar-colored walls were bare except for a spidery network of cracks, as well as a selection of graffiti, inventive and otherwise, penned on the wall by the bed. For furnishings I had an old wood dresser from which the mirror was missing; two wood straight chairs, and the single spavined bed.

I reached for the floor, found my jeans, and pulled them on. I lighted a cigar with a kitchen match, inhaled gratefully, then got to my feet and walked to the window. Out there, from five floors up, the city of Detroit looked peaceful at this early Thursday hour. Directly below was Twenty-third Street, more of an alley, which ran north and dead-ended into the broad expanse of Michigan Avenue that knifed due east to the heart of Detroit. In the urban plain out ahead the Jeffries Freeway flowed by in an expanse of concrete. I could see Southwest Detroit Hospital, Tiger Stadium, and the train station. To the south I could see the towers of the Ambassador Bridge. To the north a ways was the suburb of Berkley, where Carole was probably up already, drinking coffee, getting Will ready for school, wondering about me.

I chased those thoughts, folded my bare arms, smoked my cigar, and scanned the landscape. The sky hung thick with haze, another cloudy, gloomy, excessively humid day. And lucky me with an airless Buick! I told myself to quit whining. Just because the job at hand is impossible doesn't mean you can't do it. All you need—in addition to coffee, of course—is some kind of plan.

I had the Buick, sixty bucks (make that forty now), my .45, and clean underwear. Hell, I'd done a lot with much less. All I needed now was a plan.

I dragged one of the straight chairs over to the window, sat down heavily, and started going through my notes.

Angie. No matter what I did, it all came back to Angie.

Clearly, the whole thing had started when Paul found Davey Jackson's cocaine in the Gremlin car seat he'd bought at WorldWide. One of those evil coincidences, the type of thing that supposedly keeps life interesting; such as John Jacob Astor taking the *Titanic* and W. Averell Harriman being persuaded at the last moment not to.

The otherwise clean and straight Paul saw a chance to make a quick buck. From the get-go, his luck was not so good. He tried to peddle it at Jugg Poltiss's Texas Time Saloon and, for his pains, made contact with a state police undercover. Had that deal gone through, Paul would have been in jail instead of dead. Better? Debatable.

But I'd never know, because at this juncture Angela Barnes came onto the scene. She got to Paul by means of that Gremlin car seat—she'd persuaded Charnelle Blais, at knife point, to tell her where Jackson kept it while on courier runs. Exactly why she wanted it I didn't know. Maybe, as a free-lancer, she was hired to retrieve it.

I knew that Angie had, in fact, found Paul; they'd been seen together. I knew that a matter of days later, five thousand bucks had appeared in Paul's secret savings account. And shortly after that he was dead.

Theory A: Angie had killed him. There was a lot to like about this one. I knew she was a killer; Goforth had told me she was a professional free-lance assassin. I knew she was working for Savastano, because she'd used Savastano's pet lawyer during her interview with the Detroit police. Theory A said that Savastano sent her to track down the cocaine that disappeared when Davey Jackson was killed. She traced it to Paul Reardon and he had either refused to give it to her, or had already sold it (which would explain the five grand), so she'd blown him up.

Like I said, a lot to like. Theory A also had some troublesome holes. Goforth had insisted that Angie's MO was purely traditional, .22 with a silencer: "*Phip-phip* and out of there." This didn't square terribly well with the bombing.

Another hole was the five grand. If Angie gave it to him (say, in return for the cocaine), it wouldn't make sense for her to blow him up. If she blew him up, then where did the five large come from?

Another problem was squaring Theory A with the whole drug war scenario. Savastano had lost three distributors in addition to Jackson. They'd been dropping like flies since spring. I reread the notes I'd made of my talk with Dennehy and read off the cities: St. Joe, Grand Rapids, Ann Arbor. Goforth thought a war was brewing. Savastano was clearly under a lot of pressure. What was Angie's role in all of this? Was she investigating the killings for Savastano?

Or was she the perpetrator?

Could she be working for Savastano and, at the same time, knocking off his people? Dangerous. But do-able.

I hadn't looked at it quite that way before. It didn't really sing. But it was a possibility. As I thought about it and leafed aimlessly through my notes, my glance fell once again on the scribblings I'd made on the talk with Dennehy and there it was. Not a smoking gun. Not even much of a clue. More of an indication that time was getting short and I'd be wise to get on Angie's tail. Quickly.

I folded up my notes and stuff and prepared to leave the room. I was sick of wondering and worrying and theorizing. I was sick of trying to puzzle this miserable thing out. It was like trying to grab a specific minnow out of a pailful of them.

I would go with my gut, which said that Angie was in back of Paul's death, somehow, some way. I was going to get on her and watch her and, when the time came, fix her—put her in such a jam with either the cops, or with Savastano, that her best recourse was to come clean, clearing me of suspicion and avenging Paul's death.

As a plan, it wasn't pretty. But not every case lends itself to the niceties of inductive or deductive reasoning. Sometimes you just have to hunker down, gut it out, and outlast the bastard.

There was every likelihood that I would, in the end, fail. Which meant I'd end up in jail and on trial for Paul's murder. But why go quietly? Why shuffle along like a meek little sheep, wrists out and head bowed?

Moreover, thanks to Ellen Reardon's betrayal (and where the hell did *that* come from? Another thing to hold for later, like the business with Carole), I'd been driven out of my job, my home, my very life. I had lots and lots of time to fix Angie now. It was, in fact, all I had to live for.

It was still fairly early when I hit the street, and Michigan Avenue was just starting to hum with inbound commuter traffic. I walked up the sidewalk past a liquor store, two resale shops, a sidewalk Baptist temple, and a gaggle of strung-out guys lined up to give blood at a clinic. At the corner I went into a sandwich shop named Sub Rosa, bought an egg-salad sandwich, two large coffees and the *Free Press*, and carried it all back to the Buick, which I'd left parked and unlocked on the sidewalk in front of the Czar Nicholas. I mean, who'd steal the thing? Nobody was that desperate, not even in this neighborhood.

The expansive front seat of the Buick became my dining room. I ate, drank, smoked, and consumed the *Free Press*, which, to all indications, either had not learned that I was a wanted man, or didn't care. Let's face it: as murder suspects go these days, I was pretty small potatoes. Compared with most of today's crimes, whose grisly ingenuity seems designed with the front page in mind, the killing of Paul Reardon was almost quaint.

But I had no doubt that the cops were out there looking for me. They were watching Norwegian Wood and Under New Management. They were touching base with my friends and checking all my regular haunts. They were distributing my description to every police agency in the Detroit area. But they would not find me, not unless they either got very lucky or I got very stupid.

I finished breakfast. Then I gave my .45 automatic the once-over and loaded it up, seven in the clip, one in the chamber, resolving not to leave the car without it for any reason. The important things taken care of, I then popped the Buick's hood and checked the oil. Down a half quart already. Jesus. Sucker was as bad as Carole's misbegotten Thumper wagon. I started up the engine and watched blue smoke collect in a cloud around the back end. I peered underneath and saw a slick black puddle under the pan. The sucker was burning it *and* leaking it. Christ.

Well, first things first. I drove west on Michigan till I found a CHECKS CASHED/MONEY ORDERS joint open for business. Through the ghetto glass inside I was able to negotiate a two-hundred-dollar cash advance on my Visa card—all the weight the thing would take. Cops'd have to be really on the ball to trace me here through the credit card, and even if they did, I'd be long gone.

From there I went to a strip mall on Grand River and bought supplies. Weird variety of stuff: motor oil, duct tape, wide-mouthed mason jar, an eclectic (and mostly nauseating, except when you're starving) variety of snack-food items, a couple jugs of bottled water, trash bags, a clipboard, pad, and box of pens. I also rescued several large cardboard cartons from a Dumpster out back, flattened them, and stored them in the trunk.

After topping off the Buick's oil, I motored east to the riverfront and parked across the street and up two doors from 77 Curtin Terrace, in the heart of Harbortown and Angela Barnes's last known residence.

Then I settled back to watch. Odds were, Angie was at work somewhere. Odds were, she wouldn't be back here till tonight at the earliest. That was all right. I had nothing but time.

Two hours passed. Three. Lunchtime came and I ate a

cold burrito out of a cellophane bag. Drank some water. Smoked and watched.

At 2:00 P.M. an enormous white Cadillac pulled into the driveway of 77 Curtin Terrace. A diminutive black man in a dark pin-striped suit got out and escorted a middle-aged white couple to the front door. He was talking to them, gesturing as he spoke, but I couldn't hear what he was saying. They went into the townhouse. I saw lights turn on and off, saw faces appear at various windows. Twenty minutes later they came out onto the porch and stood there talking. I began to get a very sinking feeling.

Finally they walked back to the Cadillac. I tooted the Buick's horn and waved, and the black man looked at me, said something to the couple, then walked down the driveway toward me as the others got into the Cadillac to wait.

"Morning," I said. "Is that townhouse up yonder for rent or something?"

"For sale," he said. His face was shaped like an inverted teardrop, the eyes dark and intelligent and only slightly wary—no doubt concerned at the sight of the 1964 Buick dripping oil all over Detroit's newest stretch of upscale pavement. "Are you in the market, sir?"

"Well, sort of. My wife is, more than me, really. She's up the street looking at another place. When'd this go on the market? We hadn't heard anything about it."

"Just listed," the man said. "The owner was renting it out, but the tenant moved away this week and the owner's decided to sell. I can spare a few minutes now if you'd like to—"

"No, not right now," I said hastily. "Give me your card, I'll call you when the wife's ready to have a look. What the hell, they make the real decisions anyway, am I right?"

He smiled dutifully and gave me his card. "Riverfront Realty, Stuart Sims, Owner/Broker." We exchanged farewells and he returned to his Cadillac and drove his real paying clients away.

I drove away, too. There was nothing to hang around for. Angie had flown the coop.

*   *   *

I could always try Titanium Tower. That was where Savastano's organization was based, which meant Angie might be working out of there. But finding her there—if she was there to find—was a virtual impossibility. I had one other possibility to check out first.

I took Grand River to Livernois and went north several blocks to Pulaski Street. I did not turn down it. I remembered Gail Barretta's bay window, her telescope, her comment about recording license plate numbers, and I decided to keep the Buick where she couldn't get a look at it. Instead of parking at the curb on Pulaski, I parked behind a vacant gas station on the east side of Livernois and then walked down and around the corner to Barretta's building.

The conditioned air of the foyer was so cool and dry, it made me feel like I'd dived into Lake Superior. Inside the foyer the layout had changed about as much as an oil painting. There was the desk; there were the video cameras; there was the uniformed Bruce, in his faded football-player glory, sitting there with only the phone console for company. "Good afternoon, Mr. Perkins," he said pleasantly.

"Just barely. Listen, I don't need to bother the honcho upstairs this time. I'm just wondering if the woman I'm after, Angela Barnes, has been around since I stopped by last week."

Bruce's very black face was as expressive as a cave opening. "I'm not authorized to give out information," he said in his gentle, faraway voice. "I'm sure Ms. Barretta—"

The phone purred. Bruce snatched the receiver, listened for a long moment, then said "Very well" and hung up. "She'd like a word with you," he reported. "She has some information that you'll be very much interested in."

"Well, okay. I'm kind of in a rush, so—"

"She'll send down for you directly."

"Okay. Thanks."

Bruce sat at his desk, somehow relaxed and alert at the same time. I felt fidgety for some reason, and to keep busy I took myself on a small and very boring walking tour of the featureless foyer. When the sound came from behind me, I just barely heard it. A single, metallic *snick*.

I looked at Bruce. He watched me, face empty. I remembered Barretta's obvious interest in technology. The video cameras, the metal detector in the doorframe upstairs, and all the rest. Oh yeah. Sure. She'd do that, all right. What amazed me was that she evidently thought I'd sit still for it.

I reached back and under my shirt and pulled my .45 automatic from its resting place under the waistband of my trousers next to my spine. Two-handed, I swung it on Bruce, who had started to push himself back from the desk. He froze.

I smiled. "Hands on the desk, Bruce. Far apart. Fingers spread." He didn't move. I wheeled, drew down on the left-hand video camera, and took it out with two shots. I only needed one shot to blow the other one to hell. Practice makes perfect. I trained the .45 back on Bruce. "What I said, pal. Now."

The stink of gunpowder filled the room. Bruce's large throat worked once and then he obeyed me, brown eyes on me all the while. I jerked my head back, indicating the door. "Electric lock, huh?" He didn't answer. "What," I said, "she hear from her cop buddies that I'm hot?" Once again Bruce spilled his guts. "Yeah, well," I said. "Go ahead, pal, unlock the thing and let's be done with this."

"Can't do that, man."

I stared at him. "What do you think, you're dealing with some twinkle-toes here? Do it or I'll blow your fucking head off."

"I need this job," he whispered.

"She worth dying for, Bruce? That fat bitch? Shit, no. No boss in the world's worth dying for. Unlock the thing."

For a moment I thought he'd stay stubborn and I'd have to shoot. At the door, of course, not at him. But a tiny bit of strength seemed to go out of him as he said, "Button's on the underside of the desk, need my hands to hit it."

"Use your knee," I said, gesturing with the .45. "Make like a contortionist if you have to, but keep your hands where I can see 'em." He wiggled, and then I heard that metallic *snick* behind me again. "Thanks. One more thing. Angela Barnes been around here this week?"

Bruce shook his head slightly. "Lease just ran out. We cleaned out her place this morning."

I lowered the .45. "Very good," I said, grinning as I stepped toward him. "Now stand up and turn around. Easy now."

He rose, hands raised with pale palms facing me. "What're you gonna do?"

"Turn around, like I said."

"Oh, no, please," he said as he began to turn, ducking instinctively. I swung the .45 in a sweeping right and hit him flush on the head with the flat of the piece. He grunted and bellyflopped onto the chair, which revolved under his weight and dumped him with a heavy splattering sound onto the slate floor.

Good. Let her think he went down fighting. Without the video cameras, she'd never know he weenied. I put my .45 away and bounced out the door at a quick trot. I cut to the right through a big hedge into someone's yard, vaulted two chain-link fences, crossed an alley, and reached the Buick by coming around the back side of the abandoned gas station.

I started the big 300 motor, pulled over to Livernois, waited while two white Detroit police scout cars made whistling turns onto Pulaski. Then I headed north.

Once again, no Angie. And a disquieting pattern was emerging: her lease had run out on her townhouse, and her lease had run out on her hideaway office. Sounded as though she was getting ready to blow town—if she hadn't already.

Just one more place to check.

Chapter 20

The Titanium Tower is the centerpiece of a group of five massive steel-and-glass skyscrapers, which, thanks to their spacing and their varying heights, have become known around town as "The Five Fingers." It sits on Northwestern Highway in Southfield, that most venerable of metro Detroit suburbs, which, like a buzzard, hovers above Detroit, waiting not so patiently for it to die.

Just as Southfield is more a state of mind than a city, the Titanium Tower is more a complex than a building. There's the skyscraper itself, thirty stories of reflecting glass that is the blue of a Vicks VapoRub jar. There are three two-story wings that jut out every which way, to Evergreen on the east, Culex Drive on the north, and Northwestern on the west. There's a Bon Chance Hotel, an all-glass atrium shopping mall, a three-screen theater (showing *St. Elmo's Fire, About Last Night,* and *The Big Chill* the day I was there), and several multistory parking decks out of the Maginot Line school of architecture. All this is attended by a veritable rat's nest of driveways, ramps, switchbacks, kitty-corners, and dead ends. There's even a skywalk leading to an exclusive apartment tower at Culex and Evergreen. Evidently, the complex's designers employed the time-honored "flypaper" strategy: once you're there, you never leave.

I found my way into the complex from the Northwestern side and lucked into a loading-zone parking space near the north entrance. I backed into the space, shut off the motor, then sat there for a moment reviewing what I remembered about the place from the last time I was there several years before.

That was the first time I ever tangled with Rick Savastano and the Detroit organization. He'd sent a couple of goons down to Norwegian Wood to escort me up here for a meeting. I remembered that the mob's offices occupied at least one of the top floors of the tower. I remembered that you accessed those floors by means of a public elevator, but there was no floor button; you had to use a special key. I remembered that the mob's offices up there looked about as threatening as a CPA's—but, all things considered, I still didn't think it would be wise or healthy to go busting in there wild-eyed, even if I could figure out a way to get up there.

I almost gave it up right then. I mean, what did I really have to go on here? Elvin Dance had connected Angela Barnes to Savastano by means of Hite, the alleged mob lawyer. The address Angela had given the police for her employment was approximately the same as Titanium Tower. Plus, Carlo Infante had not specifically denied a connection between Angie and Savastano's group.

On the other hand, Carlo hadn't confirmed it, either. The Hite bit, the similar address—flimsy. Plus, Ezra Goforth, claiming to have a mole in Titanium, had said that Angie did not work in Titanium. And even if she did once, she could be long gone by now. But in the end I pressed on—not because any spiritual voice encouraged me or anything, but because I was damned if I'd quit till I'd run every possibility, no matter how remote, into the ground.

I walked through the revolving doors of the north entrance. To my left was the multistory atrium mall and one of the parking structures; to my right was the foyer of the tower itself with its banks of elevators and double row of glass-enclosed shops. I checked out the foyer first, threading my way among the elevators and shops, counting exits, staircases, and doors. Then I walked over to the atrium mall and bleakly surveyed its layout.

Finally, I went back out to the Buick, sat in the front seat, lighted a cigar, and reviewed my findings. It seemed to be borderline hopeless. There were at least a dozen entrances to the complex and no fewer than three vantage points that would have to be covered if I was going to have a prayer of spotting Angie either coming to work or leaving. I'm considered fairly resourceful, but I couldn't possibly be in three places at once.

Once again the let's-give-it-up idea hit me with even more compelling force than before. I mean, it would be one thing if I was positive Angie was even here. But I wasn't. And—

A distant reflection in the rearview mirror caught my eye. Three women, walking beside the tower toward the atrium entrance. I focused on them and my breath caught. The center one was Angie.

I had the Buick door open before I could think. What do I do now? If she's headed for her office, it's no good following her. If she's headed for her car, there's no point following her on foot. I should stay here and pick her up as she drove out.

But three parking decks served Titanium Tower, each with maybe two exits, and she could drive out any one of them. There was no surefire, risk-free way to get on her tail here and now. And in most surveillances the most important rule is: it's better to lose the followee than to let her catch you following her.

I pulled the car door shut and sat back in the seat, feeling my heartbeat ease back to normal. A break, damn it, I'd gotten a break. About time. Angie was here, and if my half-baked idea was at all correct, she'd be here tomorrow, too. I'd be back, and ready this time.

I checked my watch. Pushing three. Reached for the keys, then let them go. Relighted my cigar and decided to face the problem once and for all, think it through, and take action.

Carole.

The look on her face after she heard Ellen's tape . . . I couldn't get that out of my mind. I knew what the last twenty-four hours must have been like for her. And the next twenty-four were going to be no better. Tomorrow was Friday. She was going in for her abortion, and she was doing it all alone.

At that moment I felt about as rotten and as small a human being as I ever had. Good old Ben Perkins, the legendary smoker and joker, had a terminal case of the guilts. And, so far as I could see, there was but one way to fix them. Maybe it was for naught. Maybe this was the end for me and Carole, at last. But if I was ever to sleep really well again, if I was ever to think of Carole again without flinching, I had to try.

I couldn't just go to see her. I was a fugitive, and she was an officer of the court. I wasn't positive that she'd turn me in, but I didn't want to put her on the spot. There was the phone, but that seemed sort of cold. The mail's even colder, telegrams scare hell out of people, and if FTD had something covering this situation, Merlin Olsen hadn't chirped about it yet on TV.

Which left one other idea. What the hell, I thought. Go for it. Now, before your nerve runs out.

I fired up the Buick and wheeled it over to Culex Drive. The memory of spotting Angie just now flitted across my mind again and I smiled. If I was a mystical guy, I'd have called that a sign that maybe things were going to work out after all. If I was a Catholic, I'd have thanked the patron saint of private detectives. But I'm neither a mystic nor a Catholic; I'm a lapsed Southern Baptist. And there probably isn't a patron saint of private detectives anyhow. Who'd want the job? Bad pay and long hours.

"May I help you?" the very young, squinty-eyed woman asked.

"Yeah, hi. I'm here to see one of the summer camp kids. Will Somers."

"Are you a parent?"

"No."

She stared at me vacantly. Evidently she had to go deep into memory to retrieve the proper response in this situation. "You'll need to see Dr. Kinsbo," she said. "One moment."

I stood back from the counter as the young woman hoisted herself up from the desk and disappeared into a back room. The office of the John R. Williams Elementary School was empty and silent except for the distant sounds of young voices in classrooms. Edgy though I was, I found myself thinking about Holcomb Elementary in northwest Detroit. It had been a lot of years, but the sounds and the smells of paste, disinfectant, and moldy paper had not changed a bit.

Presently a dark, severe-looking woman in her thirties came out of the back room. She was tall and thin and, from the set of her carriage and her mouth, used to getting her own way. "Yes," she asked briskly, "how may we help you?"

"Hi, Dr. Kinsbo, I'm Ben Perkins." She had nice eyes but at the moment they were glacial, and I found myself wondering how many days of detention I was going to get.

"I'm a friend of Carole Somers, whose son Will is in the summer camp here, and I need to see him for a minute."

"May I ask why?"

"Well, it's personal. I just need to talk to him."

She looked me up and down. I admit I was starting to look a little scroungy. Hadn't shaved in thirty hours and on me it really shows. "I can't allow you to take him from the building," she said.

"I understand that. Can I—"

"You may speak with him, but I'll have to be present."

"Look. Doctor. I've known him since he was a little baby. His mother and I are—"

"I understand that, Mr. Perkins, but I have my responsibilities." She went to a World War II–vintage intercom unit sitting on a table in the corner, consulted a clipboard of notes, then hit a switch and spoke into the mike: "Mrs. Rogers, please send Will Somers to the office."

We waited a few moments. Two teachers breezed in and out. The young clerk spilled a bottle of White-Out. Dr. Kinsbo got into a phone argument with someone about a broken copy machine. Then Will, wearing a T-shirt bearing the cryptic information "I Saved the Princess" as well as jeans and sneakers, came into the office. He looked expectant as well as nervous, his expression as readable as a sign: *What did I do now?*

His large brown eyes widened when he saw me. "Hi, Ben. What are you doing here? Where's Mommy?"

"She's at work. Everything's okay, Will, I just need to talk to you for a minute."

"You two can come back here," Dr. Kinsbo said. I put my hand on the boy's shoulder as we walked into her office. She shut the door and then sat behind her cluttered desk.

I sat Will down on a straight chair and took one facing him. My heart was trying to kick my chest out. I didn't know where to begin. Will took care of that problem. "Mom said you're in big trouble. She said we might not see you again for a long long time."

I was aware of Dr. Kinsbo watching us intently. "There's a lot of problems, Will, I won't kid around with you. But don't worry about it, that's not what I'm here about. I want you to give your mom a message for me, okay?"

"Okay." He cocked his head. "Why don't you call her?"

"It's a long story. This is the only way I can think of to handle it, but I need your help real bad. Can I count on you, big guy?"

"Sure."

"Okay. Here's the message for your mom." I drew a breath. "'I won't leave you to deal with this alone. I love you, and I want to marry you.'"

My words hung in the still air of the office. I'd heard myself say them, in front of two witnesses yet, and I still didn't believe it. I'd never thought I'd ever propose marriage to anyone, let alone this way.

Dr. Kinsbo had turned into a statue. Will was dead serious. "You're gonna marry Mommy?"

"Up to her now, big guy."

"Are you gonna live with us?"

That caught me off guard. "I don't know. Could be."

"Well . . . what about this bad trouble you're in?"

I looked into his earnest eyes and said, "Don't worry about it. I'll take care of it. I'm a real good fixer, remember?"

"It's just not *fair*," he said unhappily.

"What isn't?"

"You fix things for people. You help everyone else. But no one ever helps you."

"Well . . . you dance with who you brung," I said, quoting my old buddy Jack Hatfield.

"Why can't you come home with me and see Mommy?" he asked.

I put a hand on his shoulder and looked intently into his face. "I can't do that now, Will. That's why I need your help. You're going back to class in a minute, and then after school you go home. Wait till Mrs. Miracle leaves and let Mom have a chance to eat something. Then tell her what I told you. Can you repeat it?"

He did so, word for word.

I stood. "Okay, kid, better get back to the learnin'."

He stood, too. "Good-bye, Ben. Come home soon."

"Count on it."

Suddenly he ran over to me and hugged me hard. I bent and hugged him back, for one fierce instant. Then he turned and trudged to the office door and, with one sad look back, was gone.

Dr. Kinsbo was on her feet. The hard planes of her thin face had softened and her eyes were different as she looked at me, as if she was seeing a person now instead of just another pain-in-the-ass problem. I said, "Thanks for the help, Doc."

"Not at all. In fact—Mr. Perkins, I owe you an apology. I'm sorry I was so curt and suspicious toward you when you came in."

I shrugged. "Not to worry. You got your job to do, taking care of all these kids." I started for the door. "I mean, what the hell? You never know when some kinda murder suspect toting a concealed .45 automatic is going to come barging into your school, now do you?"

She looked just a little pinched and pale now. I just grinned at her. She asked, "Is there anything I can do for you?"

"Yep. Forget I was ever here."

Like everything else along that stretch of Michigan Avenue, Sub Rosa looked, from the street, like a dump. It had a version of the White Castle look, bright white block-shaped siding, a flat roof, a blue awning above the double door. Unlike your typical White Castle, it had bars on the windows, graffiti on the walls, and a tattered, home-made banner that said NOW SERVING HOAGYS N HEROS TOO!

But inside it wasn't too terrible. The order and pickup windows were on the left, and the narrow dining area had booths with high partitions. The patronage was a mix of working-class stiffs, mind-your-own-business types. The food smelled palatable. Despite the incessant Muzak, so inoffensive it made you want to kill something, the Sub Rosa seemed like an ideal place for a meeting.

The problem was finding someone to meet with.

I mean, Elvin Dance and Dick Dennehy were obviously out. Ditto for Jack Hatfield and Carlo Infante. I did try to raise Darryl Rockecharlie, a strong-arm buddy of mine, only to be told by his wife that he was in alcoholism treatment again but would doubtless be delighted to lend a hand once his twenty-one days were up. I got hold of Norris Johnston, who was entirely too interested in learning exactly where I was, so I hung up on him. I tried a half-dozen other people, all of whom were on vacation, indisposed, or otherwise not available.

So forget the professionals. I ended up signing on a couple of rookies. Shortly after I finished my sandwich and first beer in the corner booth of Sub Rosa, the first recruit arrived.

"Jesus, Ben!" Brian said, sauntering up to the table with a small cloth sack in his hand. "Think you coulda picked a more down 'n' dirty neighborhood to get lost in?"

"Have a seat. Pour yourself one." Brian dropped the sack on the floor. The Muzak switched to an accordion cover of "Blue on Blue." As Brian slid into the booth across from me and loaded a mug from the pitcher, I peeked into the sack. There were five pieces of triangular two-by-four wood in there, each with long glinting spike driven through it. Perfect.

Brian wore tight acid-washed jeans, a tan athletic shirt whacked off at the navel, and a tiny earring in his left lobe. His long earnest face had picked up some tan and he was very fresh and vigorous for a guy who'd been at death's door from a gunshot wound just two months before. Oh, to be twenty-two again. "Trouble finding the place?" I asked.

"Nah." Brian drank and wiped foam from his lip. "Everything's going good out in the place, Randy and I are covering. Doug couldn't make it in today, though."

"Oh? Why?"

"Called in at noon, said his cat stepped on his alarm clock and shut it off, so he overslept."

"Oh, shit. He still could have come in."

"Well, he said he was going to take the afternoon off anyway, so he figured he was through for the day."

"Swell." I lighted a cigar. "Cops hassling you guys?"

"They're around. Questioned us about your hangouts and so forth." He glanced around the quiet sandwich shop.

"Even if we were going to rat, we'd never have known about this place."

I tapped ash in the big tin ashtray. "You play double-back and stuff, make sure nobody tailed you?"

"Yeah. I was clean. But listen, Ben, something weird happened."

"What's that?"

He leaned toward me. "Belleville PD and state police are on your case. But that ain't all. Other cops, too. Canadian."

Chapter 21

"Blue on Blue" gave way to a Muzak knockoff of a Whitney Houston knockoff of a Phil Collins knockoff of some old song.

"Canadians?" I growled at Brian. "What the hell do they want with me?"

"Dunno. All I know is, some detective from the Ontario Provincial Police came by yesterday, asking all kinds of questions about you."

"Jesus. As if I don't got enough to sort out."

"You got a plan?" Brian asked.

"Yeah, I guess you'd call it that. Let's wait till—oh, okay, here she comes."

The jingling of all the fake jewelry—bracelets, necklaces, and earrings—made Barb Paley sound like an approaching chuck wagon. That, plus the flaming red hair exploding around her head, made everyone in Sub Rosa turn to look as she came in, and there was plenty of her to see. She was inserted into prewashed jeans and sandals and stretched a black Detroit Pistons "Bad Boys" T-shirt to extremis. When she spotted Brian and me, she came to us at a near trot.

Brian got a playful head rub, I got a hug that nearly knocked me over, and both of us got gassed with a piercingly sweet scent that, no doubt, had some sort of naughty name. Then she seized my chin and examined my face with worried eyes. "Ben, how are you, hon? Are you all right?"

"All in one piece, Barb. Have a seat, load up." Brian slid out of the booth, allowed Barb to slide in, then sat on the end. "I'm glad you could make it."

"I'm glad you called," she said, filling her glass with beer. "How'd you know to try me at Under New Management?"

Probably because you virtually live there, I thought. "Just a hunch." I grinned. Barb's a sweet lady with one hell of a good heart. She was born in party mode and has stayed there all her life. She and I had had a fling earlier in the year—before Carole—and it had fallen apart when it became obvious that she took it more seriously than I did. Since then, her partying had become, if anything, more frenzied. This did not bode well for the task at hand. The heavy boozing was starting to get to her; she was, sad to say, no intellectual giant anyway, and there was every chance that she'd inadvertently screw something up. But I needed help badly and I knew she'd do her best.

"All right," I said to the two of them, "here's the scoop." And I laid it all out, chapter and verse.

"Eight A.M.?" Barb wailed. "I got to be in god-awful Southfield at eight A.M. tomorrow?"

"We got to be ready," I explained. "No telling when things'll start to pop. Can you get the time off work?"

"Sure, hon," she said absently, glaring at a chipped fingernail. "I'm working at Heritage Hospital now, didja know that?"

She's been a typist there since before Jerry Ford was in. "Yeah, I heard. Good for you. How 'bout you, Brian, got any problems with the plan?"

"No," he said. His eyes were alight and I knew he was excited. The very notion of detective work still thrilled him, which surprised me since it was detective work that got him shot the last time. "What about equipment?"

"I've got it in my room. We'll go over it tomorrow up

there. It's probably gonna be an all-day gig, people, so be ready. And be sure to dress like you belong in the joint. It's Oakland County, remember, the pseudo-straight crowd: yups and fat cats. Okay?" They both nodded. "Okay, then, that's it. Y'all better head back out to the 'burbs. And thanks a lot. You're real pals, the both of ya."

We exited Sub Rosa and hit the Michigan Avenue sidewalk. The broad avenue was crowded with the tail end of the afternoon commuter traffic, all surging westbound. Brian shook hands with me and headed west up the sidewalk. Barb stood beside me, very close. "Where'd you park?" I asked.

The exhaust-tinged breeze made her red hair dance. "Across the street over there. Where are you staying?"

For an instant I felt suspicious, and then guilty. "The Czar Nicholas. Right up there at—"

"Michigan at Twenty-third." She nodded, looking around. "I know. I grew up in this neighborhood. Roosevelt, just east of the Boulevard. My dad worked at Cadillac Motor Car till he got killed and then we moved out to Taylor." She took my hand in her two small ones, equipped with more rings than fingers. "You really all right, Ben?"

I looked down at her and gently disengaged my hand. "I'm fine, kid. Thanks."

She looked into my eyes. "Want me to stay? I can spend the night. If you want."

I felt bad for her, standing there on the streets of her youth, which was, by most definitions, just about gone; offering herself to a man who'd held her and then spurned her, however gently and diplomatically. She tried to hide it, but her desperation to be wanted was growing stronger with each day that passed.

And I did want her. She had the exact earthy qualities that had attracted me all my life. I was lonely and depressed and more than a little scared just then, and it had been, shall we say, a while. The notion of taking her back to my seedy little room and screwing the night away had its attractions.

But the last time we'd gotten involved, Barb had dug herself such a deep emotional hole that digging us out was one of the hardest things I'd ever done. I wasn't about to go through that again. Plus, there was Carole. In some sense, anyway. What are the protocols with women you've made pregnant? I wondered. Do you stay faithful to them till they're no longer pregnant, even if they don't want you?

"Can't do it, darlin'," I said quietly.

She looked down and gnawed the inside of her cheek. "Yeah. The big strapping blond, right?"

"Partly."

"Well," she said after a moment, managing a smile, "just so you're happy."

Which remained to be seen.

"I mean to tellya, Ben," Brian said, guzzling at his paper cup of Donut Hole coffee, "Debra had a fuckin' fit when I told her I was doing this with you today."

We sat in the front seat of my big old Buick in the west lot of Titanium Tower, near the entrance to the Bon Chance Hotel. It was 8:20 and Barb still hadn't arrived. "Ya dumb shit, why'd you tell her?"

His long honest face flushed. "'Cause we have an honest relationship, that's why."

"That's right, you're young yet," I said patiently. "But what I mean is, what if she blabs? I don't want to get nailed. Not yet anyway."

"She won't blab."

"Hope not. And I hope Barb gets here sometime this month."

She actually made it ten minutes later. Came roaring up in her fire-engine red Ford Escort and bounced jiggling and breathless into the backseat of the Buick. "Hi, guys," she puffed. "I'll have you know, this is the middle of the night for this gal. I want you to feel real guilty, Ben."

She wore a full-cut, pleated cotton twill skirt under a blue shirt that was baggy everywhere but across the front. She'd toned down the makeup and the jewelry, restricting herself to just two gold chains. Brian looked good for Titanium Tower, too, in a white shirt, narrow tie, and navy blue Levi slacks. We were just about ready.

I opened the bag on the seat next to me and passed out

the small walkie-talkies. To get their tiny size you sacrificed range—they were good for a couple hundred yards, at best—but they'd do for what I had in mind. We tested them and they seemed to work okay. Barb had trouble with the buttons, though. The sequence and the combinations puzzled her at first, and her long fingernails reduced her dexterity. I drilled her till she seemed to get the hang of it.

Then I handed each of them two prints of the snaps of Angela Barnes that I'd taken outside her Harbortown townhouse. One was profile, one was full face. I described her as best I could and made each of them repeat the descriptions.

"When you see her," I said, optimistically omitting the word "if," "you trail her. Keep her in sight but do not let her catch you. As you get chances, report to me where she's headed. You're to follow her as far as her car and that's it. You describe the car and you tell me where it's at, and then you get clear. Don't go near her. Don't call attention to yourselves. No heroics," I added, eyeing Brian sternly. "Got it?"

They nodded solemnly. I led them into the tower and positioned them at the places I'd picked out before: Brian in the lobby near the elevator banks, and Barb on the mezzanine, where she could watch the atrium mall and the umbilical hallways that led into the tower's wings. I then took up position back in the Buick, where I could watch the main entrances as well as the front of the hotel.

And I waited, and watched. But mostly I waited.

It was a long, grueling seven solid hours of steady vigilance. No breaks. No relief. Nothing but faces and profiles, false alarms and tedium. Occasionally, Barb and Brian would call me on the walkie-talkies. Sometimes with a false alarm, mostly just to bitch. Brian was jumpy, wanted to pounce on every blond or near blond he saw. Barb was bored and her mind kept wandering. At one point she asked me why I didn't think to give them code names, and informed me that if I decided to, she had dibs on Danger One.

The radios seemed to work okay. Brian came in loud and clear but Barb's transmission garbled up from time to time. Either she was still having trouble with the buttons or the steel structure of Titanium Tower was interfering with her transmission.

By 3:30 I was glumly preparing myself for failure. So you blew it, I thought. It happens. You can turn yourself in and put yourself at the mercy of the lawyers and the cops—maybe they can figure out what gives—

"Ben!" crackled the walkie-talkie: Brian whispering urgently. "I got her. Dead bang fer sher."

My heart raced. "Talk to me, Brian."

"She came out a utility stairway." Sneaky Angie: didn't use the elevator. Long walk if she'd started on the thirtieth floor. "She's headed, uh, east."

Toward the atrium mall. "Barb, are you there?"

"Ten-four, hon," came her voice. Ah-ha. An "Adam-12" fan.

"Move to the right, toward the big railing, and look down. See if you can spot her."

Commotion. Then Barb, excited, through heavy static: "I see her. She's entering the mall now."

Brian's transmission stepped all over Barb's. "Into the mall. But she's . . . going across it, continuing east. Could be going up on the mezzanine, could be headed for one of the parking decks."

I fired up the Buick and as I shot forward out of my parking space I made a general announcement: "I'm coming around to the east side. Stay with her. Do not lose her."

"I'm on her," Brian returned.

"Barb, you stay put up on the mezzanine there."

"Ten-four. Mayday," she answered amid the static.

To get around to the east side of the Titanium Tower complex, I had to wheel the Buick past the drive-through bank, over to Culex Drive, east a ways, and then south. Here was the less attractive back side, composed of parking lots and decks plus the apartment tower, which was connected to Titanium by a pedestrian skywalk. There were three separate exits from the parking decks and I took up position opposite the center one.

I fingered my walkie-talkie. "Talk to me, Brian."

"Second level," he reported, voice low and urgent. "I'm following parallel, two lanes over. Lots of cars and dark—"

"I've got your twenty, Ben!" Barb broke in excitedly.

"What? Gimme that again."

"I can see you from up here!" she bubbled. "Wow, this is like watching a spy movie or something!"

I figured she was getting a little punchy from being on her feet all day. "Good, Barb. Keep an eye out now."

"Six-two and even, over and out!"

"There it is," came Brian's voice. "Ready, Ben? Gold Mercury Sable station wagon. Very clean, could be this year's model but who can tell anymore. Can't make the tag from here but definitely standard, not commercial or dealer. She's backing out now. Headed east. Bound for the east down ramp now, Ben, watch out."

"Stay put, Brian." I watched the three exits anxiously. "Barb, you stand by."

"She went down the east ramp, Ben," Brian reported. "Can't see her anymore. She's all yours."

Though it was just four o'clock, there was a fairly steady stream of cars from the parking decks. I sat rigid in the Buick, hunched over the big steering wheel, eyes blipping endlessly, like a radio scanner, from one exit to the next, checking out cars as they exited. Nope. Nope. Well, maybe— nope. Nope. Maybe? Is this it? *Bingo*.

"Got her," I broadcast. "Y'all're clear. G'wan back to the barn and hoist a few brewskis on me. And thanks. I'll catch you on the flip side or sometime."

I threw the walkie-talkie on the seat, shoved the tree shifter into drive, and punched the gas. The big hungry 300 motor slung the heavy Buick toward the parking deck as the gold Mercury Sable station wagon turned north on the access road, headed for Culex Drive. I took the access road, too, and followed about a hundred yards back, studying and memorizing the back end of the Sable, which seemed so dainty and make-believe compared to the big-shouldered brute I was driving.

Behind the Mercury's wheel I could see a single female head. Could have been anybody. I only had Brian's word that it was Angie. First thing you do on a tail is make damn sure you're tailing the right subject, not some poor dumb schmuck from Muddy Boots, Michigan. What a laugh, what an absolute fucking *riot* it would be if—

She abruptly swung left on another access drive instead of going to Culex. I obediently followed and we continued around the Titanium Tower complex toward the west side, Northwestern Highway, and the Lodge Freeway. I hung back at a prudent distance, thinking through the geography: she must be going northwest, like out to Farmington or Novi or—

"Ben!" Barb's voice crackled on the walkie-talkie. "I . . . sure, but it looks . . . following you."

The Sable turned left and zipped along the parking lot past the tower and hotel entrances. I drove with one hand and worked the walkie-talkie with the other. "Come back, Barb, the static chewed you up that time. What's cooking?"

The interference seemed to grow worse, probably because I was getting farther away from her by the minute. Urgency bordering on panic colored the words I could hear. ". . . Man . . . Dodge . . . watching you in the . . . now, and when you start . . . U-turn . . ."

The Sable swung right, then right again onto Northwestern Highway. I had to wait for a kamikaze truck. "Try again, Barb. Slowly now."

"Right . . . look in the . . . Dodge . . ."

The Sable lunged down the entrance ramp onto the northbound Lodge Freeway. I gunned out onto Northwestern and followed her down the ramp. "Forget it, Barb, we lost it," I said into the walkie-talkie. "Thanks anyhow." The Sable was in the center lane. I stayed to the right, in her five-o'clock blind spot, and threw the walkie-talkie over my shoulder into the backseat. Barb's voice, drowning in static, continued for a few moments to sputter back there, like an animal that refused to die: "Please . . . trouble . . . careful, Ben . . . careful . . . careful . . . careful."

Finally—at long last—the hands of my watch met straight up, and I decided to call it a day.

I was in the parking lot of the Michigan Inn, a deluxe

hotel just a stone's throw from Northland Shopping Center in Southfield. It was very warm, very humid, and Friday night; the Michigan Inn parking lot had been hopping for hours. Cars came and went. Drivers argued over parking spaces. Men heckled solitary women. Lovers quarreled. Drunks pissed between cars, looking around nonchalantly as they did so, as if they were fooling anybody. A stoned young woman in red leather hot pants and halter top roamed the lot for a while, plaintively calling for someone named Edgar. I had a feeling her cause was hopeless and that she knew it, too.

As for my cause, who knows?

Angela Barnes had driven straight here, gone inside, and vanished. I checked the desk and learned that she was not registered there, which meant nothing. She might be visiting, or staying under an alias. Or—dreadful thought—she might have pulled the ultimate pro slipperoo, gone out the opposite entrance and driven away in another car.

If that was the case, she was long gone and there was nothing I could do about it. I sat and watched the gold Sable wagon for three uneventful hours. I smoked cigars. Ate some peanuts. Sipped a little water and made use of the widemouthed jar. Listened to the radio, which was, unfortunately, only an AM. Picked up an open-line call-in show on KLOE, a station that catered to Detroit's substrata of cranks and crackpots. One guy spent five minutes preachifying on the merits of a life devoted to Jesus and sex.

To my vast relief, Angie came out about 7:30. She was dressed to the nines in a blazing red suit, a smoldering number that could stop the city dead in its tracks. She also wore a gold choker, a solid gold bracelet, and a thin gold chain around one gorgeous ankle. Her blond hair was pinned and bunned up back and she walked to her car with a gait that was confident to the point of being menacing: a Theresa Russell lookalike on the prowl.

She didn't just get in the car, start it, and drive away like everyone else. Instead, she unlocked the driver's-side door and kind of sat half in and half out: her right leg and haunch inside, her head, shoulders, left leg, and most of the rest of her outside. Only when she had started the Sable did she get

all the way in and close the door. This tickled me because it's
an old mob trick, a precaution against car bombs. The idea is
that if the car is rigged and you're all the way inside, you're
dead; but if you're only half inside, you'll probably survive.
That's the idea, anyway.

I followed her up to the Ten Mile Road, where she
parked and went inside a restaurant called the Golden Mush-
room. I was about to do likewise, but one look at the menu
posted in the glass case beside the door changed my mind.
My attire was not appropriate, nor was my credit card.

Ninety minutes later Angie came out, drove sedately
back to the Michigan Inn, and went inside for good. It was
midnight, I was exhausted, I didn't think she was going
anywhere anymore tonight, and I was prepared if she tried.

I opened the cloth sack that Brian had given me, extracted
one of the spike blocks, got out of the Buick, and walked
down the lane and across to Angie's car. I glanced around; no
one was watching. I dropped the block and used my foot to
shove its business end up against the tread of the left rear
tire. If she backed out, she'd flatten the tire instantly: *poof!*

Back at the Buick, I opened the trunk, took out the
flattened cardboard cartons, and dragged them into the backseat.
I worked for better than twenty minutes, using scissors,
knife, and duct tape, backing off from the car periodically to
inspect my progress. When I was done, I had created what
appeared, at a glance, to be a stack of cartons in the backseat
of the Buick, rising almost to the ceiling.

Perfect. I closed the trunk, climbed into the back,
pushed the cardboard aside, and slid into a sitting position
beneath it. Then I arranged the cardboard back around me.
I'd been afraid that police or private security people would
get curious about a man sitting or sleeping in a car in the
parking lot all night. Now I was out of sight.

It was like being inside a cardboard coffin. It was hot and
close and very uncomfortable, and I didn't like it a bit. I used
my pocket knife to slice a couple of slits at eye level. Through
one of them I could see Angie's Sable wagon, across the lane
from me. Okay.

I leaned back in the seat, trying to get comfortable. For a

while there I didn't think I'd get to sleep at all, despite my exhaustion.

The next thing I knew, I was in flames.

Chapter 22

I'm bobbing and weaving at treetop level, but my Nieuport is getting increasingly hard to control. A rudder wire must have kinked up. That isn't the worst of my problems. My goggles are gone and the blast of wind is making it almost impossible to see. My leg is in agony and filling my boot with blood. That bastard Jerry son of a bitch of a fucking Boche Fokker D-7 had scored a lucky hit, coming at me out of a cloud bank with dual guns blazing. I am out of ammunition and, worst of all, the Fokker is still on me. He knows all my tricks. I can't shake him.

Yet the sadistic Hun does not close in for the kill. He hangs back maybe six hundred meters, at five o'clock to me, following, watching, waiting for me to go down. If I can just make it to the Somme Valley—maybe I can lose him—

Suddenly the hard, full-throttle drone of my Hispano-Suiza motor breaks up, commences briefly, then breaks up again, and with a building, roaring *whoosh*, a fount of flames, brighter than bright, shoots out of the engine. I lunge back, my heart in my throat. Look down, nowhere to land, nothing but trees. No parachute either. Parachutes are for weaklings like the Jerries. Only real men fly for the Royal Flying Corps.

Any instant my petrol is going to go. I'm losing altitude and the Nieuport is not responding to the stick. I look to my right and there's the Hun again, drifting closer now, enjoying the sight. Only now it's not a D-7 anymore, it's a Triplane. It's no longer red but black. Its fuselage, which bore the usual Maltese cross, now carries—what the hell?—a big red maple leaf?—

I must have screamed. I opened my eyes and blinked in the blinding beam of sun, which reached like a dagger through the slit in the cardboard. I was hot, incredibly hot, and drenched in sweat. My right leg was twisted, the big thigh muscle in the furious grip of a charley horse, and the foot had gone numb.

Without thinking, I pawed the cardboard back and away from me and gasped air that was cooler, if only slightly. Then I popped the door open, struggled out, and nearly fell in the parking lot since my right leg refused to take my weight. I used the open door as a crutch and stretched and massaged the leg, enjoying the cool breeze and the feel of the morning sunshine on my face. Only when the pain in my leg had lessened did I look for Angie's car.

Still there.

Babying my leg, I hobbled over to the Sable and retrieved the spoke block. Then, making like "Gunsmoke's" Chester, I limped back to the Buick, opened the driver's door, and fell inside behind the wheel. It was 7:45 A.M. Another wonderful Saturday morning in metropolitan Detroit, promising to be a bright, sunny day. The kind of summer day we live for through our hard, cold winters: brilliant and beautiful and perfect for the beach, for lounging around the pool, for a beer and barbecue party with your friends.

I felt unrested and grungy and viper-mean. How many more nights like that one could I expect to endure? How many more?

Angie did not appear till noon.

I killed the time with cigars and the radio. I had no coffee, nor the means of getting any. Just as well; coffee's a diuretic. I dared not snack because that would trigger a digestive necessity that I had no means of dealing with at the moment. So I smoked and twisted the station knob of the AM radio in a forlorn search for something I could stand to listen to. One station was doing a special on the anniversary of the Barbie doll. Another seemed to be playing "We Are the

World" over and over. I finally stumbled onto a panel discussion with a bunch of professor's answering phone-in questions and giggling a lot. Better than nothing.

When Angie finally did appear, she looked as fresh as the summer day. She wore a white camp shirt with vertical blue stripes and rolled-up sleeves, over a matching pleated skirt that plunged nearly to her ankles. Her blond hair was still bunned tight—don't even loosen up on Saturdays, huh, gal? She wore impenetrable wraparound sunglasses and carried a large canvas tote bag that swung from her shoulder as she strode to her car.

As she performed her half-in, half-out starting ceremony, I found myself staring at the way her skirt hugged her rump. I remembered two movies I'd seen recently, in which men on stakeouts ended up in bed with their sexy subjects. I wondered why that kind of thing never seems to happen to me.

I started the Buick, let her get a small lead, then trailed along, glad to be doing something at last. She didn't go far. First stop, to my eternal relief, was a gas station on Nine Mile Road. She pulled up the full-serve pumps; I grabbed a self-serve. The place was busy and I knew she'd have to wait, so I took the chance and went into the john and did all the business I could, followed by a whore's bath in the sink that ended with a disconsolate look at my bristly, weary face in the mirror, which seemed to be wondering if I was getting too old for this.

I trotted back out to the Buick. Angie's car was being filled. She sat behind the wheel, motionless. I started filling the Buick and picked up a small contact high from the gas fumes. Imagine that, I thought: a car that still uses regular gas. Mustang doesn't use regular. Mustang would giggle if you gave her regular. I popped the hood and checked the oil. Jesus to Jesus, over two quarts down. Son of a bitch! I was leaving a slick trail of multi-vis all over Detroit. Sort of a four-wheeled *Exxon Valdez*.

Angie paid with a credit card. I ran inside, paid cash for the gas as well as for four quarts of overpriced Calvin Klein motor oil, and got back to the Buick just as Angie was pulling away. In this work, timing is everything.

The next stop in our exciting episode of "Afternoon with Angie" was Northland Mall, right across J. L. Hudson Drive from the Michigan Inn. Northland holds the dubious distinction of being the world's first shopping mall—another item on the list of things first made in Detroit. I'm no mall crawler, but entering this one was blessed relief. At least I'd be on my feet now for a while.

I trailed Angie at long range as she threaded her way through the mobs of people. She browsed window displays, occasionally stepped inside a store to finger a hem or hold something up against herself, but didn't actually buy anything till we reached a leather shop. I watched from a distance as she held an earnest discussion with a saleswoman, inspected a set of calfskin luggage minutely, and then did the paperwork bit. She didn't take anything with her. I assumed she was having the stuff delivered.

Hm. Got a trip in mind, Angie, old gal?

Then she backtracked her way toward the other end of the mall. Evidently the luggage buy had whetted her appetite because now she went on a silent, intense buying binge. By my count she made eight stops and bought what had to be well over a thousand bucks of stuff: mostly clothes, plus four pairs of shoes.

Then, with her canvas bag full to bursting, she walked back out to her car. I stayed closer to her than I would have liked, but I didn't want to lose her. She seemed oblivious to her surroundings, anyway. She motored out of the lot, north on J. L. Hudson Drive past the Michigan Inn, and left into the Northland Theater complex, where she parked. I did likewise and followed her inside.

I took a line two over from hers, roughly parallel with her. I heard her buy a ticket for *A Fish Called Wanda* and did likewise. I trailed her past the ticket taker and into the theater itself, where I stood in the back watching Angie take a seat about halfway down, in the middle. I counted rows and seats, then sat down and waited till the movie was fifteen minutes under way. She stayed put.

Time for another calculated risk. I slipped out of the theater and grabbed a pay phone at an island of them that stood in the lobby. From there I could see the theater exits. Of course, if she left through one of the back ones, I was sunk.

So I punched the number as quick as I could. At the female robot's request I fed a bunch of change to the chrome mouth, then waited.

"Under New Management."

"Bill? Ben."

"Benjy! How the hell are ya?" He lowered his voice. "I mean, *where* are you? You all right?"

"Yeah, I'm fine, and never mind where I am. Barb around?"

"Yep, but I'm not entirely sure you really want to talk to her."

"Lemme decide that, okay? Put her on."

"Okay," he said doubtfully. The phone clonked in my ear as he set it down. The familiar sounds of the jukebox, the Foosball machine, and the din of laughter made me feel like I was a million miles away.

"Well, hiya hon!" came Barb at last.

"Hey, sweetheart, howya doing?"

"Well, I'm just—" She lowered her voice. "Things are satisfactory, O Spymaster. What instructions do you have for me?" She exploded in gales of laughter.

"No instructions, Barb. Now listen up."

"That was so great, Ben! I felt just like Mother Harry or somebody!"

Sounded like she got Mata Hari mixed up with Dirty Harry—typical for her even when sober, but at the moment she was better than half-drunk and going downhill fast. "Listen up," I repeated. "About what you were hollering at me at the end there."

"What's that?" she asked blearily.

"As I was driving away from Titanium Tower," I said patiently. "You were hollering something about a Dodge, and some kind of trouble or whatever. I couldn't understand it because the reception went to hell."

"Oh, that," she said disdainfully. Then, a sharp intake of breath. "Oh yeah! There was somebody following you, Ben!"

"What do you mean? How do you know? Take it slow, now."

"A Dodge minivan. I saw it come around when you came around to park that first time. Remember?"

I guessed I understood. "Go on."

"Well, it parked a couple rows over from you. I dint think anything of it. But then, when you started following Angie, it started up again and followed you." She giggled. "It was almost like a parade. Angie and then you and then this Dodge—"

"Sure it was a Dodge?" I asked urgently.

"Or a Chrysler. Or a Plymouth. It definitely wasn't a Toyota. My sister has a Toyota and—"

"What color was it?"

"Some dark color, I think. For God's sake, hon, I wasn't filming the thing." Suddenly she'd gone from giggling to whining. "I was trying to work the buttons on that goofy walkie-talkie you gave me. I broke three nails, you know."

I decided to let it go. What the hell, it could have been anyone, it could have been no one. Not much I could do about it but keep an eye out. "Not to worry, kid. Thanks anyhow. Put Bill back on." After a moment the big bartender answered. "Hoo boy," I said, "you better pour her home pretty soon, partner."

"Got it covered. Elmer Kent's doing the honors this time. Least that's how it's shaping up. They been making goo-goo eyes at each other all afternoon out here. How's life on the run, Benjy?"

"Sucks like a Hoover, quite frankly."

"Well," Bill said heavily, "you better be thanking your lucky stars you're upright and breathing. You remember that guy dropped dead of the food here?"

"Yeah, what about him?" I was getting impatient to get back inside the theater and make sure Angie hadn't ankled me.

"Health people were here again, beating on Eddie. Had some more poopy. What the poor bastard died of was our chili, which he ate on Sunday, the sixth of July," Bill said. "That date mean anything to you?"

It seemed like eight billion years ago. "The day Paul died," I murmured, realization dawning.

"You were here!" Bill said intently. "You ordered chili, remember? Then you changed your mind and this other guy ate it and that was curtains for him." For a moment neither of us said anything. "You realize how close you came?" Bill asked.

I remembered the grease monkey in the jump suit, his whiny voice and skeptical sneer as he thumbed the cardboard menu at Under New Management. The living-color memory made me feel nauseated. "Yeah," I whispered. "Guess I dodged the big bullet again, huh?"

"The biggest one of all. So keep in mind, however bad things are for you right now, they could be a lot worse."

We said our seeyas and I hung up. Stood there for a moment, watching the concession stand with unseeing eyes. I remembered the bowl of chili, bubbling hot and pungent, and the way my stomach suddenly said no thanks. At the time I'd attributed my loss of appetite to the early beers and the tension of the day. Now I wasn't quite so sure.

Add to this the tampering with the Mustang. Throw in the Dodge van that Barb thought was trailing me. All these little things going on around me—was it all coincidence? Or was I stumbling around half-blind in a much bigger and uglier picture?

Six hours later it was the same old story: back in the Buick in the night-drenched parking lot of the Michigan Inn.

After the movie, Angie drove the two hundred feet to the hotel parking lot, parked, and went inside. I didn't see her after that. She must have eaten in the hotel, one of the restaurants or maybe even room service. As I scarfed down a stale ham sandwich out of a baggie, washed down with lukewarm water, I thought about how nice it would be enjoy a room-service cheeseburger with a side of fries and a fistful of something really tasty, like maybe Michelob chasing some Jack Daniel's black.

From there on it was radio, and watching Angie's car, and monotony. Shifting around in the seat. Stretching half-

dead limbs as best I could. My left foot kept wanting to fa
asleep. Radio got four bars into "We Are the World" befor
I could switch the station. I was really starting to sme
myself now. Kept smoking cigars to camouflage it. Som
writer on the radio was talking about his new book, *How t
Get Rich and Famous Overnight*. I sat there and let h:
nasal N'Yuck voice bounce off my ears. God, this wa
getting old.

At 10:30 I called it quits. Waited till I was unobservec
then trotted over to the Sable and slipped a spike bloc
under the left rear tire. I arranged the bogus box pile aroun
me in the Buick's backseat and relaxed as best I coulc
hoping that I wouldn't have to spend another night flying fc
the Twenty-seventh Squadron—

Chapter 23

Click, uh-*click*, uh-*click* . . .
Plang-a-lang.
(Gluey eyes open. Just the palest light. Smell of card
board and night air and my own body. The hell time is it
Still dark.)
Uh-*click*, uh-*click*.
My left eye didn't want to see. I squinted it closed ane
jammed my right eye against the slit in the cardboard. Th
Sable was a little cockeyed, left rear hiked up some. I mad
out just the hint of a shape in the gloom, down low by th
rear bumper. Could have been female. Probably was.
Very very slowly and silently, I inched my wrist up to m
face and checked the time: 1:30 A.M.
Well! I thought with sudden, savage joy. And where are
we off to so early in the morning, young lady?
I didn't dare move. Angie had, no doubt, discovered th

cause of her flat. Hopefully she'd conclude that it was a fluke, something that had fallen off a truck. Something she'd backed over by accident. But sabotage would also occur to her, pro that she was. She would have checked the surrounding cars. She would be extra careful for any sign of surveillance, at least till she was out of here.

So I sat and waited as she changed her tire. Fifteen minutes later the Sable motor cranked and purred. She backed out, swung right, and headed for the exit to J. L. Hudson Drive.

I flung the cardboard off me, tumbled over the seat back into the driver's seat, fumbled the key into the ignition, and started the Buick up. With lights still off, I rolled over to J. L. Hudson Drive in time to see Angie making a right on Northwestern Highway. I powered on down there with headlights on now, made the right, and followed along, allowing Angie a substantial lead.

I *knew* it, I thought. I *knew* there was a pattern there, in the dates of the deaths of the cocaine distributors. Starting with the St. Joe victim on May 11, a cocaine distributor had bought the farm precisely each two weeks. The most recent death had been Paul Reardon on July 6. Tomorrow—today, really—was Sunday, July 20. Two weeks since Paul's death. And Angie was on the loose, just as I'd hoped.

And I had a ringside seat. Hot damn. Soon now. Very, very soon . . .

WELCOME TO

OHIO

THE HEART OF IT ALL!

TOLEDO

CORPORATION LIMIT

I couldn't believe it.

We crossed the border about 3:00 A.M. All the way down I-75, across the glacier-flat plain of Monroe County and the Lake Erie shoreline, I cursed and fumed. I had to hang way back, as much as two miles in places. If Angie got real cute real sudden, I'd be dead out of luck. I had no idea where she was headed; I hoped it wasn't far, like Florida or someplace.

Toledo. Jesus.

Just the faintest mist hung in the night air as we followed the practically deserted freeway into the city. Presently Angie guided us west on I-475. I don't know from Toledo—it, along with the rest of Ohio, is foreign country to me—and I had to stay somewhat closer to Angie than I would have liked.

She got off at the Monroe Street exit. The end of the ramp had a red light that, thank God, she ran; otherwise I'd have had no choice but to come right up on her bumper. She motored northwest on the six-lane commercial strip, then angled due west on Sylvania Avenue, past a couple of intersections, the Michael Mall, and the bucolic grounds of what looked like a monastery. Half a mile farther, she slowed and turned right into the driveway of a dark, gaunt school building.

A school yard in the middle of the night! How interesting.

I continued west a short piece past a large complex of single-story apartment buildings, then U'd as sharply as the Buick would let me and came back gingerly. In the weak light of the randomly placed security lamps I saw the asphalt driveway, the play equipment, the clusters of tall oaks, and the gaunt, three-story brick school building. The carved inscription above the door said HORACE MANN SCHOOL 1930. No sign of Angie anywhere.

I U'd again and came back. I did not follow her up the same lane into the school grounds. Instead I turned into the driveway of the apartment complex that neighbored on the west. This lane ran along a high, vine-covered chain-link fence that separated the complex from the school grounds. I proceeded to the back of the complex to an area of Dumpster wagons, then swung the Buick around in a tight turn, pointed the nose toward the exit, shut off the motor, and got out silently.

It took a moment for my ears, attuned to the glass-pack rumbling of the big Buick motor, to adjust to the powerful silence outside. Evidently there were a lot of forests in these parts, because I could hear the rustling and calling of birds and frogs, the occasional howling of a dog, and the incessant chant of crickets. Now, at two-something A.M. on a Sunday morning, nature had taken over for the moment. Everyone was asleep—everyone but Angie and me.

I retrieved my .45 automatic from its hiding place under the front seat and stuck it under my shirt in the waistband of my jeans. Then I walked as silently as I could across the gravel-strewn asphalt, past the Dumpster area, and onto a deep strip of bristly lawn that separated the apartment complex from the chain-link fence. This, I saw now, was twelve feet high and topped with a spiral band of razor wire. I couldn't tell if this was to keep apartment dwellers out of the school yard, or school kids out of the apartment complex. Nor did I care. I had no plans to jump it. I was here to observe.

I gently tugged at the thick leafy vines till I had fashioned myself a peephole into the school yard. The view was not exactly ideal. A single-story segment of the school building Ld out toward me; to the left of it I could just make out half of the tail section of Angie's car. I moved left about twenty feet, made myself a new peephole, and looked again.

Perfect. Angie's Sable sat in the protective shelter of the school building, well out of sight of the roads to the east and the south. Its light-colored roof caught just a lick of light from the apartment complex's security lamps; aside from that, everything was grainy and muddy and dark. The car sat silent. It could have been abandoned, but I didn't think so. She was inside, waiting.

And wait we did, for over twenty minutes. My legs and eyes were getting tired from the strain and from the lack of sleep. A vindictive voice inside whined, *And you're not even getting* paid *for this*! My back, facing the apartment complex, felt exposed; any minute I expected to hear a voice call, Hey you! What're you doing? Get over here.

Then, in the distance, I heard the faint hiss of turning tires. The hum of an approaching motor. And a car, with lights out, appeared to my right, headed toward me, bound for the back of the school building where Angie waited. It was a Mercedes-Benz. As it came toward me I blinked, not believing my eyes, but there it was, sure enough: a vanity plate on the front that said VIP ON BOARD. It was tough to tell the color in the poor light, but as the car swept by my vantage point I concluded that it could very well be candy-apple red.

Marty Stempel. Mrs. Sturtevant's "godson."

"I'm doing high-class work with high-class people," he'd told me. People like Angela Barnes. Very interesting.

The Mercedes swerved around sharply, eased up next to the right side of the Sable, and stopped. The engine died. For a moment I wasn't sure what was happening; the light was that lousy. Then I realized that the passenger-side window of the Sable had come down; ditto for the driver's window on the Mercedes. I clearly saw a large athletic bag go from the Mercedes to the Sable; then a thick brown paper parcel went the other way.

Then nothing. The cars just sat there. I blinked and stared, trying to make out what was—

Phip-phip.

Silence again.

For a minute I wasn't sure. The sound was muffled; it could have been a loud cough from inside one of the cars. But I doubted it.

The driver's door of the Sable opened and Angela Barnes got out. In the bad light she was anything but angelic: a ghostlike figure, indistinct, light above, dark beneath, her movements appearing jerky as if lighted by a strobe. She walked around to the passenger side of the Mercedes, opened the front door, reached in, and came back out clutching something—it looked like that parcel she'd handed over before. She started to close the door, then changed her mind. She raised her right hand, which had been obscured till now, and aimed into the car. Two flashes, no brighter than the rapid flick of a Bic. *Phip-phip.*

Insurance shots.

As she walked briskly back to the driver's side of her car, I thought numbly: Well, there it is. What more do you need? I realized I'd jerked my .45 out of my waistband. I put it back. No need for it. My job was not to avenge Marty

Stempel. He'd assumed the risk of his business and he'd lost—a fact that would not break Mrs. Sturtevant's heart and certainly didn't break mine.

Nope. My job was to nail Angie. And I could do that now, if I got the drop on her, and—

But what the hell is she up to? *Really?*

As I stood there debating, Angie got inside the Sable. The engine came on but not the lights. She pulled forward and began a tight turn that would take her back to the exit from the school yard.

I turned and jogged to the Buick. Fired it up and barreled up the lane to Sylvania Avenue. Angie's Sable was just a blur of taillights to the left, half a mile away and gaining. I turned and gunned hard onto Sylvania. As I did so, I caught just a blink from the dashboard. The oil pressure idiot light had flashed for an instant. Jesus: running low on oil again! No time to fool with it now.

I pushed the Buick hard and gained gradually. Angie was beating gears; I had to run the light at Monroe, but by the time we reached the I-475 entrance I was back within good tailing range.

She led me east on I-475 to northbound I-75. Ten minutes later we crossed the line back into Michigan, bound for Detroit.

The powerful purr of the Buick motor sounded fine. No more idiot lights flashed. But I'd have to top off the oil soon. If I got the chance.

In the meantime, false dawn was lighting the rim of the eastern horizon. Angie motored comfortably north ahead of me, in the center lane, at sixty mph. I imagined her up there, listening to easy music on the radio, enjoying the afterglow of another job well done. I wondered how much cocaine and cash she'd collected in her six hits. I wondered at the courage— bordering on insanity—it took to work for the mob and rip them off at the same time. I wondered what she was planning to do now.

And, most especially, I wondered how I was going to take her down.

* * *

The Greyhound Bus Terminal occupies a small city block in the heart of downtown Detroit, almost smack on a line between Cadillac Square and the gleaming towers of the Renaissance Center. Normally you can whistle Dixie finding a place to park around there. But at 5:00 A.M. on Sunday morning there was parking aplenty. Angie circled the block and took a spot on Congress, across the street from the terminal. I continued past Bates and took a loading-zone spot just before Woodward. As I got out of the Buick, Angie was entering the bus terminal, the big blue athletic bag swinging in her hand.

I trotted down there. Full summer daylight was building fast, promising another spectacular day. For a Sunday morning, the city sidewalks were pretty busy, and not just with loafers and vagrants. Several cabs disgorged travelers bound for the bus station. A couple of joggers panted along, hastening their heart attacks. A squad of cabbies bunched around the lead taxi in the bus-station pickup line, smoking, talking Detroit Tigers, and laughing in high hoarse voices. Delivery trucks threaded their way amid parked and double-parked cars.

I pushed my way through a heavy door into the bus terminal. The air was stuffy and smelled like disinfectant; the color scheme was shades of green—tile floors, walls, fixtures—and not all that pleasant. The waiting area to the right was about half-filled with people, most of them black, several of them stretched lengthwise on the bolted-down chairs, sound asleep.

To the left, off a hallway running to the Randolph Street exit, was the entrance to a Burger King restaurant. It looked incongruously new and bright and cheerful in the otherwise shabby building. The concourse straight ahead was empty except for a couple of people leaning against the wall. The ticket counter was the most popular place and there was Angie, leaning on the counter as her athletic bag sat like a dog at her feet.

This was my first look at her in good light since yesterday, and I saw that she was dressed for action, not for the office. She wore a simple white crewneck top with red-trimmed cuffs turned back at her elbows, over loose, comfortable prewashed jeans that looked newer than new. Her white deck shoes looked pristine also, and her blond hair was bound in a loose ponytail. She wore dark sunglasses and no jewelry and she was talking to the ticket agent, who was shaking his head regretfully. Christ! I thought. Hope to God she isn't taking a bus anywhere.

Evidently, she wasn't. She picked up the athletic bag and strolled out to the waiting area. I busied myself buying a *Free Press* from the yellow box just inside the door. Angie walked right by me, looking for all the world like a lady killing a few minutes. Then, after completing a circuit of the waiting room, she walked to the far wall, which consisted of large green built-in public lockers.

I stuck my newspaper under my arm and leaned against the wall, pretending to loaf. Angie dug a key out of her jeans pocket, used it to open one of the center lockers—four right, three down—and loaded the duffel bag in. Then she locked the locker and strolled casually across the waiting room and into the Burger King. After a moment I sauntered by the entrance and saw her taking a booth by a window looking out at Congress Street. She'd bought herself a paper cup of coffee, a danish, and a newspaper. Evidently, she now had time to kill.

I didn't.

I peered through the doors inside the bus station. Everything looked normal to me. I turned to Elvin Dance, who was lighting a Kool cigarette, and asked softly, "How many people you got in there?"

"Three," he answered, grinning as he puffed smoke. "Pretty invisible, huh?"

"I'm impressed."

"You're also under arrest," Elvin said. "Just thought I'd mention it."

"Yeah, yeah, yeah."

"Hey," he growled, "according to Belleville PD, you assaulted one of their detectives. That's a felony on top of the escape, which is a misdemeanor, on top of the murder, which is, of course, the big enchilada. You done hit the jackpot this time, boy."

It was past 5:30 A.M. now, and Congress Street was getting noticeably busier. Several convention-oriented hotels are located around there, and well-dressed early risers were getting in their morning strolls, power walks, jogs, and runs. The cabbies were getting busier as buses arrived and departed, conveying interchangeable passengers. Last, but certainly not least, there was Elvin and me: a study in contrasts.

It being the weekend, Elvin was decked out a little more casually today. He wore bright white trousers and a light blue sport coat over an open-necked red dress shirt. He also wore an admiral's cap with gold braid and gold trim on the patent-leather brim. He looked crisp and natty, possibly a powerful and well-connected downtown businessman, which, in a sense, he was. I, on the other hand, was still in the outfit I'd started out in Thursday—jeans, blue pullover shirt, high-topped safety shoes—and was not only starting to feel like a vagrant, I was starting to look like one. Well, with any luck, I'd be enjoying a hot shower at Norwegian Wood just a few hours from now.

"I hope this works," Elvin said, peering inside the bus station to see if anything was happening.

"Well, you got it all set up, right?"

"Yeah. We'll take Subject A inside there at the locker. We'll take Subject B when she hits the sidewalk. Should go fine. But you never know." He looked at me. "This is a throw-it-all-together team I've got here, best I could scrape together on a Sunday morning. You better be right about this chick."

I wandered toward the curb and glanced over Elvin's shoulder. Angie still sat in the Burger King's window. She was smiling at the comics page. I wondered what Hobbes and his buddy was up to today. "I saw her blow a guy away down in Toledo earlier this morning," I told Elvin again after waiting for a gaily chattering black family to stroll by. "I figure she's whacking the 'caine distributors and peddling their inventory. What she took off the victim last night is in that locker in there. Be interesting to see who picks it up."

"Yeah," Elvin said impatiently. He stood very close to me and spoke softly. "And you think when we nail her behind that hit down in Toledo, and she'll just roll over on blowing up your buddy, too?"

"Something like that. Hopefully."

He snorted. "You're dreaming. She's a pro, remember? She'll get Hite in the picture. She'll deny everything. In the meantime, you're still under the hammer for that bombing."

"Her own people are gonna want her bad," I said stubbornly. "Maybe when she looks at that, she'll turn state's and roll over a hundred percent in exchange for protection and a new identity and stuff."

Elvin rolled his eyes. "This ain't no storybook," he grumbled, "but you hope for whatever you want. Meantime, let's hope we can get this done clean." He went to the doors again and glanced inside, then strolled back to me, eyes bright. "I think we got a live one."

I drifted over there as Elvin wandered to the curb. A man in a beige raincoat stood near the lockers, glancing around casually. He was bald, wore a scraggly Fu Manchu mustache, and winked gold from his teeth. I looked away swiftly, not wanting him to make me as I'd made him: JoJo, one of Ezra Goforth's goons. The man who, with the oh-so-friendly Gracie, had kidnapped me on Ecorse Road.

Well, then. How interesting. It looked as if Angela, who worked for Savastano, and JoJo, who worked for Goforth, had set traditional and violent rivalry aside and were doing business together.

Some kind of Baptist church group was trooping by on the sidewalk, all smiles and Sunday bonhomie. "Our friend has arrived," I called to Elvin, who was crushing his cigarette on the sidewalk.

He looked at me and smiled. "Well, let's go inside and say hello, shall we?"

Chapter 24

I followed Elvin through the two sets of double doors into the bus terminal. The lobby was getting crowded. As planned, Elvin and I separated; he wandered to the left, toward the hallway that ran to Randolph; I hung back by the door, pacing, hands in pockets, checking my watch often as if I was waiting for someone.

JoJo did not lunge for the locker. He was too slick for that. He strolled the terminal from the Randolph entrance to the Bates entrance and back. I had no idea who Elvin's undercovers were, but it's possible that JoJo's keen underworld instinct smelled trouble. It's also possible that he was just following routine precautions. Who knows.

Finally he went to the same locker Angie had used—four right, three down—opened it, and hoisted out the heavy athletic bag. From the pocket of his raincoat he withdrew a slim cardboard box, the kind you get your blank checks in, and tossed it into the locker. He was just locking the locker when one of Elvin's disciplined, highly trained undercovers went gung-ho and screwed up the whole thing.

"All right! Hold it right here! You're under arrest!" The rookie was young, dark-haired, and burr-cut, dressed in slacks and a pink sport shirt. He stood between me and JoJo, his back to me, and from his posture I could tell he was aiming a handgun at the mob grunt, expecting everything to stop right there just like in the movies.

I'll never forget the expression on JoJo's face. He was a little perplexed, a trifle annoyed, the look you get when you find you've been shorted a dime. The undercover was barking the line about hands in the air when JoJo did something fancy with his right arm and the concealed sawed-off shotgun swung up from under his raincoat, black snout aimed at the undercover, and exploded flame.

The blast took the undercover full in the chest, driving him back and down in a sliding, spinning, bloody mess right toward me. I dived to the floor as people screamed. One of the other undercovers charged at JoJo from the right and JoJo, after working the pump action, calmly blew her away, too. Then he turned and sprinted past the ticket counter for the bus concourse.

I was up on my knees, .45 automatic out, as panicky screaming people rushed past me and through the Congress Street doors. I saw Elvin and another undercover race toward the concourse as JoJo reached the doors down there. Elvin stopped and aimed his .357 Python. He took JoJo out with a single shot dead between his shoulder blades. Instead of opening the door, as JoJo had planned, he crashed through it and lay inert, facedown in a lake of bloody broken glass.

I didn't hang around, however, to enjoy the view. There was a loose end that Elvin and his people seemed to have overlooked. Angie.

With my .45 out, I ran into the Burger King. As expected, she was no longer there; her paper coffee cup still steamed on her table. She couldn't have come back into the terminal without my seeing her. Which meant she must have ducked out the Burger King exit onto Congress.

I ran out the door. Sirens whooped in the distance and groups of angry, frightened people were chattering shrilly on the sidewalk. On the crowded street I saw a blond head bobbing in the distance. It was Angie, walking briskly toward her car.

I ran after her. Damn if she was getting away from me now. Not after all this. Pedestrians, noticing my .45, shouted and pointed and ducked away, giving me wide berth. Angie must have sensed my pursuit, because as she reached her car she looked over her shoulder, saw me, and understood. Calmly she bent, fumbled with her cuff, and came up shooting: *phip-phip*.

I don't know where her shots went. All I know is, they didn't hit me. By the time she aimed, I was already on the way down, and I hit the pavement rolling, bashing up elbows and hips and knees, stopping only when I collided with the curbstone. People were screaming as I got up hands and knees, .45 at the ready, but I was too late. Angie was already diving into the Sable. The range was too long for my .45 and the area was too crowded with civilians; unlike Angie, I wasn't going to take a chance on hitting any innocent bystanders.

The Sable tires shrieked as Angie popped it into gear and roared away, west on Congress toward Woodward, cutting in front of a red Toyota. A headlong ten-second run later, I was in the Buick. I powered it up and jammed it into gear. Angie had not turned at Woodward, but continued straight on Congress. I raced west and, honking like a madman at the cars and pedestrians, ran the red light at Woodward. Up ahead I saw the Sable barrel through the Second Boulevard intersection; evidently Angie didn't see the entrance to the Lodge Freeway just south of there, which was a good thing. I felt I had a better chance of running her to ground on surface streets.

Congress ends at Third Boulevard. Angie swung right wildly as I ran the red at Second. As I swung north on Third, I saw her turn west again on Fort Street. I made the turn, too, violating my third traffic signal in sixty seconds.

And the Buick's oil-pressure light blinked on, then off. Shit.

Angie was standing on the gas. She must have been doing seventy or eighty, casting subtlety to the winds as she used all three westbound lanes of Fort Street, dodging the occasional car and jaywalker. The best I could do at the moment was keep pace.

But that was fine. I felt great. Despite the exhaustion, frustration, tension, and literal imprisonment of the past few days, I felt, at that instant, better than I had in the two weeks since Paul died. At last I was operating. At last the cards were on the table. No more tailing at a distance, burning my eyeballs out; no more endless hours of sitting. Now it was bare-knuckles time, competitive on several levels: driver versus driver, man versus woman, working grunt versus suit, private detective versus mob killer, fancypants Sable V-6 versus my old relic of a Buick V-8.

Despite the bigger engine, the Buick had definite disadvantages. The suspension was about gone and the thing couldn't corner for diddly. There was a lot of play in the wheel, making precision steering impossible. The thing drank gas and was obviously getting perilously low on oil. To Toledo or somewhere I could not chase her. I'd have to take her down soon, in Detroit.

Once you get out of downtown, Fort Street cuts a wide swath through a bleak warehouse and factory district. For a while it parallels the Detroit River as it runs southwest. I kept the Buick at seventy and, by the time we passed under the Ambassador Bridge, was only about a block back of the Sable. At West Grand Boulevard I got my first break; a gigantic semi tractor-trailer rig was stalled in the center of the intersection, and Angie had to stand on her brakes and kind of skid her way around. By the time we broke free of that, I was two car lengths back of her.

Only problem was that the oil-pressure light blinked again. Longer, this time.

On we went, between sixty and seventy, southwest on Fort Street. I kept lunging the Buick at her, hoping to tap her into some kind of spin that would take her down. I didn't care if she got hurt, but I didn't want her dead. I wanted her alive, to cut deals, to testify, to clear me, to resolve Paul's murder and pay some sort of penalty for it, I didn't care what. So shooting at her was out, even if I was a decent shot, even if I had a secure platform to shoot from.

We raced past the Produce Terminal, Cadillac Fleetwood, the Fisher Freeway, and Woodmere Cemetery. Traffic was picking up and we were both doing a lot more dodge 'ems. Angie was obviously not as experienced at this as I was. Several times she almost lost it. I thought she was getting rattled and scared and had no idea what to do, no idea of how to get rid of me.

Just past the Rouge River, there's a fork where Fort Street bears left and Oakwood Boulevard continues straight. Angie jinked left to stay on Fort, and I knew why. Up ahead a piece was an entrance to the Fisher Freeway. If she got on the freeway, I knew I was finished; as I made the turn on Fort Street the oil-pressure light came on and stayed on a good five seconds. The Buick was just about done. Any second the motor would seize up. I had to take Angie out now, before she got on the expressway, come what may.

As we approached the Norfolk & Western railroad crossing, I gave the Buick all the gas pedal there was. The 300 V-8 howled through the red-hot glass-pack muffler and lunged up to eighty, gaining rapidly on the Sable now. I swerved into the left lane as the train tracks came at us, pulled abreast of the Sable, and, as we flew over the tracks, jerked the wheel right, smacking the Sable broadside.

It was no contest. The Buick was half again the weight of the Sable, and the shiny new Mercury just couldn't take it. Angie hopped the curb, charged down a grassy verge, sideswiped a light pole, mowed down thirty feet of chain-link fence, and then, still flying, charged into a field parked dense with semi trailers, where I lost track of her.

By the time I hauled the Buick down to a stop, I'd shot beneath the gigantic overpass complex of the Fisher Freeway interchange. The oil light came on and stayed on, and the motor developed a hard, whiny tone that signaled the end of the line. Sorry, babe. I jammed the car into reverse and backed up, fishtailing, most of the way to the spot where Angie had bought it. Now the oil-pressure light was off and the engine sounded better. I powered the car up onto the shoulder, shut it off, and got out, .45 ready.

All was quiet except for the steady hiss of traffic passing by up on the Fisher Freeway overpass. There was no traffic to speak of on Fort Street. No cars, trucks, or pedestrians. No houses in sight. Nothing but the street, the expressway, and industry, as far as the eye could see. I stood in the sunlight, .45 automatic in hand, then started down the grassy verge toward the ruined chain-link fence, to find Angie once and for all.

The semi trailers were parked in long rows that seemed never to end. Each was gray and orange, with the word BUTWELL printed in giant letters on the side. I clambered carefully over the collapsed fence and entered the yard. Up

ahead about a hundred feet sat the crumpled remains of the
Sable. It had buried itself under the back end of one of the
trailers. The roof was punched down, the windows shattered. I
stopped and waited and watched, but there was no sign of life.

No sign of Angie, either.

Automatic at the ready, I started slowly for the car. As I
veered to the right, I could see that the passenger-side door
was open. There was nothing on the front seat, no Angie
living or dead; just a ton of busted glass.

The yard was silent and spooky. The back ends of the
trailers stood open, like hundreds of hungry dark mouths. I
was jumpy and dry-mouthed; my palms were slick on the
butt of the .45. Where are you, bitch? Could be hiding just
about anywhere—

Then a voice, female, up ahead, out of sight. Speaking in
a conversational tone. "—kill you. I'll just put one through
your knee. That will give you more pain than you've ever felt
before, but it won't kill you and it won't even knock you out.
So behave yourself."

What the hell?

I started forward, gun at the ready. Gingerly stepped
around the corner into a new lane of parked trailers that
yawned away into the distance. To the right, three trailers up,
stood Angela Barnes. On the ground to her right was a large
blue athletic bag, like the one she'd left in the bus station, as
well as a small, knapsack-style handbag. To her left, half-
sitting and half-lying, was an older man in dirty, shabby
clothes—olive drab army pants, ratty old boondockers, and
what was once a white dress shirt that was ten sizes too big
for him. His thin dirty gray hair was cropped at the jawline,
his whiskery face was bloated and bleary, and his jaw moved
spastically, chewing something that wasn't there. His bleary
eyes goggled in amazement at the sight of the statuesque
young blond woman aiming what looked like a Beretta Model
84 automatic pistol at his head.

Reflexively I drew down on her and we locked eyes at
last. She did not budge. "Do it and he dies," she said
tonelessly.

I confess I almost did it. Came so damn close. I mean,

maybe she wouldn't really shoot an innocent man. Maybe she'd only wing him. Maybe she'd miss him entirely. But she hadn't hesitated to shoot at me back there on Congress Street, imperiling all kinds of innocent people. And I remembered what Ezra Goforth had said about her: "She can put one up your nostril at a hundred feet."

I relaxed the tension on the trigger but maintained the bead on her. "That thing aims anywhere near me," I said, "and I'll splatter your ass all over this part of town." Brave talk, considering who I was and what I was carrying. But Angie couldn't know I was a lousy shot. And she would, as an experienced shooter, have a healthy respect for the mess the .45 can make.

She'd lost her sunglasses during the chase. Her blond hair was loose, and damp at the temples. Her eyes were large, widely spaced, and a luminous, compelling green. "Who the *hell* are you?" she asked. No petulance, just curiosity.

"Ben Perkins." The .45 automatic was getting heavy in my hand, so I wrapped both fists around it and held it at my belly, aimed roughly at Angie's face. "And it's all over, Angie."

"I hardly think so." Her voice was smooth and polished, well-bred Oakland County all the way. "In a minute my new gentleman friend and I will be leaving, and you're going to assist us, Mr. Perkins. But first, please enlighten me. What in the hell do you think you're doing?"

"I'm taking you out," I said roughly. "I know all about you. I know you've been zotzing Savastano's white-lady distributors, the people working the upscale circuit. I know you been keeping the dough—my guess is, that's what's in the athletic bag there—and selling the 'caine to one of Goforth's soldiers. Poor old JoJo, *requiescat in pacem*, you should have seen him try to open glass doors with his face back there at the bus station."

I paused for breath and to get my voice under control. "I saw you ace that guy in Toledo last night. Or this morning. Whatever. I was behind the one-way window in the cop house when they hauled you in for questioning. I been living in your rearview for almost three days now, and in your backfield for a couple of weeks—"

"But why?" she asked. She wasn't nervous, tense, or upset. Just intensely curious. "What did I ever do to you?"

I gripped the pistol tightly to control the shaking in my hands. "You blew up my friend," I said. "Two weeks ago today. Don't tell me you've forgotten."

"Two weeks ago?" she murmured. "I was in Cleveland."

"Sure. Maybe you went there after you put the bomb in Paul Reardon's car. The bomb that blew him away on his wedding day."

At the mention of Paul's name, Angie squinted. Her mouth opened and closed. Her pistol remained pointed at the hobo's head. She said, "I knew Paul. We did a little business together. All those other things you say I did are true, of course. But I didn't kill him." Her eyebrows arched and she smiled at me. "You're barking up the wrong tree, Mr. Perkins. I wasn't the one who killed your friend. And I have no idea who did."

Chapter 25

The hobo honked, spat nothing, looked up at Angie through rheumy eyes, and asked, "Hey sweetheart, you want to fuck?"

She barely glanced at him. "Sorry, I can't. It's that time of the month, I'm afraid."

"Come on, honey," he sang in a quavering voice. "I can throw a real good fuck into you."

"Some other time." Her green eyes were steady on me. "So," she said softly, "what do you think, Mr. Perkins?"

"I think you're bullshitting me," I said.

She smiled. "Of course you do. You've obviously got a lot of time and energy invested in your theory. I don't know how you tracked me down, but I must say I'm impressed. It's too bad we had to meet under these conditions. In fact, in a way it's too bad I'm not the one who killed Paul. I hate to see such initiative and tenacity and skill go to waste."

"You do something to me," the hobo sang, "and I'll do something to you."

We stood there in a tableau: Angie aiming her Beretta unerringly at the hobo's head; yours truly pointing the .45 in the general vicinity of Angie's prominent chest. Sunday morning was building to brilliance, bathing us in sunshine as we stood there in the view of the black maws of hundreds of semi trucks. Birds fluttered and sang overhead. Traffic roared in an unending river on the Fisher overpass in the distance behind us. I was strung out to heart-thumping tightness, trying to figure how to take her, fighting the disquieting notion that I'd been terribly wrong all of these days. The woman was convincing.

"Paul stole your dope," I said.

She shook her head impatiently. "He got Davey Jackson's dope by accident, in a car seat he bought. Of course you must know that. I tracked Paul down through that junkyard. Simplicity itself. I offered him five thousand and he accepted eagerly. A good deal for him and an acceptable deal for me—the 'caine was worth eight times that."

"And you were screwing him, right?"

She blinked. "Heavens, no."

"That's not what I heard."

Her eyes flashed. "I can't help what you heard. I don't fuck men who are involved. Too messy. And he didn't want me in any event. He loved his girlfriend. He told me so, believe it or not."

I knew Paul, and I believed it. "Be that as it may, I still think you killed him."

"You can screw her, too," the hobo sang to me.

"Shut up," I advised him. "Can't you see we're busy having a tense showdown?"

Angie ignored that. With her free hand, she smoothed strands of her loose blond hair as she spoke rapidly. "I want you to believe this, Mr. Perkins, because I have vital business today and I would prefer that you and I disengage cleanly. I am a professional. I don't kill for fun or in the heat of the moment. I kill for two reasons only. Mostly for pay, occasionally in self-defense. Paul was no threat to me; nor was he an assigned target. He was a civilian who happened to wander into the picture. We had a pleasant negotiation and concluded our business amicably. Besides, I'm into firearms. All I know about bombs is that the mere thought of them makes me feel icky." The hobo, humming low, had reached for her ankle. She said, "Keep your scabby hands off me, pukebag, or I'll cut your cock off and feed it to a minnow."

"Nice story, Angie," I said nastily, "but it won't hold up." I was, of course, bluffing. Under the circumstances, she was as believable as anyone I'd ever met. It was beginning to look like I'd screwed up, big time. I was angry and embarrassed and just this side of doing something rash.

"I liked Paul," she said in a low voice. "I was sorry when he died. If I knew who killed him, I'd tell you."

"Yeah, sure. You say you were in Cleveland? Prove it."

She considered. "Well," she said slowly, "you could check the papers down there. I'm sure they wrote about the mysterious shooting death of Clara Wellman." She winked. "Another of the distributors, like Stempel and the rest."

Obviously I couldn't run out and verify that now. But it rang true and it fit. According to Fat Bob, the state police computer, cocaine distributors had been dying every two weeks. I'd assumed that Paul's death was part of that pattern. I'd considered myself ingenious for having figured that out. But now it seemed that Angie had been doing an out-of-state killing that day, a killing of which Fat Bob knew nothing.

"You can fuck till you fall out," the hobo mumbled.

Angie, watching me thoughtfully, said, "So what do you say, Mr. Perkins? Put the gun down and I'll move on, out of your life. This doesn't have to get ugly and bloody."

Her wheedling rekindled my anger. I hefted the .45. "Sorry, babe. I may have screwed up a detail or two, but I'm not letting you walk just on your say-so."

"Well, that's too bad," she said mildly. "Here's what we'll do. My car's kaput, so I'll take yours. You toss the keys over here. Then my gentleman friend and I will go to the car. We'll get in, start it up, and drive away. You're free to watch. If you try to interfere, I'll shoot him through the head. You may get me, but I'll certainly splatter him. And if your first shot isn't good, I'll shoot you, too." She cocked her head, half-smiling. "Is that clear?"

I looked at the hobo. He still lay in a half crouch, sunken eyes blurry, chewing on something invisible. It all came down to, did I believe she would really kill him, and did I care if he died. The answer was yes on both counts.

I fished out the Buick keys and tossed them in Angie's direction. She caught them with her free hand. She did not gloat. "Now the pistol," she said.

"Nope," I answered. "You can go. You can even take him with you. But for some reason I don't trust you. If I even think you're fixing to shoot either him or me, I'll blow your fucking head off, swear to God."

She nodded, frowned as she filed that information away, and prodded and hobo with her foot. "On your feet. Let's go."

He shambled vertical. He was a little man, fine-boned and wasted under the grime and the scraps of clothes. He'd seemed oblivious to what was going on, but now I saw that his dark trousers were hanging even darker with dampness that speckled the gravel beneath him. "Nice place in the van there, baby," he said breathlessly. "Sleeping bag and everything. You'll love it."

"Move it," she ordered. "Down the lane there." With the Beretta trained on him and one eye watching me, Angie slung her handbag over her shoulder and picked up the heavy blue athletic bag with her free hand. She followed the vagrant, matching his slow shuffling pace, staying always where she could watch both him and me without turning her head. Pro, all the way.

We moved up the lane between the rows of trailers, an odd-looking procession. I kept my .45 trained on Angie. She walked half backward, Beretta aimed at the vagrant, watching me. I itched to shoot. She knew it and was half-smiling, enjoying the competition, enjoying the sport on this bright summer morning.

We passed the wrecked Sable and came out into the open grassy approach to Fort Street. It would have been pleasant indeed to see a cop car or two there, stopped to investigate, but there was nothing at all, no cars or people in evidence, except for the traffic way up on the Fisher Freeway overpass and a small van that was just disappearing around the southbound curve of Fort Street. Angie escorted her hostage over the crushed chain-link fence and then to the Buick.

I stopped when I reached the fence—still aiming, still waiting for a chance, but I'd given up by then. The bitch was going to get away. Sure, the Buick motor was nearly out of oil and could seize at any moment, but it probably had enough to get her a mile or two up the road and that was all she needed. She could then call a cab or steal a car and be long gone in mere minutes, while I stood here, wheelless and beaten.

Angie took no chances. She walked the hobo around to the driver's side of the Buick and had him open the door, climb in, and slide over, keeping the Beretta trained on his head all the while. Then, with a weather eye on me, she shoved the blue athletic bag onto the front seat next to him. Finally, out of habit, she climbed halfway in, one leg in, one out. I saw her switch the Beretta to her left hand. There was a pause as she evidently groped the key into the ignition.

Then the Buick went.

The blast jumped the front end a foot off its tires, buckled the hood, shattered the windshield, and instantly filled the interior with smoke. An instant later the sound reached me, a clap of gigantic hands that nearly punctured my eardrums. Before I knew it, I was running toward the car. I heard a huge, curiously metallic ripping noise and then a second explosion obliterated the rear as the gas tank went, sending a noxious and oily wave of heat over me as I ran around the front end of the car. The initial smoke cleared and I could see flames raging inside, immolating the vagrant who sat erect at the passenger side, as well as the athletic bag packed with who knows how much cash. The driver's door stood open still, and Angie lay on the grass about a dozen feet from the inferno. Maybe the explosion threw her there, maybe a last-instant reflex caused her to fling herself there. One thing was for sure: she didn't crawl there.

Braving the heat, I darted to the killer, kicked the Beretta out of her hand, and dragged her back from the car. I eased her onto her back. She muttered, her eyelids fluttered, and she looked up at me, the green not so vivid now as the light behind them faded.

"Where's my leg?" she asked.

"Back there in the car."

She coughed. "Don't need it now."

"Reckon not."

She grimaced, then smiled. "Told you I didn't do Paul."

"So you convinced me. Happy now?"

"Sweet Jesus mercy," she said, and died.

The next thing I knew, I was running through a field of dry, waist-high grass toward the gargantuan Fisher Freeway viaduct. I had my .45 in one hand and Angie's handbag in the other. Didn't remember when I stripped that off her, or why. I secured the .45 in my waistband and slowed to a walk as I reached one of the huge cylindrical poured-cement pillars of the viaduct. Fastened to it was a rusted steel ladder that ran up fifty or sixty feet to the freeway deck. I slung Angie's handbag over my shoulder and began the climb.

I realized that my ears were ringing so hard that the sounds of my shoes clonging on the steel rungs, and the hard roar of vehicles on the overpass above, were muffled and indistinct.

But I could hear myself think all right.

Number one—now I knew what happened to the rest of the dynamite stolen from Norwegian Wood.

Number two—as far as I was concerned, this proved Angie's contention that she was not the bomber. She'd paid for that with her life. . . .

As I climbed, I saw the black oily smoke from the blazing Buick rising into the sky, creating an oddly appropriate funeral pyre for the late Angie Barnes. Several cars passed by on Fort Street but no one stopped, even though Angie's body was plainly visible on the grass near the car. . . .

Unless I believed that some random person had just happened along and decided to rig the Buick, the inescapable conclusion was that I was the target. Whoever rigged the car had been on my tail for a long time. I could buy this. I'd been so intent on following Angie, I'd never once considered that someone might be stalking me at the same time.

With myself as target, a lot of what had happened the past two weeks suddenly made a lot more sense. Going all the way back to Paul.

Someone wanted me dead. Saw me working on the Gremlin, assumed it was my personal car, and rigged it. Good-bye, Paul: in the wrong place at the wrong time . . .

Now I was better than halfway up, and straight ahead I could see the hazy skyline of downtown Detroit: a spectacular mix of new steel/glass structures with the old ornate buildings from the city's heyday. Out of nowhere I felt an almost overpowering surge of affection for the old gal, unobstructed by any of the facts. That's when I knew I was getting very tired. . . .

Since killing Paul instead of me, the perpetrator had been in and out of the picture: tailing me, looking for chances. I'd been on the move so much that his—or her—chances had been slim. Swipe the lug nuts. Take a long-distance shot at me on Ecorse Road and kill someone else instead. Good-bye, Del: in the wrong place at the wrong time.

When I'd used the ultralight to escape from the cops, I'd inadvertently shaken off the stalker, too. Somehow he—or she—had gotten onto me again. How? ("Some detective from the Ontario Provincial Police came by yesterday, asking all kinds of questions about you," Brian had told me at Sub Rosa. Maybe this was the character. Maybe he followed Brian that night.) The stalker had stayed on me during the wild ride to Toledo and back, the showdown at the bus station, as well as the chase out to the truck yard. There the stalker had

found his chance at last. Good-bye, Angie: in the wrong place
at the wrong time . . .

At last I reached the deck of the viaduct. I climbed
clumsily over the cement New Jersey–type barricade onto
the littered shoulder of the freeway, feeling the native breeze
and the hard winds from passing vehicles tearing at my
clothes. I was on the southbound side, which was unfortunate, but I stuck out my thumb and hoped for the best. . . .

The question was: who? Suddenly I felt very naked,
standing there on the wide-open overpass. Unless the bomber was totally convinced that he'd gotten me this time, he
could still be hanging around. I had to get clear as fast as I
could. I gestured with my thumb with additional urgency,
only to hear the bray of a truck horn behind me. A Snapper
Tools van had pulled over and was backing up on the pitted
shoulder. As I trotted down to it, my mind, momentarily
freewheeling, locked onto another recent incident—yet another ugly occurrence that I'd written off as a coincidence.
Not necessarily so, I thought. In fact, most likely deliberate,
most likely the stalker again. If true, it would be easy enough
to find out. I decided to make that the first order of business,
once I got clear of here.

I reached the truck and swung up into the cab, purse
and all. The driver, a middle-aged stringbean in gray twill,
barely looked at me, which was a good thing. Otherwise he
might have had second thoughts about picking up an unshaved,
unwashed man in dirty bloodstained clothes and carrying a
woman's handbag. "I'm going to Monroe and then over to
Dundee," he announced.

"I just need to get to the next exit," I said, slamming the
door, grateful to be sitting down and, relatively speaking,
safe.

"Roger," he said, jammed the truck into gear.

"Ben," I answered.

He gave me an odd look. "What's with the purse, pal?"

I leaned back in the hard jostling seat as he worked up
the gears. "Oh, this?" I asked lazily. "Found it back there.
Wonder what's inside?" I unzipped it. A compact. A big
yellow comb. Sunglasses. Then, in plain view, a gold money

clip embracing a thick wad of bills. The top one was a C-note.
The driver, noticing, whistled. I tossed the wad into his lap.
"For your trouble," I said.

"Hey, I can't keep this," he said. But his eyes lit up.

"Don't worry," I said distractedly, "I'm sure whoever lost
it got no more use for it." Tissues, a Tampax, a change purse,
and then a business-size envelope, thick and unsealed.

"More dough?" the driver asked.

I opened the flap. On top was an airline ticket in the
name of BARNES, A. Delta Airlines. Leaving Detroit at
10:00 A.M. today, nonstop to Miami, connecting on something
called Lacsa Airlines to San José, Costa Rica. "No extradition
treaty," I mumbled. This tied in nicely with the expired
rentals on her townhouse and her hidey-hole office.

Beneath that was another plane ticket. Same airlines,
same schedule, same destination. Different name, though.
Someone called HERSHEY, D. Diane? Duane? Demosthenes?

The last items in the envelope were a pair of passports. I
flipped open the first one and saw Angie's unsmiling face.
The other passport was in the name of David Jefferson
Hershey. The name was still unfamiliar to me, but the
passport picture made my gut clench and my spine straight-
en. I reverently put the items back into the envelope and
returned the envelope to the purse.

The driver was coasting the truck up the exit ramp at
Outer Drive at the border of Lincoln Park. "This okay,
mister?" he asked as he squealed the truck to a stop.

"Fine, thanks. Keep the change," I added, and left the
truck with a slam.

A Total gasoline/pop/grocery station sat next to the interchange. I trotted over there, found the open-air phone booth,
dropped some silver, and punched numbers. Bill Scozzafava
was up already—naturally—and agreed to round up Eddie
Cabla and meet me at Under New Management in an hour.
He didn't ask any questions, which was a relief.

The gas man gave me a cab-company number, and I
called and arranged a ride. While waiting, my mind wandered
back to those airline tickets. The flights were to leave at ten,

and it was pushing nine now. I jammed more coins into the phone, got the number from information, and punched.

"Page Mr. David Hershey, please," I said to the man who answered. After a long wait, another voice grunted a hesitant greeting. "Mr. David Hershey?" I asked.

"Yes," the voice said warily.

"The trip's canceled," I said. "Angie just got blown up on the southwest side."

Pause; then: "Who is this?"

"Never mind who this is. Just go on home and wait to hear. It's all over."

"I asked who this is," the voice said.

"This is the guy who, as of now, owns you," I replied. "But don't worry. The price of freedom will be high, but affordable."

A rickety yellow cab clattered into the gas-station driveway and honked. The voice on the phone was asking urgent, angry questions as I hung up gently. That'll keep him, I thought as I sauntered out to the cab.

Chapter 26

"Tell me about the cook," I said.

Aside from the lack of customers—it was just after 10:00 A.M. Sunday, two hours from opening—Under New Management was the same as always, right down to the rebreathed air. That's one of the great things about bars. They're predictable.

Though he wasn't on the clock, Bill Scozzafava stood behind the bar. Force of habit, I guessed. He wore a three-piece navy blue suit, expertly tailored to accommodate his massive body. From somewhere I recalled that he was an inveterate churchgoer and was probably headed to the 11:00 Mass at St. Mary's after this.

Eddie Cabla, on the other hand, looked like he hadn't changed since last night. He wore canvas shorts and a purple tank top from which graying chest hair peeked. His bullet head was polished smooth, as usual, above his small, beady-eyed face. His black-framed glasses with their near-zero correction factor made him look like a diminutive, bald-headed Michael Caine. The bar owner answered me with familiar gruffness; he doesn't like getting up early, he doesn't like being dragged to work on his day off, and he doesn't particularly like me. "The cook? What the hell you wanna know about him for?"

"Who was he?" I asked quietly. God, I needed a smoke. I spotted the cigarette machine by the hallway leading to the johns and wandered over that way.

"Vinnie Sutton," Bill replied.

"Where'd he live?" I asked, digging for change.

"Down in Romulus someplace," Eddie said. "Listen, Perkins, if I'm not mistaken, you're a fugitive, right? So why are we sitting here talking to you instead of siccing the cops on ya?"

"We're doing it," Bill said quietly, "because Ben's our friend. That's why."

I quit feeding the machine coins as Eddie looked at the big bartender. Like most small-time bullies, he caved in to what he took to be a threat. "All right! Okay!" He looked at me. "He only worked here a few weeks. Then one day he just quit showing up."

"Okay," I said. I pulled the handle under Camel and retrieved the pack as it thunked out. "Now. This guy who died from the poisoning. He ate here on the sixth of July, right?" Bill nodded. "When did this Vinnie guy quit?"

"I don't know"—Eddie shrugged—"a few days after that, I guess. 'Cause then the guy died, and—"

"What did he look like?" I prodded, opening the pack.

"Look like?" Eddie exploded. "Just a guy. Tall, bushy-haired, middle-aged. Pretty good shape, I'd say."

Bill said thoughtfully, "Wait a minute, Ed. You've got a

stat of his ID around here someplace, don't you? You always get that from the help when they hire in."

Cabla was shaking his head. "Nah, nah, nah. Health people took all that away."

"You gave them copies," Bill reminded him. "You still have the originals."

"Guess so," Eddie grumped.

I fired up a cigarette and inhaled so deep I thought the drag would get stuck down there. Suddenly I felt light-headed. No doubt from the smoke, but only partly; I think it was also from the realization that I was about to get to the bottom of this mess at last. "Shall we have a look?"

Eddie, shaking his head, led us through the door behind the bar. Funny, in all the years I'd been hanging around Under New Management, I'd never been in the back. There wasn't much to see. There was a supply room, the keg closet, the now-dormant kitchen, and, finally, in a space the size of a walk-in closet, the office.

Eddie, muttering, led us there, opened the file drawer in the battered green desk, and began flicking along the manila tabs with his fingers. I glanced at Bill, who was leaning on the wall near me, watching; he gave me a wink. I looked back as Eddie, who'd extracted a file folder from the drawer. He peered inside it officiously, then handed it to me.

I opened the folder. On top was a standard employment application form, filled out in a looping longhand. Beneath it was a photostat of a Michigan driver's license in the name of Vincent Sutton. To this day, I don't remember what the address said, because my eyes were seized by the grainy black-and-white picture staring up at me.

The Vincent part was right. But the man who'd been Under New Management's cook, the man who'd tried to poison me and shoot me, who'd twice tried and failed to blow me up, was Vincent Wakefield.

I blinked and looked at it again. Still Vince. I was only vaguely aware of the men watching me. I said, "Oh yeah. Uh-huh." I turned and strolled back into the barroom, looking at nothing.

When Bill spoke from behind me, I was pulling myself a Stroh's dark from one of the taps. "You know him, huh, Ben?"

"Knew him once, yeah, years ago," I answered, words a half mumble from the cigarette hanging in my lips. I finished drawing the beer, strolled out into the seating area, leaned on the edge of a table, and looked back at my friend. "We got tangled up in a case together. Never were friends, though. We needed each other, was the thing. Hell," I said, making a grin that I knew did not look nice, "I never did trust him. Hit him a few times, in fact." Eddie had come into the barroom and he lingered by the jukebox, watching me. "He killed some friends of mine, in the end," I added quietly. "Got away clean."

"Good Lord," Bill said.

I drank the top off the beer. It was chilly and tasty and kindled a friendly glow in the floor of my stomach. Nothing's as good as beer in the morning, which is why I hardly ever do it. "I always said—I told my client—I said I'd kill the son of a bitch, I said I'd get him back for what he did to my friends." I remembered the conversation I'd had with Joann Sturtevant just a couple of weeks ago, about this very thing. I shook my head and looked away from the men, determined to keep my vision from blurring. "Never occurred to me he'd double back at me. I mean, all I took from him was money. God*damn* he carries a grudge a long time."

Eddie stirred. "So," he said with sour disbelief, "I'm in a shitpot of trouble with the bar here all because this asshole was after *you*? I got *you* to thank for this mess I'm in?"

"You know what's weird?" I said suddenly, looking at Bill. "I've been dreaming about this guy. I dreamed about him in the hospital with Carole. And then there was France— that Fokker D-7 had a maple leaf. Vince is Canadian." I shook my head and looked away. "My subconscious must have sensed something."

"Whatever," Bill observed. "It looks to me like your luck in this thing has been just a shade better than his."

I was only half listening, because a little voice was whispering in my mind, making a grin as big as all outdoors spread across my face.

"Yeah," I said, "and you know what? His luck just got a whole lot worse."

Monday morning, 8:00 A.M. Another brilliant day had dawned in downtown Detroit. I stood in the center of the cylindrical skywalk that runs between the New Center One and New Center Two office buildings. Through the porthole windows I could see the massive Fisher Building and the General Motors Building, as well as the boulevard dense with morning commute traffic. I was right on time; it looked like the men I was there to meet were going to run late, but that didn't upset me. I felt pretty lucky I'd been able to arrange this meeting at all.

The day before, Bill Scozzafava, foregoing Mass, had driven me up to the Shine Inn, where I'd rescued the last serviceable junker I owned: a rust brown Mercury Montego with no spare tire and a bashed-in, rusted-shut driver's-side door. I'd limped it out to the suburb of Inkster, where, on a whim, I registered at a tiny transient motel called the Dexter Lakes. It was cheap and anonymous, but a step up from the Czar Nicholas—by which I mean that my room had a private bath, its own telephone, a coin-operated vibrator bed, and no cockroach scoreboard on the wall. After taking my first shower in nearly five days, I'd occupied myself with phone calls and negotiations. No doubt Camp David had been easier to arrange than this meeting.

After ten minutes of loafing, I spotted a man at the north end of the skywalk, standing there watching me. Though he wore a business suit just like the other people who'd strode purposefully through the skywalk, there was an edge in his eyes, a wariness in his posture. I gestured. He disappeared for a moment, then appeared again with another man, who walked along the skywalk toward me.

"'Morning," I said as Rick Savastano reached me.

The mob boss was dapper as ever this morning: dove gray suit, glossy black shoes, gold stickpin in his tie, and gold chain across the vest. I caught the aroma of Brut 33 from him, and he was freshly talced, manicured, and polished. But all the cosmetics in the world could not hide the weariness in his eyes and the loose skin of his fighter-pilot face. The man needed a vacation. Badly.

"Where is he?" Savastano asked neutrally.

"He'll be—oh. Here he comes now."

Ezra Goforth approached us from the south end of the skywalk. He wore a short-sleeve red check shirt, canvas pants, and high-topped black leather work shoes. His compressed face looked even tanner than it had before, setting off those very cold blue eyes; and unlike Savastano he was jaunty and grinning, with a spring in his step. As he approached us his hoarse metallic voice rang in the skywalk. "Jesus H. Christ, either the feds have this place surrounded or those are Ricky's fuckin' entourage hanging around the joint trying to look inconspicuous. Oh, hi there, Ricky, how's tricks?"

"'Morning," Savastano said coldly. They did not shake hands.

"Hey, hey," I said brightly, "the gang's all here."

Neither man found this funny. "Let's get on with it, Perkins," Savastano said edgily.

The three of us stood there, almost elbow to elbow in a casual conversational arc, looking out the portholes of the skywalk at the boulevard. "Okay," I said. "This is about the person who killed the string of drug distributors." My glance took in both men. "That person is dead and will be causing no more trouble. Further," I said, fixing on Savastano, "you can take my word for it that the perpetrator did not belong to the Pontiac operation. Goforth and his people are clean. If you want to go to war with them, by all means be my guest. Kill each other to your little hearts' content. But don't do it on a misunderstanding. Okay?"

The mob bosses stood thee silently, looking out the windows at nothing. Savastano broke the silence. "Who was the shooter?"

"If I answered that, you'd be very sorry you asked. So let's just let it go, okay?"

Goforth turned on me, grin unpleasant. "Well then," he said hoarsely, "s'pose you tell *me* then."

"Same answer goes for you."

Goforth jammed his hands angrily in his back pockets

and looked away from us. Savastano stared at me, long lean face pale and showing his age. A couple of businessmen strode past us, hardly giving us a second look. When they were out of earshot, I said, "Look, guys. There's some things you're better off not knowing. Let's let bygones be bygones and get on with our lives. Whaddya say?"

They glanced at each other. Goforth said, "Yeah, screw it, I got too much to do, how about you, Ricky?"

Savastano said in a low, strangled voice, "I don't like it. But yeah, let's go make some money."

"Warms my heart," I said. "Now. Let's talk about how you two are going to reward me for having effected this, ah, truce."

"You got our most fervent thanks," Goforth said, grinning. "That'll suffice, won't it?"

"Not hardly." Three brightly chattering women swept past us. I gestured the men closer and we looked out the windows again. "There's this guy. Vincent Wakefield. Canadian; works out of Windsor. He's gotten to be a real annoyance. In fact, it's fair to say that he's a genuine threat. I want him out of my face and out of my life." I took a deep breath and said, "I want him dead, and I want you guys to arrange it."

My feelings were the same as when I proposed to Carole via Will: I couldn't believe I had uttered the words. A long, silent minute passed as my heart pounded. My answer came from Goforth, in the form of a snicker. "You're putting out a *hit*? Ben Perkins, man on the white horse, is putting out a *contract* on a guy? Lordy mercy."

"You need expert help," I answered, "you contract with professionals."

Savastano was not so amused. "You're out of your mind, Perkins. We don't do that sort of thing these days."

"The hell you don't. Come on, fellas, I came through for you, now you come through for me."

Goforth looked at me, ruddy face grinning. "In return for your efforts, what you get is the satisfaction of a job well done. Be happy with that. S'long, guys, it's been real." He turned on his heel and sauntered away, whistling "Camptown Races," *do*-dah, *do*-dah.

Savastano was headed the opposite way, shaking his head regretfully. "Too bad, Ben," he called back to me. "Better luck next time."

I trailed after him. At the end of the skywalk, waiting by the door, was the goon I'd spotted before. He was a study in incongruity: shoulder-length brown hair, Rollie Fingers mustache, finely tailored Savile Row business suit. He was wall-sized, probably armed and evidently unhappy at the way I followed his boss. "Rick," I said, "we're not done with our business, pal."

"Afraid so, Ben," Savastano answered without looking back.

"Better think again."

Savastano spoke quietly to his associate. "Make him disappear, please. Don't bother being polite about it."

The goon started for me in a heavy, lumbering step, eyes bored now that he had instructions that he had carried out hundreds of times before. I stood my ground but took no steps to defend myself. "I think it's in your interest that I stay healthy, Mr. Savastano. Or, should I say, Mr. Hershey of San José?"

The mob boss stopped suddenly at the end of the skywalk. Just then the thug, unaware that things had changed, bumped me, hard. I didn't take offense, just pointed past him and said, "I think maybe Mr. Savastano has had a change of heart, Igor. What do you say, Rick?"

Chapter 27

The boss turned and faced me, face expressionless, eyes dead unreadable holes.

"Ah," I said. "I thought so. Do me a favor, Rick?" I thumbed at the thug. "Make him disappear, please. Don't bother being polite about it."

Savastano opened his mouth, cleared his throat, and said, almost inaudibly, "Go smoke a cigarette, Rodney."

On cue, the thug lurched past his boss and disappeared into the skywalk stairwell. Savastano and I regarded each other for a minute. "Can we talk?" I asked.

He nodded, once, abruptly, and walked with me about a third of the way back into the skywalk. I got out a cigar and lighted it. He winced and kept his distance but made no comment. The skywalk was virtually deserted now. I figured the suits were all at their desks now, ready to begin a brand spanking new week.

Savastano broke the silence. "That was you on the phone? At the airport?"

"Yep. That was me." I exhaled smoke. "And, just for the record, I have the passports and the plane tickets."

"What about the money?"

"For shame. I'd have thought you'd be asking about the last moments of your lady love, first."

He breathed through his open mouth. "Did you kill Angela?"

I couldn't tell if it was a statement or a question. "Matter of fact, no. Just so happens this Wakefield guy I was talking about? He did it. He was aiming for me, got her instead. Blew her leg off. Don't worry, she didn't suffer much. As for the money, well, sorry. It got fried along with the Buick."

"Awful," he whispered, in what had to be the only word of honest emotion I ever heard out of him.

"Yeah, you're right," I said, examining the glow of my cigar. "Money you can always replace, and another shooter you can always hire. But they don't make cars like that Buick anymore."

Savastano turned, hot-eyed, and his hands came up reflexively, his body coiled as if he was about to lunge at me. I stepped back and spread my hands, suddenly pumped, ready to throw him through the wall of the skywalk. Almost at once he dropped his hands and straightened and looked out the window, safe inside that rock-hard shell that, evidently, only Angela Barnes had ever been able to penetrate. "What do you want?" he asked quietly.

"Well, let's see. Hit the Lotto for a couple mil. A dusk-to-dawn with Stephanie Zimbalist. High-test at thirty a gallon. And, like I said before," I added, "I want Vince Wakefield dead."

"I told you. We don't work like—"

"You must have been really hung up on her," I observed. Savastano didn't answer. "Was it that, or was it you wanted to retire from a business not known for its retirement plans? Or was it both nooky and retirement that drove you to kill your own people and steal your own product?"

The mob boss whispered, "You can't squeeze me."

I knocked off a hunk of ash. "Buddy, you're hanging by gnawed fingernails from a cliff that's steeper than a cow's face, and you fucking well know it. So don't be impolite to me."

He turned away. I stayed still and silent. When he looked back at me, his face was resolute. Whatever heart the man had was shut away. It was all business now. "If I make the arrangements? What then?"

"Then we're square."

"You'll return the items."

"I didn't say that."

"You'll destroy them?"

"I didn't say that either."

His voice got an edge. "There must be a quid pro—"

"And there is. What you get is, the documents stay private."

"That will not do. You could squeeze me forever."

"True, if you assume I want anything to do with you or your business, which I don't. Trust me."

Savastano glowered. "Maybe," he said in a very low voice, "I'll just have you taken out if you don't do as I say."

"There's that," I admitted. "But then, you never know. There might be, say, copies of the stuff in a safe-deposit box. I just might tell my lawyer to see to it that in the event of my demise, the stuff gets distributed to certain people." I smiled.

"Such as one Mr. Tagucci. That name familiar to you? How about Steve Ricci? Think he'd be fascinated?"

There was no clean way out for him and he knew it. Suddenly I was no longer enjoying this. I wanted the sordid business done with. Savastano evidently felt the same. He said, "Vincent Wakefield. From Windsor, you say?"

"Once lived on John Donne Close over there. He's positioned himself as a labor consultant, I gather. Street operator. Posed as an OPP detective. Six-two, one-ninety, curly dark hair—"

"We'll find him," the mob boss said. "Anything else?" he asked, voice remote.

"One other thing. Make it conspicuous, so it gets in the papers. That's how I'll know it got done."

Savastano nodded, his mind elsewhere. After a moment's silence he said neutrally, "This really surprises me, Ben."

"Well, it's a funny line of work I'm in." I didn't bother to explain that, to me, this was equivalent to picking up a gun and shooting back. Wakefield had made several attempts on me and killed one of my best friends. He'd given no warning, so I owed him none. This was a street matter, governed by street rules, of which the first is that there aren't any.

There was no percentage in taking Wakefield on myself. As I'd told Mrs. Sturtevant, I'm no killer. I needed the expert services of one, and I'd just contracted for them. Had Wakefield used the same common sense, I'd be dead now. And Paul would be alive. Something I would always remember.

As I looked at Savastano, it occurred to me that I might never see him again. Word of his disloyalty wouldn't leak from me, but if this was any indication of what his judgment had been like lately, he might very well be facing, shall we say, forced retirement. I wondered if he cared. Somehow I sensed that he didn't, much. "If you need a personal reason to take care of Vince, keep in mind that he's the one who blew up your one-and-only true lady love."

"I haven't forgotten," Savastano answered.

"Neither have I. He killed mine, too, once." Ignoring the flicker of surprise in the mob boss's eyes, I hooked my cigar in my teeth, turned, and sauntered away from him, waving. "Seeya, Rick. Would love to buy you lunch, but I got a date with a prosecutor."

"The people versus Benjamin Perkins," intoned the clerk. "This is on for preliminary examination, your honor. Charges are aggravated murder, resisting arrest, and assaulting a police officer, Defendant is free on fifty-thousand cash bail."

"Very well," the iron-haired judge said, rippling officiously through some papers. "For the people?"

"David Fence, your honor," the assistant DA said, rising briefly. He was an emaciated young man with thick glasses and whispery-thin permed brown hair.

"For the defendant?"

"Shaughnessy Levin," my chief counsel said politely, rising to her five feet four. "Assisted by Carole Somers."

"Very well. Motions?" There were none. "Prosecutor?"

"People call Chief Jack Hatfield."

As the beefy chief lumbered up to the stand and took the oath, I glanced around the courtroom. It was modern and Spartan with a low ceiling, unadorned wood paneling, and room for perhaps sixty spectators. The air-conditioning was hopelessly outmatched by the heat, and I was awash in perspiration under my navy blue pin-striped suit. The chairs were half-full with people who were paying scant attention to the proceedings. The public-address system was barely able to overcome the steady din. Jesus Christ, I thought. The scariest moment of my life, and I can hardly hear what's going on!

The DA took Hatfield through a brief recitation of the facts surrounding the death of Paul Reardon. My two lawyers sat attentively down the table from me. Shaun Levin was her usual vivid self, dressed today in an electric blue pantsuit expertly cut to fit her butterball body. Carole wore a wine-colored suit over a white blouse.

It felt good to see her. Levin had been handling the nitty-gritty since I surfaced; she took care of the arraignment, where I was charged and where bail was set. I'd had to pay a bondsman five thousand nonrefundable dollars to end my three-day stay at the luxurious Wayne County Jail. My only contact with Carole, till today, had been on the phone, and she'd resolutely avoided any personal conversation.

Carole caught my glance and gave me a tiny wink. I returned it. I wondered how she was handling the aftermath of the abortion. I wondered what she thought of my proposal, once she got done laughing. I wondered if I'd ever—

"No questions, your honor," Levin said.

"You may step down, Chief Hatfield. Prosecutor?"

"People call Ellen Reardon."

Here she was, the Judas of the piece. She strode to the stand past the departing Hatfield and took the oath without looking my way. She didn't seem the least bit rabbity or scared today. She looked calm and purposeful and summer-casual in her khaki shirtdress and flat shoes. She looked tanner than when I'd last seen her, and her short blond hair was streaked even whiter in places. Been doing some beaches, huh, bitch?

As if reading my mind, Levin touched my arm lightly. I gave her a nod. All's cool. I'm not going to kill the bimbo. Yet.

"Mrs. Reardon," the skinny prosecutor began, "what is your relationship with the victim in this matter?"

"Paul was my husband," Ellen answered. Her voice betrayed tension, but the words came trippingly enough. She'd been coached.

"And what is—or, shall I say, was—your relationship with the defendant?"

"Mr. Perkins managed maintenance and security at the apartment complex where we live." After a pause, she added without inflection, "Where we lived."

"I see. More to the point, Mrs. Reardon—and I realize this is not easy for you; your husband has been deceased only a few weeks—what was your personal relationship with the defendant?"

"We were friendly. Actually, he was more friends with Paul than he was with me. But we all went out together a lot. Bowling and out to the clubs and such."

The prosecutor, watching Ellen keenly, missed a beat.

That was my first indication that something unexpected was happening. My lawyers felt something in the wind, too. They looked really involved in the exchange, for the first time.

The prosecutor cleared his throat and smiled indulgently. "Please tell us about your *personal* relationship with Ben Perkins, Mrs. Reardon."

"I just did," Ellen said blandly.

The prosecutor gave her a cross look. "Your honor, a fifteen-minute recess to confer with the witness?"

"I object," Levin said, tone puzzled. "Counsel should prepare his witness before the proceedings, not during. Let's get on with it."

"I agree," the judge said. "I'll let you struggle along for a while longer, Mr. Fence. Please proceed."

He turned on Ellen. "Isn't it a fact, Mrs. Reardon," he said, tone harder now, "that you and Mr. Perkins were involved in a lengthy and illicit sexual relationship?"

"That is not true," Ellen said, a catch in her voice.

I hardly dared to breathe. What the *hell*?

The prosecutor had the same thoughts. His voice went up a half octave. "I remind you of your taped statement, in which you—"

"Oh, that," Ellen said, waving a hand. "I was . . . well, that was just a few days after my husband was killed. I was on prescribed tranquilizers. And, frankly, I was drinking a lot." She still did not look toward the defense table. "My mind wasn't tracking so well. I was angry and scared. I said a lot of things I shouldn't have, that I didn't—"

"But," the prosecutor said hotly, "you *testified* that you and Mr. Perkins—Now look here—do you understand what the word 'perjury' means?"

"Objection," Levin said mildly. "Counsel is arguing with his own witness."

"I object to *that*," the prosecutor sputtered, "as irrelevant."

The judge held up both hands, face a study in patience. "Order, please," she said calmly. "Mr. Prosecutor, where are we going with this witness?"

He blinked owlishly. "Well, I—"

"I see. Are there any other witnesses?" She asked it almost kindly.

He stalked back to his chair and dropped into it. "No, judge."

"You may step down," the judge informed Ellen. "Motions?"

"Move to dismiss all counts," Levin said promptly, "with prejudice, if it please the court."

The prosecutor was already putting his folders away, head bent to listen to Jack Hatfield, who was whispering in his ear. "No objection, your honor," he said.

The judge asked, "The people agree to dismiss the resisting and assault charges as well?"

"That's right, your honor."

She rapped her gavel once. "So ordered. The defendant is discharged. We'll take a ten-minute recess."

And, just like that, it was over.

Shaun Levin faced me and shook my hand as the interminable courtroom buzz, which had never abated, went up a notch. "How's that for superior lawyering?" she asked with a cherubic smile.

"You done good, kid," I answered. "Thanks." Carole was next. Her smile was remote. She gave me a swift and very prim hug, which surprised me. I eased her back, holding both her hands. "Doesn't this violate courtroom decorum, or whatever?"

She released her hands and reached to the table for her briefcase and portfolio. "Why don't you come out later for dinner? We'll put on a good feed and celebrate. Okay?"

"Sounds like a winner."

She joined Shaun Levin and the pair of them walked out of the courtroom, threading their way through the crowd. The defense table was already being commandeered by other people, briskly laying out file folders and exhibits and stuff. I picked up my pad and newspaper and headed for the door. Nobody gave me a second look. The drama, it seemed, had passed almost unnoticed in this room, and I was history already.

Except to some people. Jack Hatfield, beefy and burly in his baggy gray suit, stood just inside the double doors, arms folded, tiny beady eyes on me as I approached. "Now," the old cop rumbled, "what in the hell was that all about? You get to her somehow?"

"No way, not me, Chief," I said. We pushed our way through the doors and into the hallway. "We weren't even going to contest the arraignment. Ellen's switch came as a total surprise."

We cleared the crowd and emerged into a vacant stretch of hallway, the green tile floor drenched with sun that poured through large windows. I fired up a cigar and applied my match to the ratty little stump of one that Hatfield produced from his coat pocket. He puffed it to life and then said quietly, "Well, truth be told, I never thought you done it, even after the little bitch come up with that cockamamie story."

We stopped between the center window and the door of a vacant courtroom. "That why you persuaded the DA to drop the assault and resisting charges?" I asked. "'Cause you felt guilty?"

"No. Figured I owed you one." At my surprised look, Hatfield said, "Detective Portman needed an attitude adjustment real bad. Too many old TV movies gave him a bad case of mouth. Appreciate your adjusting him for me."

"Hey. What can I say. Anytime, Chief."

He examined my face bleakly. "Just try to stay out of trouble for the rest of the summer. Please."

I raised my right hand. "Scout's honor."

Hatfield rolled his eyes and turned to the window, squinting as he looked out at the courthouse lawn and the traffic that teemed up the broad granite steps. "So, we ever gonna know who killed Paul Reardon?"

I thought for a moment. Then I said, "Well, Chief, let's put it this way. Lot of people die in this mean old world. In fact, pretty near everyone. Some die peaceable, some not. We try our best, but in a lot of cases, there's no accounting for why."

I folded the morning *Free Press* and handed it to him. "Like for example, that story at the bottom there."

The article, accompanied by a color picture, occupied the lower third of the front page:

MAN GUNNED DOWN "GANGLAND" STYLE ON PEOPLE MOVER

In a page torn out of a script of the old "Untouchables" TV show, a man was machine-gunned to death yesterday while disembarking from the People Mover at the Times Square Station downtown.

The man, identified by police as Vincent Wakefield of Kitchener, Ontario, was alone on the People Mover car as the automatic doors opened. Two men in 1930's style suits, complete with snap-brim fedoras and wielding .45-caliber Thompson submachine guns, pushed through the crowd, aimed their weapons at Wakefield and...

The old cop looked up from the paper. He was no fool. "This have anything to do with anything, Perkins?"

"What makes you think that?" I asked, offended. "Haven't you ever heard of a analogy? That's what this is, a analogy. A f'rinstance. I'm using it to illustrate a point."

"Uh-huh," Hatfield said, folding the paper. "I think I'll just hang on to this."

He lumbered away, paper under his arm, and I didn't argue. I still had my own personal copy. It had, as usual, been delivered to my apartment door that morning. There was just one unusual thing about it. Felt-tipped in savage printing next to the article were the words THIS CONSPICUOUS ENOUGH FOR YOU??

That didn't surprise me. What did surprise me was another article entirely, about the knifing of an Ann Arbor ad-agency receptionist. What surprised me was not that David had done Della in; it was that he'd waited this long.

I stubbed out my cigar in a wall-mounted ashtray and headed up the hall toward the main entrance. I was tired and felt only a sour sense of semisatisfied resignation. I'd spent three days in jail and was now five grand poorer, but for better or for worse, the mess was as over, as over as it would ever be.

As I trotted down the courthouse steps, a tentative female voice behind me called my name. I turned. "A moment of your time?" asked Ellen Reardon, smiling uncertainly.

Chapter 28

"Moment's about all I've got, darling'," I answered. This was a lie. I had nothing to do except get back to work and start putting my life back together.

She folded her arms tightly and walked down the steps toward me, angular and hesitant. "I want to explain," she said nervously.

"Yeah, you might want to clear up what you said about being all crazed up from booze and drugs," I said. "I never seen you drink or take anything stronger than Anacin 3."

She reached me, as we started down the steps, she reached for my arm. I edged away from the touch of her cold damp hand. "The part about being angry and scared, about not tracking so well—all that was true," she said quietly. "In fact, I was in shock. Hysterical and out of control. And then Paul's father, he came and talked to me and I went to stay at his place for a few days, and—"

"That's where you disappeared to?" I cut in, incredulous. "You went and stayed with *Lance Reardon*?"

"I was all alone!" she flared. "I had no one. He was nice to me. He said if I helped him 'fix' you, as he put it, he'd see to it that I got Paul's inheritance even though I wasn't entitled to it. I had no choice."

"Yeah, that's nice, all right."

"So," she said in a small voice, "I made the tape for the

police. And said I'd testify. But when I got up in there, and
saw you, and remembered—"

"I get the idea." We reached the sidewalk and proceeded
down it a piece to an old-fashioned green park bench, which
sat amid a clump of bushes. "Ya got religion," I went on, "and
say hey, good for you. But you know what I'll never forget,
Ellen? I'll never forget what you said on that tape, but I'll
especially never forget how controlled and assured you sounded.
Hell, you almost convinced *me*. Pretty good job for someone
who was, as you put it, hysterical and out of control."

She sat on the bench and crossed one long leg over the
other, leaning forward with her hands folded in her lap.
When she looked up at me, I could see that her eyes were
reddened under the makeup. She licked her lips. "That's
because the things I described on that tape were things I'd
thought about a lot."

Suddenly I understood. "What? Us?" She nodded and
looked down. "Well, forget it," I said.

"Oh, I know," she said coolly. "I'm only telling you that
to make it easier for you to understand."

"Well, it doesn't make it easier," I said roughly. "Makes
it harder." I almost said it then, told her the thing I'd been
thinking about ever since those endless nights in the Wayne
County Jail, but I decided: screw her. She doesn't deserve it.
"See you around, kid.".

I started up the street for the Mustang. I'd taken but six
steps when her voice reached me, thin and sad. "Ever since I
was a little girl, nothing has ever worked out for me."

I turned and faced her and started back on feet that
seemed to stick to the sidewalk. Part of me wanted to hit her.
Part of me wanted to hug her. Then I thought, Oh hell,
what's the use? People do what they do. All you can do is
deal with it. I'd have preferred that she hadn't fingered me to
the cops, but it had all worked out, regardless.

"Look at the time zones," I said.

"What?"

I folded my arms and looked away, rushing the words to
get them over with. "Nova Scotia's in the Atlantic time zone.
Hour ahead of us here in Eastern. Paul's birth certificate said

he was born at five-thirty. That's Atlantic time, which means he was born at four-thirty Eastern time, which means he'd been twenty-five by a half hour when he died. With that and a tough enough lawyer, you ought to be able to pull down that inheritance."

She gaped at me. Her mouth moved but nothing came out. I turned on my heel and walked away, leaving her there in my increasingly crowded, and ugly, past.

There had been many surprises the past few weeks. But the biggest came that evening, when I walked into Carole's kitchen and saw what she had prepared for dinner.

"Good God," I whispered. "Look at this! How'd you know? Where'd you find out?"

Carole looked a little tired, but her smile lighted up her face. "You've always talked about the great southern meals your mother used to make. Well, I decided to tackle one myself. So I called your brother Bill and asked him what kinds of things you liked. He told me, and then put Marybeth on, and she gave me the recipes. I hope you enjoy it," she added, "and you'd better, because I may never do it again."

"Oh boy," I said reverently, inhaling the aromas.

"Do I have to eat this stuff?" Will asked.

"Your life will be immeasurably better if you do," I told him. "And, if you don't, well, that'll just leave more for me. Let's go."

And so I got lost in a meal that took me back, back to those long-ago Sundays in the big old Bennett Street house. We started with a cream of chestnut soup, went from there to a genuine Etowah ham loaf, stuffed with things like bell peppers and onions with eggs and celery. On the side, Carole served enough fried okra to feed an army, as well as a minty, fruity Bessie Tift College salad. We topped it off with a black fruitcake, which I knew Carole must have started to prepare the day before.

I ate till I was full, then I ate some more. Finally I staggered up from the table and ambled into the kitchen, where Carole was boiling a pair of hot dogs for Will. "Not bad for a damn Yankee lady," I said. "Must be a Confederate wandered through your great-grandmother's backyard one time."

"Yee-ha," Carole said agreeably.

"It was great, darlin'," I added, lighting a cigar. "Thanks. I'll help clean up."

"Nonsense," she said. "You go out on the patio. I'll be there directly," she trilled in a god-awful Scarlett O'Hara accent.

I appropriated a pair of Stroh's Signature beers from the fridge, strolled out to the patio, and sat down heavily in a lawn chair. The long hot, humid spell had finally broken and it was pleasant that evening, in the low seventies with just a trace of breeze whispering through Carole's sycamore trees. I leaned back in the chair and closed my eyes in a rare moment of contentment. Oooh good, I thought. I could sit here all night—

My eyes opened and I straightened in the chair as the realization dawned. Suddenly I had the sneaking suspicion that I'd been set up. What the hell is Carole up to?

I was half-done with my first beer when my hostess herself appeared. She was barefoot, dressed in a pink split skirt under a white-and-pink knit top. She carried a wineglass in one hand and a bottle of Gallo Hearty Burgundy in the other. She took a chair and sat a half-dozen feet from me, at a slight angle so we didn't have to look directly at each other, and poured herself a glass.

"News," she said, after taking a large sip.

"Yeah, I figured. You been awful quiet since I came back to the world. Even tonight, we're having a nice party and great dinner, and all you wanted to talk about was the Thumper needing wheel alignment, and Will busting out his shoes, and what a pain in the ass your mother is. So go ahead," I said gently. "What's on your mind?"

"Shaun Levin and I are merging our practices, effective right after Labor Day."

"Huh. I'm surprised. How come?"

She spoke without moving, as if needing all of her energy to pick just the right words. "Economies of scale, mainly. Solo shops are murder, the overhead just eats you up.

Plus, Shaun's a better litigator than I am and she'll be doing most of the trial work. I'm going to assist with that and handle most of the nontrial work, plus lecturing. I also have articles to do for *Working Woman* and the *ABA Journal*, and I've been approached about doing a book." She looked at me, her smile mischievous. "Nizer and Haynes and Bailey have had theirs. Now it's my turn."

I drew on my cigar and exhaled a narrow stream of smoke. "That's great. I'm proud of you," I said quietly.

She drank some more. "Another thing," she said, crossing her legs. "I've hired Mrs. Miracle as live-in housekeeper. I can't be sending Will to my mother's all the time anymore, it's making the poor kid crazy. So I need you to finish the replastering in the north bedroom."

"Okay," I said, wondering if this meant what I thought it meant.

I heard a clink and slosh as Carole recharged her glass. I felt her eyes on me. "I'm having the baby. That's final."

I looked at her. "I see," I said, dry-mouthed.

She held her wineglass in both hands, looking reflectively into it. "I wrestled with it for days. Well, you know, I went back and forth. What it came down to was, there's a lot of death around. An awful lot. I thought, maybe this was meant to happen to me. Maybe I should do some life, while I've got the chance. So here goes nothing." She smiled crookedly. "Kind of scary, you know? I feel like I've forgotten everything I learned about babies."

My mind was going off in all kinds of directions, but my mouth worked fine as usual. "You'll do great. I mean, look at Will, how he's turned out."

"That's your doing, too. You've been part of his life since just after he started walking."

"Jesus. That's right. Well, yeah, I guess I've had an influence on him. Boy knows not to shake up my beer when he brings it to me."

"And," Carole said, "he knows to raise the lid before he starts, and to lower it when he's done."

We laughed together, the first honest laugh we'd shared

in quite a while. I said, "We'll do at least that good this time. 'Cause remember what I said. I'll be around. I'll help out."

She left a silence in there, then remarked, "That isn't all you said. Will did give me your message." Her smile was gentle and indulgent. "I was surprised."

"Shouldn't have been. You know me, you know how I was raised, utmost of strictness. You play, you pay."

"That's not what I mean," she retorted. "I'm talking about the part about how you love me."

"Well, I do, goddamn it," I flared. "Why the hell else would I still be around after all the shit we been through?" I looked away from her, across the yard to the corner where the shade is deepest.

"Good Lord," she breathed, "you're sweeping me off my feet."

"So billing and cooing ain't my strong suit. Doesn't mean I didn't mean it, 'cause I did, okay?"

The words sounded insufferably lame even to me. Carole refilled her wineglass, which was acting like it had a hole in it. "I've been thinking a lot about you and me," she said. "Understandable, right? We're going to have a baby together."

"Yeah," I said, and the realization hit me, really hit me, for the first time. A *baby*. A small person with part of me in it, and parts of people going all the way back to that debtor who hit the Georgia shores with James Oglethorpe in 1733.

"And I've been thinking about what a roller-coaster ride it's been," Carole said. "How different we are, backgrounds and so forth. And how complementary in some ways. In bed, of course; there's always been that. Plus your physical skills and toughness, and my intellectual skills—"

"And toughness," I put in.

She ignored me. "We've always fallen apart, though. And I know why. It's because we get too close. We forget what's probably the most important thing we have in common. An appetite for remoteness. We both need lots of room in our lives."

I knocked a knuckle-long hunk of ash off my cigar. "You been reading *Shrinks Illustrated* again?"

She held up a hand. "Hear me out, okay? I don't think

I'm off target on this. I have my own life, and it's mostly okay because it's mostly the result of my own decisions and actions. No one on earth knows all about it, and I don't want anyone knowing all about it. Not even you, dear heart." She drank some more. "And the clearest evidence that you feel the same," she said, seeming to pick her words carefully, "is that you've been out of hiding for a couple of weeks now, and you haven't told me the first thing about what you did or what happened while you were gone. Officially, the Reardon murder is still open, but I have a feeling you resolved it one way or the other. I know you, Ben, you're too content for it to be otherwise."

Surprised, I said, "Well hell, I'm not trying to hide anything. I'll tell you all about it right now, if you want."

She shook her head. "Too late. It would be coercion. You instinctively don't want to share it with me. And that's all right. I'm not offended, because I'm the same way. There's a lot of me I don't want to share either."

She took a deep breath and fixed me with those dark brown eyes. "That doesn't mean I don't think you're a good man. That doesn't mean I don't think you're strong and able. It doesn't mean I don't love you with all my heart. What it does mean is that I won't marry you."

A warm breeze came up then and seemed to carry the words away, but they echoed in my head, as gentle and final as a drug-induced death. Hard to say how I felt. Disappointment, a sense of loss, of rejection. On the other side, a surprise visitor: relief. Go figure.

I couldn't think of anything to say, so we sat there at the prescribed distance and watched the evening deepen into night.

By eleven or so I was back home at Norwegian Wood. Carole, in what she called her last big binge before the long dry spell, had polished off her bottle of Gallo, which had the inevitable effect of making her terminally sleepy. I finally tucked her and Will in, kissed them good night, locked the place up, and left.

Carole didn't ask me to stay over, so I didn't bring it up

either. I had the sneaking suspicion that our carefree love affair was over—it was all business now. Which was just as well. Being close to me was hazardous to people's health lately.

I got home too late to do anything, but too early to hit the sack. I felt jumpy and at loose ends, and sleeping was out of the question. I needed something to do, anything to calm the noise in my mind.

So in desperation I turned on the radio to WJR. The Detroit Tigers, nineteen games out and in free-fall, were at Oakland that night, and I came in at an inauspicious but all too familiar moment: Sparky Anderson taking the ball from Guillermo Hernandez in the top of the eighth with none out and the go-ahead run at third.

I cracked a beer, lighted a cigar, and was about to collapse into my easy chair when I belatedly noticed the message light blinking on the phone box. Against my better judgment I went over there and mashed the PLAY button.

"You know who this is," came the soft slurry female voice from the speaker. Of course I did: Joann Sturtevant. I wondered about the cloak-and-dagger, and why she was calling me half-crocked. "I just wanted to tell you I heard about what you did in Toledo, and . . . You took care of it for me, just as I asked you to. I knew you would. I knew you wouldn't let me down. I want to thank you. . . ." When she resumed, her voice was more its usual cold, formal self. "We won't speak of this again. Good evening."

Oh Gawd, I thought as the machine whirred its way through a couple of hang-ups. The old ditz thinks I stalked Marty Stempel and whacked him for her. I'd have to straighten out that misimpression, someday.

I went back to my chair and collapsed into it, half listening to the baseball game. The mistake about Stempel shouldn't have surprised me. Lots have people had been wrong about lots of things in this case. Old man Reardon had been positive I killed his son. Ezra Goforth thought Savastano was gay. Curt Goldflower had been certain that Paul was screwing Angie. Dick Dennehy was convinced that Paul was a big-time cocaine dealer. I myself had been sure that Paul was absolutely straight and wouldn't touch cocaine with a ten-foot pole.

All wrong. And now, at the end, I only knew two things for sure. One: Paul was dead, and would stay dead. Two: I was going to be a father. I wondered how I'd handle it. Probably like everything else: make it up as I go along.

Mike Henneman had just finished his warm-ups when the phone rang. I didn't move a muscle. After four rings I heard my own voice from the box: "Perkins here. You've got just thirty seconds to tell me who you are, what you want, when you called, where I can reach you, and why I should bother. Be convincing." *Beep.*

"Ben," came a hesitant female voice, "it's Ellen. Ellen Reardon. You know?" She sounded drunk. I wondered if it meant something that the three women I came in contact with tonight were drunk. "I just—I want you to know that, well, I realized I forgot to apologize. At the courthouse. For what I did. For that bad, uh, stuff I told the police? It was an awful thing to do to you, and . . ."

I was on my feet, walking toward the phone.

"To make amends," she went on, "I want you to have the five thousand that Paul put in that bank account. Don't get all huffy and proud on me. Take the money. Stop by whenever, I'll give you a check. . . ."

My hand was reaching for the receiver. I froze without touching it.

"Let me do this," she whispered. "Even if you don't want to be my friend anymore, let me do this. Okay? G'night. G'bye."

I stared at the phone box for a minute. Then I walked through the kitchen, down the hall, and into the bathroom. Out the window, in the blackness of a moonless night, I could see Building 3 and the apartment that had to be Ellen's, second from the right on the third floor. Light shone through the window for a moment, then shut off.

And I thought: She said she had fantasies. God knows I had them, too. And here we are, tonight, each of us alone— What sense does this make? What harm could there be? Paul's still dead and Carole doesn't want me.

I spun and walked resolutely out of the bathroom, up the hall, through the kitchen, and to the front door. I took the knob in hand, and held it till it grew warm, and thought: What's the problem, stupid? Haven't had enough trouble this summer already?

I let the knob go, slammed the dead bolt home, and secured the chain. I shut off the TV and the lights, went back to the bedroom, and arranged myself horizontal, facing the ceiling.

And I thought: Sure, Ellen. Of course I'll take the money. Some might consider it Mafia money, drug money, dirty money. I saw it as five grand that would replace what I lost to the bail bondsman.

My daddy always said: If you do as good as break even, be happy.

So I was happy, sort of. Because I'd broken even, sort of.